TOM BRADBY has been a correspondent for ITN for almost two decades. He is currently ITV News' Political Editor. He is the author of six thrillers: *Shadow Dancer*, *The Sleep of the Dead*, *The Master of Rain* (shortlisted for CWA Steel Dagger for Thriller of the Year), *The White Russian* (shortlisted for the CWA Ellis Peters Award for Historical Novel of the Year), *The God of Chaos* and *Blood Money*.

He has also written the screenplay for the new adaptation of *Shadow Dancer*, directed by Oscar-winning James Marsh, which previewed at the Sundance and Berlin Film Festivals to critical acclaim. He is currently writing the screenplay of his novel *The Master of Rain*.

Acclaim for
Tom Bradby's novels:

SHADOW DANCER

'Quite exceptional . . . a taut, compelling story of love
and torn loyalties'
DAILY TELEGRAPH

'A remarkable first novel . . . Bradby handles the tension with skill
to produce a gripping tale'
THE TIMES

'The best book on the northern conflict since *Harry's Game* . . . An
excellent read on any level'
IRISH INDEPENDENT

THE SLEEP OF THE DEAD

'Intriguing and emotive, this is a slow builder that proves to be
well worth the wait'
THE MIRROR

'Elegant, spooky and a compulsive page turner'
DAILY MAIL

THE MASTER OF RAIN

'A moody, murder mystery with all the style of a noir classic'
THE MIRROR

'Nigh on impossible to put down . . . This intelligent thriller brings
Shanghai to life as *Gorky Park* did for Moscow'
TIME OUT

'The atmosphere and menace of Twenties Shanghai is brought to
vivid life as the backdrop to a gripping tale'
DAILY MAIL

'Does for Shanghai what Raymond Chandler did for Los Angeles –
stylish and cool – debauchery at its most elegant'
TIME

By Tom Bradby

SHADOW DANCER
THE SLEEP OF THE DEAD
THE MASTER OF RAIN
THE WHITE RUSSIAN
THE GOD OF CHAOS
BLOOD MONEY

and published by Corgi Books

SHADOW DANCER

Tom Bradby

CORGI BOOKS

TRANSWORLD PUBLISHERS
61–63 Uxbridge Road, London W5 5SA
A Random House Group Company
www.transworldbooks.co.uk

SHADOW DANCER
A CORGI BOOK: 9780552167000

First published in Great Britain
in 1998 by Bantam Press
an imprint of Transworld Publishers
Corgi edition published 1999
Corgi edition reissued 2012

Addresses for Random House Group Ltd companies outside the UK
can be found at: www.randomhouse.co.uk
The Random House Group Ltd Reg. No. 954009

Penguin Random House is committed to a sustainable future for
our business, our readers and our planet. This book is made from
Forest Stewardship Council® certified paper.

Typeset in Palatino by Falcon Oast Graphic Art.
Printed and bound in Great Britain by Clays Ltd, Elcograf S.p.a.

For Claudia and Jack

ACKNOWLEDGEMENTS

First and foremost, I would like to thank my wife Claudia, who has been a brilliant partner in the production of this book. When I lost the first five chapters of the first draft in a domestic computer crash, she had the good sense to tell me that it might be no bad thing. Writing a first novel and, more importantly, striving to make it good, is an arduous and long process. I came to think of it as a little like climbing a mountain; every time you think you have got to the top, someone taps you on the shoulder and points to the real peak miles above you, up in the clouds. Without Claudia, it would have been a lonely ascent.

I owe a great deal to Mark Lucas. He was recommended to me as the best literary agent in London and everything I have experienced suggests that may very well be true.

Bill Scott-Kerr is an excellent editor and his team at Transworld extremely professional and enthusiastic in every aspect of the publishing process. Thanks, too, to my early readers: Tom Vail, Sophie Janson, Fiona Mackinnon, Mark Davey and Letitia Fitzpatrick.

Thank you to my parents for their early comments and their endless support.

Finally, thank you to the many people in Northern Ireland and London – officers in the RUC, MI5, Army Intelligence and current and former Republicans – who helped, but would rather remain anonymous.

'I am in blood
Stepp'd in so far, that, should I wade no more,
Returning were as tedious as go o'er.'
Macbeth, Act III, Scene IV

SHADOW DANCER

PROLOGUE

The bodies in front of him rose and fell rhythmically. The men were tired and wet. He watched as they widened the hole once more, struggling and slipping in the wet earth. He knew they thought this exercise was pointless and he wished that he didn't know better.

He listened to the sound of the spades being driven into the dark earth and he shuddered. He knew with some certainty what they were going to find.

It was freezing cold on the mountain and it had been raining for hours. He thrust his hands deep into his pockets and felt the damp there too.

It was a miserable place.

He half turned and looked back towards the entrance to the quarry. The woman was still there, wearing only a thin coat, her head bowed, her face shielded by the shawl. He didn't understand. Why would anyone want to see their child pulled from the earth?

He heard the shouts and began to run down the muddy path, struggling to stay upright.

As he arrived, the youngest of the constables shouted at him like an excited child. 'We've found it, sir. I think we've found it.'

Allen felt his anger surge, 'Shut up, Hawkins. For

Christ's sake.' He stepped into the hole beside them and muttered quietly, 'Well done, well done.'

The mud was thick and two of the men were pulling at the end of a plastic sack, trying to free it from its grave. The top was neatly tied and Allen watched as they began to brush the earth away. It was a black bag and he could make out the shape of a body. He turned away and clambered out of the hole, thinking he was going to retch. He stared into the mud for a few moments and watched the rain running in rivulets down the hillside. He felt black despair and he heard himself mutter, 'Christ. Christ.'

He tried to gather himself. He looked back up towards the top of the quarry. The road was empty, the woman gone.

CHAPTER ONE

The bag was in the hall, the newspaper was open on the kitchen table and time was running out.

Colette stood over the paper, her weight on her left leg, chewing away at her fingernails.

She wanted to shout out, 'It wasn't me, you silly bitch! It wasn't me.'

She sat down and tried to calm herself, burying her forehead in her hand. Her eyes were drawn back to the page in front of her. This morning she hadn't been able to resist buying the newspaper, now she couldn't resist reading it.

The banner above the headline on the front page said, AFTER THE IRA'S BRIGHTON BOMB. The article on the features page consisted of an interview with the wife of a senior Tory politician. It was the first interview she'd ever given and she said she'd agreed to it only because she wished to promote a new scheme to train those who care for the disabled. Colette couldn't drag her eyes away from the picture. The fucking woman was in a wheelchair, her hand – the wedding ring still visible – balanced calmly on the top of the wheel.

'We tetraplegics' – she read with a laugh – 'envy the paraplegics who are only paralysed from the waist down' – only! – 'because they can dress themselves, even stand . . .'

Colette covered her eyes with her hands and began to press hard, the pain blurring her vision.

The sound of the doorbell made her jump. She tried not to look at the bag as she passed it. She opened the door abruptly and almost shouted at the young man standing there. 'You're early.'

He looked confused and stammered uncertainly, thrown by her sudden and unexpected hostility. 'Er . . . I . . . don't think so . . . It is the time I was told.'

'Wait here.'

She shut the door again and went back into the kitchen, leaning against the wall and shutting her eyes. She tried to breathe in deeply and force herself to relax. She told herself again, 'One more day. Just one more day.'

After a few minutes she'd gathered herself as much as she was ever going to. She grabbed her small overnight bag from the kitchen table (two clean pairs of knickers and her toothbrush, cigarettes and make-up) and then stooped to pick up the grip in the hall. She handled it gently, being careful not to bang it against the door before slowly placing it on the back seat of the car.

As they moved away from St Swithun's Villas she looked round briefly to take a last look at the house. Then she shut herself off and tried to keep calm.

She told herself that this was the end of the line, that it was all over. She tried to think about a new chapter, to envisage what she would do with her life. She would swim more, she decided. She'd loved sport at school and wanted to get fit again. She'd learn to sew and to knit and make clothes for the children. She would, she thought, get a job, perhaps, but as what she wasn't sure, since she didn't have any qualifications. She wondered if she might be able to train as a teacher, a career she'd considered once, years ago.

She thought about how pleased her mother would be. There would be no more tense silences, no more pointed comments about how clingy and insecure young Mark was, no more accusatory goodbyes.

She opened her eyes again. They were turning off the motorway now and the young man seemed to be concentrating hard. As they pulled into the entrance to Southampton Parkway station, Colette felt a sudden surge of uncontrollable panic, and she grabbed the young man's arm, sinking her fingertips into the muscles on his forearm. 'Go round again! Go round again!'

He looked at her, bemused.

She gripped his shoulder. 'Go around again! For Christ's sake.'

She pointed ahead through the windscreen. He did as she demanded, the car lurching as he thrust it hurriedly into first gear and accelerated away. Colette looked over her shoulder and the young man pulled back onto the main road and headed towards the roundabout.

'What was it? What did you see?'

She couldn't meet his eyes. 'I'm sorry . . . I thought I saw something. I mean . . .'

'Shall we go round again?' His voice was gentle, reassuring.

She hesitated a moment before replying. 'Yes, yes. Drop me on the main road outside. It's better.'

As he pulled off the roundabout he stopped by the side of the road, flicking on the hazard lights. He seemed to have a maturity and calmness about him that belied his years.

'Are you all right? Are you *sure* you're all right?'

She nodded silently and he touched her shoulder. 'Have you still got your ticket?'

She nodded again, not trusting herself to speak.

The young man turned back to the wheel and switched off the hazard lights. 'OK. I came down the motorway just to check we weren't being followed. I've been looking out. It's all right. Everything has been done meticulously.'

She took the bag out of the back gingerly and tried to make sure it didn't rub against her leg as she walked. She didn't say goodbye because she had turned her mind away from him.

She walked through the side entrance to the platform, oblivious of the details of the station and the specific age, shape or size of the other passengers. She saw figures. She felt them. A couple to her left, a man to her right. She was convinced they were watching her and she stood stock-still as their eyes bored into her. She didn't dare look up, lest she catch their eyes. She knew they would *know* immediately, if they didn't already.

The train had pulled up before she registered it. She tried to put the bag out of her mind and to summon up some anger for that fucking woman and all her kind, who were screwing her people and had been for years. The train was pretty empty and she saw a seat and gently lowered herself into it, positioning the bag carefully between her legs. She closed her eyes and sighed deeply, her mind suddenly conscious of the sweat on her brow.

She could feel the gun pressing against her breast.

After a few minutes she loosened her grip on the bag and leaned back on the seat. It had been a long night without sleep and she was very tired. She felt a kind of calmness descend and she looked down to check that her clothes were still clean, neat and unruffled.

She'd taken great pains with her appearance and it showed. She was wearing a dark-brown suede jacket, a white shirt and a plain black pair of trousers. She wasn't wearing make-up because she knew she was pretty and didn't want to attract unnecessary glances – and to that end she wore a black suede hat that she pulled down onto her forehead.

She closed her eyes now and thought briefly about arming the bomb. It was the work of a few seconds in the ladies' loo in Waterloo and then she would be away. She would make one phone call to Dublin and they would place the warning with the police. The police might play silly buggers with people's lives and lie to the media, but what was it to her? Not her fault if they wanted to see people killed. But nobody would be killed, she told herself. That wasn't what it was meant for.

She picked up the local evening paper and tried to concentrate on the words in front of her. Eventually she got bored and lowered it slowly, allowing herself to look around the carriage.

It was nearly empty. For the first time, she noticed the old woman sitting opposite was staring at her intently. Colette found her gaze unnerving and irritating and she snapped the paper back up over her face. But it was too late. The woman had seen her chance. 'It is awfully hot in here, isn't it?' she said. 'They do so often get the temperature wrong.'

Colette lowered one side of the paper slightly and smiled over the edge of it. It was a forced smile, polite rather than interested, but the old woman smiled back and continued. 'Are you from London?'

Colette shook her head and would have said nothing, but the woman looked as if she would go on.

19

'I'm just coming up for the night – to see friends,' she said, and then pulled her newspaper higher to indicate the conversation was terminated.

The woman's inquisitiveness worried her. If this had been the start of a campaign she wouldn't have thought twice about it, but it had been going on for two months and people were getting suspicious. She'd been especially careful in the last few days not to be drawn into conversation with anyone.

She tightened her grip on the bag. It was close now. The neat semi-detached homes and carefully tended gardens of suburbia had given way to drab office blocks. Waterloo was only a few minutes away.

She felt more nervous than she had ever been. She tried to tell herself it was stupid because it should be simple to leave the bag beneath a bench and quietly slip away. Then it would all be finished and she could have a hot bath and scrub herself clean at the flat in Clapham.

The train slowed and the passengers were on their feet. Colette sat still, but so did the old woman. She could feel panic rising now and she wanted to stand up and scream. She fought to control herself. She almost shouted to herself to keep calm. She told herself there was nothing to be afraid of but an interfering old-age pensioner. She waited for her to rise and leave the train before she picked up her bag and slowly walked to the end of the carriage, pausing at the door for twenty or thirty seconds.

The moment she set foot on the platform she knew that had been a mistake. They were close to the exit and the other passengers had cleared through. Only the old woman was there, talking to a guard whose head was bent low to catch her gentle voice above the noise of the train.

She walked on, but waves of panic were beginning to overwhelm her. She tried to convince herself that nothing was wrong, that it would be as it had been so many times before. She saw the policeman as she heard the voice. He might have said excuse me, she couldn't be sure, but he looked startled as she broke past him into the packed concourse.

She heard the shout, but by now she was running, her heart pumping and her head bursting.

The platform exit was in the middle of the concourse and she ran left, past W. H. Smith.

Somebody shouted again. She saw only blurred faces. She lost her hat.

She passed a line of people staring up at the departures board and then saw an exit and ran for it, experiencing as she did so a momentary sense of relief.

She burst through the glass doors, jumped off the top step outside and crashed headlong into a woman carrying home her shopping. She recovered her balance and started to run again, turning left. The pavement was full of commuters and she dashed out into the road and ran alongside the traffic, cutting across the lanes as she went. She reached the corner and turned towards Westminster Bridge. Her lungs felt like they were bursting and she was tiring fast. Halfway across the bridge, in the shadow of Big Ben, she stopped and forced herself to look back.

Nobody was following.

Her feet were hurting because her shoes had heels and were not designed for running. She could feel the blood in her face.

She realized with a jolt that she still had the bag in her hand. The commuters plying to and fro were set for home and took little notice of her as she leaned over the bridge and dropped the bag over the side. She saw it hit

21

the flat surface of the Thames and walked on. She looked behind her again. Still nothing.

She had no time to plan or think, but she realized she would have little chance of escape on foot. The roadworks at the centre of the bridge had brought the traffic to a standstill, so she turned round and walked back the way she had come. She knew she had to get away quickly.

On instinct, without reason, she hailed a taxi. The man pulled down the window. 'Where to, love?' he asked easily.

He had grey hair and a pleasant face. She hesitated. He didn't push her.

She heard a siren and felt the sense of panic return. 'Battersea,' she said, without knowing why.

'Where in Battersea?'

She didn't understand. 'I'm sorry?'

The man shook his head. 'Whereabouts in Battersea?'

'Battersea Park,' she said. She got into the back and felt instantly safer.

On the radio, the presenter was grilling the British Home Secretary. She listened to his silky voice.

'But surely, Home Secretary, there must be something that can be done to prevent these attacks. As you are well aware, they do seem to be able to strike at will. Is it time to consider introducing internment again?'

The Home Secretary sighed audibly. 'Well, the legislation remains on the statute book, but whatever the frustrations – and I know it *is* very frustrating – I don't personally favour that. After all, if we bring them all in, sooner or later we have got to let them all out again.'

'Home Secretary, thank you very much. For those just joining us, the latest news is that London's train stations have once again been disrupted by a series of real and hoax bombs. Commuters face another night of chaos.'

They were nearly at Chelsea Bridge now, but the traffic had ground to a halt and she could feel the panic rising again. 'Can I get out here?'

The man turned round slowly and pulled back the connecting window a little further. 'You can do what you like, love.'

'All right. I want to get out here.'

She heard him sigh as he turned back to face the road ahead. He edged over in the traffic and she had her hand on the door handle as he did so. It wouldn't open.

'It won't open until I stop,' he said.

As he came to a halt, she got out. She looked about her. There was no-one else on the pavement and no sign that anything was amiss.

She fumbled in her side pocket, but could find no change. She reached inside her jacket and felt the weight of the gun as she reached for her purse.

'How much?' she said.

'Two pounds eighty.'

She only had ten. She wanted to get away from there fast, but couldn't bring herself to let him keep the change. It was too much money. She waited while he counted out the cash and then began a fast walk, looking over her shoulder as she did so.

He was looking at her.

She broke into a run, slowly this time, as if trying to convince herself there was nothing to escape from.

She crossed the bridge. Sirens wailed further down the river, but they seemed a long way off. She jogged slowly through Battersea Park, keeping close to the river. She turned back onto the road by the south end of Albert Bridge and then stopped.

What to do?

She thought walking was easiest, and then public transport.

Which way?

She hesitated. So much at stake – and simply the thought of it led to a renewed sense of panic. So close to being caught.

She heard another group of sirens, closer this time, and she wanted to run, but forced herself to stay still. She needed to get as far away as possible as quickly as she could. She felt the gun in her pocket again and then walked forward decisively. She waved airily at the driver of a red Rover, opened his passenger door and climbed in.

'Christ!'

'It's all right. Please, I need a lift, not far.'

The man was big. He seemed to fill the car, his sandy blond hair pressed against the roof and his huge hands covering the steering wheel.

'What do you want?' He sounded calm, his voice gentle and level.

Colette also spoke quietly. 'I just want a lift a short distance.'

'Why? What are . . . ?'

'Somebody was chasing me. I'm sorry, I just want to get away.'

'Somebody was chasing you? Who?'

'Just somebody. I don't know . . . I just ran . . . I need to get away.'

The man's voice was still level. 'I'll take you to the nearest police stat—'

'No.'

He looked at her sharply. They'd been moving forward gently, but he put his foot on the brake and brought the car to a halt. 'Battersea Park can be dangerous. You ought to report . . .'

'No. Please. I need to get away, please.'

She pointed forward, through the windscreen, as if

24

indicating the direction she wished to go in. She could feel the panic returning. She could sense this man was not going to be hoodwinked. He had the feel of a . . . she didn't want to think about it.

His voice was still steady. 'I don't understand what has happened to you – and perhaps it's none of my business. But you're in my car and I think I should take you to the police station, don't you?'

'I just want to get away.' She was gesturing beyond the windscreen again, as if willing the car forwards. 'Please. I want to get away.'

'I'll take you away – but I really think I should take you to a police station. I mean, I don't know anything about you. I mean, I just think it would be best if—'

She snapped and pulled out the gun, pushing it into his side just above the belt on his trousers.

He exhaled deeply. 'Fucking hell . . . now I see what this is all about.'

'I asked you. I just want to get away.'

They were inching forward again now, but Colette could not still the tempest in her mind. She wasn't sure what to do because the whole situation had spun rapidly out of control and she was desperate to save herself, but scared the odds were mounting against her.

She could sense the man beside her wasn't frightened. What was he: a policeman? A soldier? She'd spent too much time with them not to sense something familiar.

It was his calmness that disturbed her.

She tried to think clearly.

'You won't escape, you know,' he said. 'They're sealing off this area of London – it's just been on the radio. Roadblocks, the works.'

Colette didn't reply. He was a policeman. She cursed inwardly.

'It's because of the bomb scares.' He looked over at her, his face calm and impassive. 'You're not one of them, are you?'

She turned towards him and pushed the gun into his ribs. 'Shut up.'

'I'm not frightened.'

'Shut up.' She could hear the desperation in her own voice and she could hear sirens again in the distance. They seemed to be getting closer.

She held the gun at waist level so it wouldn't be seen by passers-by. The streets were busy with people who'd decided to walk home to avoid the chaos. The sirens grew louder, and up ahead she could see the cars moving onto the pavement to try to clear a way through.

She was peering anxiously out of the windscreen when she felt a blurring pain in her cheek as the man punched her. Her head smashed against the side window and she felt him grip her wrist, the pistol already pointing harmlessly towards the roof. She struggled, but he had his other hand on her throat and he was strong. She tried to yank her right hand down and fire, but the shot went through the roof, the noise deafening both of them. He pushed her hand back and smashed it repeatedly against the window behind her. She struggled, but the pain was intense and she couldn't keep hold of the gun. When she sat up, she was looking down the barrel of her own pistol and the man was reversing slowly out of the door and gesticulating wildly to the approaching police car.

She closed her eyes and began to sob quietly, her body hunched over the dashboard.

On the other side of the Irish Sea, Trevor Long was driving fast. It was raining, it was dark and the roads were narrow and slippery. He knew he was pushing it.

There had been no fuss, just a single bleep, followed by a telephone call. He felt hollow, tired and dirty. At times like this he always felt dirty. And, if he was *really* honest, he felt sad and bloody disappointed. He had lost players before, but never one who'd been going for so long and risen so high.

Assistant Chief Constable Trevor Long rarely had dealings with the man now, but the officers who handled him on a week-to-week basis still acknowledged that, ultimately, he was *his* man. They told Long to his face that, as head of the RUC Special Branch, and thus the man responsible for all intelligence operations, he was far too senior to be taking risks. Long told them bluntly he still believed in coming to the coalface. He'd lost men before and he was determined not to lose this one. He couldn't afford to. Gingy Hughes was the best agent they had. Or had been.

Long felt awful. Over the years this hadn't got much easier. He thought of his man, with his gawky teeth and ginger moustache and he could picture him exactly in his mind, his hands shaking with nervousness and fear. He'd been a difficult bastard to handle, all arrogance and insecurity by turns, and Long had had to use all his powers to control and keep him, his manner sometimes encouraging, sometimes cold and cruel and ruthless. Their relationship had resulted in a range of feelings, from hatred to grudging respect. It had been a peculiar kind of friendship.

He stopped for a minute and studied the map again. He knew he was lost.

He tried the road ahead, but realized he was going nowhere, turned round and came back to the crossroads. Two hundred yards down the road to the left he saw the thin red light of a soldier's torch and pulled the car gently to a halt. He wound down the window as the soldier approached and pulled out his wallet. 'Trevor Long, E Department.'

'Up ahead on the left, sir.' The soldier's accent was raw Glaswegian.

There were three men at the gate in civilian dress. They recognized him immediately and the tallest one came forward. He seemed surprised by the sight of the hooded, angry eyes and appeared to recognize Long's mood. He stretched out his hand, pointing into the darkness. 'The other side of the field, sir, by the light. The Army have checked. There's no booby trap. We thought you'd want to be the first to look.'

Long grunted his thanks.

It had been raining for days and the field was like a bog. Long was still wearing his neatly polished office shoes, but he didn't care. Through the darkness, he could just make out the hedgerows, and he walked steadily towards the light in the corner where they met. Normally he would have made this journey during the day, after a lone farmer or walker had discovered the body, but tonight they'd received a call, a tip-off from the IRA – that fact alone suggesting the man in the ditch was important.

The men by the light recognized Long and made way for him. He knelt down. 'Hold up the light,' he said sharply.

The man was on his front, his hands tied tightly behind his back. He was wearing jeans and a jumper – scant protection against the bitter cold. He was bare-foot, the removal of shoes the final indignity. For the tout, there was no sympathy and no warmth, not even at the end.

They'd have forced him to walk, barefoot and blind-folded, to this point. He might have stumbled, or cried, but there would have been nobody there to hear him. They'd have made him kneel on the side of the ditch and then placed the gun against the back of his head. Long thought they might have enjoyed his desperation and walked home to dinner feeling a good day's work had been done. His man *would* have stumbled and cried and begged. In his final moments he would have been a coward; pathetic, frightened, alone, his arrogance long since beaten from him by the IRA's feared Internal Security Unit. Long thought of the split-second when a finger squeezed on a trigger and a life was ended.

The body beneath him had a grey hood, the cord pulled tight around the neck. Long gripped him and tried to turn him over, struggling to pull him round in the mud. He looked up briefly. 'Give me a hand, for Christ's sake.'

Long knelt over the man's head and tried to loosen the cord. He didn't have a knife to cut it and his hands quickly grew cold as he fumbled with the knot. It was frozen solid. He looked up again. 'Has anyone got a knife?'

The man holding the light produced a Swiss army penknife and Long eventually managed to cut through the cord. He felt bitter and angry.

The blood from the wound had stuck to the sack and he had to pull it up from the front. Finally he looked at the man's face. He felt weak with relief.

Whoever the poor bastard was, it wasn't Gingy Hughes.

CHAPTER TWO

Colette curled up into the foetal position and rocked slowly to and fro on the bunk. She stared straight ahead of her, oblivious of her surroundings, her mind numb with shock. She clutched her knees closer to her chest and gently rested the side of her face on them in a child-like gesture of despair.

She tried to blot out the images of Mark and Catherine, but their faces kept on shining through; bright, happy faces, imploring her to come home. She could hear Catherine crying out, 'Mammy, I love you,' and the words reverberated round her head.

For the last number of hours – she'd lost all sense of time – everything had been noise and aggression and hostility. First she'd been taken to Battersea police station and then pushed into a van and driven at high speed to the secure cells here at Paddington Green. At least she assumed that was where she was, though she'd not been able to see anything as they arrived.

Wherever she was, she knew what to expect. It was always the same: the bullying detectives seeking an easy confession, and then the weasels from Special Branch. In Belfast, indeed all over Northern Ireland for all she knew, it was the detective constables from

Special Branch who were considered to be the real enemy. Just thinking about them stiffened her resolve. They inspired fear and hatred in equal measure and she shivered involuntarily as she remembered some of their tactics. The worst had come after she'd left prison. They'd brought her into the interrogation centre in Castlereagh and placed a brown envelope on the table in front of her. She hadn't moved and they'd opened it for her, gleefully spreading out the photos. She'd wanted to close her eyes, but shock and horror had got the better of her and she'd stared wildly at the pictures of her husband Davey in bed – in every position – with the slut from the other end of the street.

Apart from anything else, she couldn't believe the quality of the pictures.

The episode had left her with a corrosive bitterness that had dragged on for years and poisoned her relationship with Davey, her anger amplified by the knowledge that, if their situations had been reversed, she'd have been expected to behave impeccably. If Davey had been in gaol and she'd been on the outside, people would have watched her and they would have talked, but they excused Davey as they excused the other men who strayed whilst their wives were locked away in prison.

But, in the end, she'd been lucky. A friend in the same street had strayed – 'Only the once, for Christ's sake,' she told Colette – whilst her husband was inside, and she'd got pregnant. Special Branch watched her go to England to get an abortion and threatened to present her husband in the Maze with evidence of her infidelity unless she agreed to become an informer.

The woman knew it would kill him, but she held out. Colette sometimes wondered where she found the strength.

Colette thought of her own years in prison and shivered again. It was not so much the hardship of it, though it *had* been hard. It was simply the isolation. She'd enjoyed the friendship and comradeship of the other women on the Republican wing, but she'd found it almost impossible to maintain her relationships with Davey and her family. After a while, she'd come close to asking them to stop visiting, because it was so hard after they left. She used to lie on her bunk and look at the ceiling for hours, trying to remember what it was like to be free.

She thought that going back in there was more than she could bear.

She thought about how you tell two children that you're going to prison for the rest of your life.

She wondered how you explain why.

She heard a loud bang outside the door and looked up to see two scruffily dressed detectives of opposite sizes filing into the cell. They looked tired and hostile, and for a brief moment anger displaced her despair. She tried to follow her training and concentrate on every detail of her incarceration and interrogation. She knew that afterwards, after it was all over, the IRA debriefing would be extensive.

The men took her to a small interview room down the corridor – armed guards in the corridor, she noted, at least three of them – and sat her down on the opposite side of a sturdy table with a Formica top.

The thin man spoke first. 'Life for attempted murder, I would say, and twenty years for conspiracy to cause an explosion.' His tone was matter-of-fact and he sounded tired.

She looked down, determined not to catch his eye.

'You can listen to this or not, we don't give a shit, but you are going to go down for a twenty-year stretch – I mean serve twenty years – and you're going to serve it in an English gaol.'

The words crushed her defiance.

'Twenty years in a gaol in England. None of this cushy life in the Maze or Maghaberry, where you run your own show and control your own wings. And English gaols with English criminals are not noted for their love of the IRA – but, then, I'm sure your bosses will have gone *out of their way* to warn you of the consequences of your actions. Anyway, you were caught red-handed and that's the reality.'

He leaned forward on the table, but she did not look up.

'I know what you're told, but you're old enough to understand what makes sense. The IRA can't help you now. It's over for you. If you help us, if you make it easy on yourself, I give you my word it'll not be forgotten. Maybe it will ease your transition to a gaol in Northern Ireland, help you get back to where your children can see you.'

He lowered his voice and spoke softly. 'You'll want that, won't you? You'll want your kids to be able to see you? Maybe you're tough, but you wouldn't want to hurt your kids any more than you have to, would you? You'd want to make it easy on them, wouldn't you?'

She kept her head down and tried to shut out the noise. She thought it was the sound of the devil and she searched deep within herself to try to find the strength to remain silent, as the IRA demanded.

Trevor Long found it hard to push the image from his mind. He could feel himself cutting, ripping and tearing. When the sack came off, he saw a white face, curiously expressionless in death, the skin cold to the touch.

33

He tapped the steering wheel with one hand and fondled the bleeper between his legs with the other. The rhythmic beat of the windscreen wipers should have been comforting, but wasn't. He had the engine on and the lights off. He couldn't see a thing.

He could hear the wind in the trees above him and occasionally a strong gust would gently rock the car, lashing the rain against the windows. He was worried at the mud and wet. In a hurry, the drive out would be slippery.

He waited. He could feel his mood souring further. If the little bastard hadn't been getting difficult, he wouldn't be here. Insecurity and arrogance; a bloody awful combination, but perfect too.

Not for the first time, he wondered what he would do without Gingy Hughes.

He caught the first flash of headlights in the distance and felt his chest tighten slightly. He breathed in deeply.

The car was coming fast. He turned on the lights, picked up the Heckler & Koch machine-gun with his left hand and, on instinct – he hadn't planned this – opened the door and got out.

The wind and rain whipped into his face, blinding him. He took off his glasses and thrust them into his raincoat pocket. He could make out a large tree behind the car and he walked towards it, slipping in the mud as he did so. He wished he had changed his shoes.

He watched the car come. It skidded to a halt and the lights went off. The door opened. He could just make out a figure.

Silence.

He heard a voice. 'Long?'

'*Here*. Get into my car.'

Gingy obeyed and Trevor Long walked forward and

got into the driver's seat. For a brief second, he could see Gingy's face – pale skin, frightened eyes, ginger moustache – then he killed the lights and they were plunged into darkness again.

'So, to what do I owe the pleasure of a meeting with you?'

'You've been getting difficult, Gingy – and careless.'

'Don't send me out with amateurs.'

'Your handlers are the best. It's *you* that's the problem.'

'I've had enough.'

'You'll have had enough when I say.'

'You don't control . . .'

'Shut up. Shut your fucking mouth.' Long felt his power. 'You'll do what they tell you. They answer to me – and so do you.'

'You need me now.'

'I don't need *anybody*. Whilst you're useful, whilst you co-operate, you're safe. Betray me and you're finished.'

Silence, but for the beat of the windscreen wipers and the hum of the engine.

'Body on the border couple of nights ago. One of yours?' Gingy's tone was different now and Long sensed his fear and insecurity.

'One of ours. Not a serious player.'

'I heard Internal Security did him over good and proper.'

'You'll be all right, Gingy.'

'Is that what you said to him?'

Long sighed. 'I never met him. He wasn't a serious player.'

'What makes you think I'll be all right?'

'Because you're good. This boy was just a kid.'

'They don't discriminate.'

35

Long tried to sound reassuring, lowering his voice an octave. 'Come on, Gingy. We've been at it too long to get frightened now.'

'You mean *I've* been at it too long.'

A sudden gust of wind lashed the rain into the windscreen with extra force. They were silent for a few moments.

'Perhaps we are near the end,' Long said eventually.

Gingy didn't reply. Long could hear him breathing. He could smell his breath. Gingy appeared to be sitting awkwardly in his seat – right on the edge of it – and Long had to prevent himself from recoiling at their physical closeness.

'There's been an Army Council meeting,' Gingy said eventually. Long knew, but allowed his man to continue.

'It was agreed that there would be absolute discipline about targeting. We're going to concentrate heavily on the security forces and avoid civilian casualties at all costs. The bombing campaign in London is being wound up for the moment.'

Truth or fiction? Long asked himself. He said, 'What about the overall picture?'

'There's a belief that the political situation is on the move. There's a feeling the Brits are finally starting to grasp what this is about, that's why there's the emphasis on careful targeting.' Long could tell he was looking at him. 'I'm bringing people round, trying to help it along, but it's a slow process.'

He turned his face to the window and began to draw patterns in the condensation. Like a child, Long thought.

'It's damned difficult and it isn't going to get any easier. Nobody trusts the Brits. We've broached the idea of a ceasefire somewhere down the line, but even suggesting it stirs things up. A lot of them are dead against it unless the Brits come up with some cast-iron guarantees. South Armagh, East Tyrone and even some in Belfast are already talking about the possibility of a split. They think the leadership is misjudging the climate and misjudging the political situation in London.'

'So what happens?'

'I don't know. I don't know. I'm pushing it as far as I can, but you know how it is. I've got to bring it along very, very slowly.'

There was a self-congratulatory note in his voice, but Long had grown used to his arrogance and he continued to listen in silence. Gingy always exaggerated his own influence.

Outside, the wind appeared to have died down. The silence was unnerving too. Long forced himself to concentrate on what his man was saying.

'They're paranoid about the dissenters. Gerry McVeigh is one of the main problems. He's difficult and stubborn. He's been working on a plan in England – something really big – and maybe he'll get mad when they turn it down.'

'What is it. Who's the target?'

Gingy shifted in his seat, as he always did when he didn't know something. 'Something big, somebody big.'

Long's voice was sharp. 'Who?'

'Somebody big, that's all I know.'

'You don't know anything more?'

'I wasn't told. Sometimes it happens. I'll find out.'

'A politician?'

'Maybe. Big fallout, they said.'

'A royal.'

'Big.'

37

'But it'll be turned down?'

A pause. 'I think it has been, but—'

'But what?'

'Maybe better if something ... I mean if Gerry McVeigh were to meet with an accident, or were to fall victim to the Loyalists ...'

'No. We don't go in for that—'

'Like hell you'se don't.'

Long didn't respond. He could tell Gingy was riled.

'We're not pissing about here. We get this war stopped and it goes wrong, I could be finished ...'

'Watch him.'

'I'm warning you.'

'Watch him.'

Silence again. Eventually, Gingy spoke quietly. 'It feels close, somehow.'

'We've been here before.'

'No, no, there's something different—'

'Has something happened?'

'No, but—'

'But what?'

'I don't know. They're not going to bloody announce it ... It's just ... I don't know. Nothing has really changed, but maybe there's a slight coldness. I can't say anything has changed. I'm still told things. Questions are still answered, but maybe not as fully, or not as openly.'

'Could it be your imagination?'

'Could be.'

Silence again.

'I'm scared to shit.'

'You'll be all right.'

'What the fuck would you know?'

'We'll be all right, Gingy.'

Long groped for his arm in the darkness. 'Get a grip

of yourself. We've been going for a long time. It has never been more important. We're near the end.'

Gingy fumbled for his hand and held it. He waited for a few seconds, then let go, opened the door and walked back to his car.

After the headlights had disappeared, Long waited for ten or twenty minutes. He tried to fight off the sense of foreboding.

Colette felt like crying. She had held the line, but only just.

When the two men had started to question her she'd felt bullish. She'd been questioned, abused and sometimes beaten by policemen before, and the arrival of two new tormentors had sparked a rush of adrenalin which fuelled her hatred. But she wasn't as strong as she'd once been and their constant battering had brought her close to cracking.

The battering had been mental and emotional rather than physical. They appealed to her conscience, her sense of family and her instinct for self-preservation. Sometimes they shouted, sometimes they whispered, but they took it in turns and kept the questions coming.

She remained deadpan. She gave them nothing. She felt that the wall of silence was all that lay between her and oblivion. That was her training.

She didn't know if they could see her weakness and she feared their intuition.

She didn't know what they had, didn't know what they could do.

She told herself, 'Silence, silence, silence,' but when the thin one looked at her quietly – as if to say, 'I know you, I know what you're thinking' – then she wanted to talk, to let it all come spilling out, to beg for clemency.

She wanted to tell them about her two young

children. She wanted to convince them she could be a good mother.

She wanted to say sorry.

The fat one was easier because she knew he'd laugh at her. The thin one was harder. She thought he might understand.

They both said if she confessed they'd do their best for her, though they could make no promises. The thin man was talking at her now, blowing smoke in her face. 'We've got a long way to go. This can go on for days, as you well know. Then, of course, there are the boys from Special Branch who'll be wanting a pop at you, no doubt, though they're a bad lot, to be honest. Be a lot easier if you talked to us, of course. Make things a lot simpler.' He took another long drag on his cigarette and then blew the smoke out into her face again.

The big man stepped forward and slammed his fist down on the table, shouting. 'I've had enough of your silence, you stupid fucking bitch!'

He sat down heavily on the chair opposite her and sneered across the table. 'I don't know who the fuck you think you are, or who you think you represent, but you damn near killed a whole lot of people in that station there today and I'm going to laugh my little nuts off when you go down for a life sentence.' He picked up the packet of cigarettes on the table and threw it into her face. 'Don't just fucking sit there. You don't give a fuck. Mothers with babies, children, you don't give a fuck who you could have killed. And what did they do to you, eh? What the fuck did any of *them* ever do to you?'

The thin man reached out and took his colleague's arm. 'Hold on. I think she's going to help us.' His voice was soothing. He stubbed out his cigarette and took the ashtray off the table, sweeping it away briefly with his hand. 'Come on, Colette. We know who you are. We know *all* about you from our colleagues in Belfast. Don't be like this. It won't get any of us anywhere.'

He looked at her in silence, his eyes and expression pleading with her to speak and to break the spell. 'Come on, Colette. We can go on like this for days, but there's no point, is there? There's no *point* in it. We've got you. You *know* we've got you. So why make it harder on yourself? Why make it difficult?'

He offered her a cigarette, but she didn't acknowledge him and he took one for himself and lit it. 'Suit yourself.'

He breathed the smoke in deeply.

'I have to tell you what it's going to be like. I've got young kids too, you know, and I have to say, honestly, I would do anything – and I mean *anything* – to avoid being parted from them.'

He leaned forward again and tried to catch her eye. 'You know what it's going to be like, don't you? It's going to be fucking hell on earth. I hope you've got understanding parents, because they're going to have to look after your nippers and then ship them all the way over to England just to see you. And, of course, when they get here – when they get to the prison, always supposing they can afford to come – they'll maybe find you've been moved, or the visit's been cancelled. What's that going to do to the nippers, eh? By the time you come out, you'll be a total bloody stranger.'

Colette wished she could shut out the noise. The questioning went on and on and they changed the level of their voices to make it harder for her to close her mind to what they were saying. She could feel herself weakening. She felt helpless. Perhaps they were right. What was the point in staying silent now and making it harder on herself?

Then, suddenly, they lost patience, got up and went. She didn't feel relieved because she was sure they would be back.

When they came back, they were more relaxed; she was more tense. She was lying flat on the floor like a corpse, her legs close together, her toes pointing towards the ceiling and her arms pressed rigidly against her sides. She didn't know how long she'd been there because she'd lost all track of time.

Without any visible surprise, the thin man lowered himself down and lay on the floor beside her, pushing aside the chairs and table as he did so. The hairs from his moustache tickled her ear and his voice was soft. 'Come on, Colette. This isn't going to get you anywhere, I give you my word on that. I don't mind if you lie on the floor or sit in the chair. I don't mind if you hang from the ceiling or stand on your head in the corner . . . It makes no difference to me. It makes no difference to me whether I sit opposite you on the table or whether I lie here on the floor beside you. In fact, to tell you the honest truth, I'm quite enjoying lying here beside you, because you're an attractive woman. But then, I'm sure you know that, don't you? I'm sure you've been told that many times. I bet questioning you is quite a treat for the boys up at Castlereagh, eh? I bet there's quite a little celebration when they hear you're being brought in. Not above a bit of sexual harassment when an attractive lady like you comes into their clutches . . . eh, Colette? That's the truth, isn't it? I bet it is. But I have to tell you, we're not interested in that, you see. Don't get me wrong, you are an attractive woman – any idiot could tell you that – but it's not about that. We genuinely want to help you. Excuse me—'

The man belched gently, but Colette didn't flinch. In

other circumstances, lying on the floor might have been comic, but it was a tactic she'd created years before when the questioning was becoming too much for her.

'No, as I was saying, we want to help you. We're not inhuman. I can see you're a decent individual, an attractive woman. Two lovely kids. A lot to live for. I can see that – and what I'm saying to you is that I want to help you do that, as far as I possibly can.'

Out of the corner of her eye, Colette saw the fat man bend down and tug his colleague's trouser leg. She winced involuntarily as the thin man continued.

'I'm afraid that's my friend wanting another word. He's not very gentle, is he? I know it's a kind of cliché – nice cop, nasty cop – but that's the way he is, I'm afraid. I don't suppose the others are any better, are they? Lying on the floor doesn't help, you know. I'll grant you it's novel, but I don't think it helps. I'd ask you to see reason, Colette. In my opinion, you've got to speak to us. You've got no choice. You don't want a living hell, do you? Not seeing your kids for twenty years. Christ, that's a tall order for anyone, isn't it? I don't think you'd find your bosses prepared to go down for that, would you? I mean, they've hardly ever been in bloody prison.'

Colette saw the big man tug his colleague's trouser leg again and she mentally braced herself for the renewed onslaught. He'd been shouting obscenities in her ear right from the start.

She tried to focus her mind again. This was the second time these two men had interrogated her. In between, another similar pair had taken over, and she believed the four men would be working in rotation. She knew that as soon as she was let out, the solicitors would be after the custody record, and she knew that somebody in Dublin would want to check it and debrief her in detail on exactly how the men behaved and what they asked.

She tried to concentrate, but it was so hard.

It was hard because she knew they were right. She was looking at twenty years. A living death.

When the fat one and the thin one left, she slept. She knew they'd only let her sleep for ten- or twenty-minute stretches all night, but she was so tired.

She slept deeply.

She dreamt. The dream was incredibly vivid. It was frightening because she knew it was real.

It was a hot summer's day and the bright sun was sparkling off the soldiers' helmets as they trotted slowly towards her down Hyde Park's South Carriage Drive. They were Blues and Royals troopers of the Queen's Household Cavalry on their way to the daily mounting of the guard on Whitehall, resplendent in blue tunics, white buckskin breeches and silver breast-plates, the tips of their unsheathed swords resting on their right shoulders.

As they approached, Colette looked around her. Because of the weather, the park was full and small groups of tourists had gathered along the route to watch the soldiers' passage.

Colette didn't know what to think. She felt she should hate them, but for some reason the feelings just weren't there. She felt unsettled and uneasy and was alarmed to find she was actually enjoying the sunshine and the pageant.

She looked at her watch. It was ten forty-three exactly and, as she looked up, the soldier carrying the regiment's scarlet and gold standard came alongside a parked blue Morris Marina sedan.

The car exploded with a deafening roar, filling the air with 4- and 6-inch nails which tore through the detachment, blowing the flesh of men and horses hundreds of yards into the park.

For a few seconds she could not see or hear anything, but then her senses returned. Nobody was screaming and there was just a deathly, deathly hush. She could feel the flesh and blood on her face and taste it in her mouth. All around her, she could see the dead and the dying, their bodies torn apart. She could see a head and an arm and she wondered vaguely if they were from the same man.

And then she heard the screaming – the awful, heart-rending screams of men in terrible pain, crying out for release. She could do nothing. She put her hands to her ears, but she couldn't shut out the noise.

She stood transfixed. She wanted to run, but her legs were frozen beneath her.

Finally, she saw and heard the horses. They seemed to have appeared suddenly, their bodies torn, their faces pleading for help. She could see their eyes; hopeless, helpless eyes that tore at her heart. She wanted to scream, but she opened her mouth and no sound came out.

Colette sat bolt upright, her body bathed in sweat. She stood and breathed in deeply.

She heard herself say, 'Fuck. Fuck.'

She wanted to say sorry – not to them, because Christ knows they deserved it, but to somebody, to God – to the horses, because they were such gentle creatures.

She sat with her head bent, still able to see their eyes.

CHAPTER THREE

She was beautiful. That was his first thought. The photographs didn't do her justice and he took in the smoothness of her skin, her pink, perfectly formed lips, and a small dark mole to the left of her mouth.

For a few seconds he was thrown, but he took a step forward and sat opposite her, looking down as he pulled the files and notebook from his bag. He raised his head and met her stare. Her look betrayed nothing, neither defiant nor submissive, but she held his gaze.

He could feel his heart beating faster.

He noticed her clothes. Not what he was expecting. A chunky gold-coloured necklace, fine gold earrings, a suede jacket. A bit dishevelled, perhaps, but feminine and elegant. She looked like one of his friends, only with something more.

He sat in silence for a few seconds, then began. 'My name is David Jones,' he said. It was the name he'd written on the custody record. Even if this went well, he didn't think she'd ever learn that his real name was David Ryan. 'I'm sure you're intelligent enough to know who I am and why I'm here.' He paused, wondering if she would know where he was from. 'I'm not from Special Branch,' he said. 'How have you been treated?'

He looked for a reply, and knew from her expression he wasn't going to get one. She held his gaze for a few seconds more and he thought he saw hostility or hatred in her eyes. Then she turned in her seat a fraction and fixed on a single point on the wall behind him.

She sat stock-still. The room was silent. It was almost comic. He waited fifteen seconds, perhaps thirty.

He leaned back in his chair and smiled gently. 'I apologize for the police. They're not very gentle ... a necessary evil, I'm afraid.' He leaned forward again. 'But perhaps you wouldn't agree?'

Silence.

'The police tell me you've not asked for a solicitor.'

Silence. Longer this time.

'Why is that? I should have thought you'll be needing one.'

Silence. She stared at the wall, her head still, her face expressionless.

'The police tell me the case is clear-cut. They say conviction is inevitable.'

Silence.

'It will be an English court, of course.'

Nothing. Not a movement. Not a flicker. He spoke quietly. 'I don't think I'm telling you anything you don't know, but you're going to go to prison for a very long time.'

Nothing.

'You've been to prison before, I know. I think this is going to be much harder.'

He kept his eyes on her face.

'You have children. I should imagine that will be the hardest part.'

Silence.

'How do you tell your children that you're going to be in prison for the rest of your life?'

He saw a flicker, of recognition, perhaps, or fear, in her eyes. There had been some sort of reaction, he was certain.

'Mark is five. Is that right?'

Silence.

He looked down at the file in front of him. 'Sorry, no, Mark is four and Catherine is three. Is that right?'

Nothing. She sat absolutely still. Perhaps it had been his imagination.

'So, by my reckoning, Mark should be about twenty-five when you get out.'

He felt like a bully, but he was comfortable with it.

'That is supposing you *do* get out, of course. What have we had now, twenty-five years of terror? That's a hell of a long time. People are so *sick* of it. They want life sentences to mean life. The climate in England is not in your favour. I'm sorry to say that, but it is a fact.'

He tried to speak gently now. 'You and I know, of course, that there are extenuating circumstances; you were born a *McVeigh*. Your father was in the IRA, your eldest brother is head of the Belfast Brigade, your second brother is head of a unit in the Lower Falls. What chance did you have?

'I understand that. I also understand that you only became reinvolved after your husband was killed – murdered, possibly – by the SAS down at Coalisland.

'I understand that, Mrs McGraw, but a court won't.'

He leaned back again. 'Twelve good men and true. Isn't that what they say? Not in this case, though. Mentally, they'll have convicted you before they even start.'

He leaned forward, his voice animated. 'Mrs McGraw, I don't want to patronize you, but it is going to be hell. I couldn't do it. I *could not* do it. You are going to miss your children growing up.'

He paused, trying to see a reaction in her face.

He waited patiently. The silence dragged on. A minute? Two? He felt comfortable waiting now. He had nothing to lose. He tried to think carefully about what he was saying. He tried to think about what might make her want to reply – what might make her unable to resist talking. He knew he had so little to go on, the file suddenly seeming flimsy and inadequate. He wanted to *know* her and needed to know her pressure points.

'According to our files, you joined the IRA in 1980. It's been a long time. Do you still believe in it?'

Silence.

He looked into her face, moving his head to try and catch her eye, without success.

He changed tack. 'Since I don't think you're going to tell me about you, perhaps I can tell you about me?' He sat back in his chair, as if visibly relaxing. 'I served in Belfast in the Army. Several times, in fact. Always west Belfast. Perhaps that makes you hate me? I can understand that, but the feeling's not mutual. I did a job, but I'm not sure I liked it. It's not much fun being despised. But perhaps you understand that?'

Silence.

'I read a great deal when I was there and after I came back – and I think I can say I came to sympathize with your point of view in many ways. Ireland is partitioned in 1921, the northern quarter or so is given to the Ulster Protestants, effectively. But nobody bothers to ask the Catholic minority in that quarter if they are happy about being fed to the wolves so that everyone else can live free from British rule. The Protestants rule badly. They're bigoted, deny Catholics their civil rights and attack peaceful protests that are only designed to demand equality of treatment. So you rebel, in the only way you can. You try to sap the Brits' will to stay – their

49

willingness to go on underwriting what you see as a Protestant mini-state.'

He leaned forward again. 'Now you might say the IRA has gone a long way to achieving that, but I believe – and it is a sincere belief – that you have damaged what could have been a noble cause. You may not believe me, but I think the English – the British – are a reasonable people and would have been willing to listen, and don't forget that in 1969 we were beginning to really enter the television age. The demonstrations were being broadcast to a mass audience. I do not believe that all this bloodshed, all the terrible tragedy, has got anyone anywhere, do you?'

He looked for a response, but her eyes didn't flicker. He could not tell if she was listening, but he continued. 'All this bitterness . . . atrocity, counter-atrocity, tit-for-tat – for what? Nothing is clear any more, is it? Except that it will continue. Or will it? Is all this peace talk going anywhere? Maybe you can *help* us finish it.'

He lowered his voice. 'You tell me, Mrs McGraw. Are your children going to die the same way your husband did? And your children's children? How long is this war going to continue? Are my children going to join the Army and be shot by your children? Or yours by mine?'

Silence.

He took his arms off the table. A soliloquy. He felt self-conscious, but there was no other way. 'There has to be a way out of this. There *has* to be. There has to be a way out for you, too. Now, God knows, I don't know you – and you're certainly not helping me, so I've got to make a few guesses. I don't know why you came back in. I don't know if it was because your husband was killed. I can understand revenge, but there has *got* to be an end to it. There has got to be a

50

way to stop it killing your children and mine.

'I have to say, and I get no pleasure out of this – you can believe me or not, to me it is immaterial – but you are going to get several life sentences for this, plus twenty years for conspiracy to cause an explosion. You are not going to see your children for *at least* fifteen years. You are going to miss their entire childhood and come out not knowing who they are or how they got there.

'I don't have children, but I know enough to know I couldn't stand that. It would kill me. I would do anything to avoid it. *Anything*.'

Colette moved and, for a moment, Ryan thought she would speak, but she simply leaned forward, took a cigarette from the packet on the table, lit it and drew the smoke deep into her lungs. She didn't once take her eyes off the wall behind him.

Ryan had no idea at all whether he was getting through and he paused for a moment, looking closely at her, as if she were a statue. He noticed how wide and sensual her mouth was and how clear her skin. It was almost perfect.

He wondered if she'd already guessed they had nothing on her. He wondered how he was doing. He wondered what the hell she was thinking. He could feel the frustration growing, but kept his patience and waited. Another minute, perhaps two. He sighed. 'You're not really helping me. I fail to see how refusing to acknowledge my presence here is going to help either of us. You know I'm not a police officer. You can see nothing is being recorded. You know what I'm offering. How can you gain anything by refusing to discuss it. Aren't you *curious*?'

He swept the file off the desk and put it in his bag. He looked directly at her. 'I'm not going to bully you,

51

Mrs McGraw, like those thugs in the police force. We're both human beings and I've told you frankly I couldn't face what you face. I couldn't risk being taken away from my children for half a lifetime. Not for anything. Nothing, to me – no cause, no work, certainly not the shit I have to do for a living – is worth that. You know what I'm offering. It is an honourable and simple way out.

'You're intelligent enough to know that it is not without cost, so I won't patronize you. But from my perspective, it is a cost worth paying.'

He stood up. 'Think about it. I'll be back tomorrow. I don't know how long the offer will last.'

As he reached the door, he paused and looked back. Her head was bowed, as if in defeat. He thought she might be crying.

He waited quietly outside in the corridor for a few minutes. This was his first big break and he thought he should feel elated, but he didn't. To begin with, he'd had a strange desire to reach out and touch her. To feel her. But the sales pitch had made him feel queasy. He walked away and was grateful he could. He wanted to go home.

It took him twenty minutes to get to his flat in Clapham's Latchmere Road. Nobody was in, but there were three pints of stale milk on the sideboard, a huge pile of washing-up in the sink and debris all over the kitchen table. There were three messages on the answering machine. None were for him.

His bedroom was the smallest, the noisiest and the nastiest. In the summer, when it was hot and he needed to open the window, the noise of the street was overwhelming and the sound of a lorry grinding down a gear always figured prominently in his dreams.

He switched on the bedside light and noticed the

flowers and the note. 'David. You looked a bit low this morning and I thought these might cheer you up. We've gone to a club in Brixton, but I can't remember the name and I know you wouldn't be interested! Sorry about the mess. Love, Claire.'

He opened his bag and pulled out a file and a brown envelope. He sat down and opened the file. The first page read:

Subject: Colette McVeigh/McGraw
Born: Belfast, 3 September 1960.

Note: this file was last updated on 20 March 1992, following the death of McVeigh's husband David Sean McGraw (Davey) during an IRA operation in Coalisland, County Tyrone. Despite the involvement of the SAS, there is no indication that the resulting bitterness has led her back into active service with the IRA. She appears to have been outside that organization consistently since her release from Armagh prison in 1987.

Ryan smiled to himself. Perhaps that wasn't *so* wrong. Having seen her, his own guess was that she was too good – too presentable – to risk too often.

He thought that if he'd been an IRA commander, he'd have wanted to keep her away from suspicious eyes. She didn't look anything like an IRA terrorist, but then what was a terrorist *supposed* to look like?

He closed the file again and put it on the floor. He shouldn't have taken it out of the office, but it was one small rebellion amongst many.

The brown envelope underneath was thin and he turned it over. It had been given to him by one of the management secretaries with whom he remained on

53

friendly terms – largely, from her point of view, in the hope that they would become more than friendly.

It contained two sheets of white A4 paper, stapled together in the top left-hand corner. In the centre of the page were the words 'Annual Assessment' printed in bold. He read.

TO: ALAN GRANT, DIRECTOR OF COUNTER-TERRORISM.
FROM: DESMOND JENKINS, HEAD OF PROVISIONAL IRA
SOURCE UNIT.
CC: PERSONNEL.

DAVID RYAN.
GENERAL INTELLIGENCE GROUP.

In his annual appraisal interview, Ryan identified himself as a motivated and determined individual, who was prepared to take risks in order to get results. He described himself as hard-working, patient and independent-minded.

Ryan has developed well over the past few years and has shown a certain mental toughness. He is self-confident (bordering on the arrogant at times) but he remains a reluctant team player and sometimes seems curiously immature – unable to adapt to what he describes privately as 'the Service mentality'.

He has performed a useful subordinate role in the running of one or two minor assets on the UK mainland during the past year and he has indicated he is impatient to be given the chance to recruit and run assets himself. He has expressed a strong desire to return to Ulster.

Our own assessment is that, whilst Ryan is competent and capable and has made a significant contribution to 'T' branch this year, question marks remain over his suitability for high-level field work at this stage. We would hesitate to use the phrase 'maverick' so early in his career, but several officers have expressed reservations about his attitude.

Ryan took his clothes off, climbed into bed and turned off the light. For a few minutes he lay awake, thinking about Colette McGraw. He could see her face vividly.

McIlhatton had picked his target carefully and, as she left, the woman didn't see him leaning against the wall reading his paper and didn't notice that he followed her.

She walked towards the tube and he watched her slip her pass into her handbag. She bought a copy of the *Evening Standard* at the entrance and then joined the crush inside, apparently lost in thought.

The platform was busier than usual and, as the tube arrived, she had to force her way into it. It was packed inside and she was crushed between two men.

At Embankment station she was propelled out of the train like a champagne cork and switched to the Northern Line. The next tube to arrive was packed and she decided to wait. She noticed the man but did not seem to register that he made the same decision.

She only had to wait a few minutes and the next train was slightly emptier. She got in, pushing herself to the middle, and the man got in beside her.

She tried to read her paper, but there wasn't much space, so she gave up and stared blankly ahead.

The train started to empty at Clapham North and by the time they reached Clapham Common she could read her paper comfortably. She got off, ignored the beggars and made for the shop on the corner.

She bought herself some supper and chatted amiably with the shop's Indian owner. Business was good, he said, as he always did.

She turned out of the shop and began the short walk up to her flat in the centre of Clapham's Old Town. There were only a few people on the street and she looked over her shoulder.

She saw the man behind her.

She broke into a run. The man was faster. He gained ground. She felt the impact of his shoulder and the impact of the pavement, sudden pain mixed with fear. Then he was gone. She picked herself up, confused. He was still running and she later told the police all she could remember were his eyes – and the fact that he was limping, favouring one leg, though she couldn't remember which.

She felt numb. It took her a few seconds to realize she'd been clutching her handbag to her chest and it had now gone.

She almost wept with relief. Only the handbag.

Later, the police listened to her politely, but held out little hope of getting her bag returned. She said she was annoyed. She didn't care about most of it, but her Commons pass was in the bag and it meant she'd have to spend hours going through security on Monday morning.

By the time she had finished with the police, McIlhatton was on his way back to north London, stepping off the tube train at Highgate and walking back to his small terraced house with no discernible limp.

The contents of the handbag were stuffed deep into the pocket of his trench coat and he was pleased with the night's work.

CHAPTER FOUR

Ryan woke early. He thought of Colette McGraw. The image from last night was firmly imprinted on his mind. Had she been crying?

Outside, Claire's clothes lay in a pile on the stairs and he wondered how he could not have heard them come in, since he was usually a light sleeper. He cleared a space on the table, poured a bowl of cornflakes, realized there was no milk and sat in silence.

As he picked up the phone, he wondered why Grant had said to call him in the office, since it was a Saturday and Grant always spent the weekend in the garden.

There was no answer in the office and Grant picked up the phone at home on the second ring. He had clearly been up for some time and had other things on his mind. 'Well, I wasn't expecting anything, David, so don't worry. Ask the Met to hold her for the weekend and give it another try. Be gentle, she's been in it a long time and I don't think the rough stuff will cut much ice.'

Ryan briefly pondered going to see Colette McGraw immediately, but he decided to leave her isolated until the evening.

He spent several hours in a coffee shop round the

corner, reading the morning papers. When he got home, Claire still hadn't surfaced, so he decided to go for a walk, trawling over Albert Bridge towards Hyde Park. He walked once round the park, feeling a little lonely as he did so. Not for the first time, he noticed how many couples there were in the world – and how many Arabs there were in this part of London. He wondered if that was a racist thought, but decided it was simply an observation.

It was a long walk and he felt exhausted by the time he got home. He went back to bed and slept again.

At seven o'clock that evening he returned to Paddington Green. He chatted to the uniformed sergeant in custody and went in again at seven sixteen.

He was shocked. She looked terrible, her eyes red and puffed up. She obviously hadn't slept. She didn't look up. He sat down. He wondered if there had been mistreatment. Nobody else should have been allowed anywhere near her.

'Are you all right?'

She put her face in her hands.

'Are you all right?'

She still didn't look up. He thought for a second that she might be crying, but there was no sound. The room was silent.

He began to ask again, but this time, as he did so, he put his arm forward and gently touched her shoulder. As his hand made contact, her head sprang violently backwards. She was sitting upright and staring at him. He was shocked. His heart was beating fast. He had lost control and felt awkward. For a moment, he couldn't meet her eyes.

'Why don't you people *leave me alone.*' She'd spoken slowly, deliberately and viciously, but the words saved him. He recovered.

'Mrs McGraw, you are going to go to prison for the rest of your life. I am offering you an alternative. A real alternative. If you don't want to consider it, I will leave.'

He held her gaze. He waited for a bitter rejection. She stared at him. There was a wildness in her eyes. She looked down. He said nothing more. They were silent for several minutes. She seemed to be wrestling with herself.

'You've got nothin' on me.'

'I'm afraid we do.'

'I'll not be convicted.'

'You will be.'

'You've no evidence.'

'The police say the evidence is cast iron.'

She looked down again. He waited. He studied her, noticing for the first time that she had a small tattoo on her forearm, just above her right hand. He also noticed her fingers, which were unusually long, thin and elegant. Bomber's fingers, he thought. He pushed his chair back.

'I'll give you a few minutes. I'll be outside. Shout if you want me.'

He stood in the corridor, finding it hard to contain his excitement and hide his nerves. He paced up and down slowly. Every time he was about to return to the room, he forced himself to wait a little more. Time crawled by. Ten minutes. Twenty. Thirty.

Eventually, he went back in. She sat with her head bowed. She looked frail.

She raised her head as he sat down. She looked resigned, he thought, like a wife who has been beaten black and blue accepting her remorseful husband back in the knowledge that he will do it again. He wondered if that had ever been her story.

'You're like vultures,' she said. 'Always hovering over the dying and the wounded.'

'We don't normally find ourselves in this situation.'

She shook her head, smiling. 'Right, that's the Special Branch. *You* wait till people go on holiday and then miraculously turn up in the same hotel . . .'

'It's more subtle, I agree.'

She laughed and Ryan couldn't help noticing how attractive she was when she smiled.

'It's a waste of your time.'

'We do better than you might think.'

'You tried Davey's brother in Benidorm.'

'Before my time, perhaps.'

'He complained to the Spanish Foreign Ministry.'

They lapsed into silence again. He wanted to keep her talking, but he sensed she had more to say and would only be put off by a leading question. Her head was down again.

'I don't know how you can live with yourselves,' she said.

He didn't reply. Her hair was dirty, her face drawn from lack of sleep, but she was still unquestionably one of the most beautiful women he'd ever seen.

She shook her head. 'You know who I am. You know who my brothers are. You know what my family is and you want me to betray everything that ever meant anything to me to save my skin?'

He held her gaze. 'If people could hear what you just said – with the greatest respect – I think they would find your sense of moral equivalence very hard to get to grips with.'

She didn't respond.

'Betrayal saves lives,' he went on. 'Murder is irreversible.'

'You're proud of what you do?'

'Sometimes, yes.'

'You can look at yourself in the mirror?'

'Can you?'

'No.'

She stared at him. The room was silent. He held her gaze for ten seconds, perhaps longer, and then she looked down.

'What are you offerin'?'

'What do you want?'

'I want out for me and the kids – a new life for me and the kids.'

'That should be possible.'

'I want a new life for the whole family – Ma, too, if she wants it.'

Ryan nodded.

'I want to go to Cyprus, Australia, somewhere like that.'

'Anything is possible. Eventually.'

'Why do you want me?'

He was surprised by the question and saw genuine uncertainty in her eyes. 'Because we think you can help us save lives.'

It was too po-faced an answer for her, but she didn't seem to notice. She seemed to be fighting a battle within herself, but he didn't think it was over the decision. He sensed that had already been made.

She looked at him again. 'I want money.'

'You'll get money.'

'Fifty thousand, to begin with. More later.'

He wondered if she'd been thinking about it all day or whether she had just made the figure up. 'That is a lot of money.'

'I'm worth it.'

'You're not in any position to bargain.'

It was a mistake and he knew it as soon as he said it.

61

The atmosphere had become easy, jovial almost, but he saw her changing mood clearly in her face.

'If that's your fucking attitude . . .'

'It's a lot of money.'

'It's chicken-shit for you.'

'We don't often pay upfront.'

'You offered Davey's brother a quarter of a fucking million *upfront*.'

'All right. I'll ask. I'll have to get authorization. It is not in my hands.'

'Well *get it*.'

'In a minute.'

'*Now.*'

Ryan looked at her. He leaned forward. 'All right, Mrs McGraw, I'll get you your money. But understand this: mess me around – *ever* – and you're finished.'

She met his gaze.

There was a phone in the room at the end of the corridor. Grant answered on the third ring. He was surprised and reticent at first, as if he didn't really want it to be true. Ryan was puzzled, but he promised Grant the woman genuinely appeared to have turned. Grant said he would bleep Jenkins and told him to wait.

Ryan waited. He paced up and down the corridor endlessly. He felt deflated and worried. He was annoyed with himself for losing control at the end. What if she changed her bloody mind? Time dragged again. At the end of the first hour, he went in briefly to reassure her the matter was being dealt with. She said nothing and his anxiety increased.

He didn't want someone in to help him. He wished it was anyone but Jenkins.

Jenkins arrived an hour later. He began talking as he entered the corridor. He looked like he'd just got out of bed.

'I opposed this.'

'What?'

'Your involvement.'

'Thank you.'

'Don't take it personally. You just lack the experience required.'

'Everyone has to get a break.'

Jenkins shook his head. 'I told Grant he should have called me straight away and left it in my hands. I told him that if there is a mess, I'm not going to clear it up.'

'There isn't a mess and there isn't going to be one.'

'Well, I'm glad you're so sure. That is *very* reassuring.' Jenkins smirked. He was wearing the same faded corduroy jacket, but he'd taken off his tie since he'd left the office and a few ginger hairs poked out of the top of his shirt.

'You know why Grant put you in, I suppose?'

Ryan shook his head.

'Bait.'

'Bait?'

'Yes, bait. Vulnerable woman. Good-looking, sympathetic young man. That doesn't mean she's going to be any bloody good when we get her back over the other side. She may very well decide to change her mind and set us up. *Then* there will be a mess.'

Ryan was stung. He was tempted to fight back, but he knew this was not the time. 'I think you'll find there's real potential here. I think you'll find she's worthwhile.'

'And what makes you think that?'

He shrugged. 'Intuition.'

'Intuition? Christ!' Jenkins shook his head. 'I think we need a *little* more than that.'

Then he appeared to realize he'd gone too far. He

sighed. 'OK, let's see what we've got. She believes she's going to go to prison. That's the pressure point, right?'

Ryan nodded. 'She thinks we've got her on conspiracy to cause an explosion and attempted murder.'

'And she's turned?'

'Not yesterday. She said nothing yesterday throughout a lengthy interview. I think she must have been turning it over in her mind today. She may even have made the decision before I came back tonight.'

'But she's definitely turned?' Jenkins's manner was now businesslike rather than condescending.

'She's begun to set out her terms.'

'Which are?'

'Er, resettlement for herself and her family – including her mother when the time comes . . .'

Jenkins snorted. 'Fat chance of her mother wanting it.'

Ryan continued. 'She wanted to get out soon, but that was only a vague wish. I think she knew that wasn't realistic. Other than that, she asked for money. That's when I called in.'

'How much?'

'She asked for fifty thousand upfront.'

Jenkins nodded. 'They're getting greedy, these people.' He turned. 'This door?' He led the way in.

There was only one spare chair and Jenkins took it. Ryan stood to the side. Jenkins leaned forward, placing his arms on the table.

'Mrs McGraw, my name is Dennis Peters. I am able to agree terms. Can I ask you how long you've been in England?'

'What about the money?'

'I will agree to the fifty thousand upfront.' Colette looked surprised. Jenkins continued. 'Let me ask you another question. You are clearly very well connected back in Belfast, so perhaps you can tell us exactly what is going on at the moment. What plans do you have? Is all this talk of peace serious? Is it going to happen?'

'There will never be peace.'

'That is not an answer. What is happening, please?'

Colette looked uncertain. 'I don't know. I haven't been there for months.'

'That is not an answer.'

Ryan looked at Jenkins sharply. He didn't understand why he had to be so patronizing. He didn't see how it would help. He looked at Colette's face. She looked confused, but she answered. 'I don't know. I haven't been there for months. There were rumours, but the leadership go their own way. We'll be the last to know. It won't happen – and if it does, it won't work.'

'Why?'

She shook her head. 'Work it out.'

'Who were you working with here?'

Colette looked at Ryan. 'Why is he asking all these questions?'

Jenkins answered. 'Intelligence, Mrs McGraw. You know as well as I that that is the basis of the deal.'

Colette still looked at Ryan. She seemed to want him to intervene, but he said nothing. He kept his face impassive.

Jenkins asked again. 'Who were you working with here?'

She paused before answering. 'His name was Magee. That is what he's known as.'

Jenkins pulled out a file from the bag he had with him and pushed a black and white photograph across the table. 'Is this him?'

She looked at it and nodded.

'Who else?'

She pointed at Ryan. 'I'll take questions from him.'

65

Jenkins continued. 'Who else, Mrs McGraw?'

'No more questions.'

Jenkins met her stare. 'This is how it works, Mrs McGraw. This is the nature of the agreement.'

'There is no agreement.'

'I thought we'd agreed to your demands.'

Ryan watched the harshness fade from Colette's face. She spoke quietly. 'I know nothing about it.'

Jenkins's manner was still brusque. He made no concessions to her changing moods. 'My colleague here will brief you on the ins and outs of what we require. In essence, it is simple. We will require you to return to Belfast and continue with your activities. We will require you to meet us on a regular basis, in a place and manner which we deem to be safe for both of us. You will be required to provide us with intelligence – both specific military intelligence, information about certain personalities and as much as you can tell us about the broad strategic and tactical direction.'

Colette said nothing. She was looking down.

'And I would remind you, Mrs McGraw, of the nature of your position here. You are about to escape a very, very serious charge. You could be preparing for a lifetime in prison at this point. We expect something in return. When the time comes, we will take you out and look after you, but in the meantime we need results.'

Ryan looked at Jenkins. He wasn't sure this was working. He could not read Colette's face. Jenkins looked up at him. He was still talking.

'My colleague and I have to justify our actions to our superiors and, in this case, that is not going to be easy. If you let us down, the consequences could be very severe.'

Colette was looking down now, as if uninterested. Ryan thought they'd lost her. Jenkins was on his feet.

'Please give us a few minutes, Mrs McGraw.'

Outside, Jenkins strode down the corridor and Ryan was forced to trail after him. He was still worried and considered saying something, but once again thought better of it.

Jenkins took them along to the room occupied by the custody sergeant. He asked for a copy of Colette's custody record. The sergeant looked dubious, but didn't argue. Jenkins then led the way back to the small room at the other end of the corridor that contained the phone. He sat down, opened the custody record and began writing. Ryan stood and watched. He was confused.

'What are you doing?'

Jenkins didn't look up. 'I am writing her confession, which she is bloody well going to sign. It may be useful later on.'

'Do you think we should be a bit easier on her?'

Jenkins looked up. 'Leave it to me, if you don't mind.'

When they went back in, Colette still had her head down. For the first time, Jenkins spoke quietly and relatively gently.

'Mrs McGraw, we are on the point of departure on this. I know this is difficult but you must understand what you are doing. You have to be sure of your decision.' He leaned forward. 'There is no turning back and there will be many times when you will want to. It is a brave step for you and the children, but you must know what it means.'

She didn't move. Jenkins pushed the white booklet across in front of her. 'Sign at the bottom of this page, please.'

She looked up. Ryan thought she might have been crying again. She looked down at the booklet in front of her and slowly opened it. They waited for a response.

'I'm not signing this.'

Jenkins's voice was calm. 'I'm afraid you have to, Mrs McGraw, if this is going to work.'

'It's lies.'

'It is a factual account of what happened at the train station and your role in it.'

'It's lies.'

She looked at Ryan for help. He gave none. Jenkins continued. 'Mrs McGraw, I'm not sure you really appreciate the gravity of your position. You are going to prison. There is no doubt about that. Now, if I am to go to my superiors and justify my decision, I need to have everything that they will ask for. This, I'm afraid, is one of those things. There is no choice.'

'You'll use it against me.'

'There has to be trust on both sides.'

'I won't do it.'

Jenkins's voice was confident. 'Then the deal is off.'

She looked down at the page again. They waited.

She looked up. 'I need to think about it.'

'There is no time.'

'I need to think about it.'

'There is no time, Mrs McGraw. We need to get you back to Belfast as quickly as possible or suspicions will be aroused.'

She looked down again. They waited. Ryan watched her. He didn't know which way she would go. As the minutes crawled by, the tension increased. Nobody spoke.

She picked up the pen in front of her slowly and deliberately, held the paper with her right hand and signed with her left.

* * *

68

Later that night Ryan came back, this time to her cell. She looked up at him, but didn't speak, and he sat down quietly on the other end of her bunk. The cell was tiny and Ryan noticed its white walls were shorn of anything that could be used for the purposes of suicide or escape. Ryan wondered which option she had really chosen. For perhaps a minute, they sat together in silence. When he began, he spoke softly. 'I'm sorry. I know it's difficult.'

She didn't respond.

'You'll be all right. It is for the best, though I'm sure it doesn't feel like it now.'

Colette sat cross-legged, the smoke from her cigarette spiralling up towards the ceiling.

He looked down at the file in his hand. 'I'm afraid I've got to take you through a few things. We'll go through more tomorrow, but we need to get you home quickly.'

She looked up and nodded dumbly, so he went on. 'I'm afraid I'm going to have to ask you to remember a few things – code names, emergency numbers and so on.'

He relayed some of the points he had agreed with Jenkins. They'd decided her code name would be 'Shadow Dancer', which was his own idea. It had once, a long time ago, been the name of his parents' boat. He also made her memorize the emergency number she would need to call in the event of a crisis, or if she had something to tell them and wanted to set up a meeting that had not been scheduled. He told her she would be provided with a small bleep, in case of a real emergency, which would, he said, sound an alarm at the local police station and prompt immediate action.

To everything he said, she nodded, but he wasn't convinced she was concentrating. Once or twice, he asked her gently to repeat back what he'd just told her. She kept on stumbling uncertainly.

When he asked her to run through the emergency numbers again, she broke, putting her face in her hands and sobbing gently. He didn't know what to do, but he edged forward on the bunk and put his hand on her shoulder. He said, 'I'm sorry.' He could feel the warmth of her body through her shirt and he could smell her; a strong, distinctive, feminine scent, mixed with the faint odour of stale sweat. She made no effort to shrug off his hand and he left it there. With a conscious effort, he forced himself to stand and knocked on the cell door. As he heard the guard turn the lock, he looked back at her, but she didn't raise her head. He said quietly, 'I'll see you tomorrow.'

McIlhatton sat, slouched in the armchair, watching *Neighbours*.

The flat he was in had one bedroom, one table, one armchair and only one person. Himself.

In the beginning, he'd been pleased to have been selected by McVeigh, but that had worn off.

He stood up and walked to the window. The street outside was horribly familiar and he wondered how many boring, lonely minutes he'd spent standing here.

The handbag was by his feet and he'd delivered the pass to the man in Hammersmith, as instructed.

They'd always said it would be tough.

CHAPTER FIVE

They walked out of Paddington Green into the winter sunshine.

The car was waiting and Colette clambered into the near side. She was wearing the same clothes, but she'd showered and applied some of the make-up a female police officer had given her.

She'd barely spoken, but he could sense her mood had altered. She seemed more confident and more buoyant.

It was 7.30 a.m. and Ryan knew that time was short.

They drove out of Paddington Green and down towards Oxford Street. The driver spotted an Italian café that looked open and pulled up outside it. Ryan turned and touched Colette's arm.

'I thought we might have some breakfast.'

She smiled. 'OK.'

The owner of Mario's was a tall, grey-haired man with a strong Italian accent. The cappuccinos, when they came, were frothy and thick. Ryan picked up his teaspoon and drew small patterns in the froth.

'You seem to feel better this morning.'

'A bit.'

'Good.'

Silence – awkward. He sipped his coffee and was considering what to say – how to make conversation – when she said quietly, 'I'm going to die, aren't I?'

'No.'

'But you say that to everyone.'

'Yes.'

Silence again.

'Shouldn't you be a bit more reassuring?'

'Probably, but I sense that lying to you isn't going to help.'

'Do you always tell the truth?'

A pause. 'As often as I can.'

'That's not terribly reassuring either.'

'You'll be all right.'

'Oh yes. Like all the other touts.'

'Well you agreed, so you must be confident.'

'That's what I thought, is it?'

He leaned forward. 'You will be all right. You *will* be all right.'

She looked down. 'I don't know why I should believe you.'

'Trust.'

'Do you?'

'Do I what?'

'Trust *me*.'

'Yes.'

'Why? You have no reason to.'

'No, that's true. But I do.'

Colette leaned back in the seat. 'So tell me about you.'

'Me? Not much to say.'

'There must be something. Married?'

'No.' He felt awkward. 'I don't think we should be talking about me.'

She smiled again. 'Oh, come on. You seem to know all about me.'

'I know very little about you.'

'Would you like to know more?'

'I don't think this is a productive avenue of conversation.'

She looked irritated. 'You're to be my handler, right?'

He nodded.

'So I'm not supposed to know anything about you?'

He nodded again. 'That is the general idea.'

'Right. So I'm supposed to trust you with my fucking life and yet I'm not allowed to know the slimmest details . . .'

'All right. It's not very interesting, that's all. I'm twenty-nine years old. I'm not married.'

'Would you like to be?'

'No comment.'

'I was married.'

'I know.'

'Aren't you going to ask me what it was like?'

'No.'

'Your boys killed him.'

'Not my boys.'

'Sometimes I think they did me a favour.'

Silence again. A dangerous area, he thought. 'Why do you think that?'

She shrugged. 'I think you'll have to work that out for yourself.' She took a sip of her coffee and went on without raising her head. 'You're not very experienced, are you?'

'Experienced enough.'

'And I'm supposed to have confidence in you?'

'I think you'll want to concentrate on whether I'm committed to you above all else.'

'And are you?'

'I think you know the answer to that.'

'And what about your superiors – that other man . . . dick-features.'

Ryan couldn't suppress a smile. 'Mr Jenkins.'

'I thought he said his name was *Peters*.'

Ryan cursed himself silently.

She looked at him directly with an amused, ironic grin on her face. 'And what is your name, Mr *Jones*?'

He waited for a few seconds and then, slowly, smiled back at her. 'My name is Ryan.' He took a sip of coffee. 'And I don't think you need worry about Mr Jenkins or Mr Peters, because we will be working with people from the RUC.' He watched the grin fade from her face.

'The RUC?'

'Yes. I'm sorry if you don't like it. It was decided above me.'

'I won't do it.'

'I'm afraid you have no choice.'

'They'll burn the likes of me just for the hell of it.'

'No, they won't. They're very professional. I'll be there to protect your interests.'

For a moment he thought she would argue further, but she picked up her teaspoon and began to stir her coffee. He could sense her confidence was slipping away.

'If they catch me they'll kill me.'

'Possibly.'

She leaned forward again, suddenly animated. 'For Christ's sake, not possibly! There's no fucking *possibly* about it.'

He knew he'd made a mistake. He put up his hand, as if imploring her to keep her voice down. 'They won't catch you. I'll make sure you're all right. There'll be no risks taken, I give you my word. You *have* to trust me. You've got no choice.'

She sat up and took a sip of her coffee. He tried to

move the conversation away from potential consequences.

'We need to go over some more ground—'

She interrupted. 'I had a dream last night.'

He didn't know if she expected him to reply, but he simply stirred the dregs of his coffee and left her to continue, unsure of where this was suddenly leading.

'In it, I worked in an office in Belfast, sorting income-tax forms.'

She paused, but didn't look up. 'My boss was called John and he was an attractive-looking man with four kids and a very nice wife called Sheila.

'I knew she was nice, because we always went to their house before Christmas – the whole load of us in the office and got drunk and . . .

'And that's how we knew he was an army reservist . . . because there was a photo on his bedside table and I had to go to the loo in his bathroom there one time.

'His kids were great.

'He kept it quiet, no-one knew about it.

'He was shot outside the office one cold afternoon the following February. The police reckoned one of us must have called to say he was preparing to leave.

'We all went to the funeral.'

Ryan stirred in his seat. 'If that was a confession, I suggest you . . .'

'It was a *dream*.' She lifted her head and stared at him again. 'There's another. Can I tell you about the one with the horses?'

'Can I ask you why you're telling me this?'

'You don't know me.'

'There are bits of you I don't need to know.'

'Let me go.'

He sighed deeply and shook his head. 'There is a lot of ground to go over,' he said.

She looked down and didn't speak. Eventually, she said, quietly, 'The first day will be the hardest.'

'We'll go through it now – again and again – and we'll put you down at Heathrow this afternoon.'

She shook her head. 'No, I think I should get the tube.'

'Why?'

'You never know ... international airport. You just never know.'

Ryan nodded. 'OK. We've dealt with what happens after you get back, but we need to go through exactly what you've been doing for the past forty-eight hours.'

Colette pulled herself up in her seat, as if consciously turning her mind to a practical problem. Ryan watched the emotion and uncertainty slowly disappear. She spoke deliberately, her story gathering steam. 'I ran from the scene ... down to Battersea Park ... that much as it happened. Then ... I heard the police sirens ... lots of them. I was worried. It was dark. I decided to spend the night there – in a shed perhaps. That's what I *should* have done ... Then, perhaps, I made my way to the flat in Clapham and spent last night there. We'd have to go there to check.'

Ryan watched her as they drove down the Embankment towards Battersea Park a few minutes later. She didn't acknowledge him. There was a coldness between them now.

They found the hut just next to the tennis courts, and she watched as he broke the lock and checked the inside. It was comfortable enough, they both agreed, the discarded netting made a reasonable bed.

By the time they reached Clapham, their moods had darkened further, but they found the keys to the flat and Colette spent twenty minutes making sure it looked as if it had been used. She assured him there was no possibility of someone else having been there. She said it never happened after an operation, just in case she'd been followed. She put the keys back and they made the last drive in tense silence. Ryan asked her once if she was all right, but she didn't respond; it was as if she'd already gone. When they got to Baron's Court tube she left without saying goodbye and without looking back.

Colette had never seen the man before and that surprised her. She couldn't place the accent exactly, but she thought it was Cork or perhaps Kerry. He greeted her warmly and waited patiently as she paid the waitress for her coffee.

She followed him across the road with her heart in her mouth. So far, it had been the strangest of homecomings. She'd felt a rush of affection for Dublin. There was a certain comfort in the anonymity of a big city. So many strange faces. She thought none of them would ever have even begun to guess and, initially, she had found herself almost enjoying her secret. That feeling hadn't lasted.

The pavements and streets were crowded and she followed the man into St Stephen's Green with a growing sense of dread. She remembered waiting outside Sister Theresa's office at school before she'd reached the greater self-confidence of puberty. It was the same feeling, only a thousand times worse. She knew this man could sign her death warrant. There were quite a few people in the park, some feeding the ducks, some ambling, all enjoying the brief afternoon sunshine. They walked past a couple arguing on a park bench and watched as a young man got up from another, his lunch apparently finished. They sat down.

Colette struggled to control her nerves.

The man started gently and that helped her. She found reserves of strength she didn't know were there and she told herself she was a volunteer back from the front. He had no right to question her loyalty or commitment. He was a back-room soldier. Nothing to be worried about.

As he talked, she looked at him. He was unremarkable in every sense. He stood just under 6 feet, was clean-shaven, softly spoken and wore a padded peaked cap with flaps at the side.

Gradually, he probed deeper, though he didn't seem to be trying to catch her out. Why had she aborted the operation, he asked. Why had it gone wrong? Why had she disposed of the bomb? How had she got away? Where had she gone to? Where had she spent the first night – and the second? Why had she not called in? Why had she not requested assistance?

She stumbled over her answers and tried to muddle through with studied vagueness. He didn't let anything drop. When she said she'd spent the first night inside Battersea Park, inside a small wooden hut, he'd wanted to know where the hut was, how it was locked and how she broke in.

She felt grateful to Ryan for the thoroughness of their preparation.

How long it went on she'd have found it hard to say, but eventually he let her go with an affectionate pat on the shoulder.

She didn't know his name and didn't know if he was convinced.

Later, she woke as the train shuddered to a halt. Outside the window, she noticed the red paint and hanging flower baskets of Belfast's Central Station. On the journey back, she'd thought of Catherine and Mark and little else, now with foreboding. The encounter in Dublin had given her back a degree of self-confidence, but the man was a stranger. She didn't dare ask herself whether her family would be convinced.

She turned left out of the station, away from the great yellow Harland and Wolff cranes towering over Protestant east Belfast. It had been raining and the water was running in rivulets by the side of the road, but the sky was clearing now, the sun sinking down towards the mountain ahead of her. She wanted to feel happy at the familiarity of that view and just couldn't. It was a horrible sensation.

She cut through the city centre and tried to think of the joy of being reunited with Mark and Catherine. She thought they, at least, would not suspect her.

As she passed the city hall she saw a newspaper stand. The headline on the billboard caught her eye and she froze. It read, LOYALIST ATTACK ON FALLS. The banner line underneath added, MCVEIGH HOME TARGETED AGAIN.

For a moment she didn't move, then the impact of the words hit her and she began to run – fast, as if demented.

Up Grosvenor Road, crashing into somebody, but not looking back. She felt the impact of the pavement through her shoes. She felt short of breath, but kept running. She slowed as she approached the round-about. The traffic on the other side was waiting for the light to go green and she ran out just as it did. They honked, but didn't hit her. She turned right. Past people she knew now. She recognized Cathy – from next door – but didn't acknowledge her. She turned left into the street and saw the white tape and the soldiers. She slowed. She could see the one in the middle was a head taller than his colleagues. She tried to brush past him, but he grabbed her roughly and forced her back.

As he began to ask questions, she saw Paddy, her middle brother, detach himself from the crowd in front of the house and come running towards them. He hit the soldier powerfully from behind and sent him sprawling towards the pavement. The others moved to close in, but Paddy pointed at Colette and began shouting.

'Just fuckin' keep your hands off her.'

Before the soldiers could react, their officer arrived. 'Mr McVeigh.'

'She's my sister – just keep your bloody hands off her.'

The threat was unmistakable. A large crowd had gathered and the officer was painfully aware that the situation could deteriorate quickly. 'She was running towards us. It could easily have been Loyalists.'

Paddy looked at him with contempt. 'Sure you'se would know if they were coming back.'

He took Colette's arm and led her gently forward, leaning to whisper in her ear. 'Pipe bomb through the window, but it's OK, the kids were at Auntie Margaret's. Nobody's hurt. Ma's frightened, but they didn't get us.'

Colette felt dazed. It was like a dream now. With each step, she was assaulted by the familiar: the street itself, with the rubbish swept up against the pavement, the stray dogs, the crowd outside, the soldiers, the new wooden front door – replaced after the last police raid – with the number six written roughly in white paint at the top.

The door seemed to open automatically as they approached and she was conscious of several men grunting a greeting. Paddy released her arm. She stopped dead. She saw Mark's striped T-shirt hanging at the bottom of the stairs and felt her stomach

80

lurch. She saw the carpet – dark purple swirls – and the poorly framed landscape of a view she had never placed but knew to be somewhere on the west coast.

It was home.

But there was no warmth here today – nothing safe or comforting or secure. It was sordid.

She turned into the front room. She saw the damage, but what she noticed was that the television, which was not broken, was new. There was a large hole in the floor and the room was littered with glass and debris, but otherwise it was the same; the same mottled blue wallpaper, the same dark wooden bookshelves, the same picture of the Madonna and child on the far wall.

She stood still again, trying to find her bearings but failing. She heard the music in the kitchen and took a step forward.

She saw the spools of the white cassette recorder slowly turning and heard the clear, sad voice of Enya – the tape she had given her mother last Christmas. She noticed the top of the aerial had broken off the tape recorder. She saw her mother, hunched in the chair, with her head in her hands. She looked at her shawl, at the grey hairs poking out of it, the blue trousers and the flat-soled brown shoes that she had worn for so many years. She looked beaten. Defeated. Colette felt her betrayal so acutely she almost collapsed. Her mother looked up, tears in her eyes, and Colette wanted to hesitate. But the guilt wasn't enough to stop her. She didn't want her legs to move, but she found herself in her mother's arms.

She wanted to cry but couldn't. She wanted to feel safe but didn't. As her mother's embrace tightened, she tried to hate her. She stopped hugging first. She couldn't remember the last time that had happened.

She realized she was shaking violently.

She stepped back and her mother looked at her with sorrow and grief in her eyes. Her face was weather-beaten and lined, but she still managed to look elegant, and there were traces of the beauty for which she had once been renowned.

'The kids are OK – they're at—'

'I know, Ma.'

Her mother still had tears in her eyes. 'Bastards,' she said simply. 'Bastards.' She hugged Colette again. 'It's got to stop, love. It can't go on. It's *got* to stop.'

When Colette pulled away she did so with her face averted. She went back to the hall, where Paddy was talking to their eldest brother, Gerry.

Gerry smiled at her. 'You OK?'

She nodded and smiled back. He looked at her, but without scrutiny and, for once, she felt grateful for his indifference. She noticed his pebble glasses were dirty and his chin was unshaven.

He was a quiet man, who generally kept his emotions under tight control, but she could tell he was furious. 'We'll have to move her – the Loyalists will keep coming here now.'

She felt contempt. She wanted to say, 'It's your own fucking fault,' but she didn't flinch.

Paddy leaned back against the door, his face suddenly catching the evening sunlight. 'Ma won't move.'

Gerry said nothing, but pushed himself away from the wall. He looked as if he would say something else, but seemed to change his mind as he saw a policeman and two soldiers standing outside. They watched him in silence.

After he'd left, Colette sat with Paddy. They had always been close and neither of them had ever really seen eye to eye with Gerry. They had all played together, but somehow Gerry had kept himself apart.

They talked a little about England, but Paddy didn't probe in any detail. She tried to eliminate the hesitancy in her voice, and when she spoke she did so with her eyes focused on the ground. She looked for a reaction in his face, but saw nothing amiss. She could see tension and stress there and she told herself it was the life he chose. He did not have the intelligence to find a way out.

She congratulated herself.

When he smiled and kissed her forehead, she felt sick.

They sat in silence for a while. She couldn't help looking at him and feeling her love. His hair still hung to his shoulders – it always seemed to have been the same length – but there were tinges of grey now. Even his moustache was showing signs of age.

She smiled again. 'You're getting old.'

He grinned back at her only briefly, his expression suddenly serious. 'Do you ever wonder what life would be like without this?'

She paused for a while before replying, looking at the ground between her feet and scratching it with a small, sharp stone. 'It'll always be like this, Paddy.'

'Not everyone thinks so.'

'Gerry does. Doesn't he?'

Paddy paused. 'Yes, he does.'

She looked at him. 'What's happening? Is it coming to an end?'

'Maybe. I'm not sure. Gerry keeps his own counsel – you know how he is.'

Colette wanted to be away and she told Paddy she had to go and see the kids. As she arrived at Margaret's house a few minutes later, she could barely contain herself. The front door was a few inches ajar and she pushed it without knocking. There was nobody inside, but she could hear the sounds from the yard. The back door was open, the sun spilling into the room, catching Catherine's blond hair and making it golden.

She was wearing the pink and white dress Colette had given her before going away. She sat hunched over her doll, dressing it meticulously and combing its long blond hair.

For a moment, Colette watched. She could see and hear Mark in the courtyard. He was screaming abuse at Margaret's son Kieran and waving a plastic gun wildly in his face. 'I killed you first and you've got to lie down. We agreed!'

Kieran was a nervous boy and he was stammering weakly, 'But I got you. I got you.'

Mark began to push Kieran to the ground, but Colette's attention was distracted by Catherine, who had turned and seen her. Without speaking, she ran and curled herself around Colette's leg, whispering quietly as she did so, 'Mammy, Mammy.'

Colette bent down to hug her and looked out towards Mark. For a few minutes he stared at them, and then turned and ran, leaving Kieran stranded on the ground, relieved his torture had inexplicably ended.

Colette picked Catherine's hands off her leg and promised she would be back in a few seconds. She chased after Mark and found him around the corner, crouching against a wall. When she sat down and tried to hug him he pulled away, but she persisted and eventually he began to sob quietly.

When he'd exhausted his tears, he pushed himself closer to her. 'Why did you go away for so long, Mammy?'

For a long time, she didn't answer, but she realized

she must. 'It's hard to explain – and hard for you to understand. I'm trying to make you and your dad proud of me.' She gripped his chin. 'One day, I want you to be proud of me.'

'Is Daddy coming back?'

She hugged him tight. 'No, Daddy's gone to a better place. He's up there looking down on us. You see him?' She pointed up towards the sky. 'He's up there in the clouds, looking back down on us. Helping us when we need help and—'

'Why did he have to go away?'

Colette sighed deeply, squatted down and sat Mark on her knee. 'It's very hard for you to understand. One day you will, but he did it for us. He did it so we could have a better life. That's what I'm trying to do. That's what he'd want me to do.'

'Would he want you to be away?'

'No, he wouldn't. No, but it is something we all believe in; Davey, me – everyone. It's something we have to do.' She felt hollow as she said it, and lonely. Mark nuzzled closer to her again, pushing his head into her chest.

'I hate it when you go away.'

She tightened her arms. 'I know, love, I know.'

He began to sob again gently. 'I hate it. I hate it.'

'I do too, love. I hate it as much as you.'

He pushed away from her again. 'But why do you *have* to go? I don't understand.'

She pulled his head back down and tried to stem the tears.

'Will you go away again?'

'I don't want to, my love. I really don't want to. I hope I won't have to. I love you, Mark. I love you.'

She carried him back to the house. Catherine was sitting on the step and she seemed to understand that her mother needed to deal with Mark first. She accepted Colette's hug without any reservations and the three of them formed a small tableau by the kitchen door.

Eventually, Colette stood up and began to feed them and put them to bed. Mark remained truculent and he seemed to manage to intimidate Catherine. It upset her. She felt tired and dazed. After she'd read to them and put out their lights, Margaret suggested she stay on and they sat in the front room for a few minutes drinking tea. Colette felt uncomfortable being here. She'd shared the house with Davey and only offered it to Margaret when she'd decided to move back in with Ma. The situation was only temporary, but she wasn't sure she wanted to come back here. It held too many memories.

Margaret was very like Ma, though she talked more. She was the youngest sister in a family of ten and the closest to Ma in age. Her husband had gone to England to find work. They were not 'involved' and did not really approve of those who were, though they understood well enough the pressures that set people on that road.

Like Ma, Margaret was good with the kids. Colette knew that, in this small community, with its warm and intimate network of friends and family, the children were well cared for, even when she was not there. The fact that she thought that made her feel guilty. She felt like she was making excuses.

Eventually, she said she had to go and check on her mother. They agreed it would be best if the kids stayed where they were for the night.

In Leeson Street, the house was now full of relatives. Paddy was still there and he persuaded her to go down into the centre of Belfast. She was very reluctant, saying she had to get back to check on the kids, but Paddy insisted.

They decided to walk and were pleasantly surprised to discover there was no checkpoint at the bottom of the Falls. They were comfortable and easy in each other's company and Paddy did not seem to be in the least suspicious. Colette felt as if she must say something, but as they went on, she found herself relaxing slightly. She thought to herself, it is only Paddy. Somewhere, there was a darker thought, and she began to wonder what he would think, what he would say, how much he would hate her . . . She locked it away and, as they walked, she found herself laughing. They were brother and sister again. They were friends.

With her, Paddy was always indiscreet. He told her that Gerry had tried to go for a job in Northern Command, the organization responsible for running the IRA's campaign in Northern Ireland, but had been turned down, much to his anger and annoyance. She learned that Gerry was still playing around on his wife Christy with great regularity, but that she knew nothing about it – or at least pretended she knew nothing. Paddy's tone suggested he disapproved. He and Gerry had always been different.

Colette tried to discover if Paddy was seeing anyone, but he just laughed. He'd never married. Their mother was still waiting and hadn't given up hope.

As they entered Kelly's, the doorman gave Colette a broad smile.

'How's the form, Colette?' he said.

She felt a stab of guilt again and began to wish she hadn't come. Everything that was familiar – every individual and every street – provided a reminder and an accusation. She decided she wanted a drink and made for the bar.

Inside, the band was loud and bad, grinding out poor renditions of 'Johnny Be Good' and various other classic Sixties songs. The singer was a tall lanky man with a thick mop of greasy black hair and a thin red headband. All of them were dressed in jeans and white T-shirts. A few people were dancing, almost everyone was smoking and drinking heavily. The smoke was overpowering – choking. Paddy was accosted by a group of young men just inside the door and Colette pushed on through the throng towards the far end. The room was like a cavern and had no ventilation.

As she reached the bar, she felt a hand on her shoulder and turned to see a wide, toothless grin and an unkempt beard.

'Chico.'

'It's been a long time, pet.'

She felt slightly uncomfortable so close to him, but she didn't move. He smelled of Guinness and Chinese food.

She had known Chico a long time and for a few minutes they shouted at each other, straining to be heard above the din. He bought her a vodka and lemonade, which she drank quickly. He bought her another and continued to try to shout above the sound of the music. She nodded and drank. He'd got doubles and she began to feel light-headed. She felt better. Chico was just ordering another round when he appeared to catch sight of someone over her shoulder. He frowned and began to fumble in his pocket. He pushed a key into her hand and began shouting in her ear, 'I need you for a few seconds. There's a red Sierra round the back. Bring it to the front and keep the engine running.'

Before she could say anything, he was pushing through the crowd. She did as he said, not daring to refuse, and began to head towards the door. She saw

Paddy, but he was standing with his back to her. The doorman smiled and asked her where she was going. She smiled back and shrugged. She began to worry.

She found the car and waited outside. A few minutes later one of the side doors flew open and Chico emerged dragging a boy in a white baseball cap.

He pushed him into the back of the car and got in beside him.

'Drive.'

Colette didn't know where to go, but she knew better than to question Chico, so she took the car up towards the Lower Falls. She was fighting the effects of the double vodkas. They passed beneath the security monitoring point at the Divis Tower and continued on up towards Andersonstown. She saw a soldier to the left of her and then another to the right. A few yards further on a third aimed his gun at the car, testing his sights. The streets were pretty deserted. A black taxi stopped ahead of her to let somebody out and she had to swerve round it. She crossed over the Springfield Road and slowed as she came down the hill towards Beechmount. At Beechmount Avenue, she turned right. She passed a long, red-brick wall, which was covered in graffiti. Somebody had written in big white letters, 'Time for Peace. Time to go home, Brits.' She turned left and then slowly brought the car to a halt.

Chico dragged the boy out of the car and onto a piece of wasteland to their right. Ahead of them lay two identical red-brick terraces, built in Belfast's industrial heyday. If they were once new and neat, they now stood as a symbol of neglect, deprivation and urban decay, their walls covered in barbed wire, the streets in front of them strewn with rubbish.

Chico pulled the boy into a narrow alley that ran between the two sets of houses, pushing his face into a concrete pavement and a discarded packet of salt and vinegar crisps. The ground was damp and the air cold. Colette had followed Chico on autopilot and stood beside him, but now she realized she didn't want to be there.

The boy was crying gently. Chico banged his face hard against the pavement. Colette winced.

The boy screamed, 'I haven't done nothin'! I did what you'se said.'

'Shut up.' Chico grabbed his hair and leaned down to whisper in his ear. 'Just stay there – move and you'll be dead.' He turned to Colette. 'Hold him. I'll be a few minutes.'

'For Jesus' sake, Chico. He's only a kid.'

He looked at her. 'Just fucking hold him.'

She put her knee into the small of the boy's back, but he didn't move or speak. He was still crying and whispering to himself. He had a thick, attractive mop of curly blond hair and Colette felt intensely uncomfortable. She wanted to say something, but knew she shouldn't.

'I haven't done nothin', I haven't done nothin',' he whispered.

Chico was quick and when he came back he gave Colette the pistol and grabbed the boy's hair again.

'I thought I told you not to go back in there?'

The boy was very frightened and tried to raise his head, but Chico slammed him down against the ground and he screamed again and struggled to get the words out. Blood from the grazes on his face was thickening on the concrete.

'I wasn't doin' nothin'. I was just out for a drink.'

Chico leaned on him. 'Are you still pushing?'

'No. No. Please.'

'I've not seen any money from you. You know the

rules. Nobody plays that game without our say-so. If you want to push, you ask me and maybe I'll let you. You go freelance, you pay the price.' He stood up, but kept hold of the boy's hair. 'Do it, Colette.'

She looked up.

'Do it. That's an order.'

The boy was sobbing hysterically now. 'No, please no. For Christ's sake, I didn't do nothin'.'

Colette closed her eyes for a few seconds and then stood up, took aim at the boy's right thigh and fired. In the small alley the noise was deafening, and the two of them turned to run.

The army patrol must have been near, because as they rounded the corner the soldiers were running towards them at full tilt. They were shouting and the boy was screaming. The alley ahead was dark, but Colette could see their way was blocked. Chico leaped onto the wall, turned back and stretched out his hand.

She jumped for the top, missed and slid down again, grabbing at Chico's hand in the process. The first shot rang out and ricocheted off the wall beside her. She felt her legs going, but at that moment Chico pulled her up and she fell over the other side, landing painfully in a ditch in the corner of a field. She picked herself up and followed him, and the soldiers' shouts quickly faded into the night.

They cut across waste ground and crashed through somebody's garden, but at the back of Hill Street they stopped in another alley and leaned against a wall to catch their breath. Colette was muddy and wet.

Chico had taken the gun back and he slipped it into his pocket.

'That'll teach the fucker. Little wee shite.'

He stood up again and looked at Colette. Once, when they were kids, he had kissed her in just such an alley.

'Do you want to come back to my place for a drink?' he said casually, as if it didn't matter to him either way. Colette wanted to say no, but there was a deep, corrosive loneliness within her and she heard herself say yes.

Chico lived in a sparsely furnished house at the far end of Beechmount Avenue. As they walked in he threw his keys into the bowl and swept away the remnants of a Chinese meal that had been left on the corner of the plywood coffee table. The sofa was old and worn and Colette sat down whilst Chico went to get her a drink.

She never got anything, because, after putting the kettle on, he came back, leaned over the sofa and began to kiss her. She didn't want him, but she didn't say no. She let him carry her upstairs to the dirty, unmade bed, where the sheets looked like they'd not been changed since the last time he'd brought a woman back.

She took off her trousers and managed to restrain him whilst she removed her knickers. She lay back on the bed as he turned off the light.

He thrust his hand between her legs to stimulate her, but the foreplay was brief and quite rough. She held the base of his penis and tried to rub it around her vagina before he entered, but he was impatient and strong and he pushed hard. There were a few moments of pain when he entered her.

She shut her eyes. She clenched her knees to the man's side and thrust her pelvis upwards. She clenched the top of his hairy buttocks and pretended she didn't care that the gap between them was clammy. She told herself she enjoyed being fucked.

He let out a low groan. She whispered. 'Please, wait . . .'

His voice was husky. 'Aaaaaah . . . Christ, Colette, you're . . . gorgeous.'

Afterwards, she gathered up her clothes and left without saying goodbye.

The Falls was more or less deserted, though a black taxi sped past her as she turned out of Beechmount. The temperature had dropped further and she could see her breath on the air as she walked.

She was sore between her legs and she reflected that it had been almost a year since she'd last had somebody inside her. She wondered what in the hell she'd been doing.

Perhaps, she thought, it was self-punishment. She certainly felt inexplicably better.

She opened the door to the house in Leeson Street and stood in the hall for a few moments, enjoying the silence. The familiarity of her surroundings seemed less offensive and she looked up the stairs to the landing. The lights were off and she assumed Ma must be in bed and asleep.

She walked into the front room. The curtains were open and the light was spilling in from the street. She ran her foot round the hole in the floor, and the violence it represented seemed ugly.

Ahead of her, she could just about make out the picture of the Madonna and child and she found herself wondering at her mother's faith and conviction. She thought of that young boy – Jesus – and the pain he'd endured on the Cross. For what?

She thought that whatever you made of the Bible and whatever you thought of Jesus, there was no doubt that the man had died in horrible, terrible pain. If you took it at its worst – as Gerry had always done, for example – the reality of that death was still there. Whether He was the Son of God or not (how could you believe in God?) the reality was that He was a good man who had died for His beliefs.

A good man trying to make a better world. But what were you supposed to make of that?

She turned round and walked back upstairs to bed. As she opened the door to her room, she saw the two mattresses laid out neatly on the floor. Ma had made up all three beds and she found herself sighing with a mixture of gratitude and irritation.

She looked out of the window to the empty alley below and then suddenly yanked down her jeans and knickers and peered at them. She couldn't see them clearly and she leaned over to turn on the light. She stepped to the side of the window and looked down again. They were damp, but she couldn't see any blood.

She leaned back against the wall. How long had it been? Her body was so sensitive.

Well, at least she wouldn't be pregnant – though she'd thought that when Mark had been conceived.

She thought of Mark and Catherine and made a decision. She pulled up her jeans and turned off the bedroom light. It took her only a couple of minutes to walk round to Margaret's house, where she gingerly knocked on the door.

She stepped back and looked up at the bedroom windows, but there was no response. A dog began barking close by and then others followed suit. She knocked again – louder this time – and stepped back to see a light go on upstairs. The window opened and she saw Margaret's grey hair.

'Margaret, it's me,' she said in a loud whisper.

'Colette?'

'I just wanted to get the kids.'

A pause. 'It's the middle of the night.'

'I know, I'm sorry.'

Another pause and then the window was pulled shut. Colette watched as a light went on in the hall and the front door opened. She stepped in.

'I'm sorry, Margaret. I know it's late.'

Margaret was in a tatty old blue dressing gown and her eyes were still half shut against the light. She didn't reply and Colette shot up the stairs and into the room on the left. It was dark inside, the curtains tightly drawn, and it was a few seconds before her eyes adjusted. She began to make out the beds and she bent down to touch the one on the right. She felt a body and whispered quietly, 'Mark?'

'Mammy?' It was Catherine's voice to her left.

'It's me, love. We're going home.'

She traced her hands along the body beneath her until she got to a head. 'Mark, love,' she said.

He stirred, but didn't speak. She shook him gently. 'Mark.'

He groaned and turned over. She leaned down to kiss him and he smelled clean, his skin warm and soft. 'Mark,' she said.

She could see Catherine sitting up in bed now and she picked her up and hugged her. Like Mark, she smelled clean and soapy. Colette went over and turned on the light and, for a moment, they were all blinded. Eventually, Mark sat up in bed and looked at them. 'Where are we going?' he asked.

'Home.'

Silence. He rubbed his eyes. 'I don't want to go home.'

Colette was still carrying Catherine. 'Come on, Mark, just put on your tracksuit.'

She put Catherine down and began to gather up their clothes which littered the floor.

'I don't want to go,' Mark said.

She sat down on the bed and tried to hug him, but he pushed away her arms violently.

'Right,' she said. 'You can stay. We'll go.'

She bent down again and packed their clothes into a bag. She helped Catherine into her tracksuit and went into the bathroom to get their toothbrushes. When she came back, Mark hadn't moved.

'Come on, Mark,' she said.

She bent down and tried to pick him up. He pushed her away once or twice, but then gave up. She got him out of bed and into his tracksuit and then tried to hold both their hands as they went down the stairs, which was difficult with a bag over her shoulder.

It took only a few minutes to get back home and Colette put them both straight to bed. She went to brush her own teeth and then stripped to her knickers and T-shirt before shutting the curtains. She lay down for a few minutes and listened to the sounds of them sleeping.

She found herself resenting Mark for a moment for not understanding. But then, of course, she knew kids didn't understand and didn't want complications. She felt guilty at her inability to provide simplicity, or consistency for that matter.

Guilt had been her companion for so long, she'd forgotten what it was like to live without it. She stood up again and fractionally pulled aside one of the curtains. The alley behind was deserted.

She looked down and enjoyed the silence.

She thought about the Brit and found herself breathing in deeply and asking herself, what have I done?

Suddenly, a light came on in the house opposite. There was a loud crash – sounded like saucepans or something metal. She heard Mickey Gibbs shout, 'Bitch!' and she realized he was drunk again. She pulled the curtains shut and tried to close her ears to the row and the screaming.

She lay down and tried to listen to Mark and Catherine. They didn't seem to have been woken.

She looked up at the ceiling. She thought there was a lot to be said for the argument that all men were the same. All fucking useless.

For the first few minutes, Grant stuck to small talk. 'Got yourself sorted out? Said goodbye to the girlfriend?'

The room was warm and fairly dark. Grant never had the overhead lights on and the room was illuminated now by the desk lamp, which was pushed right down against the leather top it sat on. The curtains behind the desk were drawn, but the light from the street below was just spilling in through the middle. Ryan could hear the hum of the traffic.

The left-hand wall of the room was covered with books, except for an old oil landscape in the middle, which Ryan knew concealed Grant's safe. Anyone wanting to find it would have located it in seconds.

Grant was head of 'T' branch, which dealt with all counter-terrorism. Jenkins was head of the Provisional IRA source unit and answered to Grant.

Grant himself was standing by the window now, his glasses in his right hand, with one of the arms in the corner of his mouth. He'd always liked Ryan, right from the start, and the feeling was mutual. There was a pregnant pause.

'We have every confidence in you, David. I want you to know that.'

Then why the need to say it, Ryan thought.

'And I don't want to bore you endlessly with things I know you've heard many times before.'

Ryan was listening carefully. Grant's reputation was second to none.

'But always remember, always keep at the front of

your mind, the fact that the characteristics that make someone a good agent, and a good terrorist for that matter, are not the characteristics that make someone a decent individual. Deviousness, cunning, manipulative ability, absence of fear, courage, one might even say the ability to divorce oneself from the consequences of one's actions – all these characteristics make an individual totally unreliable. These are people who live life at the extremes, in a world that nothing in our training and background can ever really prepare us for. We *need* these people, but we have got to stay ahead of them. We have to think ahead of them – not on our terms, but on theirs.' Grant paused and came round to sit on the front of the desk, blocking the pool of light. He was still sucking one of the arms of his glasses and Ryan thought he looked old.

'So, what I am saying is, however much you think you are in control, however much you think you have a relationship with your man – or in this case woman – always remember, *always*, that they could be lying. Never trust them. Never take what this woman says at face value. Ask yourself *why* she is saying this or that. What are her motives . . .'

Ryan thought of Colette in her prison cell. Alone, apparently defeated.

'I'm concerned about the nature of the recruitment . . .'

Ryan realized that was a question. He cleared his throat and put one hand to his mouth in a gesture of thoughtfulness. 'I don't think . . .'

'The coercion, I mean.'

Ryan paused. He thought about it. 'I can't be sure, but I don't think that played – I mean, I would strongly suspect that she was expecting us and that she . . .'

'You don't think she bought the idea that she was going to prison?'

'I don't know. She might have done, but I think somewhere in there is a separate motivation – one she hasn't really admitted to herself . . .'

'To get out?'

'I would say so, yes. I don't think I'd have gone ahead otherwise. I think she realizes – well, let me put it this way, what future does she have otherwise?'

Grant didn't reply. He pushed himself off the desk again and wandered back round to his chair. Ryan wondered again at the contrast between the man's reputation and the shuffling, intellectual figure who stood before him. With his thinning white hair, ageing brogues and trousers that were too short, it was very hard to think of Grant in the front line of the war against terrorism.

Grant stood behind his chair now and stroked the leather upholstery – a distracted gesture that was actually rather odd. He put on his glasses again, the thick dark frames ageing his face still further.

'One other thing you're going to have to bear in mind; operating with the RUC isn't going to be easy and you'll need to be on your guard there too. I'm sorry about that, but it is for reasons decided above both of us.'

Grant pulled the seat back and sat down, pulling himself up to the desk and picking up one of his pens.

'The RUC are very good and we certainly need them, but their motives are somewhat different from ours, if you take my meaning. This woman seems to me to present quite an opportunity. She is close to the heart of PIRA – or at least very close to those that are – and in the current shenanigans over all this peace talk, she could be quite an asset. But I'm afraid our ways are rather different to the RUC, as you know. We look to the long term – a slow build-up – they are, not surprisingly, often concerned about the immediate short-term threat. I think you know what I'm saying. Watch out, but remember we need the RUC and this is all about bridge-building, so you'll have to be at your *most* diplomatic.'

He sighed, pushed back his chair and stood up. 'You'll need to see Personnel before you go. I've arranged for you to be picked up by one of our people, and I've arranged for the RUC to issue you with a personal weapon.' He stretched out his hand. 'Good luck. Don't let us down, eh?'

Ryan shook his hand and turned to go.

'Oh, and, David, be careful – and don't take it personally, any of it. It's a job, remember?'

As Ryan left the office in Gower Street, he could feel the fear in the pit of his stomach.

Outside, the air was cold and there were a few light drops of rain. Ryan waved at an approaching taxi and asked the man to take him to Latchmere Road. As they pulled away, the man half turned and said, 'That's the MI5 building, then?'

'Is it?' Ryan asked with an air of genuine interest.

'You one of them?'

'Not the last time I looked.'

The man laughed and turned back to concentrate on the road ahead.

The journey took about twenty minutes and, as Ryan opened the door of Latchmere Road twenty minutes later, he heard Claire's voice and felt slightly disappointed. He wanted to be on his own. She was on the phone, so he got a beer out of the fridge, sat down and lit a cigarette. Claire finished and came and sat opposite him. 'You look tired,' she said.

'I'm going to be away for a while.'

'What are you doing?' She laughed. 'You could tell me, but you'd have to kill me?'

Ryan smiled and she looked at him carefully. 'Is it a big deal for you?'

'It's a big break. Something I've done before, but the first time I've had the lead, if you see what I mean – the first time it's been *my* responsibility. Before I've always been assisting. Not everyone thinks I'm ready for it, so there'll be a bit of pressure.'

'Who doesn't think you're ready for it?'

'The guy above me.'

'The one who gives you all the grief?'

Ryan nodded. 'The one above him thinks I am and it was his call, so it'll be all right.'

'It's hard not being able to talk about it all, isn't it?'

He smiled, pulled out his handkerchief and blew his nose.

'What about Isabelle?' she said.

'That's over.'

'You said.'

'Well, it is.'

'Definitely, completely, irreversibly?'

'Permanently.'

'Shame. I liked her.'

'So did I.'

Ryan took a last drag of his cigarette. 'We kind of agreed we shouldn't see each other for a while anyway, so maybe this is for the best.' He stood up. 'I've got to pack now and I may not see you tomorrow.' He bent down and kissed her.

'Good luck,' she said as he walked away.

In his bedroom, Ryan pulled the grip down from the top of the cupboard and mechanically began to load his clothes. He went into the bathroom to get his razor and toothbrush, and then came back and sat down on the bed. He shut his eyes and found himself thinking back to the previous summer and a holiday at Claire's parents' house in Provence. It had been lazy, hot and peaceful, with long days spent lying out on the grass or beside the pool. He hadn't invited Isabelle, of course, and had been sorely tempted to have an affair with Claire. But it would have been tacky, and it wasn't really his style. He'd never been unfaithful to anyone.

It had been fun, though, as a holiday. Now, it seemed a long way away.

CHAPTER SIX

Colette felt something was wrong, but it took her a few seconds to place it. The room was dark, but the door to the landing was open and she could hear the murmur of voices below.

In fact, it wasn't that something was actually *wrong*, she thought, it was just simply that ... that what? Something had changed. Mark and Catherine almost always woke her by crawling into her bed.

And there was something else too; an acrid smell that had once been familiar. She got up and fumbled for her dressing gown at the end of the bed. She turned on the light and leaned over Mark's mattress. She pulled back the duvet and saw the large damp patch in the middle. She cursed quietly.

Downstairs, Mark and Catherine were kneeling on the floor drawing with crayons on large white pieces of paper. Mark was wearing his favourite Spiderman pyjamas and, as she put her arms around him, she smelled the urine and saw the damp patch. She picked him up and carried him upstairs to the bath. He didn't complain, in fact, he didn't make a sound.

She ran him a bath and left him to wash himself. She carried his pyjamas downstairs and put them in the ancient washing machine in the kitchen. As she went back upstairs, Catherine followed her. In the bedroom, she looked for their clothes in the old plywood chest of drawers, but couldn't find them. Catherine said quietly, 'Grandma doesn't keep them there any more.'

She took Colette's hand and brought her back down to the kitchen. She pointed to the cupboard above the boiler. Sure enough, they were all there, neatly pressed.

Colette went upstairs to put Catherine in the bath too, only to discover that Mark had put soap all over the bathroom mirror and walls. It was *everywhere*. Without speaking, she stood him up and hit him once across his backside. He began to cry and to shy away from her, but she pulled him out of the bath and wrapped him in a towel. He scuttled past her into the bedroom.

She got them dressed. Mark's silence was truculent, Catherine's uncertain. It was as if she was afraid to speak for fear of angering her brother, though she tried to show her affection by clinging silently to Colette's arm.

As she released them for breakfast, Colette's mother emerged from her bedroom – fully dressed, as though she had been up for hours. In the kitchen, she clearly noticed the pyjamas in the washing machine and seemed to deliberately avoid any comment.

Colette switched on the radio and put two bowls on the table. She opened one of the upper cupboards and rummaged through its contents. She said, almost to herself, 'Where are the cornflakes?'

Her mother said quietly, 'I got them some Coco Pops.'

Colette did not reply. She opened the next cupboard and found the cereal. She found the milk in the fridge and noticed it was full fat, not semi-skimmed.

When she turned round, Mark was staring at her with all the hate he could muster. He began to eat his cereal, then stopped, picked up the bowl and hurled it at her head.

She ducked and shouted, 'MARK!' but he had clearly seen his escape route and was out of the door before she could get a hold of him. She knew pursuit was pointless. She was covered in milk and cereal. Her mother handed her a tea towel. She brushed off the cereal and mopped up the milk on the floor. It took several minutes. She was conscious of the fact that the kitchen floor was familiar. The yellow squares were fading.

Silence for a few moments. Her mother looked towards the washing machine. 'He hasn't . . . not since Davey.'

Colette tried to keep the irritation out of her voice. 'I know.'

She sat down at the table and pulled Catherine onto her lap, stroking her nose gently and ruffling her hair. 'Hello, little miss.'

Catherine buried her head in her mother's side. 'Can we go for a swim, Mammy, can we go for a swim?'

'Of course, maybe this afternoon. We'll see how we go.'

Colette looked over at her mother. 'I'll take them up to playgroup this morning, Ma.'

Her mother smiled. 'I don't mind doing—'

'Thanks, Ma, but it's OK. I'm back now, I'll do it.'

'OK, love, but you know I don't mind—'

'Thanks.'

Colette made herself a cup of coffee and Catherine some toast. She brought out the butter and jam and placed them on the table. Catherine looked at her strangely and Colette looked across to her mother,

105

sensing a conspiracy. Ma said quietly, 'I think they prefer honey . . .'

Colette had to fight to hold her temper. She went to sit on the step by the back door to smoke a cigarette, taking her coffee with her. She wondered if she should go and find Mark, but decided against it. Her mother said she was just going out and left, only to come back a minute later, poking her head round the kitchen door. 'Sorry, love, I forgot. Paddy came around earlier, said he hadn't really had a chance to see you yet. He said he'd be at the Felon's this morning if you wanted him.'

Colette glowered at the brick wall opposite the back door. She remembered that today was the day of the first meeting and she smiled bitterly. A different planet.

After she had cleaned up breakfast she put on a clean pair of knickers, a T-shirt and her jeans and washed her face. Downstairs, Mark was now sitting in the kitchen again, and she found and put on his outdoor coat without a word. He seemed content to hold her hand for the short walk to Conway Mill. She took them up to the second floor and into the playgroup room, with its mural of *The Jungle Book*. She chatted briefly to the women who ran the group and they all said they were pleased to see her back. One woman squeezed her arm supportively and one or two others gave her knowing looks, which she found irritating. 'What the hell would you know?' she wanted to ask. She kissed Catherine and Mark goodbye and walked back past the Sinn Féin press office. She had just turned onto the Falls when a soldier spotted her and came running over. She felt her temperature rising, but she knew that, whatever the provocation, losing her temper would only make the situation worse.

'Could I see your identification, madam?'

She didn't have it and the soldier sneered. 'So we've left it at home, have we?'

Colette didn't reply. He leaned closer and whispered, 'Killed anyone today, Mrs McGraw?'

It was common enough for the soldiers to recognize her. They were told to watch, note and report the movements of any 'players' – and their relatives – in their area. Sometimes they yielded good information, but most of the time it was a thankless and relatively pointless task. A little harassment helped pass the time.

The soldier was trying to provoke her now and he pushed her against the wall and spread her arms and legs apart. He began the body search at her ankles but he quickly moved higher, groping around her crotch and breasts and breathing heavily down her neck. Colette went for his hand and bit hard.

He recoiled, clutching his hand to his stomach and screaming, 'You fucking bitch!'

The other soldiers were running towards them now and she knew she was vulnerable. She would almost certainly have ended up in the Castlereagh Interrogation Centre, but she was next to the Sinn Féin press office and, just at that moment, Gerry Adams, the leader of Sinn Féin, emerged.

The soldier had now recovered and he and a colleague grabbed Colette's shoulders.

'Hold on there.'

The men stopped.

'Leave her alone.'

The officer had run up from further down the street. He was out of breath. 'I must advise you to keep out of this, sir.'

Adams's voice had an edge to it. 'This is my country and my street and you've got no business being here in the first place.'

A crowd had started to gather. The officer nodded to his men and they disengaged and set off down the street. They were booed and jeered as they went and Adams turned to Colette and smiled. 'How you doin', Colette?'

She felt shaken. 'I'm fine.'

When she arrived at the Felon's a few minutes later, she found Paddy sitting quietly in the corner of the upstairs bar, his hands clasped around a cup of Nescafé. He was concentrating on the television screen bolted to the wall beside him and he was alone but for the young girl behind the bar. It was a long time since Colette had been in here, but it hadn't changed. It was like an attic room, with a long sloping ceiling and a wooden floor. A huge Irish tricolour covered the wall in front of her. It was warm and felt cosy. She put the incident in the street out of her mind. It was too routine to be worth mentioning and it had happened to them both hundreds of times.

Paddy got to his feet, grinning. 'What happened to you last night?'

She smiled, but didn't reply. Paddy looked over at the girl behind the bar. 'Siobhan, could you get us a coffee?' He reached forward and took Colette's hands in his own and, as he did so, she felt the sense of hollowness return. She felt her treachery. It was a cancer growing slowly within.

'Got to go, I'm afraid, something brewing,' he said.

She didn't ask what. The TV was on above them, showing pictures of Albert Reynolds and the Brit Prime Minister standing in Downing Street in London. They were talking about this 'Declaration', a document designed to convince the IRA that the time had come to give up violence. It was supposed to persuade all

Republicans that the British and Irish governments would seriously address their concerns, if they would agree to pursue their aims by peaceful means.

They listened in silence for a while. When Paddy turned back to her, he looked puzzled. 'They're hyping this – there's nothin' in it for us.'

Colette wanted to ask more. She wanted to ask him what he thought, but was afraid of her motives for doing so.

'I think the leadership is getting this very badly wrong,' he said. 'I think they'll regret it.'

She registered the implicit threat and almost pursued it.

He got up. 'Sorry, got to go – I'll catch you later.' He picked up his jacket and headed for the door. After a few yards, he turned and came back, putting his hand on her shoulder and smiling as he turned.

'By the way, what we're working on is a big one. You'll enjoy it.' She didn't ask him to continue, but he did. 'Friday, the head of CID. He's had it coming to him a long, long time. He was the one who put you away, wasn't he?'

He looked at her, but she didn't reply. He shrugged. 'We're going to take him as he leaves home in the morning. Just thought you'd like to know, that's all.'

She didn't say anything. She wondered if this was a trap and then could not believe that that was what she was thinking. She felt sick and alone.

Ryan thought of her.

He felt a sense of intimacy, almost of warmth.

When they'd talked about her in the briefings, they'd used the phrases of a faraway war and the words had washed over him. They'd talked of asset, potential, development, control, PIRA Belfast Brigade, PIRA

England Department. But in his mind he'd seen a woman with slender arms, smooth skin and a warm smile.

But he was excited now. He couldn't deny it. Even a rank amateur could tell she had potential. She had form. She was close to people. She would be trusted. If he could crack her – if he could really open her up – then anything was possible. The leadership's intentions, the England Department sewn up from top to bottom. That would wipe the smirk off Jenkins's bloody face.

The voice on the intercom told them to fasten their seat belts.

He thought about his woman. He thought of her flying back to Dublin and he thought of the men who'd have watched her. They'd never have guessed it, but then who would? That was the hope. He hoped her own people couldn't smell it. He hoped they couldn't see it deep in her eyes. He didn't know if he could have coped. To deceive a stranger is one thing, but to convince a brother or a mother?

He thought of Judas Iscariot. He thought of the instinct for self-preservation. He asked himself if there was a more noble motive within her and he didn't know the answer.

The plane bounced roughly as it touched the runway, breaking his train of thought. As it taxied into the terminal, he looked out across the tarmac to see one of the big twin-rotored Chinooks taking off from the other side of the strip. A thin line of mist hung low over the fields in the distance and the helicopter rose slowly above it, twisting away to begin the long, noisy journey across the Irish Sea.

Inevitably, it was raining.

By the time he was on his feet, he'd begun to feel the

first pangs of fear. He thought of his Judas and of what he'd told her in the café. Did he trust her? It was ludicrous.

As he watched his bag come round the carousel he thought of how little he knew of her. He wondered if he was going to be set up.

'Ryan?'

The man was wearing jeans, trainers and a loose-fitting khaki jacket. He had horribly pockmarked skin. Ryan nodded, picked up his bag and followed without a word.

In the car, the man introduced himself as Joel, but then said virtually nothing. A few minutes out of the airport, they passed a permanent police checkpoint, but the constable looked bored and waved them through. Joel turned right and took the back way into Belfast. The land was scrappy here and poorly kept. Joel was driving fast and, as they rounded a corner, he had to pull the car sharply to the left to avoid another coming in the opposite direction. They passed a Gaelic football pitch and an old man walking home with a young child. As they skirted the mountain, the city was spread out beneath them. Ryan looked over towards the big yellow cranes and beyond, across the loch. Smoke from the factory chimneys drifted across the rooftops.

It was dramatic, if not beautiful. Ryan felt the fear and uncertainty in the pit of his stomach.

A thin veil of mist still lay in the valley, but it was clearing quickly.

As they drove down towards the city centre, they crossed the Andersonstown Road. Ryan saw an Irish Tricolour flying from the top of the Felon's club to the left and he felt like he'd never been away. It was an uncomfortable sensation. He thought of the one conversation he had had with Grant about it when he had

111

raised the prospect of returning to Ulster. *Don't worry. It's irrelevant. So many events. Why should anyone remember?*

As they passed, he envisaged her walking home, a child on each hand. Then he had an image of her pretty face distorted by a bullet exit wound. Try explaining *that* to the children, he thought.

Then they were through into comfortable, middle-class suburbia – only a short distance geographically. He couldn't imagine Colette here. This was his kind of territory.

He was taken to a flat just off the Malone Road, given the key and told to wait until the afternoon, when he would be picked up.

He sat trying to convince himself he didn't feel nervous. He walked to the shops and bought a few newspapers, but couldn't concentrate on reading them. He walked aimlessly around the flat. It was neat enough – modern and characterless, but functional.

He walked into the sitting room, switched on the radio and was playing with the dial when the buzzer went. Without answering it, he picked up his jacket and ran to the door.

It was an RUC car this time and the driver wanted to talk. Ryan wished he would shut up. It took fifteen minutes to get to the RUC's headquarters at Knock in east Belfast and they swept in through the gates without stopping. Ryan wondered what he would find. His colleagues sometimes talked of the RUC as though they were the real enemy.

A young woman with a pleasant smile was waiting outside the entrance to the main building and she shook Ryan's hand and escorted him up to Trevor Long's office on the second floor.

The corridor was long and gloomy. The lights were

out and it was clearly being refurbished. The young woman apologized for the darkness.

They turned left into an office and Trevor Long rose to greet him warmly; Ryan remembered him from a seminar during the training sessions a couple of years back. The man beside him wore a thin smile and stretched out his hand in turn. 'Brian Allen. Pleased to meet you.'

'Thank you. It's good to be here.'

Allen was bigger than Ryan had anticipated. He was well over 6 feet – about Ryan's height – with a belly that genuinely appeared to be testing the buttons on his shirt. He had a thick, untidy mop of white hair, a ruddy, quite handsome face and a scruffy, double-breasted grey suit with an ancient red tie. He looked unhappy, to say the least, and it was Trevor Long who continued with the small talk. Ryan was amused by the contrast: Long, the smartly turned out, bright, polite, diplomatic senior officer and Allen, the tough front-line man, who was obviously angry at having to work with a patsy from the Security Service.

Ryan thought carefully about how he was going to get round this one.

He decided the best form of defence was attack. 'On the question of authority . . .' He was looking at Allen now and trying to sound diplomatic. 'I know that you're in charge. I have no problem with that. I've got plenty to learn.'

Ryan watched the hostility drop away from Allen. They sat in silence.

'I ran into her once before in Castlereagh,' Allen said. 'She didn't say a word for seven days. Not one word. Surprising strength, I thought.'

'She was desperate this time.'

'Desperate for real? Or desperate for a few days to get herself out?'

'Desperate for real, I would say.'

'She's well-connected enough, all right. If she has turned, she does have potential.'

'She has turned.'

'We'll see.'

Allen sat and Ryan followed suit. Allen held up a cup. 'Tea?'

'Thank you. Milk, no sugar.'

'Didn't think much of your choice of venue.'

'I'm sorry. I thought it was central and quite busy. I thought she would be comfortable with it.'

'*She* might be – if she turns up – but I'm not. It's hard to clean. It makes me jumpy.'

Ryan didn't know what to say. He thought Allen was probably right.

'We've got three of our own surveillance teams out already and we'll do our best to clean both the area and her approach. The difficulty is she could come from a number of directions and it will be very busy at that time of day. But we'll do our best. We'll have two back-up units close by.'

'Are we being briefed?'

'No, I thought we'd skip Castlereagh today. I'm not expecting to learn anything. I want to know she is one of us.'

'I think you'll be surprised.'

'I live in hope, Mr Ryan. I'm an optimist.'

Thirty minutes later, they pulled out of Knock at speed and hit the dual carriageway round to the top of the Ormeau Road. It was still windy and the water ran in horizontal lines across the window. The back of the Granada was warm and might have been comforting, but Ryan had gone beyond that.

He could feel the tension right through. His armpits

were damp. His palms were clammy.

They couldn't see out of the windows very well and he wondered if that would matter. He touched the front of his coat and felt the bulk of the Browning pistol he had been issued in his waistband.

Allen didn't say anything. Ryan hoped he wouldn't.

He tried to think about the possibility of success. He tried to tell himself it might work. She might turn up. She might be willing to talk. He wondered how he would find her. Nervous? Frightened? Confident? Professional? Treacherous?

He wondered if she'd considered treachery as a state of mind. He wondered if she'd ever thought of being a tout before that night in Paddington Green police station.

Down the Ormeau Road. Scrappy, down-at-heel houses and a building that was derelict and crumbling. Past Ulster Television. He noticed a camera and a reporter on the roof and almost smiled. If only they knew the half of it.

Linenhall Street was relatively quiet. Allen leaned forward, Ryan looked at his watch. Three minutes early. They waited just outside the back entrance to the BBC and Ryan thought the building looked like an RUC station. It had high red-brick walls and a large iron gate. The street was relatively quiet. He could see the great white dome of the city hall in the distance. It reminded him, bizarrely, of the White House in Washington.

He knew the police surveillance teams were out there – knew the area had been cleaned – but he didn't feel reassured.

He noticed the quality of the cars parked on the opposite side of the street. A Mercedes, two BMWs, a Toyota. A Toyota?

The car was shabby and blue and its engine was running. Two men sat in the front.

Ryan's heart missed a beat.

Allen said 'go' and the driver moved ahead. They passed a shop with big Ford signs in the window and Ryan looked back at the blue Toyota. It hadn't moved. A scout car?

They turned right into a side street. He was looking for movement, for a slender woman with brown hair.

Nothing. No-one.

The driver gunned down to the end of the street and turned right again. They had to wait for thirty or forty seconds before they could get out onto the main road. Then they were back outside the BBC. The blue Toyota was still there. The two men were still in the front. They weren't looking at him. He pushed his eyes away from them. On the opposite pavement, a couple – middle-aged – walked arm in arm. The same cars parked. The back gate of the BBC now opening. Back to the Toyota. They hadn't moved. They still weren't looking at him. Down the street, a slender figure, probably a woman.

Ryan watched. He could feel the fear in his stomach.

It wasn't her.

Allen said 'go' again. Ryan looked at the blue Toyota, then at his watch. They were exactly on time now.

A car coming the other way, a man with a small dog, but otherwise nothing.

Back to the beginning.

They waited. Ryan tried to drag his eyes away from the Toyota – the men looked like they were talking. He scoured the street. He could see nothing else out of place, nothing that was unusual or suspicious.

Back to the Toyota. Wishing the bloody thing would go away. Wondering idly if the back-up was close

116

enough. Wondering if they'd already be dead when the Land Rovers came tearing into the street.

Two minutes, perhaps three and they went round again, slower this time. When they got back to the end of the side street, Allen told the driver to stop. Maybe they weren't going to be hit after all. But how could one know?

The wait dragged now. Ryan kept looking over his shoulder, out of the back of the car. He thought that was going to be the blind spot. One minute. Two. Five. He tried to concentrate on the street. He wondered if he should hate her, but was still too frightened to think straight. He felt dazed. It seemed incredible that he'd eaten breakfast at the flat in Clapham only this morning.

Allen was drumming his fingers on the door. Ryan very much wanted to cut them off.

'We'll give her five more minutes.' It was an order, not a suggestion.

Silence again. Ryan concentrated on scouring the street.

'This is a bloody cock-up.'

Ryan didn't know what to say. 'Perhaps she's been held up.'

'Perhaps she has, young man, perhaps she's having tea with her granny. Perhaps she's having tea with the bloody Pope. I really don't care what she IS doing, what I care about is the fact she's NOT here.'

Ryan still didn't know what to say. He still scoured the street.

'Not showing first time. It looks bad, very bad. She could be compromised, we could be compromised. She could have turned. Silly fucking bitch.'

Allen finally seemed to lose patience. He almost shouted 'Drive!' and they powered off. At the same time, he spoke into the radio and called off the nearby support units.

Allen didn't speak on the way back to Knock and when they got there he took Ryan to the canteen, bought him a coffee and left.

Ryan sat there feeling relieved, disappointed and dazed. He had a headache and he could feel the stress in his back. The muscles down his spine seemed to have tightened noticeably. He thought he'd had enough of the RUC for one day and could feel himself spoiling for a fight, but when Allen returned he was shocked by the look on his face.

'The boss wants to see us. Now.'

Ryan followed him without arguing, speaking only when they had turned into the corridor outside. 'What does he want to see us about?' he said. He hadn't quite eliminated the truculence from his voice, but Allen didn't seem to notice. He stopped and leaned towards him.

'It's absolute fucking bedlam up there.'

'Because of—'

'No. They just lost someone big. *Really* big.'

He didn't expand and at the end of the corridor he took the stairs three at a time. Ryan had to jog to keep up.

On the top floor there was indeed a palpable sense of crisis. The corridor seemed lighter this time and Ryan realized it was because almost all of the office doors were open. In the first doorway two men were looking at an open file, in the second a man stood with his hands in his pockets. Allen stopped. 'How's it looking?' he asked.

The man had a grey moustache and thinning hair. He looked tired. 'Not too good. You in for him? Take my advice: don't bloody argue. He's carpeting anything that moves.'

118

As they approached Long's office, two men emerged wearing scruffy suits. They were ashen-faced. Something *big*, Ryan thought. Allen leaned round the door to the side office and smiled at the secretary. Ryan heard her say, 'I'll tell him you're here.'

They waited for a surprisingly long time, or so it seemed – perhaps only five minutes in reality. Ryan felt a trace of nerves again and this annoyed him. Whatever the problem was, it wasn't *his* bloody problem.

The secretary put her head round the door – a pretty blonde – and said they should go in.

Inside, Ryan felt the change in atmosphere. Long didn't bother to get up and he didn't greet them. He gestured to the chairs and then sat with his elbows on his desk, his hands gripped tightly together and his chin resting heavily on them. The charm, the carefully cultivated impression of wisdom and authority, had gone. Ryan didn't think he had ever seen anger expressed so clearly in somebody's body language. He noticed his own tiredness had dropped away.

'Well?'

Allen answered. 'A no-show, I'm afraid.'

'Why?'

Ryan answered. 'She has difficult family circumstances. I think there could be perfectly legitimate reasons why—'

'And your years of experience tell you this?' Long rubbed his face briefly in his hands and sat back. 'That was gratuitous. I apologize.' He still looked at Ryan. 'However, I'm afraid I think, under the circumstances, we would like to take control of this young woman.'

Ryan didn't know quite what to say. 'You already have control.'

'Yes, but I think it's just *simpler*—'

119

'What circums . . . With respect, what circumstances are you referring to?'

'I'm sorry?'

'You said, "Under the circumstances".'

'Well, I'm concerned that her refusal to meet you today is a sign that it could be dangerous to proceed—'

'I don't mind the risk.'

Long looked at him, Ryan thought, with what might have been contempt and might have been respect – indeed might have been anything. He was hard to read. 'I'm sure you *are* prepared for the risk. I think, though, it would just be *simpler*—'

'So you keep saying. What do you mean?'

Long leaned forward suddenly, his face animated. 'What I mean, Mr Ryan, is that things have just got a lot more serious around here. Do you understand me? This woman has just become a lot more important – a *lot* – and I want to make sure that this is handled right. Absolutely right. All the way. I don't wish to insult you – you're very capable, I'm sure – but it would simply be easier—'

The secretary had put her head round the door. 'Sorry to interrupt, but it's Mark for you, Mr Long.' Long looked at Ryan. 'One second, please.' He picked up the phone and turned his chair around, as if that somehow gave him some privacy. 'What's happened? . . . You've spoken to the wife . . . No she wouldn't be. I'd better speak to her—'

Ryan wondered who it was they'd lost. He thought Mark must be Mark Jones from – southern area, was it? He couldn't remember. He looked around the room. It was curiously old-fashioned, as though no-one had had the time or inclination to see to the decor since the start of the war. The wall was covered in plaques from different police forces all over the world – Los Angeles,

New York, Taiwan – different police forces with, he supposed, radically different problems. He wondered if policemen felt part of a kind of worldwide brotherhood. At least they all shared *some* of the same problems, but did he have anything in common with, say, the Guatemalan secret service? I certainly hope not, he thought. He looked at Long's back and felt the flush of anger in his cheeks. Everyone always said it made him look younger.

Long was winding up. 'I want you to go over this, Mark. Everything. *Everything.* If there was a mistake I want to know who made it and when. I don't want a witch-hunt, but I do want to know *exactly* what happened – every last detail. Understood?'

When he put down the phone, Ryan did not let him gather his thoughts. 'Mr Long, with respect, I don't know what has actually changed since this morn—'

'Everything.' There was real hostility in Long's voice now.

'I'm here because this woman will work with me.'

'Then where in the hell was she today?'

'I'll find out.'

'You won't. I'm afraid you're not going to get the chance. I want this sorted—'

'Look, she trusts me.'

Long looked at him. 'Mr Ryan, if only you knew how many handlers have sat in that seat and told me the very same thing about their agents.'

'I'm not speaking for any other handler.'

'You're speaking for a woman who didn't show for her first meeting.' Irritation had crept into Long's voice. 'You're speaking for a woman who could get some perfectly good men killed. You're speaking for a woman who has just become a lot more important and I don't want you involved.'

'She clearly trusts me and she doesn't—'

'Doesn't what?'

'She trusts me in a way she says she doesn't trust the RUC.'

'She's said as much?'

Ryan nodded.

'Explicitly?'

'Yes.'

'I don't think that's particularly relevant.' Long sat back in his chair again. The room was suddenly quiet. Ryan was conscious of Allen's eyes on him. He felt his face reddening again. Long leaned forward once more. 'All right, Mr Ryan, we'll keep you on board. But you understand this. We've been working on this peace process for years and I tell you now, whatever anyone says, that this hangs in the balance. It is going to happen – it *is* – but the man most likely to mess it up just happens to be your woman's eldest brother. Do you understand what I'm saying? I want to know if Gerry McVeigh *farts*. Understood?'

Whilst Allen went to get him a coffee, Ryan played with the ugly glass salt and pepper pots. The room was like any canteen anywhere, except that it had the same dated feel as Trevor Long's office, though this time in yellow and blue, not green and brown. He opened one of the paper sugar packets and then poured the contents into his mouth. He felt tired again.

Allen came back. 'You take milk, don't you?'

Ryan nodded and watched Allen open four sugar packets and pour them into his coffee.

'Well done,' Allen said.

'What in the hell was all that about?'

'He wanted you off.'

'Why?'

122

'Obvious. Just as he said. Easier.'

'Thanks for fighting for me.'

'I thought you were doing quite well on your own.'

Ryan sipped his coffee, wondering whether that was a compliment. He realized it was odd that he should have thought for a moment that Allen would fight for him, but he rather imagined that an afternoon of shared tension – if rather few shared words – should have resulted in some feelings of solidarity. But perhaps that was his inexperience showing.

He thought Allen looked rather old all of a sudden. Was he forty?

'Not a great day for the forces of law and order.'

'Who was it?' Ryan said, trying not to sound too interested.

'Gingy Hughes.'

'Christ. *He* was a tout?'

Allen grinned. 'Recruited by the boss himself years ago.' A pause and another smile. 'You want to know what happened to him? Apparently, they took him and his wife away from the children to a little house out near Carrickmore. Gingy and his wife were quite devoted to each other – that was the big weakness, the pressure point, because he was going down for quite a gaol term when old Trevor Long got his hands on him. Anyway, they took the pair of them down to this house and then they had a good go at them for a week. Tortured little Gingy in front of his missus and then tortured his missus in front of him. The poor little bastard sang his heart out into the tape – quite a lengthy confession, so they say – and then they took him out and shot him *in front of* his wife. They made her watch as they blew the front of his face off. And you know what's really good? Old Gingy's mother knew what was happening all the time – knew because they'd told her she had to look after the kids. And did she say anything? Did she fuck. Not a good old fucking Republican woman like Mrs Gingy. "All right, lads. You won't hurt him now, will ya?"'

Ryan didn't say anything for a few seconds. He looked down and took another sip of his coffee. 'You enjoyed telling me that.'

'Just letting you know the reality.'

'I think I knew that already.'

'Well, that's what will happen to your woman. *Our* woman. Maybe you *would* be better off dealing with it at a distance.'

Ryan smiled. 'You'll have to do better than that.'

Ryan left Knock shortly after five. He asked the driver to stop off at the garage on the Malone Road and felt quite absurdly self-conscious buying some eggs and bread, as if everyone in the shop could somehow tell how he'd spent his afternoon.

The flat was in a development called Malone Beeches – a fact he hadn't noticed earlier – and he realized that it was actually quite respectable. There was a hallway just inside the entrance for his umbrella, should he ever wish to have one – he wondered who in the hell furnished these places – and a bedroom with a very small single bed. He clearly wasn't expected to engage in anything as un-Servicelike as sex.

A dose of realism at least, he thought.

He walked into the sitting room, kicked off his Timberland shoes, lay down on the striped sofa and switched on ITN's *Early Evening News*. He watched a report on Bosnia and then a lengthy piece on the discovery of Gingy Hughes's body. The journalists had clearly been talking to the security forces because the details were starting to emerge. He thought they sounded like they were enjoying it.

He was just about to run himself a bath when the phone rang. It was Jenkins.

'David.'

'Who is that?' Ryan knew that would irritate him.

'It's Jenkins.'

'Hi, how are you doing?'

'I see this Hughes business is hitting the news.'

'Yes. Nasty, isn't it?'

'I gather today was a disaster.'

Ryan took a deep breath. 'I wouldn't say that. Just a minor hitch.'

'Well, that's not what I hear and I must say it makes us look pretty stupid.'

'I think it's early days yet.'

'I've said to Grant that I made my reservations known and it seems clear to me now that your briefing in London was quite inadequate.'

Ryan sat up and put the phone on the floor. 'I think it is too early to tell.'

'Well then, what *is* the explanation? Why didn't she turn up? I'm told that surveillance reports indicate she spent the whole afternoon at home.'

'We're taking steps to find out what happened. There could be any number of reasons—'

'This whole thing makes us look like *complete idiots*.'

'Look, Jenkins, I've told you, we're taking steps to find out what happened. We can't explain *until* we've had some contact with her.'

'*Don't* raise your voice at me.'

'Well, you raised your voice at me. Look—'

'I don't think there's any point in pursuing this conversation.'

'I'm simply trying to point out that there could be a hundred explanations—'

'You're being defensive.'

'I am *trying* to explain.'

'Look, David.' There was a conciliatory note in his voice now. 'We're all under a lot of pressure. We've got to get these things right. Understood?'

'Yes, but—'

'I've got to go. We've got to get it right, that's all. Find out what went wrong and make sure she doesn't duck out again. This woman has been sold. We've told people she can deliver. Please *make her do so*.'

As he put down the phone, Ryan swore loudly.

He walked round the flat, picked up the pillow from his bed and hurled it against the wall. Then he sat on the bed and told himself to calm down.

After a few minutes he went to the kitchen and made himself scrambled eggs on toast. When he'd finished, he walked back down to the garage – a surprisingly long way – to get a packet of ten Silk Cut. The pavements were dimly lit and the traffic was thin. All the way down he could make out the big houses that lined the streets off the Malone Road and he thought to himself that there were still a lot of people here doing very nicely. All the way there and back he had a surprisingly strong fantasy running through his mind. In it, Jenkins got so annoyed with him that he threw a computer keyboard at his head. This gave Ryan the excuse he had been looking for to take Jenkins apart physically. It was not a very noble thought, but then, he knew how much he hated being bullied.

He also thought about Gerry McVeigh and wondered why Long had been so interested in him.

When he got home again, he wanted to talk, but realized there was no-one he could really talk to. He thought of talking to his mother, but knew he would end up being irritable with her and then disliking himself as a result. He wanted to talk to his father.

He watched *News at Ten* and noticed it had more on Gingy Hughes. He switched off the television halfway through the report and then wondered why he had. That *is* the reality, he thought. It didn't make him feel very comfortable.

Finally, he made it to the narrow single bed. He found it impossible to stop thinking of his father and of the bullies' voices. 'Ryan's daddy's dead. Ryan's daddy's dead. Ryan's daddy's dead. Who's going to be a mummy's boy now?'

'Enough.' Colette walked forward and switched off the television. Mark and Catherine looked like they had been hypnotized. 'Dinner,' she added.

Mark scowled. 'Grandma lets us watch the news.'

'You don't like the news.'

'We're *allowed* to watch it.'

'Not any more.'

She had just got them into the kitchen when the television went on again. They were all there, for once, and Paddy and Gerry wanted to watch UTV's news.

Colette had cooked Mark and Catherine hamburgers and chips and she put the plates in front of them and got the bottle of tomato ketchup out of the cupboard.

She went back into the front room to watch the news.

A reporter's voice. Monotone. 'Detectives believe that Mr Hughes and his wife were abducted by one of the IRA's Internal Security Units . . . They were brought to this remote hillside in east Tyrone where they are said to have been repeatedly tortured . . . Early this morning, Mr Hughes is said to have been taken out – bound and gagged with a hood over his head – and marched down this lane . . .'

The camera was moving down the lane for dramatic effect.

'Mr Hughes is said to have begged for his life. Mrs Hughes, too, begged for her captors to spare him. The men forced him to kneel and forced her to watch as they shot him . . .'

Colette looked at Paddy, who was sitting closest to the door. He looked . . . strange. Frightened?

A shot of a house on an estate in Armagh. It stood in darkness, as if a ghost, the light from the houses to the left and right spilling out onto the street. 'Tonight there was no sign of life at the Hughes's home in Armagh city. Mr Hughes's mother said she did not wish to give an interview, though she told the local newspaper she believed her son was completely innocent . . .'

'Like fuck,' Gerry said.

A shot of the outside of RUC headquarters at Knock. 'The RUC would not comment on the case tonight, except to deny that Mr Hughes had been involved with them in any capacity . . .'

'Lying bastards,' Gerry said.

He was in the far chair and there was a hole by his feet where the pipe bomb had gone through the floor. 'Another one gone,' he added, and Colette could tell he was trying to get Ma to rise.

'I'd prefer it if you didn't say things like that, Gerry,' Ma said quietly. 'Not in this house.'

Colette saw the tension in her mother's face – she was sheet white – and she could tell Gerry relished the challenge. 'So you want us to be nice to the touts?'

'I don't think anything is served . . . by that kind of cruelty.'

'If we don't deal with them we're finished.'

'It is so *unkind*.'

'For Christ's sake, Ma. *You* might not have noticed—'

128

'Just leave Ma alone, Gerry,' Colette said. She hadn't meant to intervene. She could tell Gerry was in a mood to fight.

'Ah, another tout-lover.'

'Just leave it. I'm no more a tout-lover than you are.'

'Well, don't you want us to be *kind* to them too?'

Ma leaned forward. 'Gerard, this is getting to you and it is about time you realized what it is doing.'

'And you're just like the bloody rest of them. I don't know why we bother, I really—' Gerry was shaking his head.

'It is about time you stopped thinking that you know best all the time.'

Gerry exploded. 'For Christ's sake! I can't stand this. I *can't stand* it!' He was on his feet now. 'People have died for this. People have spent years in prison – and this is the result.' He mimicked his mother's voice. 'You're so *unkind*.'

Colette could see her mother was hurt. 'Just leave it, Gerry. This is not the time.'

'Well, when *is* the time? We've all made sacrifices. At least Dad wouldn't have wanted us to sell out. And what about Sean?'

'ENOUGH.' Paddy was on his feet. 'That's bloody well enough.'

Gerry sneered. 'And you as well?'

'Leave it out, Gerry. I am with you, but that is below the belt and you know it.'

Gerry looked at Ma and could clearly see she was crying. He turned on his heels and, a few seconds later, they heard the front door slamming.

Colette went to sit on her mother's chair and put her arm around her. Paddy sat and watched the television in silence.

Colette found herself thinking, not of the row but of the fear on Paddy's face – and on Ma's, too.

McIlhatton watched his breath. It was a cold but clear day, and he looked up at Big Ben. It looked staggeringly beautiful set against a blue sky and he found it dazzling. You could say what you liked about the Brits, but they certainly built extraordinary buildings.

He heard the couple next to him muttering in Japanese. He thought they must be nuts standing here so patiently in this kind of temperature. He looked at the policeman opposite and, when the man caught his eye, he looked away.

There was a sudden short burst of a police siren. There was a murmur from the small crowd. McIlhatton looked up again. The cameras clicked and the Japanese woman yelped as a grey Jaguar swept past them into the House. Eddie McIlhatton looked into the window and felt a *frisson* of excitement as he caught a brief glimpse of the man they were going to kill.

He looked at his watch. It was 3.05 p.m. exactly.

CHAPTER SEVEN

The scream made her sit bolt upright. For a few seconds she felt disorientated, and then she realized it was Mark who'd screamed. He was mumbling now, babbling incoherently. She listened but could make no sense of what he was saying. She turned over and put her hand down to comfort him. He didn't wake.

'Is it OK?' Catherine asked.

Colette got out of bed and stepped over to touch her head. 'It's all right, love. He's just talking in his sleep.' She bent down and kissed her and then lay back on the bed. She felt wide awake. Mark began to babble again. She wondered what he was having nightmares about.

She found herself thinking of the meeting that she hadn't turned up to, and for the first time she felt afraid, wondering what they would do. She thought how ruthless the Brit was. He hadn't *seemed* like the rest of them, but maybe that was just for show.

She drifted off to sleep and found herself dreaming of Davey. He was walking along a beach somewhere – it looked like Donegal – wearing jeans and a T-shirt. He was walking backwards, but she simply couldn't hear what he was saying. With each step, she could see the desperation growing on his face, then, suddenly, he was pointing agitatedly at the ground and she looked down to see Mark, covered in blood. She bent down and touched him. He was so cold and, when she looked up, it was not Davey but Ryan who was standing over her. He was smiling, but she couldn't work out whether it was compassion or contempt . . .

She woke up. She could feel the sweat on her body and she sat up in bed. The house was silent, though she could hear some dogs barking in the distance. The curtains were open a fraction and they were billowing out gently with the breeze. She heard a familiar sound faintly in the distance and then it was drowned out by the sound of the dogs again.

When they stopped, silence returned.

Then she heard it. A single Land Rover door slamming, then several. She heard shouts and she shivered, but didn't move. She didn't think it could possibly be for her. Not now.

There was a moment's silence again and then she heard the crash of the sledgehammers. Before she could gather herself, the front door gave way. They were shouting now. She heard them pounding up the stairs and she just had time to stand up on the bed and cover herself with a sheet before they were in and she was blinded by the torchlight.

'Mrs McGraw?'

'For Jesus' sake!'

'Mammy,' Catherine said.

'It's all right.'

'You'll have to come with us, Mrs McGraw.'

'For Christ's sake.'

'Now.'

'Mammy.' Catherine was crying.

Colette saw one of the soldiers stumble forward as the door behind him was pushed open.

'For the Lord's sake!' Ma said.

The soldiers turned their torches round and Colette could see them now. Two great figures, impossibly large in this small room.

'Get out of my house,' Ma said.

Colette heard a quiet voice in the corridor answer and the soldiers turned their torches back in her direction.

'Please give me a moment to dress,' she said quietly.

'Dress now,' one of them said and they didn't move.

Colette heard the voice behind them again and she watched as they withdrew. As the door shut she turned on the light and picked up her jeans off the floor. She was just pulling them on when the door opened again and she looked up to see the soldiers grinning. 'Bastards,' she said, quietly.

She put on her shoes and bent down to hug Mark and Catherine. Both clung to her. 'It's all right,' she said. 'It's all right. I'll be back soon.'

She stood up and the two soldiers grabbed her arms. As she was pulled out onto the landing, her mother said, 'No. Leave her, for Christ's sake.'

There was a commanding air to her voice and the soldiers stopped.

'Don't make this difficult, Mrs McGraw,' a big RUC man said.

'We've had enough.'

'We've *all* had enough.'

'Leave her.'

'She's going. It's up to you whether you make it easy or difficult.'

Ma looked at the man and Colette saw the strength and venom in her face. 'You'll regret this,' she said.

The RUC man turned back to her. 'Get her out,' he said and the soldiers needed no second cue, pulling her down the stairs. Colette saw her mother's face twisted in uncharacteristic hatred and heard her scream, 'Bigots!'

It was dark outside. She could see lights on in the houses opposite and saw one or two faces in the windows. There were three or four Land Rovers in the street and soldiers and policemen everywhere. As she was dragged away from the house, she found herself biting her lip and trying to stop herself crying.

They pushed her towards the back of a Land Rover. The men inside reached down for her and pulled her in. It was warm and she felt the press of male bodies.

Then she saw him. She saw his boots first, and his jeans – immediately noticeable amongst the uniforms – and then she found herself looking into his face. He didn't smile at her – he betrayed nothing – but she felt a sudden strange sense of relief.

She looked into the faces of the others and saw a mixture of hostility and interest. She looked back at Ryan. He was staring at her. She realized once again how big he was, his black curly hair crushed against the roof of the Land Rover. She noticed his hands – large, strong hands. She looked at the gold signet ring on the little finger of his right hand.

She could feel the warmth of his body because his knees were touching hers.

He turned to look at the other policemen and she studied his face again. She noticed the size of his nose and the thickness of his eyebrows.

She looked down and was conscious of his eyes on her again. She closed her own eyes and tried to think of the children. She found herself thinking of Ryan instead and, after several minutes, she looked up to find he was still staring at her.

They pulled into Castlereagh and the policemen

bundled her out of the back, away from him. She held his gaze until she was through the entrance.

The holding centre hadn't changed – it still looked like a Portakabin – and she was signed in, searched and then taken down the corridor to the women's cells at the other end. Outside the newly painted, dark-blue cell doors, the inmates' clothes hung, concealed, so that no-one could tell who was being held, but, as Colette passed, someone shouted encouragement.

'I'm Richard McIlwaine, Republican. If you're Republican, tell them nothin'. Nothin'.'

They were at the end of the corridor, but Colette broke free and dashed back to bang on the outside of the cell door. She shouted, 'Richard, it's Colette.'

The uniformed officers took her arms and dragged her away, but the man was still shouting. 'Tell 'em nothin', Colette. Nothin'.'

Then she was in the cell, sitting alone on the green iron-framed bed with its brown plastic mattress. There was no ventilation and no natural light. The bed and the chair were chained to the floor and the sheets were synthetic and disposable. At night, it was always freezing cold, and she shivered at the thought of it.

She sat in silence.

A few minutes later the door opened and two uniformed constables took her up to one of the interview rooms. She was left alone briefly and then the Brit arrived. He had a big fat man with him, dressed in a grey suit with a thick mop of grey hair.

The man placed a file on the desk and leaned over the back of a chair towards her. 'Mrs McGraw, you were let off a very serious crime and spared a long gaol sentence at the behest of my colleague here and I think you owe him an explanation.'

He looked over towards Ryan, who was sitting in the

135

corner of the room. Ryan stood. He crossed his hands and forearms in front of his chest. 'What happened, Colette?'

'I want to see my solicitor.'

'In a minute.' The man's voice was harsh.

He opened the file and pushed a white booklet across the table, turning it round so that she could read the front page. 'In the meantime, you'll want to have a look at that. It's your witness statement – your confession – and I think you'll find that is your signature at the bottom of it.'

Colette said nothing for a long time.

'I just can't do it,' she whispered.

The man brought his hand crashing down onto the table. 'You've got no bloody choice.'

'I *can't* do it.'

'You've got *no choice*.'

He twisted the chair round and sat down. 'Look, let's consider the consequences. Your family, for example. What's going to happen to them? Your kids are still young, aren't they?' His tone was patronizing. 'They were lucky the other day. But I suppose, now the Loyalists know where you live, you wouldn't really expect to be so lucky next time, would you? Terrible to think what a pipe bomb could do to Mark or little Catherine.'

She looked up at him. 'You pig.'

'We deal in harsh realities here, Mrs McGraw. You bring it on yourself. Which bit of the Bible is it? Those who live by the sword . . .' He got up to leave. 'We both have the same Bible, after all.'

Colette stared intently at the table as he closed the door behind him.

Silence.

Ryan walked over to the table to take the seat

opposite her. He lit a cigarette.

Silence again.

'What happened?' he said eventually.

'I was busy.'

'You'll have to do better than that.'

She looked up and smiled sourly. 'I was looking after my children. Understand that?'

'This isn't a picnic club.'

'Oh, *really*. I'd never have guessed.'

Ryan stood up, turned the chair round the right way and sat down again. 'How is Gerry?'

Colette was looking down again now. 'I don't know. I haven't seen him.'

'Well, that's the first lie of today.'

'If you say so.'

'What has he been doing?'

'Like I said, I don't know. I haven't seen him.'

Ryan put his right elbow on the table and leaned forward. 'Let's start again, shall we? What does Gerry think about what is going on at the moment?'

'Why are you so interested in him?'

'We're starting at the beginning. He's a significant figure . . .'

'Well, you'll have to ask someone else. I don't know. I haven't seen him and we're not close anyway.'

Ryan leaned back. 'Do you have *anything* for us?'

'No.'

'Nothing at all?' Irritation was creeping into his voice now. 'You've heard nothing at all since you got back?'

She shook her head.

'What have you been doing? Who have you been seeing?'

'My family.'

He was about to go on when she cut him off. 'There's a bit of unhappiness at the moment. All this talk of peace.'

137

Ryan continued, as if talking to a child. 'Who is unhappy and why?'

'They think the leadership is getting too tied up in politics. They think they're being conned by the Brits.'

'Who thinks this? Gerry?'

She stopped again, took a cigarette from the packet on the table and leaned back. He made no move to light it for her.

'It's what I heard.'

There was a note of finality in her voice. She looked into his eyes and could see the irritation there.

'From *whom* did you hear it?'

'It's what people are talking about.'

'People? Everyone?'

'Not everyone.'

'Names?'

She shook her head. Ryan stood.

'You'll have to do better than this.' He looked at her for a response. 'You'll have to do better than this, Colette, or this is over and we're in trouble.'

She looked up. 'Is that a threat?'

'It's the reality. This is not a game. It's not in my control. Your life *is* at risk.'

'And yours.'

'Is *that* a threat?'

'It's the reality.' She looked at him and then smirked. 'You're a 'Taig, aren't you?' She saw confusion, and perhaps anger, in his face. 'You're a Catholic, I can—'

'I heard you the first time.'

Silence.

'Well, are you?' she asked.

'That is the most stupid, irrelevant question I've ever heard. What difference could it possibly make?'

'It's a start.'

'It's loyalty that counts.'

'For Queen and country?'

'Fuck Queen and country.'

She raised her eyebrows. 'I see.'

He was looking down now and she studied him again. His hair was glossy and clean and, from this angle, his face looked exceptionally narrow.

He looked up again and she met his eyes. They were a pure clear green. There was no shyness about him, no embarrassment at looking at her. He seemed to have an unreasonable strength and self-confidence and she found herself wanting to humiliate and embarrass him, to see the certainty fade from his face.

'For the record,' he said gently, 'I am of Irish Catholic stock. My mother was born and brought up in County Mayo. But, as I have tried to explain before, there is only one kind of loyalty that counts. If we do not trust each other, neither of us will be around to regret it.'

She felt her annoyance fade. Suddenly, he didn't seem so invincible.

She looked down.

Silence again.

'There's something soon, maybe even tomorrow,' she said eventually.

'Where?'

'I can't tell you.'

'It's important.'

She shook her head.

'Come on. We have to make this work.'

Colette said nothing for a long time. Eventually, she spoke quietly, as if whispering to herself. 'I can't. It's Paddy.'

'Paddy's involved?'

She paused again and took a deep breath. 'Yes. But, please, please, don't hurt him. You'se mustn't. It must be part of the deal.'

He leaned forward again. 'It's all right. Don't worry, we can fix it. Who is the target?'

'I shouldn't know this.'

'Right.'

'I shouldn't know it.'

'I understand.'

'It's only by accident that I found out.'

'How? You overheard a conversation?'

She shook her head. 'No, Paddy told me, but he shouldn't have. Sometimes he tells me things he shouldn't. We're very close.'

'Who did he say the target was?'

'I don't want him to suffer.'

'I understand.'

'You won't hurt him. You swear to God you won't hurt him?'

'I give you my word. Now, who is the target?'

'A policeman. The man who put me away before. He's from CID – Henderson, I think his name is.'

'Henderson?'

She nodded.

'Do you know where and when?'

'No. At his house, I think, as he goes to work. That's all I know, just that it is planned and is to go ahead soon.'

Ryan got up. 'Just a minute, please.'

'Where are you going?'

'I'm afraid I'm just going to have to get my colleague.'

'Don't.'

Ryan frowned. There was a note of panic in her voice.

'Why not?'

'He's a Prod. I don't trust him.'

'Well, I'm a Brit and you seem to trust me. He's all

140

right, Mrs McGraw; he's a good man. He's a professional.'

She looked at him stony-faced. 'That's what I mean.'

She waited. She stretched out her legs, looked up at the ceiling and closed her eyes. She suddenly felt terribly tired.

Ryan brought the fat man back in. This time, his tone was much more friendly, though she was still wary of him. He took her gently through all the same questions, making notes as he did so. Ryan stood behind him and, every time she looked up at him, his eyes were on her. Once again, she found his scrutiny, or attentiveness, reassuring.

Allen strode down the corridor at speed and Ryan almost had to jog to keep up. He stopped outside a blue door marked with the sign 'Source Unit' and turned abruptly to face Ryan, his hand settled on the door handle. 'Wait here, please.'

'No.'

Ryan watched the irritation flash across Allen's face. 'I'm sorry?'

'I want to learn. I won't if you exclude me.'

'This is not the time for egos.'

'It has nothing to do with ego.'

Ryan thought Allen would insist, but his expression softened. 'All right, but just don't fucking say anything.'

Before Ryan could reply, they were in the room and striding towards an office at the far end marked 'Chief Inspector'. Allen clearly knew the man well and he didn't bother to introduce him. Ryan listened as he outlined what they knew. Allen asked that they be present at the meeting that would decide what action was taken, but the man refused and would brook no argument.

Allen took them to a room further down the corridor, where another man typed the details they had into the computer, without making any significant comment. He printed out a sheet on the laser printer in the corner and handed it to Allen to check.

Ryan needed the loo badly and decided not to bother asking where it was. He didn't know what word to use and he thought the choice of word might be divisive. Loo? Gents? Toilet? Easier not to ask.

He turned left at the end of the corridor, went up two small steps, through a swing door and into a long, wide, well-lit corridor with large drinks machines at the end. He found the Gents by the machines, had his piss and then returned to the office. He strolled the last few yards slowly and, without meaning to listen, heard Allen say clearly, 'Of all fucking people —'

Then he was in the door and there was a brief silence. Allen looked awkward. He stood up and pointed to the roof. 'Upstairs.'

He took them to a corridor on the floor above. They approached a door marked 'TCG meeting room' and waited outside. They could hear the murmur of voices inside, but nothing more.

Of all fucking people . . . What did that mean? Perhaps he was being paranoid.

Allen didn't speak – he seemed angry – and Ryan tried to get his own thoughts together. He knew the TCG – Tasking, Co-ordinating Group – had been set up in 1978 to allow the different arms of the intelligence community in Northern Ireland to liaise and plan operations based on specific information. It was staffed by representatives of the Army and the RUC who analysed all the information being gathered on terrorist subjects throughout the greater Belfast region. It acted as the permanent liaison office for all the commanders responsible for running agents or sending out surveillance teams. The information was fed into the senior level meetings, like this one, where decisions were taken on how each attack might be prevented.

The wait seemed to go on for ever and they stood in silence, Ryan's only attempt at conversation brushed aside. When the men did finally come out, Allen fell into step with the chief inspector, his manner and tone aggressive and hostile. 'Well?' he asked.

The man continued to walk. 'We await a report back.'

'Don't fuck about, Desmond.'

'Arrests.'

'No.'

He stopped. 'You knew it was going to happen.'

'Come on, Desmond. That'll finish her and you know it.'

'That's not the case.'

'Yes it is and you know it.'

The other men were filing out of the room now. The chief inspector looked at them and then continued, speaking quietly, 'It was inevitable, you know it was. With players like Paddy McVeigh involved, we've got to make arrests. We've been trying to get him for years.'

'If you go that road, she's finished. I tell you—'

'Look.' A note of irritation had crept into his voice. 'I know your concerns – and the information was good – but we've had snippets from all over the place about this attack. This was the final confirmation, that's all, and there is no reason under the sun to think this will be traced back to her.'

'Like hell there isn't. With the new rules on disclosure, she doesn't stand a chance if any of the players end up in court – and you know it. If Paddy McVeigh is arrested, she's finished.'

'I think you're being paranoid. He's not going to suspect his own sister. It's not without risk, sure, but then what in the hell is? We can't let this number of players go. We just can't. And you know that as well as anyone.'

Allen was angry now. 'What I know is that this woman is close to people who count and that she has real potential, particularly at this time, and that you're throwing her away so that this will look good on your bloody records.'

'That's enough.'

'It's the bloody truth.'

'Suggest an alternative.'

'You could move Henderson. You could stick out some extra patrols and force them to abort.'

'And what happens if they come back another time and don't bother to tell your woman?'

'If this is for political reasons, Desmond, don't try to justify it to me.'

'I'm not justifying anything. I'm telling you there is no alternative.' He pointed back to the meeting room. 'There was no debate on this in there. It was clear-cut. It was a simple decision.'

Allen sneered. 'What does that tell you?'

The chief inspector turned. 'I think this conversation has gone about as far—'

'She's too good to lose, Desmond. Honestly.'

The chief inspector looked tired. 'Brian, I've lost count of the number of times a handler has said that to me. You're not going to lose her.'

'That's bullshit.'

The chief inspector turned again and began to walk.

'I'll have your skin if she goes, Desmond.' And then to himself as he walked in the other direction. 'I'll have your bloody skin.'

They both blinked as they came out into the light. For a moment, they stood still. Ryan thought, once again, that this was a strange place for an interrogation centre – a Portakabin in a car park behind the police station, or, as Allen had enjoyed telling him, a temporary solution for a temporary problem.

It was a red Granada this time and Ryan stepped forward and opened one of the back doors for Colette. She seemed distracted and dazed now, and he noticed that, as in London, the fight had gone out of her.

He wondered if she was really strong enough to cope. He didn't know what he could do about it.

They pulled out of the gates of Castlereagh and turned left and left again. He saw a Union Jack flying proudly above the factory on the corner. He turned to her. Her face was white and he thought she looked pale and frightened. 'You've got it clear in your mind. Colette?'

She looked at him and he could see the fear in her so clearly. She seemed to be wanting – wanting what? Reassurance? In this moment, he thought he really felt for her, and couldn't quite remove a distant feeling of relief that it was her and not him.

'You understand?'

She nodded, but he could tell she wasn't concentrating. He turned himself towards her, putting his left knee on the seat. He saw the ugly concrete Central Station building behind her and knew that time was short.

'You saw Detective Sergeant Allen and Mr Jones. Mr Allen was from the RUC, Mr Jones, you don't know, but you *assume* he was from MI5. OK?'

She nodded again, but was looking out of the window at the line of new red-brick houses that formed the edge of the Republican markets area.

'What was the drift of our questioning?'

Colette spoke mechanically. 'You . . . *they* wanted to know why I had been absent from Belfast for so long, where I was, what I was doing—'

'Did we know you were in England?'

'You suspect . . . constant questions. Wasn't I here, didn't I do this—'

'OK.' He tried to make his voice sound as firm as possible. 'OK. Remember, we brought you in, we suspect you, but we've got no proof. We were rough, but we were clearly only working on general suspicions. You've got to get this right. We don't want you red-lighted. Understood?'

She nodded again and this time he thought she might be close to tears. He didn't know what else he could do. He thought of saying, 'You'll be all right,' but thought better of it. He wasn't sure she was going to make it, but he knew he couldn't find the strength for her.

They drove into the multi-storey car park at the Castlecourt shopping centre and checked carefully to make sure they were not observed.

At the top, Ryan leaned over and gripped her arm hard. He held her for what seemed like a long time, then she looked away from him and put her hand on the door. From that moment, she didn't look back.

He watched her walk away.

They waited twenty minutes and then drove down to the bottom and out again. Ryan could feel the release of tension in his body. She was on her own.

It was the afternoon rush hour now and a few specks of rain were falling against the window. Outside, it was dark and he could see people scuttling along the pavements. He imagined her walking in the darkness up towards the Divis monitoring point and tried to imagine what reception might be awaiting her. He felt guilty he had not been able to give her something more tangible.

He wondered how he would have felt if that was him – how he would have coped. He thought now that, after everything, he *was* quite tough.

As they inched past the front of the city hall, Ryan looked down at the shopping precinct to his left. It was busy, the umbrellas now up, and people were jogging to get out of the rain. He could see a newspaper board, but couldn't make out the headline.

Once again, he had a surprisingly strong mental image of his father. He thought that was where the toughness must come from. *Don't run with the crowd*, he'd said, and Ryan didn't. It was an article of faith.

There was another piece of advice and he thought of it now. *Learn from your mistakes*, the advice ran. If he made a mistake this time, he knew the price. He thought of the one-line entry in the Service accounts: 'Asset: Shadow Dancer. Controller: Ryan, D. Eliminated. Entry deleted.'

Eliminated.

He wondered how she was doing.

Colette was walking at speed, as if the pace of her progress would somehow prove something. She was cold and missed the warmth of the car.

She looked up and saw an Irish Tricolour hanging from a window on the Divis Tower above her and billowing in the wind. She almost, but not quite, smiled.

She thought of the flag, of patriotism, of childhood history lessons and heroes. She saw the faces of Patrick Pearse and James Connolly and Maude Gonne and she muttered under her breath. She thought of the poem on the Easter uprising – Yeats's poem – and she thought of the line, 'All changed, changed utterly:' only this time she did smile. 'Right, Mr Yeats,' she told herself.

The front door had been temporarily patched up with plywood and she pushed it gently. It wasn't locked. The house was warm and she could hear the sound of voices from the kitchen. She took off her coat and hung it on the stairs. She stood for a few seconds without moving. Today, it felt like home.

She could make out Gerry's voice in the kitchen. As she got to the door, she heard him say, 'I'm not for splitting—' He broke off. 'Who's that?'

She was in the doorway. 'It's me. Where are the kids?'

They were all staring at her. Clarke, Mulgrew – four or five of them. Gerry looked shifty. Colette felt angry. They seemed to hold so many of these meetings here now. No wonder the Loyalists were targeting them. 'What happened?' Gerry asked.

'The bastards did me over. Where are the kids?'

'They're over at Margaret's. Ma's upstairs. You all right?'

She wanted to say, 'What do you fucking think?' but she didn't. She turned to go.

'You'd better see Mulgrew.'

She turned back and tried to sound irritated. 'Now?'

'Best get it over with. Ma can look after the kids.'

She thought it was a good thing he didn't see the look on her face. Mulgrew was on his feet and in the corridor, jangling his car keys. He waited whilst she put on her coat and she deliberately kept her back to him. She suddenly felt terribly tired. She wondered if she should go up and see Ma, but decided she was probably sleeping.

Mulgrew drove a battered old white Escort and he

148

let her in the passenger side first. As he started the engine and moved off she tried to gather her strength. He was young, sharp and ambitious, but he'd always fancied her – had once asked her out – and she told herself it would be all right.

'Bastards broke in, they said.'

She turned to him and smiled. He was a pleasant-looking man, with ginger hair and a large chin. She told herself this was going to be simple and she almost smiled as she remembered what her friend Roscheen always used to say. *Colette's in minxy mode* . . .

They stopped at the traffic lights at the junction with the Springfield Road. The streets were busy – children still making their way home from school and mothers doing their shopping. She half expected to see Ma and Catherine and Mark.

'You've come a long way, Mr Mulgrew,' she said, smiling at him.

He smiled back. 'I don't think so.'

'I remember when you were desperate to carry my shopping home, and me married then and all.'

'Seems a long time ago now.'

'You're damned right it does.' She smiled at him again. 'You were rather sweet.' Even in the darkness, she felt sure he was blushing.

'I was thirteen,' he said, almost to himself.

'You were, but you were rather sweet – and bright then, let's not deny it.'

Silence. They were just by the bottom of Whiterock and she heard a high-pitched girlish laugh – in fact several – and she turned to see a group from St Louise's on their way home. Even after all these years there was still something familiar about that kind of group. Nostalgia, she thought.

The lights turned green and they moved off. Twenty

yards further on they passed the first soldiers in a patrol and one darted across the road just in front of them. Mulgrew slowed fractionally and then speeded up again.

'They say you're going to go right to the top,' Colette said quietly.

'Do they?'

'There aren't many in your position at nineteen – or is it twenty?'

'Twenty.'

'April fifth, right?'

'Right.'

At the junction with Kennedy Way, he turned right off the roundabout and she wanted to ask him where in the hell they were going, but she didn't say anything.

'You remembered,' he said.

'What?'

'My birthday. You remembered.'

'Yes.'

'Yours is the third of September.'

She looked at him. 'Yes, but I'm thirty-three.' She turned back to the windscreen. 'Obviously not as clever as you.'

'Or as ruthless.'

She tried to laugh. 'Or as ruthless.'

Or as trustworthy, she thought. Everyone trusted Mulgrew. He had a reputation for calmness under pressure, already tested on numerous occasions. He was the latest rising star. Colette had seen them before. Maybe he'd go on up, maybe he wouldn't. For now, he was dangerous. She shivered.

They were pulling out of west Belfast. The road had turned into a dual carriageway and some of the lights overhead were broken. There were rocks all over the road because the local kids usually gathered at night on the hill to their right and lobbed bricks, rocks and bottles at passing police Land Rovers.

At the top, just before the travellers' encampment, they turned left, taking the back route to the airport. As they pulled up the hill, Belfast was a sea of lights beneath them. Colette felt the tension suddenly in her back and neck. She could feel the sweat in her palms and she was grateful for the relative darkness of the car.

The road was narrow up here and they twisted and turned, the car's headlights bouncing off the hedges. Suddenly Mulgrew yanked the car round to the left and they skidded down a gravel track. He turned the keys in the ignition and the lights died as the car glided silently to a halt.

She could see the lights of Belfast in front of her through the windscreen. She could hear Mulgrew's breathing.

'Let's get out, Colette.' His voice was icily polite.

She opened the door gingerly and stepped out. The moon was brighter than she'd thought, though it was early yet, and she could see the outline of the gravel pits around her. She could feel the dampness on her back.

'This way.'

Mulgrew led and she followed, slowly. The ground was a mixture of mud and gravel and her white trainers shone in the darkness. She could hear herself breathing now.

He stopped and she came within a few feet of him. He had turned up the collar of his coat and was putting on a pair of gloves.

'What did they tell you to say, Colette?'

'I don't follow you.'

'What did they tell you to say?'

'I heard. I said, I don't follow you.'

'Who did you see in there?'

She sighed. 'One of them was Allen – policeman – the other one called himself Jones.'

'MI5?'

She shrugged her shoulders. He'd moved slightly and she couldn't see his face clearly. The breeze blew her hair into her mouth and she picked it out.

'What did they want?'

'Wanted to know why I wasn't here for two months. Said they'd noticed my absence. Wanted to know where I was.'

'What did you tell them?'

'Said I was staying in the south with an aunt.'

'Without the children?'

'I said it was a love affair.' She shrugged. 'I don't think they bought it.'

'What did the man from MI5 look like?'

'Tall, quite thin. Broken nose. Handsome, if you like Brits.'

'You liked talking to him?'

'They're all the same. They had nothing on me.'

'You think you should be red-lighted?'

Colette thought for a moment. A trap? The idea of being taken off duty for a few months had its attractions. She shook her head. 'I don't think they had anything.'

'Who did most of the talking?'

'Ryan.'

'Ryan?' A moment's silence before Mulgrew continued. 'Who is Ryan?'

'The Brit.'

'I thought you said his name was Jones.'

Silence for a few seconds more. Colette was conscious of the sound of traffic in the distance and suddenly of the cold. 'Ryan Jones. He kept on using his first name.'

'You were friends, then?'

Silence again. 'I don't think that kind of comment helps, do you?'

'Odd to use his first name, that's all.'

'It was what *he* used.' She sighed again. 'Look, it's been a long day. Red-light me if you want, but I'm very tired. Can I go home and look after my kids?'

Silence again. 'All right, Colette, but I think we should have a longer chat about this another day. OK?'

They stomped back to the car. Colette now felt there was something slightly absurd about this and she cursed herself for underestimating him. He was a clever little bastard and he'd rattled her. Stupid, she told herself. Bloody stupid.

She felt queasy and terribly tired on the journey back and quite unable to face the house. She stood outside for a few moments, trying to gather her strength, before letting herself in very quietly.

As she walked into the hall, she heard the murmur of voices in the kitchen once more and, opening the door, she saw Ma, Catherine and Mark standing in a conspiratorial tableau. Mark and Catherine stood in front, next to each other, and, after a moment's silence, Catherine came forward and produced from behind her back a small white packet. She grinned nervously. 'Jelly beans,' she said. 'Your favourite. Grandma said we could spend our pocket money because the soldiers were horrible and took you away—'

Colette bent down and took them both in her arms, relief suddenly flooding through her.

She stood up and put on the kettle.

'Tea, Ma?' she asked and her mother nodded. Colette took two tea bags out and put them in the ancient green pot. Catherine and Mark disappeared into the front room and for a few minutes she stood next to her mother in silence.

'What did Mulgrew want?' Ma asked.

'Questions.'

'What questions?'

'The usual.'

'But who was he asking about?'

Colette looked at her mother and saw the anxiety on her face. 'Me,' she said. 'Me and my time in Castlereagh. Talking about red-lighting me – standing me down for a while. That's it.'

'Nothing else?'

Colette shook her head. 'No, why?'

Ma ignored the question. 'What else was he saying?'

Colette felt a brief flash of irritation. 'Do you mind if we don't talk about it,' she said. And then, more kindly, with a hand on her mother's arm, 'I know you worry, Ma, but it's all right, honest it is.'

Colette poured herself a cup of tea, opened the back door, lit up a fag and smoked it in silence.

Ryan couldn't sleep in the night. He was restless again.

At three, he got up and went to the fridge to pour himself a glass of milk. He walked into the sitting room and stood by the window, looking at the hedge and the road beyond. The odd car flashed by, but otherwise it was quiet.

His bag was on the desk and he pulled out the box that came everywhere with him. It was battered now, its contents well-thumbed. He didn't always look at the letters and the photographs – sometimes went months without taking them out – but he always kept it all with him.

It was not much of a legacy really and that thought always made him feel sad, even now, after all this time. Add it all up – the pictures, the letters, the memories – and it amounted to a few scraps of advice and a faded

154

image. Not enough. Not by a long way.

He still berated himself for it. The image that was strongest was of a figure standing by a rugby pitch on a rainy winter's day. The figure was strong and warm, but the boy who approached him was selfish and self-interested. For the boy, the figure was needed, but he wasn't concentrated on or attended to.

And then he was gone and it was too late. There were more rugby matches on endless winter days, but the figure of strength was absent and the rock on which his life had been founded was crumbling.

He wondered if his father would ever have guessed at the chaos he would leave behind.

In the beginning, it had been relatively easy. Then it had all changed. He remembered the day when his mother had come down to school. The bullying was bad then and he'd wanted it all to come tripping out, but instead, she had explained that she was going to marry again. He had listened in silence.

At the end of that term, he'd been woken to the power of literature for the first time. Sitting in the gods at a theatre in Bristol, he'd been pinned to his seat by the power of Hamlet's soliloquy, 'How weary, stale, flat, and unprofitable, seem to me all the uses of this world . . . 'tis an unweeded garden, That grows to seed; things rank and gross in nature . . . O, most wicked speed, to post with such dexterity to incestuous sheets . . .'

For years afterwards he'd hated himself for wanting to deny his mother happiness. Now he told himself that was all done. Past history. But he hadn't spoken to her in weeks and hadn't had a civil conversation with his stepfather for much longer.

He looked down at the letter that had come with the will. It was torn now and in two pieces, but it had been one single page of plain A4. A single page of love and philosophy to last a lifetime.

He cast his eyes over the rest of the letters. 'I hope you're well . . . keep your spirits up, old boy . . . we're thinking of you . . . glad you won the game . . . thought the referee was completely biased . . . looking forward to seeing you at the weekend . . .'

The tears rolled down his cheeks.

McIlhatton was flirting with a small rebellion.

He was in Soho, looking at pictures of naked girls. In these streets, they seemed to be everywhere – always perfectly shaped, in leotards or suspenders or leather or nothing at all.

He was standing outside the entrance to some kind of bar, looking at a picture of a girl dancing naked and thinking about the hard-on in his trousers. He was teetering on the edge of going in – a small rebellion because the standing orders were to do absolutely nothing that might in any way draw attention to yourself – when the woman behind the counter said, 'Are you coming in?'

He broke into an instant sweat and walked away, his face colouring.

He strode down to Piccadilly Circus, pushing through the crowds on the pavement more aggressively than he needed to. At the bottom of the stairs down to the tube he fumbled in his pocket for some change and then picked up the telephone and dialled. The phone rang and he looked at his watch. Might be too late.

Eventually, he heard the girl say, 'Andersonstown Travel.'

CHAPTER EIGHT

Colette sat bolt upright, suddenly awake and afraid. Somebody had gripped her arm and she was about to scream when she smelled the man's breath.

'Ssh. It's me – Paddy.'

He still had his hand on her arm and she pushed him away. 'Christ, what time is it? What do you want?'

He sat down on the end of the bed and spoke quietly. 'I'm sorry. It's six o'clock, and we need you. Kieran Doherty was picked up late last night and we need someone we can rely on.'

Colette felt numb. There was no way to refuse. She had signed her own death warrant. They were looking out for Paddy, but they weren't expecting her.

She scrabbled round on the floor for her clothes, dragged on her jeans and came downstairs. Paddy was waiting in the kitchen. 'What about the kids?' she said.

Paddy gave her a puzzled look. 'They'll be fine with Ma.'

'But why do you want me?'

A puzzled look again, as if he didn't understand why she was questioning the decision. 'You used to gather intelligence in east Belfast. We need somebody who knows their way round and who won't panic.'

'I haven't been there for years.'

'Is there something wrong?' There was an edge to his voice.

Colette shook her head. Outside, a blue Ford Escort was waiting with its engine running. She got into the back without saying anything further. She didn't recognize the driver, but she could tell his hair was short underneath the baseball cap. He looked very young.

They turned off the Falls onto the Springfield Road and then stopped opposite the gate in the peace wall that separated Catholic from Protestant west Belfast. The road here at Lanark Way had been closed for months, ever since the last vicious round of tit-for-tat killing. On the left, the landscape was desolated, the derelict houses making this part of Belfast look like an older, more war-torn city.

Paddy twisted round to face her. 'Now listen. I've briefed the others. It's the attack on Henderson. You're to drive the getaway, right? Right, Colette?'

She nodded, not trusting herself to speak. Later, she remembered thinking that Paddy seemed excited, and she couldn't help contrasting it with the look of fear she had seen on his face only a few days before. It was the fear that was unusual.

'There'll be two cars. The getaway and a red Sierra. Got that? We'll be travelling to Winston Gardens, just off the Newtownards Road.' Paddy was emphasizing his speech, as if talking to a child. 'That's where the bastard lives. He drives a silver Granada and he always leaves home by eight thirty. Got that?'

She nodded, though she hadn't.

'As Henderson's Granada comes along, the Sierra pulls directly into his path, forcing him to stop. I'll come out of the van for the kill. By now, you are in the driver's seat ready for the getaway. We drive out back down the Newtownards Road. Got that?'

She nodded once more.

'Sure?' He was distracted and turned back to face the front. Two men had emerged from a side street and were walking quickly towards the car. They were both young and she recognized their faces, but couldn't remember their names. She wasn't introduced, but they were clearly Paddy's men and they looked like they were pumped up with testosterone and adrenalin. They both wore baseball caps and they were both chewing gum. Colette thought they were nervous and it reminded her of the first operation she'd been involved in, ambushing an army patrol with petrol bombs. It seemed a long time ago.

She shivered. The questions and the doubts tumbled through her mind. She felt a violent hatred for Allen and Ryan. They had promised to protect Paddy, but she realized that there was no good reason why she should trust them.

The driver turned off the Springfield Road into Ballymurphy and stopped halfway down one of the terraced streets that ran off the Whiterock Road. A car was sitting outside on blocks, without any wheels. Paddy handed Colette a balaclava and a pair of rubber gloves and indicated that she should put them on.

She followed him to the front door, the other two men falling in behind her.

Paddy rang the bell once. The car disappeared off down the street and an elderly face poked suspiciously round the door. Paddy stepped forward, pushing the door gently but firmly. 'Provisional IRA. We're taking over your house, but you've no need to worry.'

The woman didn't seem frightened. 'Oh, for the Lord's sake. Why can't you people go away and leave us in peace?'

159

A younger man might have been unnerved, but Paddy had the confidence given by years of experience. 'We'll be gone soon enough and you wouldn't want your son to get hurt now, would you?'

Paddy brushed past her and into the kitchen, where a young man sat at the table behind a full plate of sausages and eggs. He didn't move. Paddy pulled the pistol from his pocket. 'You'll not be needing your van today . . .'

Paddy left one of the young men behind to guard the woman and her son. Colette and the other – a spotty, stumpy, ugly youth – followed him to the yellow Toyota van that was parked further down the street. A few minutes later they stopped outside a house in nearby Turf Lodge owned by an IRA sympathizer. Inside, she recognized two more of Paddy's men, Seamus McGirr and Sean Campbell.

The AK-Ms were on the table, their butts removed to make them easy to conceal. They were ugly.

Whilst they were still talking, Colette smiled and said she needed to go for a piss. Upstairs she sat on the cracked and filthy toilet seat and tried to still the panic that was swamping her mind. She finished and was about to pull the flush lever when an idea struck her. She crept across the corridor and almost wept with relief when she saw a phone wire leading across the unmade bed.

She called the Freephone number they had made her memorize and asked to speak to 'the boxman', the code name she'd been given. The operator asked her to wait a few moments and she sat in terrified silence, listening to the voices drifting up the stairs.

She waited. The line was dead. She wanted to scream.

She recognized Allen's voice.

'Shadow Dancer?'

She was paralysed by fear, because down below, one voice was suddenly louder. Somebody was at the bottom of the stairs.

'Shadow Dancer?'

The man was coming up the stairs. Her voice was barely audible. 'I'm in. Don't shoot.'

She put down the phone gently and stood up. The spotty youth was at the door. He looked suspicious. 'Everything OK?'

She nodded. 'Yes. Just checking out front. We might have been followed . . .'

He stared at her, but said nothing. She shrugged her shoulders. 'You can never be too careful.'

He didn't reply and she could feel her face reddening. She dropped her gaze and walked forward, wanting to break the silence. He made no attempt to step back to allow her room and she had to squeeze past him to get out of the door.

She walked down the stairs. She heard him go into the loo. She went back into the room and Paddy clearly saw the expression on her face. 'Everything all right, Colette?' She nodded and stared dumbly at the weapons piled on the table – three automatic rifles and three pistols, along with a selection of balaclavas, gloves and blue boiler suits.

She waited for the young man to come down and denounce her. She heard his footsteps on the stairs. He seemed to be coming so slowly and she wondered if he was thinking and turning over what he'd seen in his mind, deciding what to do.

She sensed he'd come into the room, but she didn't look. She was leaning forward looking at the floor. She heard nothing. Nobody spoke.

Eventually, she looked up. The youth was staring at

her. She wondered if it was suspicion she saw in his eyes, or fear, or both. She almost willed him to say something and get it over with, but Paddy stood up and said, 'All right, let's go.'

He scooped up the boiler suits and gloves and took hold of one of the AK-Ms, hiding it beneath his long coat. He led from the front and Colette followed him quickly, trying to get herself out of the room.

The red Sierra left first. As it moved off, she was sure the youth looked back towards her.

In the van, they waited. Colette began to replay the incident in her mind. She saw herself lying on the bed, gripping the phone. She tried to recall what she'd said, going through it word by word and second by second, and she tried to think of exactly when she had heard his footsteps on the stairs. She didn't think he could have heard anything, since she'd spoken so quietly, but she'd seen the suspicion in his face.

Before she'd really noticed, they were moving. Paddy was driving and he was frowning, his face distorted by concentration.

Nobody spoke. They passed the security surveillance point situated on the top floor of the Divis Tower, a grubby, archaic block of flats on the edge of Republican west Belfast. Colette felt the fear grow still greater within her, but there were no security checkpoints and they drove past the Westlink and into the centre of town.

Next to her, Paddy seemed confident, and she tried to draw strength from it. Then she remembered what they were going to. For one brief, fleeting moment, she felt a sense of relief that the young man would probably be killed, but it was quickly gone.

She looked at Paddy again and wondered how he could seem so calm. She wanted to scream at him and plead with him to stop. She thought he looked like he was out for a Sunday-school drive.

They passed the city hall. The square that surrounded it was bustling with life, people hurrying to work with the early morning sun lightening their step. She looked at their carefree faces.

They turned onto the bottom of the Newtownards Road and entered the heart of Protestant east Belfast. Colette read the Loyalist graffiti on the wall to her left. 'Our message to the Irish is simple,' it said: 'Hands off Ulster.'

At the top of the road, the houses were bigger and the hedges neater. They turned into Winston Gardens and Colette could see the red Sierra up ahead. The street was deserted but for an old woman walking her dog. She looked at her watch. It was eight twenty.

Paddy pulled the van into the side of the road, opposite the red Sierra, and quietly told Colette to move across to the driving seat. He clambered into the back. Colette did as she was told and then looked across at McGirr, who nodded, started up his engine and moved forward fractionally, so they were ready to stop Henderson's Granada in front of the van. Paddy and Sean Campbell had taken out and loaded the AKs. Paddy pushed the back door slightly open. The old woman was moving slowly towards him.

The sound froze them all. It was from a window above. It was loud, the voice amplified by a megaphone.

'You are surrounded. Please put down your weapons.'

Nobody moved. The street was eerily quiet. It was too quiet to be normal and Paddy swore at himself under his breath.

'I repeat that you are surrounded. Please give

yourselves up and we guarantee nobody will be hurt.'

Next to Paddy, Sean Campbell was breathing heavily. 'The fuckers, the lousy fuckers. Somebody must have bloody touted.'

Paddy looked cautiously out of the back window. The old woman was still there, frozen.

The voice coming through the megaphone was calm and measured. 'You cannot escape. You are surrounded on all sides. Please give yourselves up immediately.'

Paddy looked out of the window again. The street was deserted save for the old woman.

'Please give yourselves up immediately. You cannot hope to escape. We know there are five of you, so please come out slowly with your hands raised clearly above your heads.'

In the front of the van, Colette sat absolutely still, unable to move, her mind and body paralysed. She wanted to scream at Paddy, but the words died before they reached her throat.

Beside Paddy, Sean Campbell was panicking, and with one sudden movement he threw the van doors open and dived out onto the street. The sound of the gunfire was deafening and he was dead before he hit the ground. Paddy lay flat on the floor and, as he did so, the guns sought out the van, peppering its thin metal sides with bullet holes. Then silence, the van still rocking gently from the force of the gunfire. Paddy turned to Colette. 'Don't move,' he whispered.

The back of the van was open and Colette turned to see Campbell's body lying still on the ground. The old woman was standing there, paralysed. She watched as Paddy lunged forward. The old woman was only yards away, but the few seconds it took him to get there seemed to last a lifetime. She thought every step should be his last.

Then suddenly, miraculously, he was there. The bullets stopped. He held the pistol to the woman's head. 'Stop. Stop, or I'll kill her.'

They could have shot him clean. But their orders were to be careful. Nobody fired.

'Let the van go.'

Silence.

'Let the van go, or I'll kill her.'

The street was eerily quiet again.

'I don't know where you are, but let the van go.'

Colette watched, transfixed. She hadn't expected him to live. She knew they were dealing with the SAS and thought they would shoot him at any minute. He shouted at her, but she didn't hear him.

'Start the van.'

Still silence. She didn't move.

'Start the van.'

She didn't react. Paddy started to pull the old woman slowly towards the van. He looked naked and vulnerable, but he shouted again, 'For Christ's sake!' She stared at his back. She could almost feel the gun-sights trained on him. She couldn't understand why they were letting him live. He shouted again. 'Start the fucking van!'

He edged slowly forwards. He could see Colette now sitting hunched over the wheel.

'Start the bloody van. Start the van. START THE BLOODY VAN!'

Colette came alive. She fumbled for the keys in the ignition and started it up. The van limped forward.

Paddy waved at her. 'Go on. Drive on. Get out.'

He gestured to McGirr and began pushing the old woman towards the car. The red Sierra's windscreen

165

was peppered with bullet holes. The youth had been hit and looked as if he might be dead.

Paddy held the old woman tightly and threw himself backwards into the car. McGirr revved the engine furiously and slammed his foot on the accelerator. They lurched forward, bouncing off the line of cars ahead of them. Nobody fired.

Colette only got a few hundred yards. She turned left into Green Road and drove straight into one of the back-up platoons. Two soldiers were crouching by the side of the road and stood up as she approached. She brought the van gently to a halt, slowly opened the door and got out, with her hands pointing straight to the sky.

She moved forward gingerly, nervous until she heard a familiar voice.

'Take it easy, lads.'

Ryan emerged and walked towards her. He took hold of her arm and gently guided her to the waiting car.

Inside, she put her head in her hands and began to sob uncontrollably. Ryan drove off, but stopped a few streets further on.

She could feel him watching her, but he said nothing. 'Bastards,' she muttered, under her breath.

The air was still damp and Colette shivered. Mulgrew pointed at the house – number ten – though it was pretty obvious which one it was. The others all looked inhabited.

They were in New Barnsley, a collection of streets close to Fort Whiterock, beneath the mountain.

Mulgrew fumbled for the keys and she bent to pick up a little tricycle that lay abandoned at her feet. A few yards away, two stray dogs were dancing round each other, but other than that the street was deserted. She looked back to see the mountain above them and, just at that moment, two young boys came tearing down the road, one chasing the other and both screaming.

Mulgrew finally managed to find the right key and ushered her in. The damp inside was overwhelming. He pointed to the left and said, 'Have a seat.' There wasn't much choice in the front room – a tatty brown sofa or a wooden chair that looked like it had been pulled out of a fire. She chose the chair and tried to ignore the smell of damp whilst she waited. The wallpaper and net curtains were filthy, the carpet worn through. She noticed the smell of the kitchen for the first time and tried to fight off the first feelings of nausea.

She waited, uncertain as to exactly what he was doing next door. She breathed in deeply and tried to think about what he was going to ask. She thought about what he had asked last time and shivered again.

She thought through how she had got back. She had walked. All the way? Yes, all the way. Avoiding the soldiers and patrols? Yes, coming slowly, taking the backstreets.

Of course, Mulgrew *would* have been waiting. She should have expected it. She wished now she had been less shocked. What in the hell was he doing next door? She breathed in deeply again and wondered what had happened to Paddy.

Mulgrew came in and smiled at her. He sat on the sofa – slightly lower than her, despite his greater height. He radiated friendliness this time and she found she had the strength to hate him. He was so smart, so trusted. I bet you're a bloody tout, she thought.

'What went wrong?'

She tried to concentrate, the hate suddenly evaporating. 'I don't know. I did what I was told, but they were waiting and ... it was chaos ... everything was confused. I—'

'You abandoned the van?'

'Yes.'

'Where?'

'Er ... I don't know. A few streets away. I thought they would be looking out for it. I thought I would be safer on foot.'

'The area was crawling with soldiers.'

'I know, that's why—'

'And none of them saw you? You didn't run into any of them?'

'I took the backstreets ... I didn't think they would be looking for someone on foot.'

'Which streets?'

'Er, I ... from the city centre I could tell you, but not over there. I was kind of panicking. Wasn't really thinking too clearly—'

'You've *no* idea how you got out?'

'I came down a lot of residential streets ... big houses. I – I thought I was getting lost, but I kept going until I came to the top of the Castlereagh Road.'

'And you didn't see any soldiers.'

'Saw a few Land Rovers racing past. But I kept me head down and kept walking.'

He shifted in his seat. 'You weren't down to be involved in this operation. When was the *first* you heard of it?'

She shivered. Paddy. 'Is Paddy OK?'

'Paddy's fine. He got out too. I've spoken to him. When was the *first* you heard of this operation?'

A trap? *I've spoken to him.* What did he say? She could feel the adrenalin in her system. She shivered again.

'Come on, Colette. It's a simple question.'

'What was it?'

168

'Are you all right?'

'Yes, yes. Sorry, it's been a ... I was just worrying about the kids, that's all.'

'I know, it must be difficult.' A gentle voice now. 'I was just asking you when you *first* heard of this attack.'

'This morning. Paddy came to my room and woke me. I was dead worried about the kids and—'

'That was the *first* time you heard?'

She nodded.

'And nobody had mentioned anything before that?'

'Not that I remember, no.'

'Not that you remember?'

'No, nobody said anything.'

Mulgrew smiled softly. 'Thank you, Colette.'

O'Hanlon put up his hand. He was short, fat, ugly and bald. He was trying to be conciliatory. 'Gerry, I'm not saying you have a tout. I'm not saying that. But you won't deny it looks that way.'

They were walking up Whiterock. They had met outside the Rock Bar and had turned right up the hill, past the Sean Graham bookie's shop. They were silent for a few moments as a man and a woman with a pram approached on their side of the pavement. The man said, 'Morning, Gerry,' and that was oddly satisfying. He couldn't remember the man's name.

But, as they turned right onto a piece of wasteland, he felt angry. This morning's operation had been a fiasco, certainly, but the men from the IRA's notorious 'nutting squad' had wasted no time. It wasn't any of their bloody business, but he knew he was going to have to be tactful and that was the worst of it.

He stopped and they gathered in a tight circle. 'It'll take time to look into,' he said. 'Paddy's in hiding. We think he might have been tailed beforehand.'

'Well, we'll wait. But this morning was a disaster,' O'Hanlon said.

'I don't believe there's a tout in Paddy's unit.'

'Oh, *come on*, McVeigh. Just because he's your brother.' O'Hanlon's voice was taunting. Gerry's instinct was to hit him, but he held his arms by his side. O'Hanlon was a leadership man, after all. Not long now, Gerry told himself.

'We'll look into it,' he said.

'Nobody is above suspicion, Gerry,' O'Hanlon said. 'Nobody.'

At that moment, there was the blast of a siren and two police Land Rovers charged up Whiterock. They were low on their wheels and Gerry could tell they were heavily laden. Without a word, they broke up and dispersed to different corners of the wasteland, away from the road.

They'd been waiting a few minutes and conversation had petered out. They were at Castlereagh, waiting to see the head of the source unit. A man turned into the corridor and slowed as he approached. He obviously knew Allen.

'You waiting to see the chief inspector?' He was pointing at the door.

Allen nodded, sniffing as he did so. 'He's taking his time.'

The man was tall – in fact, Ryan noticed, they were all about the same height. He had dark hair, a moustache and a large nose that had very obviously been broken several times. He looked at Ryan. 'Is this your friend from MI5?'

Allen gestured at him with an open palm. 'David Ryan – Johnny Brogan.'

They shook hands and Brogan turned back to Allen.

170

'He'll be all over you like a rash. The chief has already been on the phone to him—'

At that moment, the door opened and a man came out. Ryan missed what he said and found himself concentrating on the look on Allen's face. It was something between shock and surprise. The man who had come out was obviously pleased and he disappeared off down the corridor with Brogan as Allen and Ryan were taken in. Ryan didn't think about it further. The chief inspector was, as Brogan had said he would be, all over them like a rash.

Afterwards, Allen suggested they go for a drink and, as he drove out of Castlereagh, Ryan thought he looked pensive. He was silent until they were crossing Albert Bridge.

'Did you see the man who came out before we went in?'

'Yes. He looked pretty happy.'

'He's a handler.'

Allen said that with such certainty and weight that Ryan felt he should understand exactly what he meant. He waited, hoping Allen would expand.

'Now why would he be so bloody happy today?'

'Perhaps he was in about something else,' Ryan said.

Allen looked at him and shook his head. 'I don't think so.'

They went for a drink in Cutter's Wharf, a bar by the edge of the Lagan. It was big and modern inside and they took a table by one of the windows in the corner. Ryan watched as two rowing boats raced past. It was an odd sight, he thought. It didn't fit with his mental image of Belfast at all.

Allen was distracted and conversation was hard going. Ryan thought about what Allen had said. *He's a handler. Now why would he be so bloody happy today?*

Ryan thought it was better to look stupid than fail to understand. He asked Allen what he had meant. Allen paused for a few seconds before answering, his face thoughtful.

'Well, the thing is. We have a source, right? We get some information and we prevent an attack and everyone thinks we're bloody wonderful. So far so good. But then we see that *another* handler is being congratulated.'

Allen looked round to check that no-one was listening before he continued. 'Another handler means another source. The fact that he is being congratulated *today*, about the same attack, means there is every chance the other source is close to ours.'

Allen leaned forward and Ryan smelled the beer on his breath. 'Is the other source better or worse, that is what you have to ask. And if suspicion grows, will they get rid of one to save the other?'

'Who is the other?'

Allen laughed. 'We're not likely to find out. Someone close to her? Could be. Local quartermaster supplying the arms? You'd never know.'

Ryan looked round again. It was still early and they were on their own in the corner. He felt queasy now and wondered if all this was just paranoia. He was relieved when Allen said he had to get home. He finished his bottle of Budweiser and said he would walk.

It was further than he thought up through Stranmillis. He mulled over what Allen had said. He wanted to put it out of his mind, but couldn't.

At home, he switched on the television and decided he really couldn't be bothered to make himself some supper. He began running a bath, and was just about to get into it when the phone rang. It was Grant and he was very, very pleased. 'Well done,' he said. 'Very well done indeed.'

Ryan knew he should allow himself a few moments' quiet satisfaction, but he couldn't shake off the sense of unease. This was a game you could never win, a game where the best result was a postponement, not a victory, where tragedy, of one kind or another, was only delayed, never cancelled.

Whilst Colette danced alone at the centre of it all, he could not enjoy Grant's praise.

If she was a puppet, he was beginning to realize how thin her strings were. If they were cut – accidentally or deliberately – she would collapse, whilst the game went on, barely missing a beat.

Today he'd saved – or helped save – the life of a man he'd never met. An innocent man. But he couldn't help focusing on the preservation of *her* life. He knew it was the wrong way of looking at it.

He got into the bath, lying back with his head resting on the end. He shut his eyes. Today did have one result: an almost irresistible urge to call Jenkins.

He still had these amazing fantasies about Jenkins and asked himself why he was not prepared to carry them through. Logically, there was no reason why he should have held back from telling Jenkins to fuck off (God, in the context, the words had such a satisfying, brutal ring to them). He'd told himself many times that he did not wish to remain in the Service for ever, but, in moments of real honesty, he had to accept he was probably more ambitious than he ordinarily allowed himself to admit. Especially now.

There was no real logic to his hatred, of course. It was something about the structure and hierarchy of the organization – any organization for that matter – that forced you to accept behaviour from a superior that you would never tolerate in an equal. And the truth was that Jenkins simply made no effort. He was a bully; curt, sometimes rude, but never making any effort to build any sort of personal relationship with his subordinates. He relied on criticism, not encouragement. Where he could, he relied on fear as a motivational force, though he'd never really tried that on with Ryan.

Ryan thought he'd have laughed if the bastard had been hit by a bus.

He got out of the bath and towelled himself down. He got dressed and made some toast.

On a whim, he called Claire. She was in.

'Any messages?' he asked.

'No, Mr Ryan. No messages. Nobody likes you.'

'They're too frightened.'

'Oh yes.' She paused, before going on. 'How are you? Lonely?'

He put his feet on the stool in front of him. 'No, bored. Excitement and boredom in about equal measures.'

'Friends?'

'Only ones that want to kill me.'

'Perhaps we should all come over.'

'Perhaps you should.'

After he'd put down the phone, he watched television for about ten minutes, channel hopping, and then went to bed in boredom.

He lay awake for hours, thinking about Colette and wondering what kind of life she could possibly be living only a mile away. He couldn't comprehend how she could cope with it.

Gerry McVeigh pulled the front door shut and looked up. The helicopter 'eye in the sky' was right above him, a few hundred feet up, its spotlight illuminating the street. He paused. He nearly went back in, but decided in the end to continue. He didn't look up as he walked to the car.

As he got in, he could feel the tiredness behind his eyes. He might have gone back, but what he was going to do was important. It mattered to him.

The car didn't start the first time and he reminded himself to get it seen to. Or maybe he'd get another. Easy to get anything stolen in the south.

At first, he thought the 'eye in the sky' was following him, but if it was, it soon gave up, and by the time he got to Andersonstown, it had headed off to the other side of west Belfast. It was dark now and he managed to find a space right outside the travel agency. It looked warm inside, condensation misting up the inside of the windows.

The girl was packing up and she was alone. She smiled nervously and looked flustered as he came in, but she accepted his offer of a drink.

This time, when the car wouldn't start, he was annoyed, but he kept his patience and eventually it spluttered into life. He turned left and then left again, avoiding driving down the Falls. Neither of them spoke during the journey; she seemed tense. When they got to the city centre, he parked close to Kelly's and they walked the last fifty yards or so. Inside, it was quiet. Two men in suits – shabby suits – sat at the bar and Gerry took her round to the far corner. She asked for a vodka and bitter lemon and drank it at speed.

If the truth be known, Gerry found these situations quite awkward. He didn't have a whole lot of time and he wanted it, but he didn't want to make a fool of himself – and he was worried about being caught. You could never tell where Christy was going to turn up.

He struggled to make conversation. She was pretty enough, with long black hair and a slim waist and small breasts pushed into a skintight black body. She'd taken off her denim jacket as soon as they sat down.

For an hour or two he proceeded carefully, his manner polite and interested. He discovered that she was eighteen, her name was Cathy and she lived with her family in Ballymurphy. He knew her father Joe, who was one of the old IRA men who'd been involved briefly at the start of the Troubles, but faded away after Internment in the early Seventies.

She drank three vodkas and when he finally said, 'Shall we go?' she nodded meekly.

He took her to an IRA safe house in Ballymurphy – not far from her home. He explained that he stayed at various houses around the city to confuse the Loyalists and the Brits.

The bedroom was tiny and it only had a single bed. Cathy looked at it and smiled, and he realized that beneath her nervous exterior she had a sense of humour.

He stripped her body slowly from the shoulders and squeezed her small brown nipples gently in his hands. Her skin was soft and white and clean, and he unbuttoned her jeans and sat her on the bed as he pulled them down to the floor. He fumbled ineffectually with the laces on her brown boots and she leaned forward to help him, her long black hair brushing against his head. He could smell her.

He pulled down his own jeans, but didn't bother with his T-shirt. She was very wet, and he lay beside her with his hand between her legs for what must have been several minutes but seemed like a lot longer. Eventually, he pushed himself up and put his left hand down to guide himself in. She kissed him and moaned quietly as he entered her.

He wanted to come immediately, but he held back, his face a study in concentration as he looked down at the top half of her body and looked back at her legs, which were pressed neatly against his sides. She pushed her hips up forcefully, enjoying him.

She came first – he couldn't believe how quickly she came – and he followed her, thinking she was anything but a novice.

Neither of them had talked about contraception.

Afterwards, they lay together on the narrow bed, Gerry wondering how long he had to hold her before he could send her home. He'd just come to the conclusion that her time was up when she spoke to him quietly. 'I'm not sure about this, but I think we're being watched.'

'What?'

She smiled gently. 'Not here. I mean in the travel agency. I think we're being watched.'

He was on his feet. He put his knee on the side of the bed and gripped her face. 'Have you fucking blabbed? Have you fucking touted?'

He could see the fear in her face clearly. He had the uncomfortable feeling that he quite enjoyed the sensation. She said quietly, 'I haven't told a soul.'

He was impressed with how calm she was. Frightened, but calm.

'I haven't said anything, but strange things have been happening. We had a mysterious break-in the other night, the phones sound funny and I keep seeing people outside who look like they're watching us.'

'Who tipped them off?'

'I don't think it's the Brits.'

Gerry looked at her, suddenly uncertain. He had released her face, but took hold of it again now, sinking his fingers into her cheeks. 'You've told somebody.'

She shook her head. 'I told no-one. It looks like our people. I know some of the faces.'

Gerry stood up and walked over to the window, naked but for his T-shirt. He pulled one of the curtains gently to the side and looked out into the deserted street. It was pretty dark. All the street lights on this side of the road had been smashed by the local kids.

'Did you hear from the man?' he asked.

'Yes. I told him what you said.' She sounded frightened now.

He turned back to the window.

Silence.

'Ever get the feeling,' he said, 'that events are driving you . . . you know, that you're cut off from people . . .'

Silence.

'Ever get the feeling that you're being isolated from people who are supposed to . . . Oh, fuck it.'

He bent down to pick up his jeans. 'You'd better go,' he said.

He didn't speak to her as she dressed. As he walked home, he felt an explosive mixture of anger and fear. It was all so bloody depressing. Everything. There seemed to be a coldness to so many things, as if everyone had somehow lost sight of his humanity. He told himself somebody had to fight for what was right.

Not his fault if everyone else was weakening.

The house was dark when he arrived. He reckoned Christy must have been taken with a migraine and gone to bed early. She always had a migraine. He pulled a beer out of the fridge and sat in front of a Clint Eastwood film.

CHAPTER NINE

Colette felt the shower and winced. She'd been generous with the children and there was no hot water left. She stepped over the edge of the bath and stood for a few seconds under the thin stream of cold water. She picked up the soap, briefly washed herself and turned off the shower, drying her body with a damp towel. She walked naked through to the bedroom, looking at her arms and legs in the process and wondering again if she was losing weight. She found a clean pair of white knickers in the top drawer and pulled out her jeans and a green roll-neck sweater – the nice one.

She went back into the bathroom to brush her teeth. She looked at her face in the mirror and thought she saw tired eyes. She examined herself and felt a trace of self-pity as she did so. It was an oddly enjoyable sensation.

She walked down the stairs quietly and popped her head round the door to the front room. Mark and Catherine were sitting on the floor, drawing, and the television was on, with the volume down. She told them she was going for some milk.

As she stepped out of the front door, she felt a gust of icy wind sweep down the street.

There was a lot of traffic on the Falls and one of the black taxis slowed down to let her cross, the driver tooting as she did so. She saw who was driving and she smiled and waved back. It was Sean Brennan, a childhood friend of Paddy's.

The newsagent was small and she squeezed past an elderly man to get to the fridge. Once the man had paid, she stepped up to the counter.

'How's the form, Colette?'

'Good, Beano. What about you?'

'Can't complain. Can't complain. What do you make of all this talk of peace then?'

Colette looked down at the newspapers on the counter as she handed over the money for the milk. She smiled at him. 'I'm not holding my breath, Beano.'

He laughed and she turned to go. She changed her mind and turned back. 'Oh, go on, give us an *Irish News*. Better hear what the bastards have got to say.'

As she stepped out onto the street again, she turned the paper over and saw the headline 'AMBUSHED!' She glanced at the first few paragraphs.

She felt as if the blood was draining out of her.

She was suddenly cold.

Sean Campbell was dead, but the boy wasn't. It said he was 'critical'.

She hadn't even considered it. She had assumed he must have died.

She tucked the newspaper under her arm and thrust her hands into her pockets, shivering against the cold. She felt dislocated suddenly from the world around her.

She walked down the pavement to the Sinn Féin press office. The doorway had a large metal cage in it. She rang the buzzer and heard a door opening inside.

A large round face appeared and she smiled again. 'Hiya, Frankie.'

The cage opened and she stepped in, feeling the warmth as she did so.

'What's up, Colette?'

'You seen Paddy?'

They were inside now and Colette could see the warmth was coming from a three-bar electric fire in the corner. The room was small and smelled musty, the walls around her covered in Sinn Féin and IRA posters.

'It's bleeding cold,' Frankie said.

'There'll be snow, I reckon,' she replied.

Frankie rubbed his hands. 'Think Paddy's holed up. That's what they say.'

Colette raised her eyebrows in reply. There was a pile of copies of *An Phlobacht/Republican News* in the corner and she stepped forward and picked one up. 'Any news?' she said conversationally.

Frankie was shaking his head. 'The boy is bad, they say.'

'How bad?' Colette heard herself ask. Frankie was still shaking his head and she exhaled quietly as if to express her shock and sorrow.

'Bad news,' he continued, 'bad news. Only son, they say. Mrs Martin from down at the Divis Tower there. Know her?'

Colette shook her head.

'Husband left home years ago. Quite a shock, I should think. Don't think she knew he was involved, know what I mean?'

Colette wanted to change the subject. She showed Frankie the front of the paper she'd bought. Apart from the main story on the ambush, all the other front-page stories dealt with aspects of the developing peace process. 'What do you think about all this peace talk, Frankie?'

He tilted his bald head to one side and tugged the end of his dark moustache, sucking his teeth loudly as he did so. 'You want my honest opinion, we're on the way to a new world, but whether it's going to be good or bad, I'd rather not say.'

She smiled at him. 'We'll see.' She turned to go and hurried back to the house. Inside, Mark and Catherine were still in the front room – they'd been so quiet that morning – and she turned off the television. 'Breakfast,' she said.

She put the Coco Pops on the table and made herself a cup of coffee.

'Mum, Daniel says they have Batman stickers in Frosties,' Mark said.

'M–M–M–M–Mum,' Catherine said. Colette looked at her. She'd never stammered before. Not ever. 'Sarah's mummy p–p–p–p–picks her up from play-group every day.'

Colette knelt beside her chair. 'I'll pick you up from now on, love – I promise. I'm sorry about the last few days.'

Catherine smiled. 'Did the soldiers hurt you when they t–t–t–took you away?'

Colette shook her head. 'No, they didn't hurt me.'

'Why did they take you away?' Mark asked.

She stood up. 'It's just one of those things. Now finish up your cereal. We'd better go.'

'Where's Grandma?' Mark asked.

'She went out earlier. Now come on.'

Colette cleared away the breakfast. She found their coats and tried to get them dressed in the hall. They were both very clingy, though they were chattering away more now. Mark was preoccupied with whether he would be the first to play on the racing car and Colette told him to hurry. The playgroup was on the second floor at Conway Mill. They were the first in, so he got his wish. Colette descended the spiral staircase and came out through the security door at the bottom. As she turned out of the car park outside, the icy wind hit her and she pulled her coat tightly about her. In the few minutes since she'd been inside, the wind seemed to have whipped up, sweeping down off the mountain, the snow drifting across the road and beginning to settle by the curb the other side.

As she passed the Sinn Féin press office, a black taxi pulled up and Gerry Adams got out, but he was looking the other way and didn't see her. She didn't particularly want to attract his attention.

She pulled a packet of cigarettes out of her pocket and smoked one as she walked. She found herself thinking about Adams, about peace and about the argument the other night. She thought about Gerry's accusation.

She told herself she wasn't a coward. She told herself Gerry Adams wasn't a coward either.

She remembered the time when they'd all been together as a family, but it just wasn't the same now. Hadn't been for a long time, if she was honest. She thought of what lay ahead of her.

Then she thought about the injured boy.

'Christ,' she whispered.

Ryan loved his shower. The flat might not be elegant, exactly, but it was well equipped and the shower was powerful and hot. He'd been in it for ten minutes at least and was reluctant to get out. Despite the central heating, it was cold in the bedroom.

He washed and stepped out, towelling himself down quickly. The towel had been sitting on the heating rail and was warm – another luxury. He pulled out his jeans, a black T-shirt and black sweater.

The kitchen was at the other end of the flat and he walked down the corridor in his socks and switched on the kettle. He made himself a cup of instant coffee and a couple of pieces of toast with honey, and sat at the table by the window. It looked out onto a garden fence. He picked up a street map of Belfast and opened it out. He looked at the route again carefully and looked at the streets that ran off it either way. He wondered if he was completely mad.

When he'd finished his breakfast, he went into the living room and picked up his blue donkey jacket and black woollen hat and opened the door on to the small patio outside. All you could see from here was the hedge, but it was rush hour and he could hear the traffic in the road beyond. He left the door open and smoked a cigarette, which was designed to make him feel calmer, but had the opposite effect. When he'd finished he stepped on the butt and then chucked it over the hedge – he didn't know why he did that – and went back into the house, checking carefully to see that he had everything. He walked back into his bedroom and opened the bedside table. He took out the Browning, checked it was loaded, and then lifted up his donkey jacket and sweater and pushed it into the top of his jeans. Unauthorized and stupid, he thought.

He checked that he had his keys and then walked back into the kitchen to check that he hadn't left the cooker on – which he hadn't used since last night anyway. Finally he shut the door behind him.

It was windier this side of the house and he felt the cold. The snow was blowing in his face as he walked down to the traffic lights. The cars were moving slowly, their windscreen wipers working to keep the snow clear. Ryan once again found himself thinking about the quality of the cars. Some people here were doing *very* nicely.

He felt good, buoyant, and he was walking quite fast. The snowflakes were small and as he walked down Balmoral they began to gather on the front of his jacket. It reminded him of Christmas holidays in the Alps a long time ago and it was a comfortable feeling.

But fifty yards further on, it began to worry him. He looked down at the jacket again and wondered if it was simply too new. He hadn't noticed before and he cursed himself for not looking in a mirror. He slowed. Too new? They weren't all poor, these people.

He stopped. There was a development of new houses on the left of him, a comfortable-looking 'Brookside'. He turned round and very slowly began to head back. Indecision. He thought about what else he could wear. Realistically, too cold to be out in a sweater, and anyway, the Browning might easily show then. He thought the truth was that the sensible thing was to abandon this.

He sauntered slowly homewards for a few more minutes and then suddenly spun round and began striding out again. Fuck it, he thought. Jenkins would have gone home, but then Jenkins wouldn't have been doing it in the first place.

It was a longer walk than he'd expected down to the top of the Lisburn Road. He was walking on the left-hand pavement and he almost crossed over to the newsagent at the bottom end of Balmoral to buy some cigarettes, but decided that would only be a delaying tactic.

He drew level with the King's Hall and walked under the road bridge. He was walking slower now and, to him, this point marked the end of middle-class south Belfast, though in fact it continued for another hundred yards or so. Musgrave Park was on his left

185

and he watched the snow drifting across it. He looked down. It was settling in the corner of the wall by his feet. A bus hurtled past him and he realized he was close to the edge of the road.

He came to the roundabout at the end of Balmoral and had to run to get to the other side. The security barriers were open today. He put his head down and tried to walk at an even pace.

There was a garage on his left, another on the right. Two young men walked past him, talking. They didn't appear to take any notice. He looked up. He was approaching another roundabout and he could see a Tricolour flying from a rooftop in the distance. The road was terribly familiar.

As he turned into Andersonstown Road he could feel the adrenalin in his bloodstream, and he breathed in deeply to try and calm his nerves. He repeated what he'd told himself in the house. There is no good reason . . .

Twenty more paces and he could hardly believe his eyes. He swore quietly to himself and seriously considered turning back. That would be asking for trouble. He walked on, with his head down, hoping. Out of the corner of his eye, he could see the man coming towards him, opening his notepad.

'Excuse me, sir . . . EXCUSE ME.'

He had to stop.

'Could I just ask you where you are going, sir?'

Ryan kept his voice calm. He managed a smile. 'I'm just off to the Sinn Féin press office.' He watched the man's uncertainty as he heard the accent. A different kettle of fish altogether.

'Do you have any ID, sir?' The man's accent was southern English. Ryan saw the tell-tale parachute emblem on his arm.

Ryan smiled again. 'Sorry, I don't, actually – I was just looking for my wallet a few minutes ago, but I've left it at the hotel.'

The soldier seemed uncertain of what to do. Ryan watched him open the notepad. 'Better just take your name, sir.'

'David Ryan. *Sunday Telegraph*. Over to do a feature. Staying at the Europa Hotel.'

The soldier wrote it down methodically and looked up the street. The patrol was moving on. He snapped the notepad shut. 'Thank you, sir. Good luck.'

Ryan walked on twenty yards and then turned briefly to watch them go. It was oddly comforting to know they weren't far away, though he knew that was a stupid thought.

He crossed the road before he got to the Felon's club and slowed as he approached the roundabout. An elderly woman was leaving the cemetery and she nodded a greeting. He smiled and then walked in. The snow had petered out and a few rays of sunlight were beginning to break through the clouds, catching the white gravestones. He walked up a tiny slope and then the cemetery was spread out before him. He felt awed, somehow, by his own presence here more than anything else. It was bigger than it seemed on television, stretching down the hill towards the M1, with Belfast spread out across the horizon, the sky there streaked now with orange and blue, behind the big yellow cranes. There were a few figures in the distance and he stopped for a moment to get his bearings. He knew the Republican plot was down to the right and he knew the spot he was looking for was close to that – close to, but not a part of. He began to walk slowly, his progress through the gravestones made easier by the fact that the ground was frozen. He could hear the sound of his boots on the solid earth.

It took him perhaps ten or twenty minutes, but eventually he found it.

Colette thought the weather was turning. She enjoyed the brief rays of sun on her face. The cemetery was quiet and peaceful and she walked down through the gravestones lost in thought.

She felt as though she were on a different planet. She couldn't think straight.

She told herself the boy was going to die. He was *going* to die.

She walked on down past the rows of graves to the bottom of the path, where a neat plot was surrounded by a freshly painted green fence. It was raised a foot or so above the ground and had a short path running through its centre, lined on either side with small fir trees. There were a number of headstones, all listing the names of the IRA volunteers who had died 'in action'. There were fresh flowers on most of the graves, some of them catching in the wind, their vases tilting and creaking eerily.

As she stepped onto the plot, she noticed a man crouched over a gravestone about 20 yards away. There was something familiar about the figure that she couldn't place. She watched for a second, but couldn't see his face, and so proceeded into the Republican plot.

She crouched down beside one of the headstones. The inscription read, 'David McGraw. Executed by the SAS. Coalisland, 28 February 1992.'

She laid down the flowers, and, as she looked at her reflection in the polished marble, she felt a sense of loneliness and isolation. She spoke quietly to him. 'I'm sorry, Davey my love. I hope you understand. I know you probably don't. I know it wouldn't have been your way, but . . . well, we've got to move on, don't we? Got to think of the future.'

She sat back and forced herself to think of Davey, her husband, and to visualize his face.

Sometimes, now, it was so hard to picture him.

She almost smiled. 'They never found your tout, did they, love? Never found the one that did for you. Probably still looking for the bastard.'

She looked up and saw him. He was right there, not 10 yards away, walking alongside the plot. She could scarcely believe it. She felt a surge of anger. He had his head down and, for the first few seconds, he didn't see her. Then he was next to her, stopped dead and staring at her with what looked like genuine surprise in his eyes.

For a split second they both stood still. She reacted first. 'You've been following me!' There was anger in her voice.

He didn't respond.

'For Christ's sake. You've been following me!'

He seemed to recover. 'Keep your voice down, Colette.'

She felt her anger deflating. She felt a sense of sudden, inexplicable warmth at the use of her Christian name.

'What are you *doing* here?' she asked.

'Quietly—' He took a step forward, closing the gap between them, his knee now resting against the small green fence.

'Why were you following me?'

'I wasn't following you.'

There was a firmness and strength to his voice. She was confused. 'What are you doing here?' she asked quietly.

She thought he was going to say, 'None of your

189

business,' but he exhaled audibly and said simply, 'I'll be seeing you. Keep in touch.'

He turned and walked about 5 yards – to the end of the plot – then he stopped and came back again. He walked to the fence and pushed his face towards her. She saw intensity, determination, tension.

'Be careful, Colette. You understand me. Be careful, be bloody careful – and watch Gerry. We *have* to know what he's doing. The next meeting as planned.'

He was gone before she could say anything and she wondered if she should follow. What did he mean? What in the hell did he mean? She looked round the graveyard, but could see no-one. She watched him go, walking fast, his long legs driving him up the slope. *Be careful. Be bloody careful.* What was that supposed to mean? And why were they so obsessed with Gerry?

He'd called her Colette.

She tore her eyes away from him and looked down at the grave, forcing herself to try to think of Davey. How *dare* he come here, she thought. How dare he violate this place. She tried to conjure up a mental image of Davey's face, but couldn't. When she looked up again, *he* had gone.

For a few minutes she stood there in silence, her mind swimming. Then something occurred to her and she walked back out of the Republican plot and over to the area where she had originally seen the figure crouching. Had that been him? Surely it had. She walked along the rows of the dead. Rafferty. Walshe. Downes. She took a step back again. Walshe? She read the headstone and could hardly believe it.

She walked back slowly to Davey's grave and knelt down in front of it, her mind racing. What did it mean? Everything and nothing. She didn't move.

Her thoughts drifted.

The hand on her shoulder startled her. 'I thought I'd find you here, love.'

Her mother was smiling kindly. Colette leaped to her feet, her voice harsh. 'How long have you been here?'

She saw the shock and surprise register on her mother's face. 'I'm sorry, love. I arrived just . . . just this second.'

Colette felt suddenly embarrassed. She didn't think her mother would have seen anything. She dropped her gaze and muttered an apology. 'I'm sorry. You just startled me, that's all.'

She squatted down again to rearrange the flowers and her mother did the same beside her. Even out here in the open air Colette recognized her mother's scent. It was the comforting smell of her childhood. They crouched together in silence, staring at Davey's headstone.

After a while, they stood. Ma had two bunches of flowers in her hand and Colette knew what that meant. She followed her mother to the other side of the cemetery and they both knelt in front of her father's gravestone. Then they walked the last few yards – to a small grave at the very end. Ma bent her head in prayer and Colette looked at the inscription: 'Sean McVeigh. Murdered by Crown Forces, aged eleven . . .'

The grave was so well kept. She tried to focus her mind on her baby brother and the horror of that day. She shivered at the memory. So long ago and yet neither forgiven nor forgotten. She thought of what Gerry had said. It was so cruel that this of all things should prove divisive.

That's what all this peace talk is doing, she thought. Our memories – our tragedies – are dividing us.

She looked at her mother. Despite the tragedy and sadness, despite the basic bloody *harshness* of their lives, Colette felt a sudden, overwhelming surge of gratitude for everything her mother had done and everything she was: tolerant, strong, principled. She was about to say something when she suddenly imagined what she would feel if Ma was here in this graveyard, dead and buried. The thought frightened her. One of us has to go first, she thought, and the only consolation is that it will probably be me.

Eventually they stood and walked up to the gate in silence. They turned right onto the Falls Road and began walking home. The streets were crowded, families taking advantage of the bright morning to finish off their Christmas shopping. Colette had Sean in her mind now – and Ryan, the two connected. She wanted to say, 'Bastard.' What in the hell did he mean anyway? *Be careful. Be bloody careful.*

Ma spoke quietly. 'Will you be at home for Christmas?'

It hadn't crossed Colette's mind. 'Christmas. Christ! I haven't even got any presents. I was going to go shopping in London . . .'

'I've brought presents for the kids. Nothing much, but I think it's what they want.'

Colette looked down at her feet. 'Thanks, Ma. I'm sorry.'

They were passing the Falls Park now and the iron fence shook as a football hit the top edge of it and bounced back towards the makeshift goal. Colette felt the need to continue. 'I know I've not been great with the kids.'

Her mother looked at her. 'You were better before Davey died.'

It was a statement of fact and Colette didn't reply. As if they'd reached a silent, telepathic agreement, they turned into the park and sat down on the nearest

192

bench. Ma touched her shoulder. 'It's your life.'

Colette noticed her mother's hair was completely grey now. 'I know.'

'But I think you must be careful. Mark has to go to school next year and we haven't talked—'

'I know, Ma.' Colette could hear the tension in her own voice.

'You've got to think about it. They're not happy.'

'I *know*.'

'And it's no use blaming it on me.'

Colette looked at her mother and patted her leg. 'I'm sorry. I know what you're saying. I am trying.'

Ma was staring into the middle distance. 'You're always finding fault with me. Everybody seems to be these days.'

They sat in silence for a while watching the young boys tearing around their makeshift football pitch.

'What's happening with the war?'

Colette was not surprised. Her mother always asked so many questions. 'I don't know, Ma.' She paused. 'You'd better ask Gerry – or Paddy. They know. I'm just back.'

'Is it over?'

Colette sat for a few moments, staring ahead, rubbing her hands and pushing her knees together to keep out the cold.

'I don't know, Ma, I really don't. I don't think it's over, but ... there's a strange atmosphere at the moment and nobody seems to know what's going on. I don't, anyway. Gerry knows, I think. He – and maybe some others – have lost faith in the leadership and think they're preparing for a sell-out, without any guarantees from the Brits.'

Her mother sat neatly, her old, battered white hand-bag placed firmly in the middle of her lap. She looked at her daughter with tired eyes. 'It's time for it to end. It's gone on too long already.'

An idea struck Colette and she looked at her watch. 'Ma, do you mind if I run? We'll talk later, but there's something I've got to do before picking up the kids.'

Colette did run – for the first few hundred yards anyway. Then she hailed a black cab and got in for the journey down the Falls to the city centre. Even in here, everyone was talking about peace – two middle-aged women, one with a young boy. Colette said with a smile, 'I'll believe it when I see it.'

She looked at her watch as she walked down the pedestrian precinct and realized this would be tight.

She took the stairs up to Humanities three at a time.

The room was uncomfortably familiar. In her intelligence-gathering days she'd come here often. Faces in newspaper cuttings of men now dead.

She asked the woman behind the counter for the *Belfast Telegraph* for July and August 1990 and, rather puzzlingly, received two small cardboard boxes. The woman saw her confusion and said, 'It's all on microfiche now, I'm afraid.'

She struggled with the machine – it seemed needlessly complicated – and had to get the woman over to explain it to her. She got the hang of putting it on the reels, but couldn't control the fast-forward lever, which spun the pages past at the rate of about ten per second unless it was tweaked ever so gently.

Finally she mastered it. It was slow going because they included every edition. She tried September and almost yelped out loud as she found the trial. It took another ten minutes to find his evidence and, when she got to the day, she sat and stared. There was a picture of him in the back of the car. He was trying to shield his face from view. He didn't look frightened. More kind of . . .

'Hello, Colette.'

She felt a chill sweep over her as she heard Mulgrew's voice and then felt the adrenalin in her body. Adrenalin and fear. She could feel the sweat breaking through her skin. She looked at him. 'Hello, Martin.'

She had an almost irresistible urge to push the dial, but she restrained herself. 'What are you doing here?' she heard herself ask.

He smiled, his face right in hers. 'Come here all the time. You should know that.'

He put his hand on her shoulder, shifted to the right and bent down to look at the screen. '"Man was running away, claims platoon commander."' He paused and then read part of the text beneath the headline. '"Relatives of Declan Walshe had to be escorted from the court room today after the platoon commander of the soldiers charged with murdering him told the court that their son had been running away from the patrol at the time of his death. Mr Walshe's mother screamed, 'Bastard!', from the public gallery . . ."' Mulgrew paused. Colette's mind was racing as he went on: '"Lieutenant *Ryan* told the court his soldiers had three times demanded that Mr Walshe stop, before chasing him down the street and opening fire. Corporals Lawson and Jones are on trial for the murder of Mr Walshe in June of last year . . ."'

Mulgrew stood straight again and looked at her. 'Lieutenant *Ryan*. No connection, I presume?'

Colette looked at him, her heart pounding. With all the charm and confidence she could muster she smiled and said, 'I knew I bloody recognized him, then today I remembered where I'd seen him before.'

Mulgrew looked uncertain, clearly wanting to ask more, but suddenly aware of his surroundings. Somebody was sitting right behind them. Colette wound the spool back and put it into the cardboard box. As she gave it to the woman behind the counter, she turned to Mulgrew and said, 'Sorry, Martin, I'm late for the kids and I've got to run. I'll be seeing you.'

She ran down the stairs and was almost out of the door when she heard the shout. She ignored the first, but then he shouted louder, so she stopped and turned to face him. He slowed as he came down the last few steps and stopped just in front of her.

'You didn't ask about the boy,' he said. 'His name was Declan as well.'

She looked at him, unsure what to say.

'There's good news,' he said. 'Looks like he might be all right.'

Colette stood absolutely still. She realized that he was looking for a response and she managed to smile.

'We're going to try and get somebody in to see him,' he said.

She forced another smile and told him again that she had to go, saying she was late. She jogged most of the way up the Lower Falls and found it hard to get Mulgrew's face out of her mind.

She reached Conway Mill just too late. Catherine and Mark looked hurt when she arrived and she cursed herself quietly. Why did the little things sometimes matter so much?

Ryan was watching the news.

The woman on the screen was twenty-five years old and she said she did not regret marrying a policeman. Her voice was quivering with emotion. 'I hope these people know what they've done. I hope they can sleep

196

easily in their beds, because I never will. I saw Johnny lying in the hallway in a pool of blood and I held his head until he died. He told me he loved me . . . He told me he loved the children . . .' Her voice was breaking up, but she stumbled on. 'They were sitting there . . . aged three and two . . . just watching their daddy die.'

She was crying.

'I want to forgive these people . . . as a Christian, I want to forgive them, but I just can't. I can't forgive them for what they've done. I can't forgive them for what they've taken . . . I loved him so much, you see . . . Oh God help me, I loved him so much.'

The woman put her face in her hands.

The next item showed a windswept, snowy cemetery and a collection of grim-faced mourners. Ryan thought Gingy Hughes's widow looked like she was about to collapse. The big bearded reporter ended, 'Despite claims made by the Provisional IRA, Mr Hughes's family still deny that he was a Special Branch informant . . .'

Then there were pictures of Musgrave Park Hospital and a report on the condition of the young man injured in the foiled attack on Henderson. 'Under armed guard,' the reporter said, 'his condition still described as critical.'

Ryan found himself hoping the kid would die. He thought he deserved to.

He picked up the remote control and switched off the television. He thought the news was developing a nicely ironic structure. A report on hopes of peace to lead. 'Tonight, Sinn Féin says peace declaration must be clarified,' followed by a lengthy collection of murders and funerals.

He looked at the clock above the mantelpiece. Ten past six. Twenty minutes to wait.

He got up and put on his donkey jacket. He opened the patio door and stepped out again, lighting up as he did so. He hated houses that smelled of cigarettes.

He inhaled deeply and peered into the window to the left. Still no sign of life there. He wondered if that was a Service flat too.

He walked round the corner, along the line of the hedge, and, as he did so, he found himself thinking of the policeman whose wife had cried so movingly on the news.

He wondered what it must have been like to be in that fateful house outside Lisburn as the policeman's life came to an end. The family had been watching television, the children not yet in bed, when two gunmen opened fire through the window. Death on the carpet. And then the police came to your door; the forensic officers and the detective officers from CID and possibly Special Branch. Then the media, looking for interviews – a man's life summed up in thirty seconds – with the bereaved always so articulate and moving in their grief. And then what? And then nothing. Then normality, with a pale stain on the carpet, where the police couldn't quite get the blood out. Normality, except that nothing would ever be remotely normal again, for any of them.

Well, he should know about that, shouldn't he? He shivered. Not *his* fault. Strangely, the image that stuck in his mind now was not the moment itself, but the funeral on the television – with them all gathered in the one room. He remembered the laughter, the jokes. 'That'll *learn* the bastard.'

Stupid. They weren't laughing when the murder charges were laid.

He thought of the man, thought of his face on the tarmac; sheet white, in pain, blood dribbling from his head onto the pavement and fear in his eyes. A life ebbing away. Some pathetic words about his mother ... Christ.

He walked round the side to the front of the block of flats and lit another cigarette. If only he *had* been a Provo, he thought, though he wasn't sure now whether even that would have made any difference.

He saw the Granada turning into the driveway and dropped his cigarette on the stone pathway, stamping it out. He walked back round the house, stepped inside, locked the patio door and went to find the house keys.

The driver was talkative. 'What do you think Sinn Féin are playing at?' he said as they turned out of Malone Beeches and headed up towards the ring road. Ryan shrugged. It was still rush hour and the traffic was moving slowly, the pavements to the left and right of the road largely deserted. It was too cold for walking.

They pulled away from the roundabout by the House of Sport and Ryan saw one or two people walking up from the river Lagan as he listened to the driver giving his views on Sinn Féin's demand for clarification of the Government's peace declaration.

The man thought the war was ending – 'Been here for ten years, the Provos have had enough' – and Ryan hoped he was right.

But, by the time they turned onto the ring road, Ryan's mind was drifting again. He found himself thinking of Colette's face in the graveyard. Stupid to have gone, he thought. He told himself she hadn't seen him before that moment.

When he got to Stormont, Hopkins was friendly. Since Ryan had not officially been posted to the Province, and since Colette had been recruited in England, the whole operation – or at least his part of it

– was still technically under the control of the Counter-Terrorism department in London. But he needed to liaise with MI5's permanent station in Northern Ireland and Hopkins was the head of it.

His office was large, with magnificent views down across Stormont Park – melancholic views, Ryan thought, at this time of the year – and he produced a large bottle of Bushmills whiskey from beneath the desk.

After a few minutes – 'welcome' and associated small talk – a woman knocked on the door and Hopkins introduced Ryan to Alison Berry, one of the senior analysts. They shook hands warmly.

The point of the briefing – Ryan hadn't realized this was a briefing – was to impress upon him the need to push for any information regarding the Provisional IRA leadership's intentions. 'We need to know what the hell they're up to,' was the general sense of it, but Ryan found it hard to stop himself looking at Berry's legs. They were long, quite thin and encased in black tights. She was not conventionally attractive – her nose was too bulbous for that – but she was certainly sexy.

She was friendly too – and direct. She did most of the talking, outlining in detail what they believed was currently going on within the IRA. There were, she said, severe tensions between the hardliners and the moderates over the so-called 'peace process' – the hardliners arguing that this was just a sell-out. She didn't mention Gerry McVeigh by name, and when he did, she showed no *particular* interest. He wondered if Special Branch and MI5 were communicating as thoroughly as they ought to be.

Ryan thought about how many bosses he appeared to be accumulating: MI5 in London, MI5 in Belfast, Special Branch in Belfast.

His position, on reflection, was really rather difficult, and he thought about how much he hated internal politics. It was hardly surprising they sometimes lost sight of the enemy.

Afterwards, Hopkins and Berry showed him round the office. He was even given his own desk.

He got home about eight, having picked up an Indian takeaway on the Ormeau Road. He ate voraciously, realizing as he did so that he hadn't had anything since breakfast. Too much to think about.

That night, in bed, he fantasized about Berry and had the curious sense, as he did so, that he was being unfaithful.

Colette was dreaming.

She could see the youth clearly. He was spotty and really ugly and she found herself viewing him with total contempt. When she looked at his face, she saw a callow young man motivated by a diet of total certainty.

He was lying in a coffin now and he was wrapped in an Irish Tricolour, as indeed was the coffin, as indeed was the whole room – the Tricolours hanging as drapes on the wall, making the room seem like some giant, exotic tent.

She could see the boy as she walked up and down beside him. In fact, she was actually walking along *above* him, and she was draped in a Union Jack which hung from her shoulders like a regal robe. She swaggered and felt very pleased with her image as she caught sight of herself in the giant mirrors at the end of the room. She looked, well, regal, and she swung her hips as she strode down towards the man at the end.

Ryan was there too, wearing jeans and a sweater and a blue woollen jacket, and smiling and laughing at her. He was pointing to the coffin beside her and she watched now as it was engulfed in flames. For a moment, she found herself laughing too . . .

She woke up.

The room was dark, the curtains once again billowing out very slightly in the wind. She sat up and rubbed her eyes. The room was silent but for the sound of the kids breathing. She pulled the pillow from under her and put it up against the wall and then sat back.

The room was quiet.

She tried to replay in her mind the exact chronology of the events in the house before the attack and was frustrated by the fact that it no longer seemed clear. She could not remember exactly what was said and she couldn't recall at what point in the conversation she had first been conscious of the boy's presence on the stairs.

And then there was the possibility that it was all her paranoia.

Bollocks, she told herself. I saw that stare. But then, maybe that was desire?

She thought of his face. He was spotty – and ugly too. He didn't look like a patriot. She remembered her dream and hated the image of herself wrapped in a Union Jack. Somehow, that really *was* obscene.

She got up and looked out of the window. The scene was the same – an empty alley. The lights were out in the house behind them and there had been no row this evening. Not his night for drinking, obviously. Or perhaps she'd whipped him into shape and reformed him.

Fat chance of that, she thought.

She wondered if the Brit ever got drunk and, if so, how he behaved. She thought he would probably be different.

She got back into bed and tried to get to sleep, but

every time she shut her eyes she visualized the young man's spotty, suspicious face. She thought of him in his hospital bed, tied up to a life-support machine, perhaps, his life hanging by a thread. For a few moments she felt sorry for him – really sorry and guilty – and then she wondered why in the hell they hadn't managed to kill him. After all, it wasn't so much to ask.

Her mind kept on working as the hours passed. Gradually she began to realize that, somehow, she was going to have to ensure he *did* die.

McIlhatton was watching the news.

The newsreader said that a policeman had been killed in Ulster, and then she introduced a report which included footage of the man's widow giving a tearful interview.

At the end of it, McIlhatton stood up and shouted, 'Yes! Re-*sult*.'

He walked to the window and looked out at the empty street, feeling slightly better. It had boosted his morale, which had been slowly sinking again.

CHAPTER TEN

The meeting had not been going well. There had been resistance, incomprehension and even some anger, but Colette thought the leaders had been expecting it.

The man from Derry was still talking and she looked about her. Everyone had kept their coats on, though the room was getting quite warm.

There were some serious men here. She'd seen Murphy from south Armagh, Fox, McKendrick. There was one man who wasn't there, of course. She wondered if anyone else was conscious of Gingy Hughes's absence.

Poor bastard. She thought about his wife. She imagined Mark and Catherine being forced to watch *her* being shot. A weird image.

She looked to her left and felt the kind of shock that was becoming too familiar. She smiled back at Martin Mulgrew.

She looked forward and tried to listen to what the man from Derry was saying.

'The point is, as we've said before, we are now in a position of strength. We have got the Brits running scared. They're terrified of another bomb like the one in the City. They're terrified of the cost of the damage –

millions of pounds for that one alone. It is our firm belief that the Brits want to get out of Ireland, but they'll never go whilst the campaign is in full swing.'

Right, Colette thought. She stifled a cough. The room was full of smoke and the man next to her was lighting up again.

She looked over at Mulgrew briefly and was relieved to see he was staring at the floor. She looked back at the platform and the two men standing in front of a Sinn Féin 'Time for Peace' poster.

The man from Derry's voice was weak from talking too much. Despite his age, she thought, he retained a boyish look, with curly hair and bright blue eyes.

'Sooner or later we've got to stop to see whether they *are* willing to get out, as they have intimated to us in our secret talks, or whether they're just stringing us along—'

'They're stringing us along,' somebody shouted from the back in reply. Colette turned round and tried to see who it was, but several of the men were smiling. She was mentally checking people off. McConaghy from Derry, Mallon from east Tyrone.

Sean Fox was on his feet at the front. He was tall and blond and kept a hold on his beer glass. 'What you're saying is we've got nothing.' He looked round the room, but there was no response. 'So what are we going to say to all our people? I mean, we've all suffered, we've all lost people, we've all seen the inside of Long Kesh. And you're saying that is all for nothing? How the fuck are we going to sell that to our people?'

The man from Derry leaned forward again. 'I'm not saying it's all been for nothing, totally the reverse. We've achieved great things and we all recognize the sacrifices all of us – each and every one of us – have made. But what we're saying is that we'll never go the final mile, we'll never get everything we want, until we break the military campaign and try an exclusively political tack for a while.'

Fox was still standing. 'Why should we trust the Brits?'

'We don't. But we *do* trust their self-interest. We believe, and it is our firm impression, that they want to get out of here. They want to get out if we allow them the time and the space to do it. And we've cemented the Nationalist side together. With the Irish and American governments standing by us, we believe we can put enough pressure on the Brits to ensure they move in the right direction.'

'And if they don't?'

'They will.'

Fox's voice hardened. 'And if they don't?'

'The military option remains. The IRA stays together like any other army. We train and prepare for the worst.'

Fox took a drag on his cigarette.

'That's easy for you to say, but I'm telling you, if this thing's over, it's over. There'll be no mucking about. I'm not explaining a different strategy to our volunteers every fucking week. They need to know what's happening.'

Colette was conscious that she was taking mental notes of all this. She was conscious that information is power.

She looked over at Mulgrew, frightened that he would somehow be able to read her mind. He had moved a few paces further away and appeared to be looking intently at someone else closer to the front. She followed his gaze and was surprised to see he was looking at Paddy.

Paddy didn't seem to notice. He was twiddling the end of his moustache idly.

Colette moved over to her right, keeping her eyes down on the dirty blue carpet beneath her feet. She wasn't sure this was the best place for a meeting. If there was trouble . . . well there was only one exit from Conway Mill, down the spiral staircase, out of the security door and into the car park.

She considered the possibility of a bomb and felt scared suddenly. All it takes is one tout, she thought. One tout who could slip away a few minutes early . . .

She told herself not to be so stupid. She moved over to one of the high white walls and leaned against it. She could see Gerry a couple of rows ahead of her, standing straight and still.

The atmosphere in the room was tense and electric, some of the men excited, some angry. This wasn't easy for any of them. Few could remember what it was like to live without the war. It was their *raison d'être*.

Gerry spoke for the first time and Colette took a couple of paces to her left so as to get a clear view of him. He looked calm, his curly hair tidy and well kept. He was cleaning his glasses pedantically as he spoke. He sounded almost uninterested in the debate. 'What about our prisoners?' he said.

The man from Derry's voice was becoming hoarse. 'They'll be released.'

'All of them? The ones in England as well as those in Long Kesh?'

'All of them.'

Gerry's voice was icy. 'What makes you so fucking sure?'

'It's what we've been told.'

'And you believe everything you're told?'

The man sighed. 'We have the Irish behind us, and the Americans and the Brits want the war finished. They can't afford to betray us on that.'

'And our weapons?'

'We'll keep them.'

'And the Loyalists?'

'We'll always defend our own communities. Always. Nobody wants a return to 1969. I don't believe that will happen. The Irish government believes the Loyalists will come around.'

Gerry McVeigh snorted violently and made a display of putting his glasses back on. 'Perhaps I'm being stupid, but let me just go over the same ground one more time.' He crossed his hands. 'We've all read this Downing Street Declaration and we've all agreed that, on the face of it, there is nothing in it for us.'

Kevin McKendrick had been standing at the front and he stood up and tried to interrupt. 'Gerry.'

McVeigh raised his hand. 'No, let me finish. As I said, we've all agreed there is nothing in it for us, and as far as I can see all it does is guarantee us another thousand years of partition. It's a new recipe for war. And you're telling me you want to make peace on the basis of that?'

He paused for effect and Colette noticed the irritation and hostility in the faces of his opponents.

'I just don't understand it. We have never been more effective. We can place bombs in the centre of the City in London and stage mortar attacks on Downing Street. We're causing millions of pounds' worth of damage all over England and bleeding their treasury dry – and you want us to stop for a piece of paper that gives us absolutely nothing.'

McKendrick forced the interruption. 'But that's the point. We have to stop when we are in a position of strength. We know we're hurting them and we know the British people have lost the stomach for the fight. It's time to capitalize on that – and we can only do it by stopping.'

The man from Derry spoke directly to Gerry. 'It's not a question of if, but when, Gerry. We have got to stop to test the Brits out, to see what they are really willing to concede. The Declaration is a teaser, it's a carrot. But we've got to take the bait to see what is on offer in the long run.'

Watch Gerry. We have to know what he is doing . . . Colette inched closer to him.

Gerry was shaking his head. 'I think you've lost touch. Completely. What about the Loyalists? They're running riot already. If we stop, it will be right back to 1969, and our people will never forgive us.'

The man from Derry held his gaze. 'We've got to take risks, Gerry, or we'll never get anywhere.'

'And what happens if we don't agree?'

'We'll persuade you.'

'And what happens if we won't be persuaded?'

'You will be.'

Kevin Murphy shot to his feet. 'That'd better not be a bloody threat.'

Colette looked at Murphy – a fat and lethal farmer from south Armagh. A hardliner, she knew, and very influential.

The man from Derry stood again. He appeared to be growing tired of the arguments. 'Nobody is threatening anybody.' He waved his hand at Murphy, trying to persuade him to sit. 'Look, above all else, everyone is agreed that we must avoid a split. There's been enough Republican blood spilt by the Brits and the Loyalists and I'm sure none of us feel inclined to add to it ourselves . . .

'But the fact is – and it is a fact – the Brits are trying to grope towards something, hinting they no longer really want to be here and are looking for a way out.

'Are they bluffing? Are they conning us, trying to

catch us off guard? Well, I don't know and neither does anybody else. But we've got to try and push this process to see how far it will go.'

He looked directly at Gerry. 'Now I agree with you, Gerry, we are in a position of strength. But that's all the more reason to see what the Brits are willing to concede. They're not just going to sign a surrender treaty and walk out, it's got to be much more subtle than that, and they've got to save face in the eyes of the world.'

Colette looked at her watch. She'd promised the kids she would be home by eight to put them to bed.

Gerry was looking round the room. A public pitch, she thought. She began to wonder what in the hell he was really up to.

'Well, I think you're making a big mistake. If we stop, we'll not get it restarted. If you ceasefire, we're finished. You may dream of life as respectable politicians with swanky apartments and fancy government cars, but the IRA's the cutting edge of the Republican movement and don't—'

The man from Derry was on his feet again. 'That's enough bloody lecturing.'

Gerry held his gaze. 'There's people out there still fighting who think we're selling them out.'

'Nobody calls me a sell-out.'

Colette saw two little big men fighting it out in a playground. She looked round her with contempt. They were all waiting to see if either man would take it further, but McKendrick was on his feet again, talking about the need to retain unity, publicly and privately. She kept her eyes on Gerry and she saw him very distinctly nod at Murphy. A few men were slipping out of the back now and Gerry and Murphy joined them. She watched them go. She was intrigued.

210

Murphy and McVeigh – an unusual alliance. Two men with empires that usually clashed.

Watch Gerry. We have to know what he is doing . . .

She waited. She wasn't listening to what was being said. She thought about it and told herself to stay put.

She followed. Out into the cold and turning back into the Falls, the wind once again cutting through her woollen coat. This winter seemed endless.

She looked up and saw the two of them ahead. She watched them turn into Leeson Street and she realized they were going home.

There was an 'eye in the sky' above them again now. She tried to resist the temptation to look up.

She found herself slowing as she passed the Sinn Féin press office, allowing them time. She wondered what she was doing.

She got to the front door. She fumbled for her keys and found them. She waited, watching her breath in the night air. She put the Yale key ever so gently into the door and turned it. She heard a good-natured scream from Catherine upstairs and the sound of running water. She heard her mother's voice. She was standing just inside the hall now, a cold draught behind her and warmth ahead. She was about to shut the door when she realized she could hear the sound of voices. She held her breath and took a step forward, the draught from outside following her.

The door to the front room was open and she could tell they were close to it. She felt she could almost have reached out to touch them.

Gerry's voice: 'I can do it. It's almost ready and, if we go ahead, it will bury this talk once and for all.'

She found herself taking another step forwards. Murphy's voice was soft and gravelly. 'Fallout'd be big. Very big.'

211

'Perhaps,' Gerry said, 'but it would be popular with some, popular with enough to make it work.'

'All right. You'll have our tacit backing. Not open, but people'll know afterwards that we knew and approved. But put us in it *before* it happens and there'll be hell to pay.'

A sudden movement. Paralytic fear. She just managed to take a step back and get a hold of the door.

'Colette.' Gerry was smiling and looking puzzled. 'I didn't hear you come in.'

She turned her back to him and shut the door. 'I've heard enough shite for one lifetime,' she said. She heard them laugh and turned back. She congratulated herself on being smart and walked up the stairs without another word.

As she walked into the bathroom and saw Catherine and Mark, she realized her hands were shaking.

'Mammy, Mammy,' they both chorused.

She heard the front door shut and realized this was her chance. She mumbled, 'I'll be back in a second.'

She walked down the stairs and into the front room. Gerry was standing with his back to her. He turned round.

'What's up?' he asked.

'Wondering about this kid,' she said.

He waved his hand dismissively. 'Don't worry about it.'

'Well, I do.'

'Forget it. Not your fault . . .'

'Could you do me a favour?'

He scowled at her – as if even the act of asking for a favour was an imposition. 'Could you go and see him?' she asked. 'In fact, could we go together, just to see how he is?'

212

Gerry looked confused. 'What's the big deal?'

Colette sat down on the arm of the sofa and looked down. 'You could get us in. I know it's not my fault, but it's hard not to feel responsible . . .'

'Forget it, Colette.'

She looked up at him. 'Please, Gerry. I don't ask many favours. I feel guilty about this kid, you know? I mean, I'd like to go and see him, bring him some comfort, maybe . . .'

Gerry was frowning at her again. She noticed his glasses were dirty. He picked up his raincoat from the sofa. 'I'll go and find out what the score is,' he said. 'But don't lose any sleep over it. There's plenty more where he came from.'

As Gerry pulled the front door shut, Colette leaned back on the edge of the sofa and sighed deeply. She closed her eyes. She felt sick; sick at what she was prepared to do, sick at having to deal with Gerry.

She imagined the kid lying in his hospital bed. She wondered how she would do it. Would it be as simple as tripping a switch, or pulling a tube or . . . ? God, she didn't know how easy it was going to be.

She wondered how she would feel.

She thought this was slipping. She told herself the youth was an ugly nothing. But he wasn't a Brit.

She wondered if she should ask the Brit for help. She considered how he might react. Moral outrage? Or pragmatism?

Would he really arrange to kill the kid? She couldn't tell. She couldn't read him. She thought about what he'd said about loyalty and she wondered how far that went. She just didn't know if it went this far. She imagined saying to him, 'It's him or me; you choose,' and she tried to imagine his reaction. For a few moments she enjoyed the uncertainty she thought it might provoke in him.

Solve that, you bastard, she thought.

She heard the door open and watched as Gerry walked back in.

'I'm sorry, Colette,' he said, 'but the kid is dead.'

She closed her eyes for a second and, as she did so, she heard Gerry leaving again. She breathed in deeply and felt the relief flood through her.

Ryan was lying back in the bath with a hot flannel covering his face, thinking about nothing in particular. He felt tired. It was late and he had overslept. That always made him feel tired.

The phone rang. He ignored it, since he now had a bleeper. It went on ringing. 'Piss off!' he shouted, and it stopped, as though somebody had heard him.

After a few seconds it rang again, and this time he heaved himself out of the bath and wrapped a towel around his waist. He picked up the receiver. 'Hello,' he said.

'It's me.'

'I gathered that.'

'Get here right away.'

'What's up?'

'Just get here.'

The phone went dead. Ryan took off the towel and rubbed himself dry. He rummaged around in his bag for a clean T-shirt – he still hadn't unpacked – and pulled one on. He was just frantically searching for a clean pair of boxer shorts when the phone rang again. 'Yes,' he said testily.

'On second thoughts, go to Garnerville.'

'Why?'

'Just do it. Know where it is?'

He did. He finished dressing and ran out to the old blue Vauxhall Cavalier that he'd now been given. It took a few seconds to start and he swore quietly. He didn't turn on the radio because he was too busy worrying.

He turned left out of Malone Beeches and then right a little further down, up through Stranmillis and then down by the river Lagan. He had no idea if this was the quickest way, but it was the one he knew and he didn't have time to get lost.

He thought of a thousand scenarios. Mostly, they involved her death.

The worst involved her capture.

He cursed Allen for not telling him anything.

He almost drove into a young woman walking across the bottom of the Ormeau Road with a child in each hand. Calm down, he told himself.

He passed the clock tower and saw that it was eleven o'clock. The sky ahead of him was clear – blue above and to the side of the green mountain. He turned right, up over a bridge, past the big yellow cranes. They were magnificent this close.

He imagined a bleak house in south Armagh and a woman's screams. He thought about days spent trudging across the wet fields and hills of the border country, swept around in helicopters to a thousand bleak locations.

And then what would they find?

He wondered what in the hell they would do to her. Torture? Abuse her children? Threaten to? He didn't think she would last five minutes, then he thought she might be tougher than he was giving her credit for.

He was at the gate now and pleased that he'd found it. He pulled out his wallet, wound down the window and tried to smile. 'David Ryan. Here to meet Brian Allen.'

The constable at the gate pointed ahead of him to a

car parked on the left-hand side of the road, its engine still running. As he drove up to it, Ryan saw the new recruits parading to the right of him. They were brilliantly turned out and Ryan wondered what on earth he was doing here.

He parked behind Allen and got out. Allen did the same. The look on his face was quite strange. He looked sheepish, Ryan thought.

'Sorry, should have bleeped you,' Allen said. 'Panic's over.'

Ryan thought Allen was a terrible liar. He wondered how he was going to deal with this. He looked across to the lines of neatly turned-out recruits waiting patiently on the parade ground and noticed the sun was reflecting off their buttons. He pointed over to them. 'Any particular reason why we're here?'

'The boss is here. Thought we might need to see him.'

Ryan took a step closer. 'Want to tell me what the hell is going on?'

Allen was silent for what seemed like a long time. He was staring at his shoes and appeared to be genuinely wrestling with himself – that fact alone Ryan found disturbing. He thought about pushing harder, but sensed it would do no good. He waited.

'I just picked up something,' Allen said eventually.

Silence again.

A band began to play. Allen looked over at them, apparently lost in thought.

'Remember what I told you the other day?' he said as he looked up. 'Well, there *is* somebody else.'

'Does that matter?'

Silence again. Ryan felt a surge of frustration. He thought this was almost worse than dealing with Colette.

'There was a rumour.'

'What was it?' Ryan asked. He was trying to keep his impatience out of his voice.

There was another lengthy pause and then Allen seemed to make up his mind. He looked directly at Ryan. 'The rumour was that the other tout is good – *very* senior. The rumour was that they were going to let our woman go.'

'Who told you?'

'A friend.'

'How reliable?'

Allen scowled back at him. Ryan turned towards the building behind them and Allen grabbed his arm. 'Where are you going?' His face and voice were animated now.

'Where do you think?'

'It's only a rumour.'

'Then why the phone call?'

Allen let go of his arm. 'Leave it, David.'

'Leave it? Leave it?'

'It's not our decision.'

'Tell me something, Brian.' Ryan was pointing at him. 'The other day. The attempt to get me off. Is this what that was about?'

Ryan didn't wait for an answer. He walked across the face of the building, listening to the band as he did so. There was something ever so slightly farcical about this. As he walked up the steps, he sensed Brian Allen was beside him. Inside, he saw three smartly turned-out men in uniform with polished shoes and batons. He recognized the chief constable, but did not acknowledge him. There was a small group of secretaries and lesser officers in the corridor and they were staring at him. He remembered he was wearing jeans and a sweater. He spoke quietly, trying to sound humble,

217

though it was the last thing he felt. 'Excuse me, Mr Long, would you have a minute?'

Trevor Long didn't blink. He was quite calm, despite the fact that this was clearly an occasion of some ceremonial import. He showed them into an adjoining room and Ryan started to speak before the door was closed.

'There is a rumour that our woman is going to be allowed to burn.'

Long tilted his head to one side. 'Why?'

'To protect another source.'

'Where does the rumour come from?'

Ryan didn't answer. He shifted his weight uncomfortably from one foot to the other.

'All right. Let me put it this way. Who do you think would make this decision?'

Allen cut in. 'There was a rumour, that's all.'

Long tapped his baton gently against his leg. 'I'll look into it.'

'With respect, Mr Long,' Ryan said, 'we'll need more than that.'

'*Mr* Ryan. *With respect*, I said I will look into it. You can take it that what you are referring to will not come to pass as a result. Do you understand what I am saying? Now, if you'll excuse me, I have some recruits to attend to.'

After he had left, Allen nodded at Ryan and, as if to answer an unspoken query, he said, 'He's straight.'

They walked back out down the steps. The sun was shining brightly now and it was almost warm. For a few moments, Ryan watched the three senior officers inspecting their recruits – pausing, talking to animated faces beneath shiny peaked caps.

He turned away and walked back to his car. As he got in, he saw Allen walking towards him. He started the engine and wound down the window.

'I'll see you later,' Allen said. He was leaning on Ryan's door with both his arms outstretched. 'And, at the risk of sounding patronizing, don't forget that it is us against them at the end of the day. *All* of us against *all* of them. Don't make it personal.'

Ryan looked at Allen as he edged ahead. 'I don't think it's quite as simple as that, is it?'

There were three of them in the car and Gerry was trying not to drive too fast. They had come down the Grosvenor Road because the young 'dickers' he had out had told him there was no checkpoint there.

They turned left onto the Westlink. It dipped down, with high walls on either side of it, and ahead of them they could see a huge Union Jack fluttering above a tall building, with a statue of a man on a horse. Gerry thought these things were easier when it was raining and he was not enjoying the sunshine.

But he wasn't worried.

He turned left off the Westlink, taking the car up to the bottom of the Crumlin Road. He could just about see the Crumlin court and prison ahead of him as he turned right onto the Antrim Road.

There was still silence inside the car and he found himself enjoying a sense of comradeship. They were three professionals and they could look after themselves.

Eventually they pulled in through an old, shabby set of metal gates and bumped slowly over the potholes into the middle of the car park. Gerry brought the car to a halt and looked through the windscreen at the crumbling red-brick structure ahead of them.

'All right, Martin,' he said, without looking back, 'take us through it.'

Mulgrew pulled himself forward into the gap between the seat. 'Simple. She comes here to the dogs – we'll check on the night that she *does* arrive – and we shoot her in the bar where she always sits. Simple. She's pregnant as well.'

'A *pregnant* RUC reservist,' Gerry said. 'Two for the price of one.'

They stayed for a few minutes, but there was really nothing further to see and Gerry turned the car round and headed back towards the gates. 'Right, I see what you mean. Simple in, simple out. I don't want any more fuck-ups. If it is that simple, then *do* it.'

A man was walking across the face of the gate with a tiny dog and Gerry slowed but didn't stop. He wanted to be away from here.

'And if it's simple, there'd better not be any fucking tout mucking it up,' he said. He smiled and looked at them both – first at Mulgrew and then at Paddy. 'Whoever he is, we've got to find him. Understood?'

They were back on the Antrim Road now and there wasn't much traffic.

Gerry looked over his shoulder at Mulgrew. 'You're a quiet bastard, Mulgrew, do you know that?'

There was no reply.

'Make a great tout. See everything. Hear everything. Know everything. Never bloody say *anything*.' Gerry laughed. 'But then we all would, right?'

They drove back up the Grosvenor Road in silence and then down the Falls towards Beechmount. Gerry stopped outside a newsagent and looked over his shoulder. 'Give us the bat, Martin.'

Gerry put the baseball bat under his jacket and both Paddy and Mulgrew followed him across the road.

There was nobody in the newsagent except the owner himself and Gerry could see fear written all over

220

his face. Gerry slapped open the counter and pushed the man into a small back room. 'Watch the door, Mulgrew,' he said.

The man was small, with a largely bald head and thick black glasses. He was overweight and Gerry knew he had a wife and five children – maybe he needed the money and that was why he was being so sodding difficult.

'I believe there are two matters before us, Mr Macauley,' he said.

'I'm not frightened of you and your thugs.'

'Oh, *please*,' Gerry said, '*do* spare us your little show of bravery and courage.' He pulled the bat out from under his jacket and began to tap it menacingly against his leg. 'Now, as I said, there are two matters before us. Non-payment of our little "insurance" fee and – almost worse – a call made to the RUC to complain—'

'Go to hell,' the man said.

Gerry thought his fear was hidden behind his glasses. He was very small and Gerry was looking down at a few long strands of greasy black hair. He thought how much he *hated* ugly people. 'Mr Macauley, don't be brave; it really does no good.'

'Piss off.'

Gerry felt the rage explode in his head. He took out the bat and swung it across the man's back. He let out a yelp like a frightened animal and collapsed, Gerry instinctively kicking him in the process. He squirmed on the floor and Gerry smashed the bat down on his legs, hearing the bones fracture as he did so. The man was screaming now and Gerry hit him savagely again and again, enjoying the sense of the damage and pain he was inflicting. The man's screams were hysterical and Gerry lifted the bat to smash his shitty little bald head . . .

Paddy grabbed his arm. 'Enough, Gerry, for Christ's sake.' There was fear and confusion in his face. He led him out into the shop itself and Gerry saw the doubt in Mulgrew's eyes too. He felt dazed and shaken. Paddy suddenly stopped. 'Christ, you're not wearing gloves. We need to get the fucking bat.' He turned back and retrieved it, sticking it under his raincoat. 'Take the car,' he told Mulgrew, and then he and Gerry were out in the street, crossing to the other side and slowly walking up Beechmount Avenue. Gerry knew there was a safe house at the top and he fumbled in his pocket for his collection of keys. Paddy had the door open before he could find them and they were inside. The house stank of damp and decay and Paddy took them straight through to the kitchen. It was filthy, the side and sink covered in unwashed mugs and plates. Paddy turned the cold tap on and took the bat out from under his coat. He began to wash the blood off and it ran down into the dirty crockery and saucepans. He swore and smashed them about, to disperse the water and blood. He took off his jacket, which was also covered in blood, and stuffed it into the sink, before turning to Gerry and doing the same.

Whilst his brother finished, Gerry waited in the other room, gathering himself. It was filthy in here, too, cigarette ends everywhere, and his hands were still shaking. He sat down on the chair, such as it was, and closed his eyes. A kind of calmness eventually descended.

When he opened his eyes, his brother was standing before him. 'That was unnecessary,' he said.

'Fuckers need to be taught,' Gerry replied.

Paddy sat down opposite him, on a rickety wooden chair by what was left of the fireplace. 'If you ask me, I think things are getting to you at the moment.'

'I don't believe I was asking you.'
Paddy didn't reply and they sat in silence.

It was guesswork, of course, and slow work at that, but instinct told McIlhatton this man would be going in, so he followed him down the stairs to the underpass and watched carefully as he approached the entrance.

The man fumbled for his pass, put it round his neck, and then walked straight through without stopping.

The policeman didn't seem to take much notice of him and certainly didn't look closely at the pass.

It was a different policeman from yesterday, too.

McIlhatton turned right just before the entrance and climbed the stairs up to the other side of the street.

CHAPTER ELEVEN

Ryan lit a cigarette, shuffled his feet and looked at the old blue Cavalier. He realized this was becoming a habit.

In theory, on his calculation, there was little risk, but there was also little doubt that it was totally un-necessary. But was that right?

The reality was that, since his return here, the whole thing had been preoccupying (haunting, you might even say) him in a manner he didn't think was healthy. And then, last night, he'd played the whole event – the whole disastrous, tragic patrol – through in his mind. He was shocked at how strong the images still were.

And the truth was simple. Straightforward and simple. He held himself personally responsible for Declan Walshe's death. And the worst of it was that he knew it wasn't self-indulgence.

As he'd lain awake last night, staring at the ceiling, the clearest image in the darkness had been not of the incident itself, nor even of the dead boy's face.

No, the clearest image had been the look on *Smiler*'s face just before they'd gone out. He'd seen the look and he'd *known* the man was cracking up. They'd done five months and twenty-five days and, for all of that time, in the cramped, uncomfortable, filthy fucking barracks, Smiler had been bullied – relentlessly – by Jacko and the rest, and he, the platoon commander, had known then, as he knew now, that he was not doing enough to stop it. Some of it was good-humoured, certainly, and some of it was inevitable, and he'd done his best to try and keep Smiler's morale up, talking to him about his family, helping him with his divorce papers. But, in his heart of hearts, he'd known that in the last month or so it had gone beyond the acceptable. On that last day, he'd seen Smiler's face before the patrol and he'd known, without any doubt at all, that Smiler was on the edge.

And he'd still taken him out.

Ryan chucked his cigarette into the flower bed and got into the car. He thought briefly about the risk again, but he knew the car was old and shabby and he was feeling bolder. He turned left into Balmoral and slowly moved forwards in the traffic, trying not to think about it and failing.

What got to him now was not so much the death – the murder – and Christ knows he'd tortured himself enough about that, but the lies. So many fucking lies.

Lie one: that the soldiers shouted at Walshe three times to stop before opening fire.

Lie two: that Walshe had a suspicious bulge in his pocket that looked like a handgun.

Lie three: that the soldiers had asked Walshe to turn out his pockets and it was this that caused him to run.

Facts: Declan Walshe was just an ordinary Catholic boy who was stopped in a completely routine way. The RUC detectives with them were at the other end of Beechmount Avenue and he, Lieutenant David Ryan, was looking down the street, wondering if there was any immediate threat.

It was Smiler (he later learned) who stopped the boy, and Smiler who threatened to kick his teeth out. When the boy ran, it was Smiler who shouted at him ('You Fenian cunt . . .') and Smiler who shot him first. Jones, inexplicably, had also opened fire (Ryan had not been able to make sense of *his* thought processes, such as they were, either at the time or since).

He crossed the roundabout at the bottom of Balmoral and felt his mind clearing. The traffic was still heavy and it took him a minute or so to get up to the Andersonstown Road.

He turned right and edged slowly down towards Milltown, asking himself as he did so whether he would really have done anything differently. They were his people, his soldiers, and he'd lied to protect them, but Christ, fuck it . . .

Sometimes, he wanted to find Walshe's parents and apologize. No, he wanted to find Walshe's parents and tell them how fucking sorry he was. He wanted to explain that . . . explain what? That they'd been attacked three times during that tour in the same area? That one of his soldiers had lost an arm? That they only had five days to go and he'd been counting them down like his life depended on it? That the atmosphere in the barracks was crap and Smiler was being bullied and that he knew about it and that there was absolutely fuck all he could do about it except try – *repeatedly* – to talk some fucking sense into Jacko?

It didn't add up. As an excuse for all those lies, it justified nothing.

Another of his father's pearls of wisdom: 'Tell the truth. It's *always* simpler.'

And another: 'Actions have consequences.'

He was at the bottom of Whiterock now and he wound down the window a touch. It was cold outside and he thought it might snow.

He jammed on the brakes at the zebra crossing. He hadn't seen the woman and he felt the sweat in his palms again. Two hundred yards or so further on – it seemed longer when you were walking and worrying about being shot – he turned into Beechmount. He looked at the mural – a hand breaking free of its chains, set against a picture of Ireland – and pulled over on the right-hand side of the road, stopping about 20 yards further on. He kept the engine running. He thought he could hear his heart beating.

But he felt nothing. This was the spot, and he could have described, to the inch and to the second, where it had happened and when, but it was daytime now and, across the road, three young girls were running back from the shop and a man was dragging along his dog. He closed his eyes and tried to picture it, but realized the images weren't going to come. He got out of the car and leaned over the top of it. He lit a cigarette and then closed his eyes again. He could hear the shouts now and could remember turning round to see the kid running, briefly. He could see the rifle at Smiler's shoulder and he could remember wondering what in the fuck was happening, and he could recall thinking, the second it had happened, that he wasn't going to be getting home now – because, for those last few weeks, that was all that was on his mind – and then he could remember the sight of the boy's face on the tarmac and the sudden desire to vomit and . . .

'Are you all right, wee son?' The old woman was looking at him quizzically. She had a bag of shopping in one hand and a dog lead in the other. She looked concerned, genuinely friendly and concerned, and he made a sound – part snort, part shrug – designed to indicate that he was all right without actually speaking.

He got into the car and slowly pulled back onto the left-hand side of the road. He turned round a little further up – by the wall with 'IRA' written in huge letters on it – and then brought the car to a halt again. He breathed in deeply. After a few minutes he turned on the radio. The news was coming on and it told him that the funeral of Declan Martin, the young man killed in an IRA attack that was foiled by the security services, was about to begin.

There was no reason to go – and every reason not to. A few years ago two corporals had strayed accidentally into a funeral procession and had been dragged from their cars, beaten, brutally tortured and finally murdered. It was dangerous and unnecessary, but in that second, as he moved slowly forwards again, he knew where he was going.

The RUC would be there, he reasoned, and he wanted to see Colette with her own people – wanted to see who she was with and how they were together – and he was, after all, an intelligence officer.

And of course, in this moment, the truth was that he didn't give a fuck about risks and ground rules.

Almost as soon as Colette pulled the door of the house shut, she felt the tension.

She saw two Land Rovers cross the top of Leeson Street and, as she turned onto the Falls herself, she watched them join the end of a long line. There must have been thirty or forty big blue armour-plated Land Rovers in all, lining both sides of the road.

She wandered down towards them. It was snowing gently, light flakes drifting slowly into her face. She pulled her red hat and scarf out of her pocket and wrapped herself up.

Up ahead of her, she could see two great Tricolours

hanging from the top of the Divis Tower. She felt curiously empty.

As she approached, she began to get a sense of how many peelers there were: hundreds, literally, perhaps 500 or more, all dressed in full riot gear, like a black space-age army from a future century.

Briefly, she considered turning back, but she decided she ought to go on. Duty, she thought, and that almost made her smile.

She reached the foot of the tower. The peelers here had almost completely encircled the mourners, and both sides stood close to each other, the peelers standing casually behind them with their visors up and their batons idle. They had left a tunnel at one end and Colette walked through it to where Gerry and Paddy were standing at the front. They nodded to her and she took her place beside them.

She looked around her. She thought they were like two armies before a battle and she looked at the enemy and hated them.

They waited patiently for the coffin to emerge and she stamped her feet gently to keep her circulation going. Gerry and Paddy stood beside her; they all knew it was going to be a difficult day. It had already begun badly; Declan Martin's mother apparently didn't care much for militant republicanism and had agreed to a 'proper' funeral only under duress.

However he'd got involved, Declan Martin had been killed in action whilst serving in the Irish Republican Army, and Colette knew that the turnout today was designed to honour his sacrifice. All the senior members of the IRA in Belfast were there and most were preparing to carry the coffin at some point along the route.

The IRA wanted to bury him as a soldier, the RUC

wanted him buried as an attempted murderer, killed whilst attacking one of their own. She knew that any attempt to fire shots over his graveside would provoke instant and ferocious intervention. The air was heavy with hostility.

Everyone understood that Martin had been killed in the attack on Derek Henderson a few days before, but she knew their sympathies lay entirely with his family and with the IRA. Regardless of his intentions, to most of the people around Colette his death was the result of a policy of political assassination. She knew they had no thoughts for his potential victim.

The snow wasn't settling, but the air was cold and Colette rubbed her hands to keep warm. There was so much anger here, she thought. A crowd of people who would have given anything for some enemy blood.

Around her a few people talked quietly, but most stood in silence, waiting for the procession to begin. A black hearse reversed slowly round the corner, ready to take the coffin on to the cemetery after the funeral. Members of the media had gathered amongst the mourners, trying to roll their cameras discreetly on some of the faces the journalists recognized. They were quickly warned off, the bigger men walking to stand with their backs to the camera lenses. The threat was unmistakable and the cameramen switched off and waited for the coffin to emerge.

Slowly, a small group of men gathered outside the entrance to the Divis. They were all wearing black leather jackets, black trousers, black ties, black shoes and white shirts. As the coffin came towards them, they began to form into two lines ready to carry it. Gerry stood beside them, the collar of his green corduroy coat turned up against the cold.

Martin Mulgrew stood next to him. He turned and

smiled at her now and she smiled back with studied shyness.

The RUC commander had been watching carefully, standing close to the mourners, his polished wooden baton and brown leather gloves identifying his rank and role. Now he pushed his way slowly through the men in front to where they were standing. The officer clearly understood Gerry's rank and assumed he must be the most senior figure present. Colette instinctively moved closer to them. The officer raised his baton but spoke quietly. 'We agreed there would be none of this.'

Colette could feel the hostility around her as the man indicated to Gerry that they should move away to discuss the problem quietly. Gerry ignored him and looked back to wave the coffin out.

The commander took another step forward. 'We agreed there would be no paramilitary displays.'

Gerry looked back. 'There aren't any.'

The commander pointed his baton at the two lines. '*That* is a colour party.'

'It's a group of men in leather jackets.'

'Look, I'm not playing with words. Split them up and have others carry it at the same time or nobody is moving away from here.'

The woman next to Gerry spat violently at the officer. Gerry raised his hand to stop her and the commander didn't move. He retained his temper. 'I repeat. Break them up, or this doesn't go anywhere.'

Colette hated him. She knew they all did. She thought they'd enjoy killing him.

He retreated, wiping the phlegm carefully off his face and ignoring the hostile looks and mutterings of the other mourners.

Gerry, Paddy and Mulgrew disappeared inside the tower and for half an hour everyone waited expectantly in silence. Eventually they emerged again and Gerry nodded to the two lines of men and walked over to the commander. He pointed back at the men standing by the coffin who were now dispersing. 'That's agreed – but only out of respect for the family.'

Colette found herself thinking of the eyes of the young man before the attack and of his accusatory stares.

She felt the first twinges of guilt. She thought about what she'd been prepared to do at the hospital.

The procession moved off, led by the hearse. Colette walked behind the coffin, looking at the feet of the colour party and watching them moving slowly forwards, more or less in time.

She imagined the body in the coffin ahead of her. It was such a dislocating image and she found it as hard as ever to tie up the idea of a living, breathing being with a cold, inert corpse.

The sound froze her.

A burst of machine-gun fire and then an eerie silence. It seemed to last a long time and then another burst shattered the calm.

Colette heard screams. She felt her legs collapse under her.

The gunfire stopped, but this time there was no silence. There were shouts and screams still, and then another burst began.

Colette lay with her face against the tarmac. She could think of nothing. Her mind was blank.

It stopped again. She looked up and, to her right, saw that Gerry was still standing with the coffin on his shoulder, holding it with another man. All the others had fallen to the floor. She heard him shouting at people to keep calm, but the crowd was cowed and uncertain.

Then people were on their feet. There was a murmur around her; she heard one shout, 'Loyalists!' and then another. Everyone was looking down to their right, towards the peace line, and she caught sight of a car there now. Suddenly, as she watched, it moved, reversing away. Then there was a black taxi behind it, blocking its escape. The car hit the taxi and then tried to come forward. But the mourners were on their feet, some of the men standing in the front, as if daring the driver to run them over.

And then the crowd seemed to explode with rage. A few men dashed forwards and then they all surged towards the car. She could feel the anger, the lust for blood and she was swept along with it.

She wanted to tear them apart.

They were on the car now and she could see a man being dragged out of it. She saw a gun being pointed in the air. She saw him being sucked down to the ground. She was pushing to get closer when she was shoved from behind and then fell to the ground herself. She was scuffed and kicked as the policemen charged through her. She curled into a ball and lay still for a moment.

Then the policemen were past her and she stood up. She watched them beat back the crowd. She saw them dragging the man to his feet.

Then she saw his face.

He was hanging his head and she could see the blood dribbling down his cheek. He was looking at the ground as if he was ashamed or frightened of recognition.

She stared at him, scarcely able to believe her eyes.

The crowd came towards her, but she didn't move. People passed on either side of her and she was vaguely conscious of danger, but she couldn't drag her eyes away from him. At the back of her mind, she could feel the questions. What was he doing here? What if she denounced him? Who'd fired the shots?

She could see he didn't have a machine-gun.

He was in front of her now and he looked up to see her. For a fraction of a second, he held her gaze.

There was another burst of machine-gun fire, and this time it was clear that it was coming from the other side of the peace line. She heard someone shout, 'Up the UFF!'

Everyone had turned to look down the road. A Land Rover was speeding down to the wall, ten or twenty policemen in riot gear running after it. She could hear the commander shouting into his radio near her.

For a few seconds, the chaos continued. The police started trying to push the crowd back. Two policemen shouted at her, 'It's a Loyalist attack, get back!' but she didn't move. As they grabbed her and moved her away, she looked round and caught sight of Ryan disappearing behind a Land Rover. 'What about him?' she heard herself say, half shouting.

'He's not a bloody Loyalist,' one of the policemen said under his breath.

Nobody else seemed interested. Their attention was focused on the wall at the other end of the road.

Then, as quickly as it had come, the chaos receded. The policemen let go of her and she was back in the procession. The crowd was shuffling again now. The colour party had picked up the coffin. Colette looked around, but couldn't see him.

She walked on, but didn't look again. She was suddenly frightened. She felt the dampness in the palms of her hands, despite the cold. She scanned the crowd ahead of her. She couldn't see Mulgrew.

She wondered where *he* had been and what he had seen.

What if he'd seen the shock in her face?

The procession rounded the corner to St Peters. They were moving slowly, the anger and rage replaced by a solemn lethargy. It was surreal.

As Colette walked, she thought about the incident in the library and asked herself whether Mulgrew could or would have recognized Ryan. All he had to go on was that one brief glimpse of the newspaper cutting. Unless he had gone back to look another day . . .

She looked round again, but there was no sign of either of them.

They were all standing outside the church now and Colette had moved to the front to stand right beside Gerry, as though her physical proximity to him would somehow save her. Gerry himself stood facing the priest, his fists clenched by his side. His voice was icily polite, but laced with menace. 'Father,' he said, 'let me repeat. This funeral cortège has just been attacked by Loyalists and, as you can see, Mrs Martin is extremely upset. Will you *please* let us into the church.'

Father Collins was equally polite and equally firm and Colette thought she saw something like hatred in his eyes. 'Mr McVeigh,' he said, 'let me repeat to you that I understand only too well Mrs Martin's distress. She is a loyal and supportive member of my flock, but I cannot and will not allow Declan's body to be brought in here covered by the trappings of paramilitary violence.'

'Father . . .' Gerry's lips were tight, his voice strained.

'I've been here a long time, Mr McVeigh. I won't be bullied. Remove the trappings or we'll be here all day.'

'What about Mrs Martin, Father?'

'Believe me, my sympathy and my heart go out to her. Where your heart is, Mr McVeigh, God alone knows.'

'Whose side are you on, Father?' Gerry had lowered his voice now and Colette could tell he was reaching breaking point. She looked at the old priest's silver curls and worried brow and found herself admiring his bravery.

'At the risk of sounding trite,' he said, 'I am on the Lord's side. There has to be somebody you cannot bully like you bullied Declan Martin.'

Gerry visibly fought down his temper and turned to have a quiet word with Mrs Martin. The mourners watched in silence, enclosed in the courtyard by a solid ring of black. A few minutes later he turned back and stepped forward again to Father Collins. 'For Mrs Martin's sake, the cap, the belt and the beret go, but the Tricolour stays.'

For a moment the priest looked as if he would refuse him, but eventually he nodded grimly and turned to lead the procession into the church.

Colette followed, right next to Gerry. She took a pew close to the front and sat in a daze, not daring to look round.

She wondered if Mulgrew was sitting in one of the pews behind her and imagined his eyes on the back of her head. She imagined him thinking, assessing, wondering. She tried to picture what he might have seen in her face for those few moments. She couldn't say, because she couldn't know how much of what she'd felt – the shock and surprise – would have shown on her face. And it would only matter *if* he'd been watching. There were a million other things he might have been doing. She tried to take her mind off it and concentrate on what the priest was saying.

She listened. The priest talked of a life wasted; of a boy who loved Gaelic football and was devoted to his mother; of a boy who worked hard and was a good

236

student, loved by his teachers, his friends and his family.

Mostly, Father Collins talked of the tragedy that had hurt them all, but he did not spare his audience. His voice was rich with emotion. 'I must say now to the paramilitary leaders who sent Declan to his death: why?

'For God's sake, I ask you why you sent a young man to his death? What do you hope to achieve after so long, after so much bloodshed and bitterness and hatred?'

Colette looked at Gerry. He was staring at the priest impassively, but the muscles in his cheek were twitching rapidly.

'When will it end?' the priest asked. 'When will *you* end it? We know of your pain, of your commitment to justice and to freedom, but it cannot go on. I ask you, after twenty-five years, what are you achieving with this daily litany of death?'

There was the sound of squeaky trainers on the stone floor. People were leaving and Colette took her chance. She turned round and scanned the church, sweeping across from right to left and then back again.

She couldn't see Mulgrew.

She turned back and tried to listen. The priest went on, 'The future lies in your hands. You have the power to stop it, to prevent other fine young men going to an early grave. On behalf of everyone in this troubled land, I beg you to have the courage to stop—'

She tried to make sense of what she had just seen. It was a Loyalist attack, so what was Ryan doing there? Accident or design? Design, surely. It worried her. It scared her.

She realized she'd been beginning to trust him.

Next to her, Gerry was sitting stock-still, staring at

Father Collins with cold fury in his eyes.

She looked forward at the coffin ahead of her. She could scarcely credit these circumstances.

Out there was a Brit she had wanted to live.

In front of her lay a patriot she had wanted to die.

The worst of it was that she didn't feel guilty.

She bent her head and found herself saying a silent prayer.

She prayed for the death of Martin Mulgrew.

She felt Gerry moving beside her and opened her eyes. He'd got up and, instinctively, she followed him.

It was bright outside after the darkness of the church and, for a moment, as they walked towards the group of men ahead of them, she found herself squinting. As they reached the group, Colette hung back fractionally to allow Gerry to join the circle – partly out of fear and partly as a recognition that she was not really welcome.

The men were from Internal Security and she wondered if they would ask her to leave.

'One of these days Father Collins is going to get what's coming to him,' Gerry said.

No-one answered him.

Terence O'Hanlon stood in the centre of the group, dwarfed by the men around him. He measured 5 feet 5 in his trainers and did not like people making references to his size. He generally got his wish.

'The greyhound attack was intercepted, we hear,' O'Hanlon said. 'There were arrests.'

Colette felt a brief sense of relief. She hadn't known about the greyhound attack. But then, did they know she hadn't known?

'There's no doubt you have a tout,' O'Hanlon said.

'It looks that way,' Gerry replied, 'but we're dealing with it. Mulgrew is looking into it.'

'Mulgrew is your intelligence officer. He's not got the experience for a major tout hunt, so *we'll* deal with it now.'

There was a moment's silence. Gerry had his back to Colette, but she could read the tension in the faces of the men opposite her. Chico was smirking at her now and she shivered. He was so revolting.

'I think,' Gerry said icily, 'that we will deal with this if you don't mind. I—'

'We know who it is,' O'Hanlon said. Chico was still smirking at her.

Another pause. Gerry tilted his head to one side. 'Care to tell us who you *think* it is?'

'We're still checking. We'll tell you when the moment comes.' O'Hanlon smiled now and it was a chilling sight. 'We like to be absolutely sure, Gerry, as you know.'

Gerry hesitated for a second. 'Well,' he said slowly. 'You'd better be right, or you'll regret it.'

He turned and, for a second, Colette saw the anger in his face. Then he was past her and she was following. She didn't look back.

She could tell how angry Gerry was by the speed at which he walked. She had to half jog to keep up with him. He didn't say anything and, as they turned back onto the Falls, she saw Mulgrew running down towards them. He was slightly out of breath and he looked at her without smiling.

'Got a minute, Gerry?' he said.

'Not now, Martin.'

'It'll only take a second. It's—'

'Not now.'

He kept on walking and Colette tried to catch him up, but Mulgrew put his hand on her shoulder. 'How's the form?' he asked. She was forced to slow down and

239

Gerry began to pull away from her.

'Gerry's angry,' Mulgrew said.

'You don't say.'

'What's up? Is it that greyhound business?'

She kept on walking. They were close to Leeson Street now and she saw Gerry pass the turning and head on up the Falls. 'An argument with Internal,' she said.

'Ah. Well, we may beat them to it.'

Colette grunted and turned left into Leeson Street. She stopped. 'See ya, Martin,' she said.

'We're pretty sure we know who it is.'

He was looking at her. She was torn once again between finding his intensity threatening and laughable. She didn't know whether to see him as 'little Martin' still.

'Good,' she said. 'Serve the fucker right, whoever he is.' She turned away.

'Or *she*.'

Colette turned back. 'I'm sorry?'

Mulgrew was still staring at her. 'You said he, but who's to say it is a man?'

For a second she was frightened and she felt panic begin to swamp her mind. Then, suddenly, he changed his tone and mood. He touched her shoulder. 'First rule of this game, Colette: never assume anything – otherwise, you end up looking in the wrong places.' He put his arm right over her shoulder now and she felt revolted. 'Are you going to offer me a cup of tea?'

She said, 'Sure,' and wished, as she said it, that she could have thought of a credible excuse.

As she opened the door a few moments later, she was conscious of the silence in the house. Ma and the kids weren't back.

She made him a cup of tea in silence and conspicuously didn't make herself one. He said thanks, took off his coat and hung it on the back of one of the kitchen chairs.

The room was quiet, but for the sound of him slurping his tea.

'How are the kids?' he asked.

'Fine.'

Silence. There was something chilling about this, as if his presence here was somehow a violation. There was an intimacy about it that made her feel uncomfortable, frightened.

He took another noisy slurp of his tea and looked at her again, his stare naked and intense. 'We've got to crack this tout,' he said, 'whoever he – or *she* – is.'

'Yes,' she said, whilst thinking, once again, I bet it's you, you bastard.

He put down his tea on the side and stepped closer to her. He was only a foot away now, at most, and she looked over her shoulder at the back door. 'Kids'll be home in a second,' she said.

She looked back at him, aware that this could be dangerous. He was still staring at her and she smiled. 'How you doin', Martin.'

'I've always fancied you, Colette,' he said.

When she looked at him now, she could see the lust in his eyes so clearly, and she cursed herself for not recognizing its intensity before, but the threat was still there. 'I know,' she said.

He stepped forward and tried to kiss her, but she pushed him away and stepped back. 'No, Martin.'

'Why not?'

'The kids'll be back. I think . . . I think we should just be friends. You know?'

He was staring at her again. 'Chico good enough for you, but not me, is that it?'

'Been watching me, have you?'

'News gets around. Fucked anyone else? Give the Brits a good fucking when you were inside to get yourself let out?'

'Get out of here, Mulgrew.'

'I think it would be sensible for you.'

Silence. She looked down. 'What do you mean?'

'I think it would be sensible, that's what I'm saying.'

'You dirty shit,' she said quietly. 'I don't know what you mean.'

'It's a dangerous world.'

'Get out,' she whispered.

Silence.

He picked up his coat off the chair and put it on. 'All right,' he said. 'We make our decisions. I just hope you don't live to regret it.'

A few seconds later she heard the front door go. She opened the back door, sat on the step and lit a cigarette.

She noticed her hand was shaking.

The alley was quiet. She had an image of Martin Mulgrew as a little boy and it was hard to make sense of it. She felt angry, but the anger brought confidence, not fear.

She thought of the funeral and suddenly had a strong mental image of Mulgrew kneeling beside the spotty youth's bedside in the hospital, leaning over to allow the kid to whisper weakly in his ear . . .

She took a long, last drag of the cigarette and then crushed it beneath her feet. No, she told herself, he *doesn't* know. Neither of them did.

She got up and began thinking about what she was going to make the children for their tea.

* * *

As Ryan passed the city airport, he realized that he was driving very slowly. He was tired and had to struggle to focus his mind on the road ahead of him. A mile or so further on, he passed a sign for Holywood Barracks and, just after it, he saw twenty or thirty men training on a floodlit rugby pitch. He could see their breath against the cold night air.

He missed the road the first time and had to consult the map, turn round and come back. Once he was sure he had the right road, he proceeded slowly, looking out for the barrier Hopkins had warned him about. When he came to it, he waited until it lifted before completing the last twist in the road and driving underneath a clock tower into a courtyard. Hopkins's house was the first on the left and, by the time Ryan turned in, both he and Grant were standing in the doorway like worried parents. Hopkins ushered him into the sitting room without any warm small talk and without offering him a drink. In other circumstances, he might have been amused to see Grant and Hopkins standing next to each other and making a great show of being friends, since everyone knew they didn't get on. But he wasn't in the mood to see the humour in anything.

Grant spoke first. His manner was that of a cross schoolmaster. Ryan resented him for the first time.

'Naturally you will be returning to England.' He paused for a second, as if waiting for that to be challenged. 'I blame myself, to some degree. I think all this was too soon for you.'

'It was a mistake.'

'Mistakes cost lives here, David,' Hopkins said.

Ryan ignored him. 'It was a mistake. I didn't think it through. It won't happen again.'

'I don't know what the hell you were thinking of,' Grant said.

'I wanted to see who she was with and—'

'Don't bloody *answer*.' Grant exhaled deeply.

'Don't pull me out.'

'There is no choice now.'

'I don't accept that.'

'It is not up to you to accept it or not,' Hopkins said. 'That is the decision.'

Ryan felt the anger rise within him. It was a scene from his own past; two schoolmasters and a boy who had no respect for authority. He fought to keep the contempt from his voice. 'Please give me a second chance.' It was directed at Grant.

'It's not in our power. You are compromised.'

'How will she be run?' He could sense a hint of desperation creeping into his voice.

'We'll leave the nuts and bolts to the RUC. Jenkins will come in to bleed her once or twice a month.'

'You may lose her.'

'We may lose her anyway.'

'Not with me here.'

Hopkins frowned. 'You're nothing if not arrogant.'

'I'm telling it as it is. She didn't respond well to Jenkins and she doesn't trust the RUC.'

Grant looked annoyed. 'This is a professional transaction. It is not a matter of personalities. If it is, that may be part of the problem.'

'She trusts me.'

'I doubt that now.'

'Today has changed nothing. She trusts me. I'm asking you to give me a second chance.'

'I'm not sure we can.'

'I wouldn't ask if it wasn't important.'

'To you, to her, or to us?'

244

'All three.'

They didn't respond. He looked for an answer in their faces. He saw hostility in Hopkins, uncertainty in Grant.

'There's another reason,' he said. He paused before continuing. 'I think you'll find that if I go, she won't survive much longer.'

'Would you care to explain that?' Grant asked.

'I can't really, I don't think.'

'Well, in that case—'

'The RUC have somebody else.'

'So?'

'Close to her. Too close for comfort, I think. Suspicion is everywhere and they're talking about . . . there's been talk of letting her go.'

'By whom?'

'I don't think I can be more specific. I've been getting help, but if I go, I honestly think they may decide to burn her as well. I think Internal Security may be getting close to their agent. They think this could allay suspicion, you know—'

'We're aware of how it's done, Ryan.' Grant's voice was firm and slightly patronizing. Ryan looked at him and tried to hold his gaze.

'All right,' Grant said. 'Please go and wait in the car for a few minutes.'

Ryan took the dismissal and turned for the door. As he stepped out into the courtyard, he felt terribly tired. Hopkins's house formed part of a converted stable yard and light spilled out onto the cobbles now from each of the four corners. Behind his car, a couple of peacocks made their way slowly towards the archway at the other end, which led out to some fields. It was extremely pleasant and restful, but Ryan waited with a growing sense of unease. The realization of how much he cared about this and how much he wanted to stay seemed to increase with each passing minute. He cursed himself silently, with the frustration of someone who desperately wants to change a piece of immediate history, but cannot.

Grant appeared in the doorway and he felt himself tensing.

'All right,' Grant said at his car window. 'But another mistake and you're out.' He stood up straight. 'And you'd better make it worth my while.'

Grant walked slowly towards the house and Ryan reversed backwards and then drove out under the clock tower.

He felt relieved, but disgruntled.

He was out near Cultra and it took him about twenty minutes to get back to the Malone Road. There were a few drops of rain and not many cars on the road. As he turned into Malone Beeches he saw the familiar shape of a silver Granada and his heart sank.

Allen got out as he approached the front door. Ryan tried to sound friendly. 'Want to come in for a drink?'

'No thanks.'

'I suppose you're here to bollock me as well.'

'Yes.'

'Go on th—'

'Did she see you?'

'Yes.'

Allen grimaced. 'Did anyone else see that she saw you?'

'I don't know.'

Silence. Ryan was conscious of the cold. He found the right key and prepared to put it in the lock. 'Sure you don't want to—'

'If it wasn't for the trial—'

'What do you mean?'

Allen shrugged. 'It's not exactly a bloody state secret.'

'I can't help that.'

Allen sighed. 'You can help today. That was fucking stupid.'

'Look. I know that, all right? It won't happen again. Now do you want to come in and talk about it, or do you want to rub my nose in the shit out here all night?'

Allen looked at him. 'I'm going home. I'll see you at Grosvenor Road RUC station tomorrow morning. We'll see what's happened.'

Ryan let himself in and dumped his coat on the peg by the door. The flat was warm – almost too warm. He went into the sitting room and switched on the TV for company. He switched it over to *Newsnight* and briefly watched a discussion on the prospects for peace in Ireland. It was slightly surreal – and he found himself wishing he had a bottle of whiskey in the flat.

CHAPTER TWELVE

Colette opened the cupboard door and was hit by a
falling broom. Everything had been crammed into the
cupboard and, now she'd opened it, it all came
tumbling out. She picked up the broom, the mop and
the dustpan and brush and loaded them back in, before
getting hold of the Hoover and pulling it out. The
broom fell again.

The Hoover was old – *circa* 1975 – and very weak.
The bag leaked and they really needed a new one.

She began in the bathroom. The carpet here wasn't
fixed to the floor, so despite the weak suction, she had
to keep her foot planted firmly by the Hoover to prevent it rucking up.

She moved onto the landing and then into her
parents' bedroom. It was odd, she still thought of it as
her *parents'* bedroom. The bed was neatly made and she
sat down on it for a second. There was a large picture
of Pa on the bedside table in a wooden frame. He was
dressed in a black cloth cap and he was smiling. God,
he looked so young! There was a picture of Paddy, too,
aged about eleven and dressed in football kit. He had
long hair and dirty knees and he was pushing his chest
out and clasping his hands behind his back. He had a

248

huge mischievous grin on his face and Colette found herself smiling. There was a picture of Sean, too, of course – a little blond boy making a sandcastle – and even now she found it hard to dwell on it. Poor Sean.

On the second level of the bedside table was a black tattered photograph album and Colette pulled it out. She realized it was ages since she'd seen it. She opened the front cover and began to flick through it.

They were all old black and white photographs, with a white border. They were mostly out of focus and poorly framed: Ma and Pa on their honeymoon in Galway, standing together awkwardly, Ma unsure whether to smile for the camera or not. Colette thought she looked incredibly beautiful and wondered with a jolt whether they had been *truly* happy. She thought it was odd that, as a child, you never thought about these things, and now it was too late. They *looked* happy, anyway, and everyone always said they were. Ma herself had said it countless times. As a child, Colette's dream had been to find a man like Pa and have a marriage like her parents'. She felt a sense of melancholy as she considered how fucked up her life had become. Perhaps there is time, she thought, hopefully.

Looking at the honeymoon pictures, she felt sad for Ma too. She was so strong, heroic even, but Colette thought it must be unbelievably hard to love someone so much and then lose them. She wondered if there had been anyone else since Pa. Not as far as she could tell. Ma spent a lot of time with her friends and they talked about their families and argued a bit about politics, because Ma fought her corner fiercely when roused and hated the war, but that was about it. It wasn't much of a life when you thought about it. But if it depressed her, she didn't let it show – not often, anyway. She was

249

always so interested in everyone and everything that was going on. Too interested, sometimes.

She flicked on past the honeymoon, to pictures of Dad on the beach in Donegal with a baby – must be Gerry. There were shots of Gerry and Paddy, and then the three of them together. There was one picture of all six of them, taken in somebody's backyard. She wondered who'd taken that. Sean was tiny, resting his head on his father's knee.

There were not many pictures of her, she noticed. Pa had always given more attention to the boys. She got to the last page and a piece of paper fell out. She bent down and picked it up. It was crumpled and had a number written on it in pencil: 240781. It wasn't Ma's handwriting.

She heard the tell-tale banging of Land Rover doors and she stood up and went to the window. The policemen and soldiers were spilling out of four Land Rovers parked on the opposite side of the street. She watched them knocking on the doors, but she felt no sense of concern. She didn't think they would be coming here.

She walked back to the other side of the bed and put the album back in its place.

She heard the knock on the door and leaned back against the wall. She breathed in deeply and hoped it would go away.

She heard another knock. She pushed herself away from the wall and walked down the stairs. At the bottom, she glanced in the hall mirror and wished she wasn't wearing a tracksuit. She muttered, 'Arseholes,' and then opened the door.

She was stunned to see it was him.

He took a step forward, forcing her back into the hall.

'I'm afraid we have a warrant to search these premises,' he said.

She didn't reply. He was wearing the same boots, jeans, a T-shirt and a dark sweater. He seemed to tower over her.

'Are you alone in the house?' he whispered.

She nodded.

'The kids?'

'Playgroup.'

'Your mother?'

'Out.'

He relaxed visibly and walked into the front room. She followed. He went to the window, pulled back the net curtains and looked out.

'We're searching the street,' he said as he turned back to her.

'Yes, I can see.' She bit her bottom lip and looked down.

'I wanted to check that everything was all right after yesterday.'

'What were you doing there?' she asked, looking up at him.

'Surveillance. You don't need to worry—'

'You seem to follow me everywhere. You know, the cemetery, yesterday, where else are you going—'

'Don't worry about it.' He was gesturing with the flat of his hand now. His height made it forceful. 'We have a job to do and we do it. You just have to concentrate on what you're doing.'

His gaze was intense and she dropped her eyes again. She looked at his feet.

Neither of them spoke. She could hear the woman next door shouting at the policemen. 'Bigots!' she screamed. 'Bigots!'

'You talk about loyalty,' Colette said quietly. 'Well, that's what I showed yesterday.'

'I'm not sure . . .'

She looked up at him. 'You know what I mean.'

Silence. He looked puzzled.

'You want to talk about loyalty,' she said. 'Well, I let you live yesterday.'

'I'm not sure I follow.'

'There are others here who know what you've done.'

'I take it that's an oblique threat of some kind.'

'Take it any way you want.'

He took a step forward and put his hands around her face. 'Try any sort of threat on me, Colette, and this will be the shortest relationship in history. Do you understand?'

For some reason, she felt the tears welling up in her eyes. 'I was just telling you I'm loyal,' she said quietly. 'That's all.'

He released her and stepped back, turning round to look out of the window again as he did so.

'All right,' he said eventually. 'I just wanted to check you were OK.' He looked down at the table to the left of him and she followed his gaze. Ma had bought some Christmas decorations.

'I was just about to put them up,' she said. 'Want to help?'

He smiled. 'I'll see myself out.'

She followed him and, as he reached for the door, she touched his back. He didn't turn round.

She shut the door and returned to the front room. Some of the Christmas decorations had fallen on the floor. She picked them up and then twirled one end of one of the streamers around her fingers.

She heard the Land Rovers move off outside and then the room was suddenly quiet.

Colette woke and it took her a few seconds to make out the two figures sitting on the end of her bed, though she'd felt their weight instantly.

She raised her head a fraction. 'What time is it?'

'Time to wake up!' Mark said excitedly.

She raised her arm and made a show of looking at her watch. 'Five thirty! That's far too early! Go back to sleep.'

She lay back, shut her eyes and pretended to snore gently. For a moment they didn't move, and then she felt one of them crawling up the bed. It was Catherine and now she was blowing on her face. She opened her eyes. 'Go back to bed, young lady, or Santa will take your presents away again.'

Mark began to crawl up the bed and Catherine kissed her gently. 'Please, Mammy,' she said. 'Please, please . . .'

Colette sat up in bed, realizing, as she did so, that Catherine's stammer had gone again. 'Right,' she said. 'Christmas it is. Turn on the light.'

Mark turned on the light and it blinded her. She felt a sudden, dull pain behind her eyes and she remembered the previous night after midnight mass. The mass was now held at eight o'clock on Christmas Eve to stop people coming in pissed from the pub. But it didn't stop drinking afterwards.

'Mark, love,' she said. 'Get us a glass of water, would you, and then you can open your stocking.'

He ran to the bathroom and then came back a few seconds later to begin tearing into his stocking. Colette watched both of them at it and tried to quell her sense of guilt. It wasn't much – pencils, crayons, rubbers, tracing paper, wind-up mice, a couple of practical jokes, sweets – but Ma had bought nearly all of it. Still, it was a joy to see them so happy. As she got up, even her hangover didn't sour her mood.

After that, the day passed very quickly and, along

with Ma, she spent most of it in the kitchen. Paddy came round in the morning and they opened their presents. He gave Colette some beautiful brass earrings and she got a striped jumper from her mother. She wasn't quite sure about that, but didn't say anything.

Gerry and Christy came round for lunch and Christy was even quieter than usual. They looked like they'd had another row. Colette tried to keep an eye on Gerry's son Sean, who was turning into a terrible bully and who, she knew, persecuted Mark when her back was turned.

She was just drying the dishes afterwards when she heard Gerry shouting at his son. 'Sit down, Sean!' he said, his anger rising. '*Now*! Do as you are bloody well told.'

'Don't swear in front of the boy, Gerry,' Ma said.

The television suddenly intervened. It had been on all day but now, at last, it managed to attract everyone's attention. The Queen's speech had begun and everyone hurled abuse at the screen, before racing for the 'off' button.

Ma came back into the kitchen to help dry the dishes – Colette was angry that neither the boys nor Christy had lifted a bloody finger to help – and she raised her eyebrows in order to reflect a private joke they'd had over the years. Colette smiled back, but said nothing.

Catherine was sitting at the table looking at her new photograph album and Colette looked over her shoulder. She thought it was a strange choice for a Christmas present, but it *was* what she wanted. Catherine turned the pages and chattered excitedly, 'That's me, me, me.' Colette looked down at the page and corrected her. 'No, that's Mark love.'

'He's ugly!'

Colette laughed. 'He looks just like you as a baby. Does that mean you're ugly too?'

Catherine turned the page. 'That's me!'

'No, that's Mark too.' She bent down, her head resting above Catherine's. 'Here, we'll find a picture of you. *That's* you, see? Not very pretty!'

'Noooo.' Catherine smiled and nuzzled her head into Colette's side. She turned the page. 'That's Daddy,' she said.

Yes, it is, Colette thought.

Both of them had been given paper and crayons in their stockings and Colette picked up some of their drawings from the table. Catherine's was of a house, with all of them in it, surrounded by soldiers. Mark's showed a man lying on the ground bleeding after apparently being shot by a group of men. She didn't know who were the bad guys and who the good. She thought that was appropriate.

She ruffled Catherine's hair. 'You going to go outside and play?'

'No.'

Colette nudged her off her chair. 'Go on. Get some air or I'll give you to the Brits and they can keep you!'

'Aaaah!' Catherine shouted as she ran out. Colette noticed that her stammer really did seem to have disappeared today. She thought it was very puzzling.

She picked up a dirty tea towel and dried up some of the plates. Voices were being raised next door. She caught her mother's eye and frowned. Gerry was beginning to shout now. 'I don't *care* what other people say.'

She put her head round the door. 'Leave it, Gerry.'

'Oh, fuck off.'

She was shocked by the casual but brutal hostility. 'It's *Christmas*, Gerry.' Colette could see Christy was close to tears. Paddy was pretending to read the paper, Sean sat on the floor, playing and listening to his parents arguing.

'It is Christmas and I said *fuck off*.'

Colette turned round and walked back into the kitchen. She put down the tea towel and the plate. Her mother shook her head. 'Leave it,' she said quietly, but Colette ignored her. 'He's not going to get away with it,' she muttered.

She walked back into the front room and Paddy looked up, as if he could sense her mood. 'Would you come outside, Gerry,' she said.

'Pistols at dawn?'

'Please just come outside.'

Gerry got up and didn't bother to put his shoes back on. She took him out of the front door and tried to bring him further away from the house. He was reluctant.

'What the fuck is wrong with you?' she asked.

'Get a grip on yourself, Colette.'

'It's *Christmas*.'

'So what?'

'Well, of course. Why would you change the habits of a lifetime and make any effort actually to be *nice* to anyone.'

'Can it, Colette.'

'Can it yourself, Gerry.' Colette turned away, as if in frustration, and then turned back to him. 'What is wrong with you Gerry? What's eating you? You're like a man possessed.'

'I'll tell you what's wrong. If you want to know, I'll tell you. I am *sick and tired* of sitting in this house and hearing all of you – Christy, Ma, you – undermine what we are trying to do. You're all cowards, every last one of you, and I am sick of it, absolutely bloody sick to death—'

256

'Since when—'

'If it's not you, it's one of the others – like a little mafia, egging each other on. Niggling away.'

'I don't know what—'

'Oh, shut it.' He was stabbing his finger into her chest. 'I've had enough of it. It's cowardice.'

He turned and stormed back into the house. Colette stood outside for a few moments watching her breath in the cold air.

She walked back up to the front door, which was more or less shut. Inside, she heard Paddy and Gerry talking and she just heard Gerry say, 'We have to do it—' As she opened the door he turned and looked at her with what she thought was real hatred and then he pushed past her and was gone. As she shut the door behind her she smiled wearily at Paddy and he smiled back.

She walked back to the kitchen, ignored her mother and went out of the door. She stood in the alley and lit a cigarette. She could hear a group of kids playing, probably Catherine and Mark and their friends.

She looked up at the grey sky above her. 'Where are you when I need you?' she whispered.

The back of the taxi was warm and comforting. The driver didn't bother to make conversation and, as he looked out of the rain-spattered window, Ryan felt a deep sense of melancholy.

Christmas was always this way and he supposed he should be grateful for being away from home.

He paid the driver in cash and stood in the drive, facing the huge mock-Tudor house. It had a spacious forecourt and two garages. His arrival had triggered a series of floodlights that illuminated the garden and most of the neighbouring bungalow. The house was situated at the end of the cul-de-sac and Ryan could see that it had been carefully chosen for maximum safety.

He was about to knock on the large oak door when it swung wide open.

'Box!'

Ryan smiled nervously, unsure how to react to his new nickname – not very original since 'Box' was simply intelligence world slang for MI5. He had both hands full with champagne and chocolates. Allen was beaming, his cheeks flushed and his nose red. He was wearing a large, bright-red hat with Santa Claus stamped in big letters on the front.

He put his hand on Ryan's shoulder and ushered him inside. The house was warm and welcoming; the atmosphere reminded Ryan uncomfortably of Christmases at home when his father was still alive. The hall was narrow and the walls were covered in dark wood panels. It could have been quite gloomy, but had been carefully lit, with a Chinese lamp by the telephone throwing light up towards the ceiling and the stairs at the far end. Allen led Ryan down into the sitting room and, as he entered, conversation in the room stumbled to a halt and everyone stood politely. He concentrated on the names. Allen's wife, Sally, was a pleasant, attractive and jolly-looking woman, with dark hair and an easy smile. Jonathan, his son, was as big as his father and much fitter. He looked like a rugby player and had a firm handshake and a friendly, open face. Allen's daughter, Annie, looked about sixteen, with an attitude to match. She was pretty, but obviously shy.

By the time they reached the dinner table, Ryan felt a little drunk. For the first half of the meal, he remained the centre of conversation, everyone politely asking him about his family, his home life and what he thought of Northern Ireland. 'Everyone is very friendly,' he heard himself say more than once, thinking as he did so, that it was a barefaced lie. About halfway through the main course attention turned to Annie, who had barely touched her food. Sally told her gently to eat up before her plate got cold, and a heated argument ensued.

Ryan was hungry and he had seconds of everything, including Christmas pudding, which he'd never greatly liked. He drank heavily and enjoyed himself. The family was still skirmishing as the party hats came out of the crackers, and he was amused to see Allen being told off by his children.

After cheese and coffee, Allen poured Ryan a port and took him into the sitting room whilst the others cleared up in the kitchen. Ryan protested that he should help, but was rebuffed.

Allen seemed to be made for the armchairs by the fire, and he rested his glass on his belly. Ryan thought he looked like something straight out of a Giles cartoon; his face red, his eyes slightly glazed and his shirt and tie undone, with a few white hairs poking out of the top. He leaned forward briefly and stoked the fire before kicking off his shoes.

'Sorry about the other day,' he said simply.

'Which bit?'

Allen shrugged. 'The whole lot. I haven't been as helpful as I might have been and I'm sorry.'

Ryan smiled. 'I've been learning.'

Allen took a sip of his port and reached up to the shelf behind him for a box of cigars. He offered Ryan one, but he refused and took out a cigarette instead.

'It's been a bit hectic so far, hasn't it?' Allen asked.

Ryan nodded. He could tell Allen was limbering up to get something off his chest.

'It's bloody difficult, of course, and doesn't get any easier however long you do it. But you've got to be careful, you know, to see these people for what they are.'

Ryan was puzzled. 'What do you mean?'

'I mean don't get too attached to her.'

'I don't think I am.'

'I'm not so sure. Like I said the other day. In the end it *is* us against them. It's not personal.'

'I recruited her.'

'Yes, but—'

'I made promises.'

'Yes – but if . . .' Allen paused for a few seconds before continuing. 'Look, what I'm saying is this: although we may be the closest to one individual, we are not able, in the end, to see the whole picture, and sometimes it is best to leave decisions to others who can see—'

'Then why did you call me?'

Allen looked at him and shrugged. 'I've been doing this longer than you could imagine and it *is* a complicated business. She's an attractive girl. Maybe in different circumstances, *she* could be different.'

'I'm not sure I follow.'

'Just don't forget the decision she made in the first place. She wasn't signing up to join the Girl Guides.'

'So she's condemned for ever?'

'No, I didn't say that, but she'll never repent. None of them ever do. Not until they're caught anyway and it suits them to pretend.'

Allen took a large puff of his cigar and sent a thick trail of smoke billowing up towards the ceiling.

'Some of these people are intelligent, many are just thugs. I know what you think: in different circumstances, what would *I* have done, what would *I* have

260

become? Just don't forget the nature of the decisions they make. What they do is irreversible and I think that sets them apart.'

Ryan looked into the fire. 'So what happens to her?'

'She'll survive for a while, if we're clever and she's careful.'

'And then what?'

'Perhaps she'll get out.'

'Perhaps?'

Allen sighed. 'Yes, perhaps. Some of them do, some of them don't. It's a hard world.'

'So she's expendable?'

'No. I didn't say that. But, as I said, these people have made their choices a long time ago. They didn't have to join the IRA. Nobody was forcing them.'

Ryan stared into the fire for a long time before replying. The room was the other end of the house from the kitchen and it was quiet. He'd enjoyed a sense of companionship with Allen, but he thought it was fading now. He wondered if there was an agenda here.

He turned over his past, looking at the dark-red coals and feeling their heat on his face.

'I don't think anyone has a monopoly on guilt,' he said eventually, almost to himself.

'We all make mistakes, David. I don't think the two sides compare, whatever your criteria may be.'

Ryan looked at him. 'Don't they?'

Allen leaned forward in his chair, suddenly animated. 'No.' He pointed his cigar at Ryan. 'Look, I don't mean to patronize you, but maybe you'll see what I mean. When I started out, I was based down in Tyrone in a little town that has been divided for years. There was a young Catholic lad in that town – a bright, intelligent, hard-working guy. He worked on a building site, but was from a large family and they were very

261

short of money and didn't have enough to make him up a lunch worth speaking of.'

Allen gestured with his cigar again. 'Follow so far?'

Ryan nodded.

'Now Joe had a Protestant work colleague – let's call him Jim, for the sake of argument. Jim was a big-hearted man and every day he'd get his wife to make up a lunch big enough for two so that Joe would have enough to eat.

'That was fine and the two were friends. But Jim was a part-time soldier, and one day he must have let that fact slip to Joe.

'A few weeks later, Jim is at home and he hears a giant explosion outside his house. He comes running out and, to his shock and surprise, he sees his mate Joe lying on the ground in front of him.

'As he stands there he realizes that Joe is in the IRA and he has been trying to plant a bomb under his car. Now, unfortunately for Joe, the bomb has gone off prematurely. Both Joe's arms have been blown off and his IRA colleague has kindly buggered off, leaving him to bleed to death. Jim calls an ambulance and tries to administer first aid. He cradles Joe in his arms as he dies.'

'What's your point?'

Allen paused for a moment and puffed on his cigar aggressively. 'The point is this: you might say that all that shows how strong a cause these people have and how much they believe in it. But there's a human element, an element that has to say that, whatever you believe intellectually, killing your own workmate and friend is an act of supreme—'

'I'm not questioning the cruelty of it.'

'Well, just remember to see her for what she is. Don't lose your hatred just because she's got a pretty face.'

'She's not exactly Adolf Hitler, is she?'

'Isn't she?'

'Come on.'

'That's a moral question. Moral fibre. Moral decisions, not outward appearances.'

Ryan pulled out his packet of cigarettes and lit another. 'Yes, but if you want to talk moral justifications, there are plenty of people without a clean record. What about the Americans in Vietnam, or us here on Bloody Sunday? Morally wrong.'

'Don't forget which side you're on.'

'I'm not bloody forgetting. But she's a human being and I'm not going to forget that either.'

Ryan was suddenly struck by something and he looked at Allen again. 'You know who this man is, don't you?'

'Who?'

'The other tout.'

Allen shook his head. He seemed to be almost smiling. He looked at Ryan with a slightly strange expression, as if he was troubled by something.

'I may be out of line on this, but when you get the chance, why don't you take another look at our woman's file? The whole thing. It's been computerized and you should be able to access it from Stormont.'

He didn't elaborate.

McIlhatton's Christmas had been shit.

He'd never felt so depressed.

He was walking down a street in Hammersmith now – it seemed the same as every other street in this rotten town. He found the house again easily – number 47 – and rang the doorbell once.

The same man came to the door. He had a brown

parcel in his hand, and he gave it to him without saying a word. He slammed the door shut.

McIlhatton stood there for a few seconds and then turned away. He hadn't realized how much he'd wanted to hear another human voice.

CHAPTER THIRTEEN

Ryan swept the pile of paper to one side and switched on his desk lamp. It was New Year's Eve and everyone else had long since gone home. He could dimly see the hands on the clock hanging on the wall beside him. Three hours to go, he thought, and another year almost done.

There was a strange loneliness about tonight. He realized that he hadn't really spoken to any of his friends for months, indeed most of them probably didn't even know he was here. He had got into the habit of relying on Isabelle to maintain contact with all his friends as well as hers. She had always arranged things and he'd got used to fitting in as and when he could, usually at the last minute.

He realized how obsessed and preoccupied he'd been for the last few weeks.

He fiddled with the desk lamp, pulling its head up a little, and leaned back in his chair, looking around the office as he did so. On each desk, papers were piled high and keyboards were balanced above computer screens. It was like any office anywhere. They were on the second floor of Stormont Castle and the sign on the door said

'Department of Employment' in big letters. The other offices in the corridor – indeed all over the compound – dealt with pensions and social security and the environment and education and even with employment. Only this office was different.

He looked at the desk beside him, the tidiest in the room. There were no photographs on it – no husband or boyfriend visible, certainly no children – and he rather wished that its occupant was still there. Alison Berry would have filled a gap tonight.

Now that he'd cleared a space, he pulled the computer keyboard forward. Allen's words had been dancing around his mind for the past few days, and now curiosity had got the better of him. He was pretty sure he was the only person in the building, save for the security guards, because he'd walked the length of the wide corridor outside and not seen a chink of light. He hadn't turned on the main light in the office and was using the desk lamp, which illuminated only one end of the room.

He began to tap away at the keyboard. He punched in his name – Ryan – and his password – Bombay – after the city of his birth. He waited as the computer went through its slow awakening. He hadn't logged in since leaving London, so he went first to check his personal files, but there was only one message and he was disappointed to see it was from Tina, Jenkins's PA. It read, 'Behave yourself over there.' Tina never gave up.

He pressed the command key again and punched in IRA. People. M. From here he could access Special Branch files as well as the Service's own and it meant there were thousands of entries.

It was hard to know where to start. He found a file that had been written up on the attack on Henderson. It gave a factual description of the attack and the personnel involved and noted that court proceedings were underway against Seamus McGirr.

Ryan wondered how the hell Paddy had got away with it.

Then he spooled up the page and was surprised to see the detail involved in their 'backgrounder'. The intelligence for the attack had been gathered over a period of two months, the report said, and it named all the operatives involved. It noted the day – even the time – on which Gerry McVeigh had given his final approval.

Ryan knew they hadn't got that from Colette.

He flicked through the files again until he found the most up-to-date profile of Gerry. He opened it and was stunned by the first sentence, which was written in bold:

WARNING: 'Foxglove' has made it clear that Gerry McVeigh represents a real threat to the emerging peace process. He remains implacably opposed to all attempts to negotiate a solution and is attempting to foster dissent amongst other leading Republicans.

Ryan sat back in the chair and exhaled noisily. Who, he asked himself, is Foxglove? Gingy Hughes – now deceased – or someone else? The other tout?

He was suddenly transported back to his mother's garden and to the tall, stooping, mauve and cream flowers in the beds by the porch. He could remember, distinctly, her explanation of the name – 'the flowers are like little fox's gloves' – and he could recall watching the bees slipping quickly in and out of them.

Somebody was a gardener . . .

He read on through Gerry's file and saw two further references to Foxglove's warnings. On a hunch, he then opened Paddy's file and found another reference there.

He found nothing in Colette's file – it looked as if it hadn't been updated and he wondered if that was deliberate – and there was only one oblique reference in the mother's records. The file noted her background in surprising detail, recording the effect of the death of her youngest son Sean in the late 1970s. It said:

'Foxglove' has reported that there are severe tensions within the McVeigh family. Despite having been born into a Republican family, Mrs McVeigh seems to have been driven firmly away from violence by the death of her youngest son, Sean, at the hands of the Army. Her stance – in contrast to that of her oldest son – has caused repeated clashes. This is exacerbated by the death of the father from cancer four years ago. Gerry McVeigh is said to be trying to pursue the legacy of his father, a notoriously hardline Republican.

Ryan leaned back in his seat again and tapped his pencil on the desk.

His own father had died of cancer. He thought of Colette living through what he'd had to endure.

It left him with a strange sensation – a sudden sense of affinity when no new intimacies had been wanted.

He wondered if she missed her father as much as he did his own.

He flicked idly through some of the rest of the files and was just about to finish when one in particular caught his eye, reminding him of Allen's comment and the reason why he was here in the first place.

Somehow, he already knew.

The file was headed simply 'England'. He opened it

and froze. The room was cold, but the shock made him sweat. He mumbled quietly, 'Oh God.'

Ryan woke the next morning a few minutes before his alarm went off. The first shards of sunlight were filtering in through a gap in the curtains and, for once, it was easy to get up. He hadn't slept well.

He stood, naked, in the middle of the room and rummaged around in the brown duffel bag that he still hadn't unpacked. His running kit was wrapped in a plastic bag and was thus easy to find. When he pulled it out, the stench was terrible. His shorts and lycra boxer shorts were still damp with sweat from the last run weeks before and he winced as he pulled them on. He found a dirty T-shirt at the bottom of the bag and pulled a large, warm, Adidas sweatshirt over the top.

He picked up his cigarettes from the bedside table and walked out to the car, which started first time. He drove up past the House of Sport and then turned right into the car park by the river. It was a beautiful morning and there were already plenty of cars parked here. As he got out, he saw a man in a tweed hat strolling up towards him with a young boxer on a lead. As Ryan began his jog, the dog lunged playfully at him and he stroked its head briefly.

Then he was down by the Lagan and watching the smooth waters of the river. As the path and the river bent round to the left, he tried to relax. He knew he was angry, but somehow it seemed hard to tie in a slim, pretty woman with so much of his own family's suffering. He wondered if he should want to punish her. He thought about the other tout – Foxglove, or whatever his name was. He thought it would be so easy to punish her, to let her go.

It took him about twelve minutes to get up to the

bridge over the Lagan and then he crossed over it and ran back on the other side. There were quite a few people out now, running, walking their dogs, and he found it an oddly pleasurable experience to be out doing something resolutely normal. Eventually he caught sight of the old road bridge back over the river and sprinted the last couple of hundred yards. He spent a few minutes bent double, recovering his breath, and then he got into the car and switched on the radio. It was just before nine.

He found himself thinking of Gerry McVeigh in a new light. He found it hard not to empathize with a man pursuing the legacy of his father.

The news came on just as he was passing the House of Sport, but there was nothing dramatic. A couple of coffee-jar bombs in Derry and a failed mortar attack in Crossmaglen. No casualties.

As he pulled back into Malone Beeches, he heard Gerry Adams giving an interview demanding clarification of the peace declaration.

Inside the house he showered quickly and ate a bowl of cereal before nearly making himself sick with a cigarette. At about a quarter to ten he got back into the car and drove down to Castlereagh. As a concession to what the police usually wore, he'd put on a half-respectable pair of blue jeans and a tweed jacket.

The traffic was heavy and it took him nearly half an hour to get across town to Castlereagh. He showed the men on the gate his ID and then parked round the back. He waited in reception for about twenty minutes for Allen, though he thought he was approaching the stage where he might be able to go in on his own.

When he arrived, Allen looked his usual dishevelled self and, as they stepped into the corridor, Ryan asked him quietly, 'How did you know?'

Allen looked puzzled and Ryan expanded, 'The business in England. I looked at the files.'

Allen stopped dead. The corridor was empty. 'I'm afraid I didn't,' he said. 'It was a guess. I've seen *your* file. I remembered the case and saw your mother's maiden name.' He shrugged his shoulders. 'I'm sorry, I've got a memory like an elephant. A brother?'

'Uncle.' Ryan took out his cigarettes and played absent-mindedly with the packet, twisting it through his fingers.

Allen leaned forward. 'I'm sorry. I really am.'

Ryan sighed. 'It's all right. What does it mean?'

'It means nothing. It doesn't change anything. Use it.'

It was Ryan's turn to look puzzled.

'Perhaps she has a conscience,' Allen said.

'I thought you said they never repented.'

Allen shrugged his shoulders. 'Everyone has a conscience.'

Allen turned. He walked down the corridor and Ryan followed him in silence. Before they got to the end, Ryan asked, 'Who is Foxglove?'

Allen stopped again. He was smiling. 'I think you know better than to ask that.'

'But you know?'

'I might do.'

'Why can't you give a straight answer?'

'Because then you'd never let up.'

'Belfast Brigade staff?'

Allen smiled. 'See what I mean?'

'Come on, Brian, for fuck's sake . . .'

Allen touched his arm. He was standing close to him and Ryan could smell his breath. 'Sometimes the best touts are players,' he said. 'But they have their drawbacks. When they know something and we act

271

upon it, sometimes the leak is easily traced back to them. So what I'm saying is that sometimes it's people close to those that count who make the best touts. Don't know everything, maybe, but less open to suspicion because they're not meant to know in the first place – like our woman and that attack on Henderson.'

'So?'

Allen laughed and turned away again. 'That's all I'm saying.'

'Arsehole,' Ryan said and Allen laughed again.

They were at the source unit now and Allen turned in. The chief inspector was standing there, smoking and looking, Ryan thought, rather older than the last time he'd seen him. He thought this was a job that would age you very rapidly. He sat down and leaned back in the seat. He found himself staring at the wall ahead of him, which was covered by a huge map of the greater Belfast region. The map was littered with pins and and pen marks.

Ryan looked at the map and found his eyes drawn to the cubby holes on the left of it. There were about twenty or thirty in all, but two caught his attention – the two biggest holes nearest to the map.

One had 'Shadow Dancer' written under it. The other had 'Foxglove'.

The room was thick with smoke and Ryan felt so choked he had no desire to smoke himself.

The chief inspector opened the file on his desk and blew a plume of smoke into the air above him. 'Not much specific at the moment,' he said. 'Not much activity in her area as far as we can tell – a lot of operations on hold because of fear of a tout . . .' The chief inspector looked up and grinned before continuing. 'We are looking out for some arms coming in over the next few weeks – a collection of AK-Ms, some hand-guns, semtex – because they appear to be running short, but otherwise it's mostly just a question of pushing her hard – really hard – on the internal mechanics of what is happening at the moment. We know the hardliners are very unhappy, Gerry McVeigh a leader among them, and we really need to push everyone so that we can start trying to nail down where we're going.'

The chief inspector took another long drag on his cigarette, smiled at them again and pointed at the ceiling. 'I can tell you, the pressure for information is getting pretty heavy at the moment, so don't be afraid to lean on her . . .'

The briefing lasted a few more minutes and then Allen suddenly looked at his watch and stood up. As he did so, Ryan felt a brief surge of adrenalin. He followed Allen downstairs and into the front of a waiting grey Granada. He noticed they had no driver this time.

Allen took them down Castlereagh Road and, as they passed Central Station, he smiled. 'I think we need to do a bit of work on our woman.'

Ryan frowned at him.

'Have you got your walking shoes?'

Ryan nodded slowly.

'I thought we might take our woman on a little walk. Reassure her. Win her over. You know what they say about this game; it's a battle for hearts and minds.'

Ryan didn't respond.

They waited for Colette in a quiet cul-de-sac opposite the headquarters of Northern Ireland Electricity, just off the Malone Road. Allen had a small radio in his hand and the two back-up Land Rovers were hidden out of sight round the corner.

The surveillance teams were out, ready to 'clean' her

approach, and their voices were clipped and urgent on the radio.

Colette walked into the hall to get Mark's coat and, as she pulled it off its hook, she heard Catherine crying. She came back to the front room. 'What have you done, Mark?' she asked.

'He punched m–m–m–me . . .' Catherine said.

Colette sighed and stepped forward, holding out Mark's coat. He held his arms stiffly by his side and refused to put them in the sleeves.

'Come on, Mark,' she said.

He didn't budge.

She crouched down, gripped his arms and shook him. 'Come on,' she said. 'What on earth is wrong with you?'

He looked at her sulkily.

'Look, that's enough.' She felt a momentary sense of panic. 'Mummy is late, so put this on, please – and stop bullying your sister.'

He didn't move.

'Mark! Put this on. Now!' She took his arms and forced them into the anorak sleeves. She turned to see her mother standing in the doorway. 'Are you still OK to pick them up later?' Colette asked.

Her mother nodded. 'Where are you going? Why don't you take them with you?'

'I'm just going into town, but I can't—'

'Oh, go on, they haven't been down for—'

'I think it's better this way, Ma. Just as long as you're all right to—'

'Take them with you.'

'I *can't*, Ma.' Colette could tell there was tension in her voice now. 'Look, I just don't know how long I'm going to be, all right?' She looked up, saw the doubt and uncertainty – and irritation – in her mother's eyes, took hold of Catherine and Mark, and more or less dragged them out of the front door.

She walked quickly round to Margaret's and gave them a brief hug before catching a taxi down to the city centre. As she got out and began the long walk up to the Malone Road, she felt guilt and fear in about equal measures.

She felt foul. The guilt was pervasive. She resented Mark again for not understanding, but why in the hell should he? She told herself she had no choice, but at the back of her mind she felt . . .

Well, if she didn't have a choice, why did she feel guilty?

As she passed Queen's University she looked at her watch and realized how late she was going to be. She felt a sense of panic and began to run.

She ran quickly to begin with, then slowed to a walk as she passed Eglantine Avenue, then started to jog again as she passed the garage. She was out of breath and she knew the fuckers wouldn't understand.

She walked the last fifty yards or so and felt the dampness in her armpits. As she turned the corner into Stranmillis, she saw the grey Granada. Its engine was running, the fumes puffing slowly out of the exhaust.

She opened the nearside back door and got in. Her man was sitting in the passenger seat, the big Prod was driving. The Prod turned to her. 'You're late,' he said.

She leaned back in her seat and closed her eyes.

'You're *late*,' he said again, with greater menace.

She sighed loudly. 'For fuck's sake—'

'All right,' Ryan said. He looked over the corner of the seat. 'All right. Lateness just spells danger, that's all.'

'Lateness just spells two kids who won't do what they're told,' she replied.

She looked out of the window. They were silent for a moment and she watched a young woman wheeling her pram along the pavement beside her.

The Prod turned to her. 'We have some work to do. Do you have any commitments?'

Colette didn't understand.

'Is anyone expecting you?'

She shook her head. 'Ma. The kids. I said I'd be back for tea.'

The Prod spoke quietly into the radio, dismissing the back-up units and then he drove. He took them up to the ring road and then down through Saintfield to Ballynahinch and beyond. At two o'clock in the afternoon, the traffic was relatively light.

Colette didn't understand what they were doing or where they were going. The Brit turned several times to look at her, but his face was impassive and, when she smiled at him, he didn't smile back.

As they travelled further and further away from Belfast, she felt a growing sense of unease. She thought of challenging them but realized she was effectively their prisoner.

Without the Brit, she'd have been frightened.

She realized she was foolish to rely on him. What logical reason was there to trust any of them? They were still the enemy.

They passed the small holiday town of Newcastle and climbed around the coast road that stretched south towards the Republic of Ireland. It was a beautiful day, the winter sun streaming dramatically through the rolling clouds, bringing a brilliant light to the sea and to the green hills that ran down to meet it.

They followed the coast road for about 5 miles and then the Prod, Allen, turned right to head inland. A mile further on, he stopped in a lay-by at the turn of the road. He looked over his shoulder at Colette. 'I hope you like walking.'

She didn't reply. Allen pointed to a path on their right. 'It's all right.'

Colette didn't move. She was frightened now.

'It's all right,' Ryan said. But he stared at her grimly. She followed them tentatively along the track. The ground was slightly damp beneath their feet and her white trainers were getting covered in mud. She wondered how she would explain that to her mother.

Fifty yards down the track they turned towards the mountain and began to climb upwards, following a neat stone wall surrounding a green field that was full of sheep. They were out of the sun now, the wood on their left ensuring the path was still cold from the overnight frost.

The track was steep and Ryan led, with Allen falling behind in the rear. After a few hundred yards, Ryan stopped to catch his breath and they both looked back. The fields were still a bright, light green and the sea a brilliant blue. Beneath them, rows of neat stone walls divided up the plots of land and gave the scene a sense of order and purpose. They waited for Allen in silence.

When he caught up with them he was out of breath. 'Sorry, I'm bloody unfit. You go on.'

Ryan looked at him quizzically, but Allen waved his hand airily as if to say, Go on, get on with it.

They walked again.

Above them, the Mourne Wall stretched up through the valley, a wide, solid edifice which must have taken years to build. She wondered what the point of it was, if such things needed to have a point.

For perhaps ten minutes they walked in silence, him stretching out ahead of her, but eventually slackening his pace to allow her to catch up. They had reached the brow of the first small hill and the track began to slope down before picking up for the mountain ahead of them.

'What's going on?' she asked.

He pointed back down the hill. 'One of his stupid games.'

She didn't respond and for a few minutes they picked their way down the path in silence. Then Ryan turned on her suddenly. 'We're here because I read your file,' he said.

She didn't understand.

'There is one section marked England. Ring any bells?'

She shook her head.

'Well, it should. You were in London during the summer of 1982.'

So? she thought.

'I suppose you'll deny involvement.'

'In what?'

A note of exasperation had crept into her voice. He spat the words out. '*Hyde Park.*'

She didn't reply.

'I remember that summer well. It was hot, I remember, very hot for England. Lying out on the grass, carefree – until that day. My mother's face was white, like she'd seen a ghost.'

She looked away from him.

'Why, Colette? What did my uncle ever do to hurt you? He was a kind, decent man and you murdered him. You watched his troop pass every day. You made your notes and then you blew them to bits.'

She looked up. 'Look, I'm sorry. I didn't know who he was, but we've all suff—'

Ryan took a step forwards, shouting her down. 'You're damned right you didn't know who he was! Well, I'll tell you, he wasn't a soldier to me and my mother. And he wasn't a soldier to his wife and two children. You want to know about his children, Colette?'

She shook her head angrily.

'Two tiny children. About the same age as yours. One five, one four. And do you want to know what they do now? They still cry for their father in their bloody sleep. And for what? Just tell me what makes it all worthwhile?'

'Don't lecture me.' She pointed her finger at him. 'I said I'm sorry about your uncle, but he's not the only one. I didn't notice any of your people crying when they shot down Davey in a stinking churchyard.'

'He had a gun in his hand.'

'And that makes it all right?'

'It's not the same.'

'Oh, and what about the boy you and your soldier friends gunned down? Declan Walshe. He didn't have a gun, did he? He wasn't even a *provo*!' She was screaming at him now. 'Oh yes, don't worry, I know about you.'

'That was a mistake.'

'A mistake? Oh, *please*.' Colette kicked a stone in frustration. 'The men in Hyde Park, they were soldiers. They died. That's the way it is. That's the war.'

Ryan pointed at her. 'It's *your* war.'

He turned to walk away, but she yelled at him. 'It's *my* war? It's *my* war?' She ran after him and pulled his shoulder, catching him off balance and sending him tumbling to the ground. As he scrambled to his feet, she shouted at him again, her voice steeled with controlled aggression. 'I didn't put soldiers on the streets. I didn't

279

shoot unarmed protesters demanding their legitimate rights. I didn't bash down people's doors and get them out of their beds in the middle of the night. I didn't torture people and beat them and harass them . . .' Her voice had reached a crescendo. 'This is my country and you've got no right to be here, so don't ever – *ever* – say this is *my* war.'

She brushed past him and ran. The path started to climb gently again and she soon grew tired and slowed to a walk. A hundred yards on, she veered to the left and climbed onto the top of the Mourne Wall and continued walking along it.

Fucking Brits, she thought.

As she walked, the anger and hatred dissipated.

She looked around her. To her left, the white clouds clawed their way along the ridge, fringed by the golden light of the sun as it sunk slowly towards the horizon. The sky above was still bright blue. It was beautiful here, as dramatic as anywhere she'd ever been. It felt peaceful, but it didn't help to clear her mind.

She couldn't have said definitively how long they walked like that, but it might have been an hour. When she finally stopped, they were between the mountains, the wall stretching away behind them like an umbilical cord attached to the sea below. The wind had got up and, as she watched him approach, she felt the first flecks of rain on her face. It was getting cold and dark rapidly. Neither of them had coats. As he approached, she sat down on the edge of the wall and he sat beside her.

Neither of them spoke.

She realized that it was a comfortable silence. She didn't want him to move. She thought she would have spoken to stop him walking back.

He put his hands down, as though he was about to jump down. 'I'm sorry,' she said quietly. 'You don't have to believe me, but I am sorry.'

'I believe you.' He looked ahead at the mountain that was fading to an outline against the darkening sky.

'You'll get your revenge.'

He turned to face her. 'What do you mean?'

'I'll not survive long. I'll end up somewhere like this. Barefoot. Hooded. Dead. When I'm thinking straight, I know it.'

She didn't meet his eye.

'That's not true.'

'It is and you know it.'

'No, it's not.'

She sighed deeply. 'You'll keep me alive as long as I'm of use to you and then, one day, bang.' She clicked her fingers.

'That's not true.'

She looked him in the eye for the first time. She felt the butterflies in her stomach.

'You don't have to believe me,' he said, 'but—'

'I'm not stupid. I know what you think of me. When the time comes, you'll get your revenge.'

'I don't think of you like that. You said you're sorry. I accept that.'

She was frowning at him. 'I know what you think. You're all the same.'

Ryan pointed down the hill. 'Maybe he thinks that, but I don't.'

She leaned a little closer to him. His cheeks were red from the cold and his hair damp from the drizzle. She had an almost irresistible urge to place her head on his shoulder.

She looked into his face. There was a drop of rain on the end of his nose, and his hair and eyebrows looked

281

even darker than usual. She wanted to touch his broken nose and put her hand to his cheek.

He looked at her without smiling. His stare was mesmerizing.

She thought he would kiss her. She told herself she would refuse.

He turned away and pushed himself off the wall.

He held out a hand to her. She wanted to swear at him. She jumped down without taking it.

He walked, putting his hands in his pockets. The sky was darkening rapidly now and she had to look carefully at the ground ahead of her. She felt somehow deflated. Empty.

They walked in silence.

As they came back to the brow of the first hill she slipped and he caught her, holding on to her arm, she thought, for a fraction of a second longer than he needed to, without looking at her face. She wondered now if her mind was playing tricks on her.

'You're not one of them,' he said quietly.

She stopped suddenly. 'Don't kid yourself. Is it easier to accept if I'm not?'

He was standing just above her. 'I don't think you have what it takes, that's all.'

She sneered at him. 'And what does it take, Mr Man-from-MI5?'

'It takes hatred. It takes ignorance. It takes ruthlessness.'

She turned and began walking. 'You're very sure of yourself.'

He didn't reply and they fell silent again. The cloud had cleared slightly and they were able to move faster, the path ahead lit by the moon. They were coming to the point where they'd left Allen.

She stopped dead. She suddenly had a clear mental

282

image of Martin Mulgrew and it panicked her. 'They're close to me,' she said.

'Why do you say that?'

He was standing near her, above her on the hill. The light was fading behind him and she couldn't see his face clearly.

She leaned slowly towards his chest, wanting the reassuring warmth of human contact, and was relieved when he didn't push her away.

After a few seconds' pause, as if to emphasize he would respond only reluctantly, he put his arms around her.

'It's so frightening,' she said. 'Christ, it's so frightening. I convince myself I'm OK and then . . .' Her voice trailed off. She was crying. He was gripping her tightly now.

'You're all right,' he said. 'I understand your fear, but they're nowhere near you—'

'They are—'

'They're not. You're not the only one. Others have been going for years and they may be near one of them, but they're not near you. If they were, we'd know it.'

He held her tightly and she cried in silent disbelief – only half reassured, but aware that half was better than nothing. He stood her up and brushed the tears from her eyes with the sleeve of his sweater; the action seeming absurdly kind. 'Are you all right?' he asked.

She wanted to say no, so that this would continue, but was afraid of his anger. She nodded uncertainly and they began to walk again.

As they arrived back at the car, Allen was leaning on the bonnet with his legs crossed. He got in and started up without a word. For the first ten minutes, they drove on in silence.

They passed through Newcastle and, as they drew

level with the pathway through to Murlough Bay, the National Trust Reserve, Allen pulled over to the side of the road and indicated to Ryan that he should drive. They got out and Allen went to sit in the back.

'Any developments?' Allen asked carefully.

Silence. Ryan looked over his shoulder anxiously.

'Colette?' Allen's voice was soft.

'There's been a meeting,' she said firmly. 'You must know already. The leadership came down for what they called a briefing. Strange mix of people there. It was kind of by word of mouth, but only people of a certain stature and experience.'

'Who was there?' Allen asked. She could tell he wasn't going to confirm that they already knew about the meeting.

She paused for a second, as if consciously trying to recall the details. 'Gerry was there – did a lot of talking. Paddy, Sean Fox from Fermanagh—'

'He came a long way,' Ryan interjected.

'I'm telling you what I saw,' Colette said testily. 'There were plenty of significant people there from all over. Murphy from south Armagh, Mallon from east Tyrone.'

'What did they think?' Allen asked.

Colette shook her head. 'They didn't say anything. Fox queried a number of points, but I got the impression he was not opposed to the peace process in principle. He just wanted them to be sure they knew what they were doing, said he didn't want them changing their minds. In private, they're all being told that a secret deal is being struck with the Brits.'

'Do they believe that?'

She shrugged her shoulders. 'Some do, some don't.'

'Who else spoke?' Allen asked.

'Gerry.'

284

'What did he say?'

'Said he thought the whole thing was a mistake.'

'Did people agree with him?'

'Hard to say. I didn't wait around to ask them.'

'There's something else, isn't there?'

Colette shrugged. 'When I got home, Gerry was talking to Murphy in the front hall,' she said. 'I only heard a few seconds of what they said, but it was something like, "We've got to do it," or, "We have to do it now."'

Allen whistled under his breath. Ryan turned to smile at her. She felt weak. She didn't meet his eye.

Allen touched her arm. 'Is there word of a tout?'

She nodded and Allen went on, 'Any ideas who it is?'

She shook her head.

Allen rubbed her arm. 'You're all right. You're all right.'

She shut her eyes and kept them shut. After a few minutes, Allen clambered into the front passenger seat. Eventually she heard the two men talking quietly.

'Think there is a secret deal?' Allen asked.

'No,' Ryan said.

They were silent for a few minutes and then she heard Allen say, 'There's plenty of ours who're prepared to believe there is.'

'Why?' Ryan asked.

'There's plenty who believe the perfidious Brits are ready to sell us out to stop their beloved capital being bombed.'

'Are you one of them?' Ryan asked.

'I don't know,' he said and then they were silent. Colette opened her eyes briefly and saw they were entering Belfast. Despite everything, she almost smiled. Gerry and the Prod were the most unlikely potential allies she could think of.

* * *

Magee was new. They'd met at Trafalgar Square – McVeigh's orders, given via the travel agency – and then walked down here to Westminster Bridge.

They were leaning over the bridge, looking at what McIlhatton knew to be Stranger's Terrace.

'It's a long drop down to the water,' McIlhatton said and Magee grunted.

They were silent for a while as both went on looking. McIlhatton didn't like this bit of the plan. In fact, there were lots of bits that made him nervous, but this was the worst.

'They'll have to go into the water and you'll have to pull them out,' McIlhatton said, eventually.

Magee grunted again.

'The boat is sorted?' he asked, finally.

'Yes,' Magee said.

They moved off, strolling over towards St Thomas's Hospital.

CHAPTER FOURTEEN

It was her time of the month. at last, it had come.

Well, she thought, at least you're not pregnant. The idea of having Chico's baby made her shiver. What in the hell had she been thinking of?

She had always suffered badly, but a lifetime's experience and endurance had failed to bring any real sense of perspective to the feelings that washed over her at this time. She had such a strong memory of Davey's reaction. He'd always dealt with it the same way, trying to reason or shout her out of it, depending on his mood. Until there was drink taken. Then he'd tried to beat it out of her.

He wasn't a bad man, she still told herself, but she remembered with a shudder the nights spent curled up on her bed feeling like the world had come to an end – wanting a way out and yet not wanting it – Davey snoring after he'd fucked her. It was always a fucking after there'd been drink taken.

She looked across at Gerry and wondered if he was the same with Christy. Probably. He was like Davey, except without the moments of kindness.

Gerry had barely spoken since they left Belfast. He'd come round to the house just after lunch and asked her

287

to come with him. She hadn't really been able to say no. She wondered if that was guilt, but knew herself well enough to recognize that not being able to say no to Gerry was a problem that went back a lot further than this morning.

They'd been to a house just outside the south Armagh village of Crossmaglen to see Murphy, the head of the IRA's South Armagh Brigade. She'd stayed in the car, there only as cover should they run into an army patrol manning a temporary vehicle checkpoint. They were, Gerry told her, brother and sister going to see an uncle who was sick and confined to bed. He wanted company because he'd been caught alone by the soldiers too often.

She'd asked about the meeting once already, trying to probe, and had received only a grunt in reply. She couldn't make small talk with Gerry and never had been able to. They had, she realized, absolutely nothing in common bar the accident of circumstances that had seen them born into the same family. Sometimes she thought she hated him.

She felt awful. Today, her problems seemed too immense. The worst thing about it was the loneliness. She felt totally and utterly isolated. She wanted to unload her burdens onto a sympathetic soul and she wanted to talk and have someone listen. Nothing in her life had prepared her for this because she'd never been alone before. The world in which she'd lived was a community, above all else, with uncles and aunts and friends creating a social network that spanned across west Belfast and beyond. Even in prison in Armagh she'd been surrounded by her own. She'd hated the loss of freedom, but the women around her were Republicans who shared her beliefs and concerns.

Now there was nobody. She'd thought about telling

her mother, but she knew it was impossible. Her mother's opposition to violent Republicanism did not stretch to a toleration of touting. She could not be sure, absolutely sure, that she wouldn't go to Gerry or Paddy, and tell them to sort it out. She'd looked around in vain for someone to talk to. She knew that was why she was drawn to the Brit. For the moment, her family felt like strangers.

Sometimes, rarely, she was able to focus on all this and understand it. But not today. Today, she felt desperate. This morning, as she'd lain in bed trying to summon the will to get up, she'd briefly contemplated talking to little Mark and Catherine. It was lunacy, she knew, but at least they'd listen. At least somebody would hear her.

They'd taken the Newry Road from Crossmaglen and were winding through the valleys of south Armagh, the sun falling dramatically below the snowy hilltops. On each one stood a British army watchtower painted cold, dark green. Colette felt almost sorry for the Brits, who spent their lives miles away from home, watching the comings and goings of cars along the floor of the valley. She had no doubt that, up there, somebody was watching them.

The thought came to her suddenly and it made her heart miss a beat. She knew it was insane, but she felt on the verge of suicide. It was an easy way out. The Republican movement always said it would forgive those who came forward. She understood her family would hate her, make her life a living death, but she couldn't stop the thoughts and they came tumbling forward.

'Gerry?' She realized her voice was trembling. He was preoccupied and grunted abstractedly. 'What would you think if . . .'

She stopped.

He turned to look at her briefly. 'Yes. If what?'

She realized Gerry still frightened her. Even now. 'Do you believe in God?'

He snorted, as if incredulous. 'No.' He looked at her again. 'Why?'

'Nothing. I know Ma wants us to, that's all.'

'Ma wants a lot of things that are never going to happen.'

Colette said nothing and the silence drew out. She knew instinctively the moment had passed.

'Where are we going?'

He frowned. 'Back to Bel—'

'No, I mean where are we going in general? What's happening?' Her nerve had failed her and she was glad it had. Gerry had never opened up to her. He was talking to her, but she was no longer listening. She just couldn't understand what made him tick. She didn't understand how anyone could be so utterly obsessed with the idea that you could still beat the Brits into submission after all this time.

She was sinking back into the depths of her despair when she saw a small red light on the road ahead. The sun had dropped below the hilltops and it was dark in the lane. She could only just make out the shapes of the soldiers. Gerry muttered under his breath, 'Fuck. That's all we need.'

He braked hard and the car skidded briefly before coming to a halt. He wound down the window, but said nothing. A man shone his torch in their eyes.

'Good evening. Papers, please.'

It was a command not a request and Colette thought the man sounded just like Ryan. She thought they were always so bloody arrogant, the officers. Gerry reached for his inside pocket and she rummaged in her handbag. Eventually she found her driving licence and gave it to Gerry, who handed it through the window without a word.

'Nice evening.' The man was smiling, the light from the torch now illuminating his face.

Gerry smiled back. 'Nice enough.'

'Long way from home. What would you be doing in these hostile parts?'

'Just visiting relatives.'

'Relatives, eh? And who would they be?'

'Crossmaglen way.'

The man lowered his voice. 'I said who, not where.'

'Hughes. Uncle. He's a bit poorly.'

'Is he now? Is he indeed? I *am* sorry to hear that.'

Gerry ignored the man's sarcasm and looked straight ahead. He'd been at this too long to allow himself to be provoked.

'Give me a few minutes, please.'

The man turned his back and walked a few yards to talk to someone who'd been waiting behind him. Colette couldn't hear what they were saying. Gerry stared straight ahead as if he were a dummy. He said nothing, but Colette could just make out his facial muscles twitching nervously. She wondered what they had in the car that might be making Gerry nervous.

The men went on talking for what seemed like an age. Finally, the officer turned and walked back towards them. He opened Gerry's door and Colette felt the first stirrings of fear and anxiety.

'Please step out, if you wouldn't mind.'

Colette noticed the change in his tone. She sensed danger. She got out too and walked round to the other side of the car. She felt safer next to Gerry. The officer turned to the men behind him. 'OK, lads, take it apart.'

They set to work on the car, but the officer stayed

watching them. The man he'd been talking to still lurked in the background, several yards behind him. Colette couldn't work out what was going on. The man in front of them was, to her mind, clearly the officer, and yet he seemed to be deferring to the soldier behind him. Without taking his eyes off them, the officer took a few paces back. Colette could feel a chill running down her spine. The voice of the man behind froze her. A tough voice; northern English, she thought. Not the accent of an officer. The man came forward, smiling. An unnerving smile. He had a short but unkempt beard and she could clearly see that he was not a regular soldier. SAS, she thought. But there was only one and that confused her.

'Remember me?' he said. She didn't. He was looking at Gerry. 'Not your lucky day, Mr McVeigh.'

The threat was unmistakable. He was still smiling. Gerry looked straight ahead and carefully avoided catching his eye.

'No, very definitely not your lucky day. I don't suppose you would remember me, but in a previous incarnation I used to work in your neck of the woods. I have some pictures of that time. Not really your regular holiday snaps. No. See, there's one of my mate, John. Regular kind of guy; the two of us joined together, made corporals together.'

He had circled behind them. Gerry continued to look straight ahead. Colette could see that the muscles in his face were twitching violently.

'So there we were. The two of us together, growing up together, thought we'd grow old together. But, of course, we didn't reckon with your boys, did we? Didn't reckon on your boys blowing his bloody legs off—'

'Watch yourself, Brit.' Gerry's voice was steady.

'Watch myself? Watch myself? You piece of pig-shit.' He kicked Gerry hard across the back of his legs, an expert blow that brought him to his knees.

Fear, confusion and panic made Colette turn and shout, 'For Christ's sake—'

The man shouted back, his face twisted into a sneer and his finger pointing at her face, 'Stay there, you little fuck.'

She stopped, unsure of herself, and looking to Gerry to lead. The man took a quick step forward and punched Gerry hard on the side of the head and sent him sprawling to the ground. He kicked him in the stomach twice. Hard. Colette wanted to scream, but she stood rooted to the spot. She didn't know what to do. Gerry was groaning.

The man pulled Gerry's head up by his hair, leaving his glasses on the tarmac. He stepped on them and the sound made Colette wince. It seemed more hateful and more gratuitous than the blows.

For a few seconds, Colette thought it was over, but she saw now that the man was holding a pistol to Gerry's head, the barrel pressing into his skull.

'This is it, you little fuck. We're going to blow your fucking brains out and take your body over the border. And you know what we're going to do? We're going to put a hood on you and then we're going to take off your nice new training shoes and your family will think you've been shot by your own side for being a bloody little tout.'

Colette blanched at the word. She'd thought this was harassment, but it was starting to get out of hand. The man was unhinged. She thought he might do it, but she felt powerless to intervene. She didn't move. Gerry was obviously frightened now too. He'd sensed the man's tone. He knew he wasn't regular army. He was into unfamiliar territory and he didn't know what to expect.

'Apologize, you bloody little bastard. Apologize for being born.'

They were on their own, the three of them. The officer had deliberately walked away and the soldiers in the patrol were pulling the car apart. They were only a few yards down the road, but they were acting as if the tableau in front of them didn't exist.

She heard Gerry's voice. He was speaking quietly. 'I apologize. I apologize for being born.' His voice was level, not defiant, not craven.

'Apologize nicely and I might just decide to let you live.'

The man kneed him hard in the back and Gerry groaned. He sounded weaker. 'OK, I'm sorry. I'm sorry I was born.'

Colette had never seen Gerry like this, never thought he had a weakness, let alone exhibited one. She was shocked. The man was whispering in his ear. 'Now, I'm going to let you go, Mr McVeigh, but if I ever run into you again, I'll kill you. Do you understand me?'

Gerry nodded.

'I said, do you understand me?'

'I understand you.'

'Right. That's better. You're learning. And remember, the man with the gun has the power, and it isn't always going to be you that has the gun . . .'

The man stepped back and the officer stepped forward. He handed Gerry their driving licences. 'I'm sorry to have inconvenienced you, sir.' A polite voice; self-confident, mocking.

Colette made as if to drive, but Gerry waved her away contemptuously, got into the driver's seat and started up the car again, pulling off slowly. Colette was too stunned to speak and they drove on in silence. As they turned back onto the main road after Newry, Gerry looked at her again. 'Fucking bastards. Thought it was all over there for a second.'

Colette didn't know what to say, so she reached over and touched his shoulder. 'Are you all right?'

'Yes.' He turned to her and smiled – a warm, soft smile. 'By the way . . .' He paused and appeared to take a deep breath. 'I'm sorry . . . Look, I'm sorry about the other day, all right?'

Colette looked at him uncertainly, but didn't reply. She couldn't remember the last time she'd seen him like this. But then, she'd never seen him humbled – humiliated – like that before.

'I know I was out of line shouting and swearing at you.' He reached over and touched her leg. 'We've all been under pressure. I know it's no excuse, but . . .' His voice trailed off and they went on in silence for a few minutes, both of them staring intently at the road ahead.

'I know it's been a long time,' Gerry said eventually, 'but I still think about Sean. Sometimes it's so real. I can feel him in my arms, I can see his little face, I can feel the texture of his hair, some of it matted with blood. I just can't . . . I'm sorry, all right?' He was looking at her again now, and he reached out to touch her leg once more. 'I know you're no coward. It's just for him. Understand?'

There were many replies Colette could have given, but she did not speak. She didn't know what she felt. Sympathy and warmth, perhaps, but anger too. She wanted to ask him how many more Seans it was going to take. Then she heard herself ask how long he thought the war would go on.

He stared at the road ahead and shook his head. 'I don't know,' he said. 'I don't know. But I tell you this:

forget the bullshit talk of this peace process. At the end of the day, one side has got to win. That's what it's about. Whilst we go on, we *are* winning, because our will to fight is stronger and more durable than their will to resist, or so it will prove.' Gerry was driving with one hand on the steering wheel now and gesticulating with the other. 'And when I hear the likes of Gerry Adams, I say to myself, remember what Dad said. Never trust the Brits. Never. At the end of the day, their agenda is the antithesis of ours. And just because the enemy may try to develop a human face, that doesn't make him any less your enemy.'

Gerry looked at her. 'You tell me, Colette. Would you ever trust a Brit?'

She looked out of the window at the passing hedgerows and shook her head. They were silent for several minutes.

'You know what you were saying earlier?' he asked eventually.

Colette looked at him blankly.

'About where we are going.'

'Yes.'

'We're going for surrender. At least we are unless I have anything to do with it. That was what I was down here for today.'

She didn't know what to say, so she said nothing.

'I have in mind something that will make the leadership sit up and take notice. Something that will force them to change course. I have support from people who count, but I need a little help from people I can absolutely rely on. People who won't talk and won't question. Paddy is with me. Will you help me? There's nobody else I trust.'

She heard herself say yes. 'What are you going to do?' she asked.

296

'Something big,' he said. 'Something in England. That's all I can tell you.'

She felt cold inside. 'What do you want me to do?' she asked quietly.

'Just be ready,' he said. 'It'll only take a few days. That's all I'll say.'

The bar was full. Wall-to-wall advertising executives, Ryan thought, and a lot of them gay.

Normally, he couldn't have cared less, but tonight he could have done without the welcoming stares.

Initially, the relief had been intense. He'd been told to take a few days off and as they'd driven down into the centre of London he'd felt like a man returning to civilization, watching the smart cafés and cars, and seeing people who disliked their neighbours but didn't hate them. It had never felt so good to be home. He'd felt wonderful.

Until now. Now he felt like a stranger, surrounded by the familiar, but no longer a part of it. What did they know, these people? With all their talk of accounts and sales and careers and satisfaction, what did they know of a woman whose life hung by a thread? What did they know of his predicament and of his world? He felt petulant, like a child. He wanted these people to look at him and to know what he did. He wanted them to sympathize, to understand. He wanted them to know he was out there fucking up his mind so they could sit here and drink in safety. He felt ignored.

He leaned forward, but still couldn't hear what Isabelle was saying. She'd insisted on coming here – a date with a girlfriend arranged long ago that she wouldn't contemplate cancelling. The girl was called Charlotte, but with the music and the noise he couldn't hear what the hell they were saying. He sat there in isolation, looking at the moonlike shapes on the wall and trying to avoid eye contact with any of the other customers. He thought these London bars looked like they were on some kind of pan-European convergence course. They were all identical, with their chrome bars and tall pillars. He decided he could have been any-where: Paris, Madrid, Brussels. Anywhere except Belfast.

Afterwards they wandered down Westbourne Grove in Notting Hill and ate at a small Thai restaurant tucked into a side street just past the 7-Eleven shop on the corner. They always ate here and they were always alone. Ryan didn't know how the owners survived.

The dinner seemed to drag. Mostly, they talked about mutual friends. Ryan couldn't bring himself to say any-thing about life in Belfast, though he wanted to let it all out. He knew if he started, he'd be going all night, and he wasn't sure she would understand.

Sitting opposite her, he felt less than perfect. She was a lovely girl, but just not *him*.

He insisted on paying and they went back to her home.

They made love. He'd known they were going to, though he'd convinced himself that wasn't why he'd arranged to see her.

Afterwards, he felt deflated and thought she did too. Her bedroom was on the top floor of the house, but the curtains were open and the moon provided a gentle night light. They lay silently in the half-darkness.

Eventually she sat up and looked at him. 'What's it really like over there, David?' she asked.

'Cynical,' he said. 'Exciting, sometimes – moments of extreme excitement and fear followed by days of bore-dom. Dangerous. Confusing – that's something a lot of people wouldn't credit. And sordid sometimes. You

298

hold so much power in the palm of your hand, but then you wonder if you *really* do. It's like a hall of mirrors and you get so paranoid – so paranoid you don't even know if you can trust your own side. And then you start wondering about, you know, what your criteria are. What war are you fighting? To protect your source, or to beat the enemy? Except you know that the enemy is never going to be beaten . . .'

She was lying on her side, looking at him. The house was warm, and she was naked from the waist up. 'Perhaps you should take it less personally. Distance yourself . . .'

'Easy to say.' He felt a burst of anxiety. 'Is, you won't breathe a word of this, will you? I trust you, but they could really throw the book at me for even talking about it.'

She shook her head. 'Don't get paranoid, David.'

He laughed. 'Until you've been over there, you don't know the meaning of the word.'

They were silent again and he listened to the sound of the city outside – traffic, the honk of a horn, the distant sound of a party in a house down the street.

'Tell me something,' she said. 'These people – these . . . agents you deal with. Are they heroes or villains?'

He laughed again and stood up. 'A very astute question. I don't know.'

'Most people think we should hang the lot of them.'

'Most people could write their knowledge of Northern Ireland on the back of a postage stamp.'

'As cynical as ever, I see.'

He shrugged, thinking that he didn't see himself as a cynic.

'Tell me, then. This man that you are . . . involved with—'

'Woman.'

299

'Woman?'

'Yes.'

'Married? Children?'

'Was – and yes. I don't think I should say any more.'

'OK, well, this . . . woman. What motivates her? I mean what makes her get involved? And what makes her work for you?'

Ryan walked to the window and looked out across the rooftops, before turning round and leaning on a radiator. He looked back at her. 'The honest answer is that I don't know and I don't think we would ever understand. The first is easier; she's from a Republican – an IRA – family. She grew up surrounded by it all. Her brothers got involved – her father had been involved – so perhaps she wanted to impress them and the people around her. I don't know. Perhaps she resented the soldiers, perhaps there was some incident of harassment – probably many in their case. It's easy to see why she started.

'And then when you're in, you're hooked. It's not like . . . you know people do stupid things in their youth, they join the Socialist Workers or whatever and then they grow up a bit and realize the world is not black and white, it's a thousand shades of grey much of the time, and they leave that behind. But violence ties you in. You kill, you suffer, your friends and family get killed, you go to prison, you're badly treated, you're bitter, and then suddenly, maybe, you open your eyes a bit and wonder what the hell you're doing. But then it's too late. You're knee-deep in blood – like that scene from *Macbeth*. You begin to understand what your conscience is telling you, perhaps, but it is just easier to go on than to turn back.'

'And that's what she thinks?'

'I don't know what she thinks. I don't think *she*

knows what she thinks. There's an element of that, but there may be many other things too.'

'Do you trust her?'

'No. Logically, no. The textbook tells you they are all devious liars.'

He sat down on the bed, looking out of the window, with his back to her. She reached out and touched him. There wasn't an ounce of fat on him, his body wiry and taut.

'But?'

'But, instinctively, yes I do trust her. I don't know why.'

For a few minutes they were silent. When Isabelle spoke, her voice was quiet. 'You like her, don't you?' she asked.

'No.' He stood up again and went to look out of the window once more. 'But I'm not sure any more. I don't know whether there is a human being in there trying to get out – and I don't know if I should let it.'

'I think I'd like to sleep alone tonight, David,' she said.

He didn't argue. He dressed in silence and kissed her goodbye.

Ryan woke early the next morning in his tiny bedroom in the flat in Clapham. He spent a few minutes lying on his back and looking at the ceiling and then he got up.

He stood under the shower briefly and dressed and wandered round the corner to buy a couple of Sunday papers, *The Sunday Times* and the *Observer*.

Back at the flat, he made himself a cup of coffee and lit a cigarette.

The front page of *The Sunday Times* was interesting. The headline read, IRA HARDLINERS REJECT PEACE BID, and the article beneath it was clearly well sourced, either

301

from the RUC Special Branch or from the likes of Hopkins or Jenkins. It was accurate, too, up to a point, but the impression it gave was that the peace process was as good as over, whereas he thought the reality was clearly somewhat different. True, the hardliners had rejected it, but that didn't mean they weren't going to be forced to change their minds, though the article did leave open that possibility.

He thought of Gerry McVeigh and the meeting Colette had told them about. He wondered vaguely if the article in front of him was based on information provided by that meeting. The thought that it might be was oddly gratifying.

He thought of Gerry McVeigh again – the enemy he had never met. On reflection, he felt he knew very little about him, the files of information in the computers at Stormont and in London suddenly seeming deeply inadequate. When it came to understanding, there really was a gap as wide as the Irish Sea. He knew he could trot out the theoretical justifications and explanations as quickly as anyone, but that didn't *explain* it. He found it easiest to understand when he put it in the context of a man pursuing the legacy of a dead father, but he wasn't sure if even that was enough. The truth of it was that Gerry McVeigh and those like him were trying to condemn their people to further years of suffering for nothing. Surely his father wouldn't have wanted that and, if he *had* – or did – why was it a legacy worth pursuing?

He thought about Colette. *She* didn't think it was worth pursuing – he was sure of that now – but why not?

He thought it was what made her interesting. He thought it was what justified . . . justified what?

He asked himself a different question: was Gerry any

less human? He asked himself why he was differentiating between the two of them.

Claire appeared. She was wearing a long T-shirt and was heavy with sleep. Ryan wondered whether she was more attractive like this, or less, and then reprimanded himself for considering the question in the first place.

She asked him, sleepily, whether he wanted to come to her parents' for lunch.

Ryan finished the rest of the papers whilst Claire got up, and then they set off in her ancient blue MG. It was a clear, cold day and his ears were freezing by the time they pulled into the gravel drive of her house, just outside Newbury.

Ryan had never been here before, but it was as he would have imagined it: a modest, old red-brick cottage with a neat garden, looking a little barren in the January cold. They were met at the door by a black labrador and a large red setter and Claire knelt down to hug them and let them lick her face.

Claire's parents were also as he would have expected them to be. Mr – Peter – was about 6 feet tall, with a tangled mop of hair so white it looked like it had been repeatedly bleached, Mrs – Sarah – radiated decency and gentility. They were, Ryan thought, what everyone in the office called 'Middle England'.

He'd often noted that his less intelligent colleagues used the 'Middle England' label as a catch-all justification for their less logical prejudices (Jenkins always sprung to mind), but he thought that the people who could be said to represent Middle England were actually more interesting and diverse in their views than anyone in the office was prepared to give them credit for.

All of which was a way of saying that he was not

surprised when, after the social chit-chat and reminiscences about the family house in Provence, Peter brought the conversation round to something he'd clearly wanted to ask about to begin with.

'Claire tells us you've just gone over to Northern Ireland,' he said.

Ryan nodded. 'Yes, a few weeks ago now.'

There was a slight pause. It was almost awkward and almost funny. 'What are you doing, or are you not at liberty to say?'

Ryan suppressed a smile and looked out of the kitchen window. The view from here across the fields to the wood below was fabulous. Truth or fiction?

Fiction. Despite the presence of Middle England, on this he stuck to the rules.

'I'm just working at the Northern Ireland Office. Claire probably told you, I'm in the civil service, working on political matters.' (Truth of a sort, he thought.)

'Interesting times,' Peter said. 'What do you believe will happen?'

Another pause. Ryan took a mouthful of beef and was conscious of the fact that everyone around the table was interested in what he was going to say. 'I think a group of IRA leaders decided a few years ago that it was time to call a halt . . .'

'Some people say it's because their kids are growing up. You know, they don't want—'

'Dad.' Claire was looking at her father. 'Let him finish.'

Ryan smiled and put down his knife and fork. 'You're right,' he said. 'There were many reasons, some political – or tactical – and some personal. However, the hardliners – maybe twenty or thirty per cent of them – would rather go to the grave than give in.'

'So what happens?'

Another pause. Ryan realized he was weighing this up properly for perhaps the first time. 'I think the hard-liners will be silenced for the moment. But they'll always be there – always ready to go it alone, or strike back. I think the others are scared to death of a split and a lot of internal bloodletting.'

'Are the politicians getting it right?'

Ryan smiled again. 'I'm a civil servant.'

Peter smiled back at him. 'Well, you're allowed an opinion these days, aren't you?'

'OK. Well, I'm not sure they've asked themselves the right questions.'

'Which are?'

'What is possible and how do we achieve it.'

'And what are the answers?'

Ryan looked around. They were all still listening and he felt like a fraud – as if his views mattered. He thought about it carefully, though, suddenly aware that his knowledge was good and improving. 'Well, the first thing to understand and accept is that we cannot beat the IRA. So we have two choices: agree a deal, or let the violence continue.

'If we *do* make concessions and offer a deal, then life would get very interesting. They won't all accept it, so we would have to hope for a split with, on the best analysis, the hardliners being restricted to a tiny rump, which we could probably contain.

'I think what we have to ask ourselves, therefore, is whether we *want* to make the concessions that are needed.'

'I thought we made a lot of once-and-for-all con-cessions at partition,' Peter said.

'We did. Perhaps if the Protestants hadn't made such a mess of ruling Northern Ireland, then it would have stood.'

'But there's always been an IRA.'

'Yes, but it's the Provisional IRA we have a problem with. They're too effective. They can't be beaten. They have to be dealt with.'

Silence. Ryan took a sip of his wine and ate another mouthful.

'Interesting, coming from you,' Peter said. He looked at Ryan again and smiled wryly. 'As a civil servant myself, I can always tell a true fellow traveller.'

They moved off the subject of Northern Ireland.

After the meal and the washing-up, they went for a walk down through the wood below, and Ryan was conscious of the fact that he did not, as he might have expected, dread returning to Belfast – as he had done during his army tours, for example. Nor did he feel guilty about the fact that he was spending his only weekend in the country with a friend's family and not with his mother.

He felt a sense of well-being that seemed out of sorts with the realities that confronted him. He couldn't explain why, except that there was a peace to his independence. There are times, he thought, when one is company.

CHAPTER FIFTEEN

The helicopter clattered above them. Gerry was tempted to look up, but managed to keep his eyes firmly on the ground. He wasn't going to give them the pleasure of seeing his face.

They were three men with a football, fooling nobody. Gerry picked up the ball and began to juggle it on his right foot. He counted, 'One, two, three, four, five ... bugger!'

He looked at O'Hanlon who was frowning severely. 'Look like you're interested, Terence, for Christ's sake.'

Gerry took off his glasses and cleaned them on the sleeve of his coat. The helicopter seemed to rise a little higher and the noise abated slightly.

O'Hanlon crossed his arms. 'So, we haven't moved further on. We think we know, but we're just—'

'If you're certain, why don't you do something about it?'

O'Hanlon smiled. 'Patience, Gerry, patience.'

In moments of real honesty, Gerry McVeigh knew he wasn't as powerful as he liked to think he was. Consequently, he'd told himself that he was not going to lose his temper with O'Hanlon and Chico this time.

He was quite determined and he'd thought about it carefully. 'All right,' he said.

'Could be close to home, I would say,' O'Hanlon said.

'I wouldn't say that.'

'Well,' O'Hanlon said, smiling, 'your brother certainly knew about Henderson – his unit was involved. He certainly knew about the greyhound attack – his unit again.'

'So, what are you insinuating?'

'What I'm insinuating is blindingly obvious.'

Gerry put his hands in the pockets of his jeans. 'If you're saying my brother is a tout, then I think we're going to fall out very badly,' he said quietly.

'I'm not saying anyone is a tout.'

The helicopter descended again, the noise suddenly deafening once more. They stared at each other silently. How convenient, Gerry thought, if *you* were a tout. Turning everyone against each other.

They stood still for perhaps a minute before the helicopter began to lift again. They could all sense it climbing and moving away, though none of them looked up.

'So tell me, Mr O'Hanlon,' Gerry said sarcastically, 'just so that I can be clear about this: you think my brother, my own brother, is a tout?'

'It can happen to anyone, McVeigh.'

'You should know.'

'Watch it.'

'I think it is *you* that had better watch it.'

O'Hanlon stared at him. The sound of the helicopter seemed distant now. 'The facts aren't changing,' he said.

'What facts?'

'You've got a problem in there and it's about time

you faced up to it. You're the brigade commander. I ask myself – we ask ourselves – how the Brits found out about the operation on Henderson. You say it might have been routine surveillance, but you and I know that is unlikely, and even if that was the case – even if it was – then they certainly would have seen Paddy, don't you think? They'd certainly have spotted him, wouldn't they?' O'Hanlon paused for a moment before playing his ace. 'In that case, why have the peelers made no effort whatsoever to pick him up? Seamus McGirr was inside for days, but they never touched Paddy.'

Gerry could feel himself teetering on the edge of physical aggression. He took a deep breath and tried to calm himself down. 'All right. All right. We've got a problem, I know that. Let's talk about it. Just don't go saying my brother's a bloody tout.'

O'Hanlon tried to be conciliatory. 'Look, I know Paddy's not a tout. Everybody knows he's not a tout. But there is a problem.' He paused for effect, looking at Gerry. 'We all agree there is a problem. A major bloody problem. So we've got to sort it out. How do we do it? We do it methodically. We test everyone out. Everyone: Paddy, Mulgrew, Colette – even those close to them.' He was almost imploring now, trying to project himself as a voice of reason. 'We've got to test them out. Sure, the Brits are probably playing games with us. Paddy'll pass and then we'll know. We have to eliminate people. We can't be sure who it is without eliminating who it's not. But we've got to know, with everyone.'

Gerry sighed. 'All right. What do you want?'

O'Hanlon had obviously thought it out. 'Something simple. Some guns being brought into the city and taken to a house, say, in Hugo Street. Early morning, day after tomorrow?'

Gerry nodded curtly. 'All right.'

'Mentioned casually. No big deal made of it?'

Gerry turned to go. 'All right, but you're wasting your fucking time.'

He stalked off.

Colette sat cross-legged on the bed, with Mark and Catherine lying on the mattresses beneath her. She read, '"Thou wilt not forget that thou art a wolf? Men will not make thee forget?" said Gray Brother anxiously.

'"Never," said Mowgli. "I will always remember that I love thee and all in our cave; but also I will always remember that I have been cast out of the pack . . ."'

'Does Mowgli prefer to be with the wolves or with humans?' Mark asked.

'I'm not sure, love. I think he feels that his loyalties are divided – and, of course, that is very difficult for him.'

'But where is he happiest?' Catherine asked.

'Well, I think we'll have to wait and see.' Colette took the opportunity to close the book and stand up.

'No!' Mark said.

'Yes,' Colette replied. 'You're tired. I'll read you more tomorrow.' She bent down to kiss them both and then turned off the light.

As she walked down the stairs, she looked at the battered front cover of the book, Rudyard Kipling's *The Jungle Book*. The kids had been demanding it because of the mural of Mowgli and Baloo on the playgroup wall and Ma had ordered it from the library. Colette put it down on the table in the front room and found herself smiling at the irony of it. 'Imperialist bastard,' she muttered. She thought of that other poem by Kipling they'd read at school: 'If you can keep your head, when all about you are losing theirs ... you'll be a man, my son.' Or something like that. It was sexist crap, of course, but for some reason it had stayed with her.

She switched on the television and watched the news on Channel Four. It washed over her head. She wasn't concentrating.

There was an item on the peace process and as she saw the familiar pictures of streets in west Belfast – of soldiers, graffiti and Irish flags – she found herself thinking of what she'd been told by Gerry. The implications were so vast. If peace was really so close, she asked herself, how could Gerry contemplate throwing it all away? She thought her mother might be right, indeed certainly was right. It was time for it to end, but she asked herself how and on whose terms? There was no peace in dishonour and surrender. There would be no peace in a solution that insulted Davey's and Sean's memory and those of many like them. And if Gerry's beating had proved one thing, it was that the Brits would never change and could never be trusted.

She considered the irony of that thought. It didn't make her smile.

She thought of Gerry. He'd come to the house at teatime with Paddy, the bruises on his face still visible. They'd stood in the kitchen and talked about what they were going to do, or rather, Gerry had talked about it. He'd told them little about the operation and she still knew only that they were to go to London and that what they were planning was big enough to bring the peace process crashing to the ground.

They would be going soon, he'd said, and they wouldn't be gone for long.

Colette was already thinking about being separated from Mark and Catherine. She felt terribly tired of it all. She desperately wanted to escape, but she didn't see how she could. She wondered if she could tell Gerry she didn't want to come, but she knew she was still frightened of him and that a part of her, a small part, still wanted to win his respect.

He'd said they were going in three days, leaving separately and flying via Paris to London. He had told them to be ready.

And there was something else. When she was in the front room giving the kids their tea, she'd overheard Gerry telling Paddy about some guns coming into the city, which were to be stored at a house in Hugo Street. She didn't think it important – a routine Belfast Brigade matter – but she thought it might keep the spooks happy. She thought it might keep them off her back.

Now she was alone, she reached for the phone and dialled the number imprinted on her memory. She didn't recognize the man's voice. She spoke quietly.

'It's Shadow Dancer.'

'OK. Five minutes.'

When she rang back, the same man answered. 'I'm sorry, your men are not here, but I work with them. Can I pass on a message?'

She thought for a moment and nearly rang off. 'Just tell them there are some arms coming in the day after tomorrow. Early morning. Going to a house in Hugo Street.'

The man's voice was confident and reassuring. 'Which one?'

She was whispering. 'I don't know, that's it.'

'Fine, it will be passed on immediately.'

She was about to ring off, but held the line for a few moments more. There was genuine concern in his voice. 'Are you all right?'

'I need a meeting. Tomorrow. Same pick-up point.'

She put down the phone and sat for a few minutes

pondering whether she would tell them about London. She knew she was playing with fire – the consequences catastrophic either way – but she was almost sure now how she would proceed. It was her secret and she whispered to herself quietly, 'Knowledge is power.'

So much money.

She picked up the phone and dialled another number and waited for Margaret to pick up. As soon as she heard her voice, she cut the line. They had told her always to place another call, because the IRA had once caught a tout simply by pressing last-number redial on her telephone.

She was just about to get up when she turned and saw Mark's face poking round the bottom of the stairs. She exhaled deeply and beckoned him closer, pulling him up onto her lap and rubbing his hair. 'You gave me a shock.'

His eyes still looked heavy with sleep. She wondered how long he had been sitting there. She brushed his hair to one side and pulled him close to her chest. He curled himself into a ball as if he were about to return to the womb. He spoke quietly. 'Do you still love us, Mammy?'

'I love you.'

He nuzzled his face against her tummy. 'You won't go away again, will you?'

She stroked his hair gently. 'I'll try not to. I'll try for you . . .'

She held him close and, before long, he was asleep. She felt the tiredness in her own eyes and slowly drifted off.

Her dreams were vivid once again. She was back on the catwalk, wearing the same Union Jack robe, trailing it along as she walked. She was coquettish – that was the word everyone was using – and,

313

Christ, she loved it . . . swaggering, swaying . . .

And then she was on a different stage; it was some kind of awards ceremony and she was the queen of the hour. Somebody – no, not somebody, the Brit – was introducing her and presenting her with an award in the form of a giant bronze statue of herself draped in the flag, with the words 'A Great British Hero' stamped on it . . .

And then she was no longer on the stage. She was in a room and everybody was suddenly quiet. It took her a few seconds to work out what was going on, but eventually she realized that she was wrapped in the Union Jack now, wrapped so tightly that she couldn't move. She was lying flat on her back and it dawned on her that she was in a coffin. She felt the panic rising just as the coffin itself began to move, as if on some kind of conveyor belt. She craned her head back and was just able to make out the flames of the crematorium. She struggled and opened her mouth to let out a silent scream . . .

'Colette?'

She woke. Gerry was standing in front of her. For a second she couldn't speak.

'Are you all right?' he asked.

She thought and felt, suddenly, many things: panic at what she might have said in her sleep; anger that he kept on coming and going from the house as though this were still his home – holding meetings, sneaking in and out whenever he liked . . .

'Are you all right?' he asked again.

She nodded. 'Sorry, I was sleeping.'

'I've got to go,' he said. 'But this thing is on. It's happening. I need to know I can rely on you.'

'I don't know,' she said. 'I've promised the kids—'

'Ma can look after the kids. Please, Colette.' He

314

smiled and touched her arm. 'I must be able to rely on you. Please. It's for Pa, for Sean – for Davey. I wouldn't ask if it wasn't truly important.'

She closed her eyes again. For a second, she said nothing.

'All right,' she said.

'Thank you, Colette,' he said. 'I won't forget.'

As she heard the door go, Colette stroked Mark's head. He was still sleeping and, as she looked at him, she had to fight hard to prevent herself crying. She picked him up in her arms and slowly walked up the stairs. She opened the door to their bedroom and stood still for a moment whilst her eyes adjusted to the darkness. Eventually, she stepped forward and gently laid Mark down on his bed, pulling the duvet cover over him and tucking it in at the side.

She pulled back her own duvet and stripped off. She went to the window to close the curtains fully and, as she did so, she glanced down at the alley below and got another nasty shock.

There was a man standing there. He was dressed in a dark-green corduroy jacket. It was unmistakably Martin Mulgrew.

He looked up, caught her eye, turned and hurried away.

She found herself staring down at the alley, close to tears again and wishing it would end.

She thought that, however insane, Gerry's scheme would at least get her out of the country.

She found herself thinking of the Brit and praying to a God she had never believed in that he would make the nightmare end and get her out.

Out of what, she wasn't certain.

She lay down and closed her eyes, listening to the sound of the kids' breathing. There was peace in the

315

gentle rhythm of it, she thought, perhaps it was in their innocence. She tried to put the image of Mulgrew out of her mind. He'd looked so sinister, standing there, leaning against the alley wall. It was like something out of a 1930s gangster movie.

There was a knock on the door. She heard it clearly, but could scarcely believe it. She looked at her watch. It was nearly midnight. She didn't move.

There was another knock, more urgent this time. She got up and began to pull on her jeans and sweatshirt. She had got to the top of the stairs when whoever it was knocked a third time and she said, 'All right, all right,' loudly. She got to the door and asked, 'Who is it?'

'Mulgrew.'

She paused for a second, considering what to do. She realized she had no choice and opened the door. 'What in the hell—'

'Your presence is required, Colette – not now, it's all right. Three days' time. Seven p.m. The house in New Barnsley. I'm afraid you'll have to be there.'

He turned round before she could say any more and walked away. She shut the door and leaned against the wall, feeling overwhelmed by black despair as she did so.

'So, you're on to me,' she told herself quietly. 'In three days. That means you're turning the screw ... seeing what I'll do.'

She slid down the wall and put her head in her hands.

The following day was bright and clear and Gerry found the house easily enough, though he had only been there once before. Macauley did not like to do business at home.

The house was small, but neat. It had been newly

316

painted and the white walls were dazzling in the sunlight. The garden was well kept and tidy and there was little obvious sign of life.

He knocked once and waited. The woman opened the door a few inches and poked her head round the edge, her curly, grey-black hair crushed against the wall. Gerry tried to be polite. 'Hello, Mrs Macauley. You'll not remember me. I'm from Belfast and was just looking for Seamus.'

She opened the door a few more inches, but didn't smile. 'If you want him, you'll have to find him.'

Gerry thought she was being facetious and he waited for her to expand. She looked at him for a second before continuing. 'He's up to the top of the hill, on the corner of the woods there. You'll not miss him.'

She'd been pointing up at a thin copse that ran across the top of the hill above them and Gerry turned away. 'Thank you very much, Mrs Macauley.'

The door slammed behind him. He turned out of the gate and found the lane that led up to the start of the hill. Eventually he came to a field and walked up the edge of it, gathering huge clumps of mud on his shoes.

He felt uneasy. As he got to the top, he followed the edge of the copse, wondering where he'd find Macauley. At the end, he stopped and looked down over the rugged Cavan countryside.

It was a fabulous day, but his lungs hurt from the climb and he cursed himself for being so unfit. He hated exercise and he hated the countryside. He reached into his top pocket for his cigarettes, took out the packet and lit one.

He felt the barrel of a gun on the nape of his neck and heard Macauley's voice. 'Hello, Gerry.'

He turned round and looked at him. The barrel was touching his chest. 'Hello, Seamus.'

'To what do I owe this pleasure, if pleasure it is. . . .'

'I'm here to see you about something.'

Gerry looked at him, feeling peculiarly nervous. He sensed this could go badly wrong. Macauley was still pointing the shotgun at him, though he'd now lowered it to his belly. 'I know what you're here for. What makes you think I'll be interested?'

Gerry smiled unconvincingly. 'How do you know what I'm here for?'

Macauley laughed. 'Men talk, Gerry, as you ought to know. You know what they say about careless talk . . .'

Gerry felt the nerves in his stomach. Seamus Macauley was a small man, with scruffy, unkempt, curly black hair and an even temperament. Although he lived just over the border in County Cavan in the Republic, he was head of the IRA's Northern Command, the body responsible for running the day-to-day war in Northern Ireland. He sat on the Army Council and was enormously respected within the movement as a whole. He had a great deal of influence.

'I'm here because we're heading for disaster.'

'Says who?'

'Everyone who's got any sense. I hear that you're not entirely happy with the direction things are taking—'

Macauley cut him off, his voice suddenly harsher, his accent stronger. 'Who's been telling you that?'

Gerry paused for a moment, unsure of his ground. 'It's what I heard.'

'Like I said, Gerry, careless talk costs lives.' Macauley swung the shotgun off him and took imaginary aim out into the valley. 'It's beautiful here, is it not, Gerry?'

'Yes, it is,' he said, lying.

Macauley started walking, turning back down towards the house. 'You see, Gerry, in countryside like this, the Brits'll never win. I feel sorry for them sometimes. They come over here with their armies and their helicopters, but they'll never understand the country here. They can't look around them and understand what's wrong; the field that is ploughed out of season, the birds that aren't singing in the summer. There's always a reason. There are always signs to see if only they understood them. But they never will, you see. They'll never understand our land like we do – and that's why they'll never win.'

'So why are we surrendering?'

Macauley laughed. 'It's not a surrender, Gerry. You know what the leadership are saying. We're in a position of strength—'

'I know what they're saying. But just because they're saying it doesn't make it the truth.'

Macauley stopped and looked at him. 'I know what you're up to, you needn't worry. Murphy and I keep each other informed. I'll not support you, but I'll not stop you.'

Gerry sighed. 'It's not support I need. I need to know there'll be no witch-hunt if I'm successful.'

Macauley shook his head. 'You're an ambitious man, Gerry McVeigh, and ambitious men need to be careful.' He swung the shotgun round, pointing it at Gerry's head. 'What's to stop me blowing your head off for treachery?'

'There's nothing to stop you.'

'I'll be honest and say I think it's my duty to do so. My colleagues have worked long and hard – bloody years of work – to get to this point and it's all going to be fucked by their arrogant little head of the Belfast Brigade. I think it's my duty to stop that, don't you think?'

Gerry felt the first stirrings of fear. He now knew

coming down here had been a huge mistake. 'I could agree not to go ahead with it.'

Macauley laughed. 'A coward as well as a scoundrel. I don't think we'd trust you, would we? Trust you no more than a tout . . .' He lowered the gun and laughed again. 'You need to watch yourself. I don't believe in what the leadership is doing; more than that, I think what they're doing is dangerous. But I'll have no part in treachery or sedition. If we don't stick together and maintain discipline the Brits will finish us . . .' He paused for a moment and turned to start walking again. 'Murphy and I have agreed we'll keep what we know to ourselves. You've got that much chance, if you've got the balls to go through with it. As to afterwards, I'll be making no promises. You'll have to see.'

He didn't expand and they trudged down the hill in uncomfortable silence. Macauley paused once and pointed out a bird Gerry had never heard of on the corner of the hedge. He grunted his goodbye at the house and didn't bother to wish him luck.

On the journey back to Belfast, Gerry felt irritated and annoyed. He thought Macauley had patronized him and he hated that more than anything. He felt his resolve stiffening and he knew he had to go ahead with this now, if only to prove to the likes of Murphy and Macauley that he was as good as his word.

He drove fast. He had a brigade meeting and he'd arranged for his key lieutenants to be there early so that he could brief them on what he was about to do.

As he parked the car opposite Sinn Féin's headquarters in Andersonstown, he passed the travel agents and noticed that it was closed. He felt a momentary surge of disappointment, but pushed it aside and crossed over the road to Connolly House. The iron gates were locked, but he'd long had a key and he let himself in quietly.

The building was dark and he put on a light in the hallway and turned into the front room. It was eerily quiet and he switched on the television to break the silence.

He sat there for fifteen minutes, lost in his thoughts, until the buzzer went for the first time. He looked out of the window and saw Joey Clarke and Martin Mulgrew standing at the gate. He pressed the buzzer to allow them entry.

Joey Clarke went into the back to make them coffee and then they all sat around the table in the front room and gossiped quietly. Gerry looked at his watch and saw that time was running out. He lit another cigarette and then cleared his throat before explaining why he'd called the meeting. 'We've talked about this before,' he said, 'but the time has come to do something about it. We've all agreed this peace process is going nowhere and it's got to be stopped.' He took a deep breath. 'I've been putting together something in London. Something big – I can't tell you what – and I want you'se behind me.'

Mulgrew exhaled noisily. 'Fuck.'

'I need your backing. Both of you. There's no sanction for this and we're taking the chance that the mood will prevent a witch-hunt. Once it's done, the peace process'll be as good as dead and we can get on with fighting the war.' He looked at them. 'Well?'

Mulgrew shook his head. 'Without sanction? No official sanction? Shit, it's risky, Gerry, know what I mean? I mean, we don't know anything about it. Fuck, the leadership'll go mad if it happens. They'll go mad. There'll be the witch-hunt to end all witch-hunts.'

'I don't think so.'

321

'What makes you so sure?'

'I just don't think so. I don't think they'd dare. They'd be crushed and their strategy would be in ruins. We'd have to build an alternative strategy based on the continuation of the armed struggle. I'm not without friends.'

Joey Clarke interrupted. 'You mightn't be around to see whatever strategy anyone comes up with . . .'

Gerry looked at him sourly, anger creeping into his voice for the first time. 'I'm not without friends, but I need my own brigade behind me.'

Mulgrew shook his head again. 'You'll have my backing, Gerry,' he said quietly. 'I just hope to fuck you know what you're doing, that's all.'

The buzzer went, the noise giving them all a shock. Gerry got up and looked out of the window, pulling the shabby orange curtains aside.

'All right, it's the others.' He turned back and pointed his finger at both of them.

'Not a word to anyone. It'll be over soon enough and then we'll see. Right?'

They didn't respond and he went to the door to let in Sean Murray, the unit commander from the Poleglass area of the city. He was followed quickly by the others – Paddy was the last – and soon there were twelve men sitting around the table, almost all of them smoking. Gerry didn't like these meetings as a general rule, because he always found himself looking round the table and wondering which one of the stinking bastards was a tout. He didn't know who he could trust absolutely, but he usually went on instinct and largely dealt with the unit commanders he trusted most. That was why Paddy's unit in the Lower Falls was one of the most active in the whole city. Gerry often said, 'If you can't trust your own brother, then who the fuck can you trust?'

Mulgrew made some more coffee. There were not enough cups to go round.

They began by discussing the failed attack on Henderson. Sean Murray brought the subject up and he began by swearing to deal personally with whoever the tout was. One of his own men had been involved in seizing the house and he was acting tough, as he often did.

Gerry thought that if anyone in here was a tout, it was probably Murray. He talked too much.

Gerry was about to move the discussion on when there was an enormous crashing sound above them. Everyone fell silent, waiting for some kind of indication as to what was happening. And then the gunfire started.

The glass came flying across the room, shredding the curtains in the process, as they sought the relative safety of the floor.

Gerry crouched down next to Mulgrew. Nobody said anything. None of them were armed.

There were two, possibly three, bursts of the gunfire, the bullets peppering the walls above them, sending small bits of plasterwork raining down on their heads. It lasted only a few seconds and then a voice filled the room. 'Be warned, Belfast Brigade of the IRA. We're watching you ...' The man laughed. 'Up the UFF. Up the UFF!'

There was one more burst of gunfire and then they heard the revving of a car engine and the screech of tyres.

For a few seconds nobody moved, and then Gerry stood up slowly and gingerly. He ran his hand along the table top and coughed nervously. He stepped into the corridor and looked out of the front door. He couldn't see anything.

323

They could all hear the sirens in the distance.

A few minutes later, three Land Rovers arrived at once, stopping in the middle of the street outside the gates. Gerry heard the sound of some of the metal doors slamming shut and he looked out of the window and saw two policemen standing by the entrance. He went back into the room. Everyone was sitting in stunned silence.

'I'll have to go and talk to the peelers. They'll demand access, so you boys get out over the metal fence at the back.'

Gerry opened the door and ambled slowly down to the gate. He recognized one of the men as a sergeant from Andersonstown police station. Gerry's voice was laced with sarcasm. 'Yes?'

The man was polite. 'We'd like to gain access, please, Mr McVeigh.'

'Want to admire your handiwork?'

'I'll ask you not to make this difficult, Mr McVeigh. We've got a job to do.'

'I'll bet you fucking have. Unfortunately for you, your boys didn't manage to kill anyone, though not for want of trying.'

'I'm afraid we're going to have to insist on being allowed access to the scene of the crime.'

Gerry laughed. 'They get a free run in and a free run out. What else is the RUC for? RUC, UFF, UVF, it's all the same thing . . .'

He opened the gate and allowed them in, returning to the house and standing in sullen silence whilst they looked over the debris inside. Within a few minutes some of the local members of Sinn Féin arrived and he left them to deal with the police, pausing once in the street outside to look at the hole in the roof left by the rocket-propelled grenade. He realized that must have been what caused the first crashing sound, before the gunfire started. They'd been lucky.

As he walked home he fought to keep his temper under control. He believed what he'd said – believed that the RUC was operating hand in glove with the Loyalist terrorists – and the implications were grim. The Loyalists had clearly known that a meeting of the IRA's Belfast Brigade was to take place at that time and in that location. That meant that they had at least one tout – or it meant that the Brits' surveillance was better than ever. It also meant that at least one man in the Brit services was passing information to the Loyalists. It made life even more dangerous for him, his men and their families.

If he'd had any doubts about what he was going to do in London, they had just been dispelled.

In the house, he ignored Christy's hopeful and affectionate welcome and went upstairs to bed in a towering rage.

He couldn't sleep and lay on his back staring at the ceiling long into the night.

This time, it was for real.

McIlhatton was nervous, but not too nervous. After all, he reasoned, if it came to the worst, he could run like hell.

He took the pass out of his pocket, put the chain over his head, and walked out of the tube and turned left, taking the stairs slowly.

He walked towards the policeman at the entrance and smiled. The man bent his head to look a little closer, but didn't try to stop him.

He was in.

CHAPTER SIXTEEN

Colette sat on the back step. She'd just finished cleaning the kitchen floor and had a cup of coffee in one hand and a cigarette in the other. The radio was on and she listened to the sad, slow tune. It was John Lennon singing 'Love' – her era.

Corny stuff. But it moved her.

She got up, picked up the dishcloth and wiped around the sink. Then she went into the front room and switched on the TV to watch one of the morning chat shows. She thought she probably oughtn't to be watching this somehow, but . . .

The presenters sat next to each other and they introduced a man from the FBI, who they said was an expert on serial killers.

They asked him what kind of people were serial killers and he told them that almost all serial killers were single white men (well, who'd have believed it, she thought) and that women rarely became serial killers, though they sometimes murdered a number of people close to them.

Yes, she thought flippantly, I can see that has its attractions.

They asked the man what it was that turned these

men into serial killers. He replied that the problems were usually caused in early childhood. By the time they were in their early teens, he said, it was too late to save them.

And what were the signs in early childhood, they asked.

Well, he said. Dysfunctional families, often without a father. A male child showing signs of being very difficult – perhaps bed-wetting – and alternating between periods of introspection and moments of aggression . . .

Colette switched off the television.

She went out to the back door again and lit another cigarette. She looked at her watch and decided she was going to have to go. She stood there for a few minutes more, looking aimlessly at the red-brick wall opposite and thinking vaguely, 'This is my life.'

She went back inside and took her coat off the peg before beginning the long journey to the Malone Road.

As she approached, she realized she was going to be five or ten minutes late again and began worrying about the men's reaction. She felt a childlike desire to please them.

Allen was sitting in the back of the Granada, Ryan in the passenger seat. She didn't recognize the man who was driving, but as soon as she got in he pushed the automatic gear lever to drive and turned down towards the banks of the river Lagan. The Prod smiled at her. 'We'll just do a tour of the east of Belfast today and drop you back in the city centre. OK?'

She nodded, like a shy child with a stranger. She bit her bottom lip gently. Allen looked at her intensely.

'Thank you for the call. Made a big difference. Where did you hear it from?'

She hesitated before answering. 'I was worried about that.'

'Paddy again?'

She shook her head. 'I overheard Gerry telling Paddy. I wasn't meant to —'

'It's OK. We were careful. We're always careful. You don't have to worry.'

She smiled thinly. The driver turned right onto the Ormeau Road, heading up towards the ring road at the top. The windows were tinted, preventing anyone seeing in. She watched two overweight mothers struggling home with their shopping and their children. Allen was still talking to her. 'Do you have any other operational details?'

She turned back to him. 'No. I'm not really ... I mean, like I said, I'm not in a unit, so I wouldn't really know. Paddy's unit is quite active, but everyone still thinks there must be a tout in there somewhere, so they're not going on with most operations. You hear that Internal Security are sniffing around people ...' Her voice trailed off and, for a moment, she hesitated. Then she spoke quietly. 'I'll be all right, won't I? I mean, everything's all right, isn't it?'

Ryan had been listening silently, but he turned round and put his head between the two seats. 'You'll be all right,' he said. His voice was firm and strong.

She looked into his eyes, but saw only professional compassion.

'I know it's frightening, but it's OK. We're monitoring Internal and we know they are nowhere near you, so don't worry. Just keep on working and trust us.'

Colette turned away and looked out of the window again. They were on the ring road now, travelling fast, and she could see Stormont House up on the hill ahead of her. Its white walls shone brilliantly as they reflected the winter sun. She didn't feel reassured. Allen was still

328

looking at her. 'Did you get any more on Gerry and Murphy?'

She felt a tightness in her chest. She turned to the Prod and looked at him. She shook her head.

'Nothing?'

She shook her head again.

Silence. A world passing by outside.

'Why did you request this meeting?'

'I was worried.' She looked at him again and wondered if he could tell she was lying.

Silence. They didn't seem to know what to say suddenly.

'You know nothing more – you've found out *nothing* further?' Allen asked eventually.

She looked at them as if they'd made an accusation. She wondered if they could sense that she was withholding something. She felt the adrenalin pumping in her veins. She was very close to blurting out everything Gerry had said, but something was stopping her.

She shook her head and they lapsed back into silence.

They dropped her on the top floor of the Castlecourt car park in the city centre. As she walked into the shopping mall, she felt fear creeping over her again and she looked around carefully, convinced that she was being watched. She crossed over to the other side of the mall and browsed aimlessly through the Benetton shop, keeping her head bowed low, as if in the genuine belief that this would shield her identity.

She turned to avoid the enquiring gaze of the sales assistant and, as she came back onto the mall, she saw him. She ducked her head immediately and started to walk fast. She went down the escalator, without looking up to see if she was being followed, and hurried along the bottom mall to the front doors. She slipped past the security guards and, as she emerged onto the pedestrian precinct, she allowed herself a quick glance back. He was there. He was following.

She turned right and had to fight the inclination to break into a run, but she heard the heavy footfall of a man running and she clenched her teeth. He put his hand on her shoulder and she stopped.

Ryan's face was harsh. 'Not here,' he said. 'There is a coffee bar above the store behind me. You go there now, I'll join you in five minutes.'

She walked across the street, into the store and up the stairs, bought a milky coffee and waited, unable to think clearly. The room was empty. After a few minutes – it seemed longer – he wandered in slowly and went to buy himself a coffee. She didn't look at him.

He walked towards her, carrying a tray with a mug and some kind of cake on it, not looking at her. He made a show of noticing her, saying hello, like a long-lost friend, but quietly, and then asking if he could join her. She nodded, hating the charade.

'If anyone sees us, I'm somebody you met years ago, all right?'

She looked at him blankly.

'Think of an explanation. That can't be too hard, can it?'

There was a bite to his voice and she was about to complain when he said, 'If you're withholding, you've no idea what a dangerous game that is.'

He looked at her and she bent her head.

'What is happening?' he asked.

Silence.

'Come on, Colette. What's going on?'

'I don't know if I can trust you. I don't know if I should.'

She heard him sigh and looked up to see the irritation in his face.

'Come on, Colette,' he said. 'We've been here before.'

'It's not resolved.'

'What do you want?'

'Love.'

Silence. 'That's a serious answer?'

'It's everything, isn't it?'

Silence. He was looking at her now. 'What do you mean?'

She put her hands over her face and pressed her middle fingers into the corner of her eyes. 'I mean,' she said, 'I mean the world's so cold.'

He didn't reply and she kept her head in her hands. She half expected him to put his hand on her shoulder and offer some measure of comfort and reassurance, but when he spoke, his voice was harsh.

'Get a grip on yourself, Colette, for Christ's sake. As I've tried to explain before, this is incredibly dangerous. There are . . . there are things you don't understand . . .'

'Are you trying to frighten me again?'

'I'm telling you the truth. I'm trying to be *honest*, as I said I would be. If we discover that you have deliberately withheld information that could have saved lives, I'm going to have a lot of explaining to do. Other people might not take a very charitable view of it. If you're *one of us*, you'll be safe. If your loyalties begin to be questioned—'

'If you're not *one of us*, you're the enemy.'

'There's no room for ambiguity.'

'Not in your world.'

'Not in our world.'

She hated him. She hated him most for pretending that his world was the same as hers.

He looked over his shoulder again, but there was

nothing to see. The room was still empty. 'I'm asking you', he said, 'to think about what you promised to deliver.'

'You're threatening.'

'I'm *warning*. You'll have to trust me.'

'You've said that.'

'That's the reality.'

'I don't trust you.'

She watched the frustration in his face. 'Fine,' he said. 'Well, I strongly suggest that you think *very* carefully about what I've said.'

He stared at the table.

'They're on to me,' she said.

He looked up.

'They're on to me,' she said again. 'Mulgrew came to me. I have to report to a house in New Barnsley the day after tomorrow.'

'When?'

'Seven.'

'They're just testing you out. They're testing everybody—'

'For Christ's sake.'

He leaned forward, his face tense. 'We'll cover it, Colette. Keep your bleeper on you and we'll have our people close. They're just putting everyone on their mettle, trying to flush somebody out ... all right?'

She got up and walked away.

Ryan sat with his head on the desk. He felt Alison Berry's hand on his shoulder. She was smiling. 'Fancy a drink?'

He dropped his pencil and stood up slowly. 'Why not?'

It was late and they were the last to leave the office.

It had been quiet for a few days, for once, and everyone had taken the chance to get home early.

Berry had a light-blue Rover 620 and she drove slowly out of Stormont, onto the ring road and out towards the M1. She hadn't told him where they were going and he didn't ask.

He could smell her: a distinctive, soft, musty scent, only slightly tainted by the nicotine in her clothes and hair. Instinct told him that he wouldn't see his flat again until the morning.

Whether or not she was always so easy-going, tonight she certainly seemed to be in a good mood and he began to relax slightly. She asked him how long he'd been in the Service, what he'd been doing before, where he went to university and where his parents lived. He tried to turn the conversation round to her, but she didn't seem to be in a hurry to talk about herself. He discovered she'd been in MI5 for seven years and had been at Oxford – and then they were back to talking about him.

They turned off the M1 on the Dublin Road and then turned left into Hillsborough. Berry slowed to a snail's pace as they drove up the hill towards the castle and then pulled into the entrance of the Plough Inn, opposite the castle gates.

It was warm inside and comfortable and they took a quiet, discreet table in a raised section round to the side. A pretty, dark-haired girl brought them some menus and Berry insisted on buying the drinks.

There was music on in the bar and Berry tapped the table with her lighter. She asked him what had happened to make him look so shell-shocked when he arrived back in the office, and he thought long and hard before answering.

'Nothing really. Just the whole thing, that's all. It's

not easy . . . kind of grinds you down. Nothing is ever simple. Sometimes it's hard not to despair . . .'

She smiled at him again. 'If it's any help, it's what I did on my first tour here and you're right, it's not easy; twenty-four-hour-a-day responsibility, always wondering what's going to happen to the poor bastards, when they're finally going to buy it, when you're going to be called to some dark field in the middle of the night—'

'Who did you run?' he asked quietly.

'A Provo.'

'Still around as far as you know?'

'I hope he's buried at the bottom of a bog by now.' She laughed – a short, bitter laugh. 'But no, I think he is still alive and wandering round the south somewhere. He was a little bastard. Nearly got me killed in the end . . .'

'Did he turn back to them?'

She laughed again. 'The truth is that I honestly don't know. He was such a pathological liar. Lied about everything. Absolutely *everything*. He turned out to be totally useless.'

She shivered volubly and gulped her drink. 'An unhappy time. How's yours? The same?'

Ryan shook his head. 'I don't know. She seems all right – most of the time.'

'She?'

'Yes.'

'They're all liars – each and every last one of them. Every handler likes to think he, or she, has found the perfect agent, who is going to deliver. It just doesn't happen. They're all liars.'

He nodded. 'Maybe.'

Ryan stood up and went to get another drink, over-ruling Berry's objections. He had a sudden and very strong desire to get drunk.

Berry was drinking gin and, as he put the glasses down on the table, he found himself wanting to know about her tout. 'Your man,' he asked. 'Was he frightened?'

'No. Not most of the time. He assumed, I think, that it would never happen to him – they all do. I don't see how you'd do it otherwise. But then, sometimes, he would be so terrified he looked like he would shit himself. I recall one time when he sat with his head in my lap crying like a baby . . .'

Berry took a sip of her gin and stared thoughtfully ahead of her, as though lost in her memories. 'I was everything to him at times: agony aunt, sister, mother, mistress – he was always bitching to me about his wife.' She paused for a second before continuing. 'But that didn't stop him lying and lying and lying.'

She looked at him. 'I know what the textbooks say, but sometimes it is bloody hard not to make it personal. Something tells me you know what I mean.'

Ryan grinned. He was beginning to feel light-headed from the Guinness. He could feel the frustration and aggression in his body and he found himself admiring Berry's legs once again. She was wearing black tights or stockings and a short, cream skirt. He found himself noticing the softness of her skin.

They were there until closing time and, as they rolled out of the door, Ryan thought Berry was as pissed as he was. As they strolled down the street she took his arm. 'I think your choice is going to be between a taxi and my sofa, because I don't think I'm in a fit state to drive you anywhere and I'm not sure if our friends in the RUC would take a very enlightened view of a slightly tipsy "box" analyst driving whilst under the influence.'

Ryan knew Berry had no intention of allowing him home in a taxi. He felt the excitement in his stomach.

He thought that, if she wanted a good time, then that was what she was going to get tonight. As they arrived at the door of her house at the bottom of the hill, he felt the warmth of her hand taking hold of his. As she shut the front door, she put her arms gently around his neck and kissed him, slowly, her tongue running along the length of her lips and then finding his. She slipped off her waist-length coat and led him gently towards the stairs.

Her bedroom was small, with a sloping roof and a large pine cupboard along one wall, the doors of which were open, the clothes inside carelessly stacked in large piles that were about to topple onto the floor.

Without speaking, Berry put her arms around his neck once more and began dancing gently, rocking her hips from side to side and then slowly forward. She rubbed his hair and then sat down demurely on the large pink duvet that covered her pine bed. She took off her smart, high-heeled brown shoes and pulled up her skirt, revealing dark-brown skin, white knickers and a black suspender belt. She watched his face as she rolled down her stockings and took off her skirt. She stood up again, slightly unsteady on her feet now, and slowly undid the buttons on his trousers, tugging them down to the floor with his boxer shorts. She made as if to kneel, but he caught her under her armpits and pulled her up towards him. He wanted her unbelievably badly. He wanted to relieve his frustration.

Afterwards, they lay in each other's arms without speaking for several minutes, lost in their own thoughts. Berry had turned off the lamp, but the curtains were still open and light was pouring in from the street outside.

There were few pictures on the wall and little sign that Berry considered this much more than a place to sleep. It didn't feel like a home. There was a large silver photo frame with a picture of a young-looking man dressed in black tie. He was laughing. Ryan moved his head so that he could talk to her and he saw that she'd been watching him. He tried to sound casual and uninterested. 'Boyfriend?'

'Ex.'

'Recent ex?'

She sighed and pulled herself up onto her elbow, turning on her side and looking at him with an amused grin. 'Quite recent. We met at university. We kept it together a long time, but he's a banker and we didn't see each other very much. He got bored of waiting.'

'The love of your life?'

She sighed again and rolled onto her back. 'Maybe. Christ, who knows. I loved him, but I guess it was inevitable. It's hard with this job.'

'You could have gone back to London.'

'I could have done. Yes, I could have done, but then I'd have been stabbed in the back. I'd have struggled to get anywhere.'

'Does that matter?'

She looked at him seriously. 'It matters to me.'

Ryan leaned on his elbow and looked down at her. She had the duvet pulled up to her neck and her head rested on a single crumpled pillow. Her hair was tousled and he could feel the warmth of her body alongside him, his left knee touching her thigh. He felt the first stirrings of arousal, but he didn't want to make love to her again. He wondered if these lonely couplings would be her lot in the life she was charting for herself. He knew he wanted more and his career with the British Security Service fell down another notch on his list of priorities.

* * *

337

Gerry had mentioned the guns at tea that day in the house on Leeson Street, but he hadn't discussed it further. He *could* have told his brother that, since then, a trap had been set and that the guns had been intercepted by the peelers.

He could have told Paddy that only he had been told about the guns and that Internal Security were on to him, but there were certain conventions and rules to follow, so he didn't.

If he'd really thought his brother was guilty, then perhaps . . .

But it was simply not something he'd considered. It *looked* bad, but there could still have been a thousand other explanations – surveillance, a tout further down the line – and he was confident it would all be sorted out. He knew Internal would never dare have a go at Paddy because much more proof was needed. More traps would be set and they'd realize they'd made a mistake and go after the real culprit.

It was annoying, but he had put it out of his mind. Everyone was always under suspicion. It was no big deal.

He was with Paddy now, upstairs in the Rock Bar, but he still wasn't going to mention it. After all, it really was no big deal.

And there was other, much more important, business to hand.

Gerry was trying to instil a sense of excitement and purpose in his brother.

'The die is cast,' he said. 'We're on the road. Like I said, we have south Armagh behind us.'

Paddy lit another cigarette from the end of the last. 'Who else?'

'I've told no-one else. It's too dangerous.'

'Will you take over?'

Gerry shook his head. 'No, I don't think so. That's a dangerous road to go down. We'll have to be careful when we come back, but I think we'll see what happens. The peace process will be dead and we'll see how the mood swings. I think the leadership will be seen to have misjudged things and may have to move over.'

Paddy sucked the smoke deep into his lungs. Gerry could tell he was nervous and uncertain, but he knew he would do whatever he was asked.

'How will it work?'

'I've yet to sort out the final details. I'm to meet someone tomorrow in Dublin. He's been working for me in London and everything should be in place. I'm going to drive down there now, but we'll have a briefing in Paris or in London. You've got it clear where to meet, how to get there and what to do?'

'We meet in Paris?'

'Yes, or if we don't make the rendezvous, in London. You pick up your tickets from the travel agency in Andytown. You have to tell Colette where to get the tickets and where to meet and then we all travel separately. I'll see you there.'

Paddy nodded. Gerry gripped his shoulder briefly before climbing into his car and beginning the long drive to Dublin.

McIlhatton was slouched in the armchair again, but he was not bored.

The television showed pictures of the House of Commons chamber he'd seen so many times before, but today he felt a little stab of pleasure as he saw the prime minister get to his feet.

McIlhatton smiled.

He couldn't help himself.

CHAPTER SEVENTEEN

Ma was trying to cook and hold Catherine at the same time. The child was tired, exhausted, and Colette thought Ma was still holding her to make a point. She couldn't remember seeing her so angry.

'Why can't you tell me what you're going to do?'

'I *can't*, Ma.'

'So you run off again, leave me to look after the kids, and you won't even tell me what bloody horror you're off to commit.'

'Don't say it like that.'

'That's how it is, and I want to know what you're up to.'

'I can't, Ma.'

'You can.'

'I'm not a child.'

'Then behave like an adult.' Ma sighed and shifted the frying pan. She wasn't looking at her. 'Come on, Colette, I need to know.'

Colette felt the anger flaring within her. 'Why do you *need* to know. What right do you—'

'Don't you lecture me about rights. Right? Right? What *right* do *you* have to bugger off to God alone knows where to do some unspeakable God alone knows what and expect me – *me* – to run around after you, picking up the entrails of your life, including looking after your own children. And I am your mother, you know, though you may have forgotten, and I think I'm allowed to be concerned about what in the hell you're getting up to. Don't you?'

Colette shook her head and looked down. 'I can't,' she said. 'I'm sorry, but you know I can't. And, anyway, I don't know – and that is the God's honest truth.'

Her mother snorted with frustration and Colette studied the faded lino on the kitchen floor. She knew now that it was fixed and that there was no way out. Paddy had been this morning and she'd walked to the travel agent herself. The tickets were in her handbag.

She'd seen Paddy's uncertainty and it only deepened her own anxieties.

Ma turned the sausages and pushed and prodded them aggressively. The smell of burning fat and pork meat was pervasive. 'You don't have to go,' she said quietly.

'I do.'

'You keep saying it's going to change and then off you go again.'

'I don't have a choice.'

'Of *course* you have a choice. Everyone has a choice.' She looked down again and stirred the sausages in silence. 'I don't know why you ever started again,' she added.

Colette sighed. 'I've told you before. After Davey died, I wanted to . . .' She let her voice trail off and grunted in frustration. She turned to go.

'What about the kids?' her mother asked.

Colette turned back, her voice wistful and self-pitying. 'Sure, you'll look after them better than me. You usually do.'

Ma gently put down Catherine on the chair by the table, trying not to wake her. She still had the wooden spoon in her hand and Colette could sense she was angry and hurt. She spoke quietly. 'You're so selfish, I can scarcely believe it sometimes.'

Colette felt stung. 'Why do you say that? Why do you say that after all this time? What choices do I have, Ma? Tell me, what choices?' Colette could hear the self-pitying whine growing in her voice. 'I'm doing my best, but I've got no choice.'

Her mother's voice was harder than she'd ever heard it. 'You *have* the choice. You have the choice to look after your children and try to be a good mother for once. Look at them. *Look* at them, Colette.' She was pointing at Catherine, who was still sleeping on the chair, her head resting uncomfortably against the wooden back. 'Enough is enough. You've done enough. Leave it now. Leave it to others if it must continue.'

'What are you saying, Ma? That we shouldn't care any more?'

'I'm saying it's time to make it stop. I'm saying it has gone on too long and it has *got* to stop. I'm saying I'm tired of it and I don't want to worry about when I'm going to get the knock on my door saying that those poor children are going to be without a mother, or that their mother is going to be locked up in prison for the rest of her life.' She was poring over the stove, poking the sausages furiously. 'You owe it to the children to stop.'

Colette felt her anger flare again. 'You're saying that because I'm a woman. You wouldn't say that to Gerry or Paddy.'

Her mother didn't answer.

'I've got as much right to it as a man, Ma. Just

because you didn't do it doesn't mean it isn't right.'

'I blame myself.'

'Blame yourself for what?'

She sighed audibly and pushed the back of her hand across her eyes, as if wiping away tears. 'I blame myself for not stopping you. I blame myself for allowing it.'

Colette spoke quietly, her anger dwindling into sorrow. 'It wasn't your decision to make, Ma. I wanted to be involved.'

'You did it to prove yourself to Paddy and Gerry. You were a tomboy and you did it to prove yourself to them – and you're still trying to do it. They've wrecked your life.'

Colette felt the tears well up in her eyes. 'We didn't have a choice, Ma. None of us had any choice . . .' She looked at her mother, but she didn't respond. Her silence and her demeanour suggested she did not agree. Colette picked up Catherine and sat silently in the front room. Her mother had been a friend, always supportive, sometimes disapproving or frightened, but never judgemental. She couldn't remember the last time they'd argued and it was years since she'd seen her so upset.

After a few minutes Ma came in and sat down on the chair opposite her, the decision not to share the settee bearing silent but eloquent testimony to her feelings. 'What are you going to do?' she asked.

'I don't know, and that's the truth. Something big. Gerry . . . he doesn't believe in the peace process, as you know.'

Colette watched her mother clench and unclench her hands and struggle with her emotions and she knew there was a terrible tiredness about them both. There was no doubt in her mind what she was going to be asked and, deep down, she knew her mother was right.

Ma's voice was weak, as if articulating the words was the hardest thing she'd ever done. 'Please, I've never asked before, but I'm asking you to stop and to do all in your power to make all of them stop. Don't let another generation get dragged into this. We're not winning. We can't win. We must sue for peace with honour.'

Colette kept her head down and fought back the tears, but she could tell her mother was reaching out her hands.

'Please, love, look at little Catherine and Mark and think of them. Please, I beg of you, don't allow them to get drawn in, don't let another generation live with this.'

Colette knew she would cry, knew she couldn't stop herself, and she stood up and placed Catherine in her mother's outstretched arms. She cried as she packed and cried as she left the house. She didn't say goodbye and, as she walked away, she muttered to herself through her tears, 'I have no choice. I have no choice.'

The atmosphere in the source unit at Castlereagh was relaxed. The chief inspector, Ian Williams – Ryan had at last managed to find out his name – had brought out a bottle of Bushmills, though it was barely lunchtime.

The others were relaxed, but Ryan wasn't. They'd discussed the question of Colette's impending meeting with Mulgrew in New Barnsley and what kind of surveillance would be needed. The others had tackled it routinely, almost casually, and that had made Ryan uncomfortable.

Allen now handed him a small tumbler of whiskey and poured one for himself. Ryan lit another cigarette and leaned back in his chair, finding it difficult once again to take his eyes off the cubby holes on the wall opposite him. Foxglove's hole seemed threateningly full of loose paper.

A man walked in without knocking. He was shorter than Allen, probably around six feet, with curly dark hair and a thick moustache. Ryan recognized him immediately as the other handler.

'Hello, Sam,' the chief inspector said.

'Foxglove says all kinds of shit is going down,' he said. 'Gerry McVeigh is on his way to England to carry out some assassination plan that is designed to destroy the peace process.'

The man paused and chucked his raincoat down on the desk. 'He's been plotting with Murphy, Mallon, Macaulay, and others. He's using his family – including his sister.'

Ryan wished that the ground would open up and swallow him.

Allen didn't wait to hear any more and, a few minutes later, they swept out of Castlereagh. Allen was driving with his teeth clenched.

'Fucking bitch,' he said.

Ryan didn't reply.

It seemed to take them only a few minutes to get there. Ryan realized they had no back-up at all.

Allen rang the bell twice in rapid succession. A grey-haired woman came to the door and Ryan recognized her immediately as Colette's mother.

'May we come in briefly?' Allen asked politely.

They stood in the hall and Colette's mother kept her back to the stairs. Ryan could see a young boy sitting at the top, watching.

'Where is your daughter?' Allen asked.

'Gone south.'

'I don't think so.'

345

'Well, if you know where she is, don't come asking me.'

'Please, Mrs McVeigh, this is serious.'

'She asked me to look after the kids for a few days.' The woman was shaking her head. 'If you want to know any more, you're asking in the wrong place.'

Allen turned to go and, as he followed, Ryan thought he could hear the young boy crying.

Gerry McVeigh arrived in the lobby of the Shelbourne Hotel wearing a plain grey suit and a white trench coat and looking like a businessman waiting to see a colleague.

Situated on St Stephen's Green, the Shelbourne was Dublin's most famous hotel, frequented by artists, actors and ministers alike. Gerry found the man he was to meet in the coffee room and ushered him out of the hotel and across to the centre of the green opposite. As Colette had done weeks earlier, he sat down on a park bench and watched the ducks ahead of him, feeling a strong sense of purpose and excitement. He was no academic, knowing of the past only what he needed to know, or thought he needed to know, but he had the growing feeling that what he was about to do was going to change the course of Irish history.

It gave him a sense of power. He knew the time was right, so he'd brought his man from London to Dublin to brief him away from prying eyes.

He could tell that Eddie McIlhatton was nervous, but he wasn't surprised. He'd grown used to being feared by his subordinates.

He was direct and businesslike. 'You have the passes?'

McIlhatton pushed his hand into the coat of his

jacket and pulled out a brown envelope. 'The pictures the travel agency sent weren't the best.'

Gerry took the envelope and pulled out the white passes. There were three: one for him, one for Paddy and one for Colette. All had neck chains attached to them. 'They're OK. You used the man I said?'

McIlhatton nodded.

'Guns?'

He nodded again. 'I've had them for months. I can deliver them whenever you need them.'

Gerry could tell there was something else on his mind. 'Everything all right?'

'It's just, I've heard nothing from anyone here in Dublin, that's all.'

Gerry turned to him, his voice icy calm. 'You forget about that, you hear? You'll take your orders from me and only me. There's no need to have any connection with Dublin at this stage. I don't want there to be any risk of this going wrong.'

'But I should have heard something, shouldn't I, I mean with the current climate and everything ... they said no operations.'

Gerry cut him off, his face twisting into a sneer as he spoke. 'Forget Dublin.'

'I just don't want no trouble.'

'Forget it. Drop it. You'll take your orders from me.'

The boy nodded glumly and Gerry went on, explaining that the operation would be carried out by himself and Paddy – both guns vital in the split second they would have – with Colette to cover them as they fired. He drove the boy through the many questions he needed to ask. He wanted to know how easy it would be to get in, what the layout was – exactly – and how they would get out.

They were there for hours, the boy producing

maps and diagrams of remarkable detail.

Gerry thought he was just a boy. A shyster and a coward. But he had to acknowledge he'd done his homework and done it well.

They summoned Paddy to a house in Ballymurphy. He was expecting Gerry and Mulgrew and the Belfast Brigade staff, and when he saw O'Hanlon standing in the kitchen he swore under his breath and looked down at the floor.

He knew he should relax and play it cool.

But O'Hanlon was the enemy.

He didn't have time to think. On instinct, he turned and ran, but Chico got to him before he reached the door. There was another man from east Tyrone whose face he recognized and they kicked his legs out from under him, took hold of his hair and pushed his face into the grey carpet. He heard O'Hanlon's voice in his ear. He whispered, 'Big mistake, McVeigh. Big mistake. Only the guilty run.'

They carried him up the stairs and this time he didn't fight. He knew what was happening now – he could scarcely believe it, but he was too old and experienced to kid himself about what it all meant – and he decided to save his strength. He had a nasty feeling he might need it.

They took him to an upstairs bedroom and tied him to a small wooden chair. Chico pulled the ropes tight and he winced with pain. They were taking no chances.

The man from east Tyrone sat silently opposite him and smoked. Paddy could hear Chico and O'Hanlon talking in the room below.

Paddy's initial reaction was anger rather than fear. He knew he had impeccable credentials and he could still scarcely believe he was being held by a jumped-up

348

lowlife like O'Hanlon. He promised himself several times that, as soon as he got out, he'd finish O'Hanlon for good, no matter what the consequences.

The man from east Tyrone sat and watched him, resting a Browning pistol on his knee with the barrel pointing towards his stomach.

Paddy ignored him.

But as the minutes stretched into hours, the silence began to grate on his nerves. Doubt began to creep into his mind. He'd assumed Gerry would arrive sooner or later and the whole thing would be quickly sorted out, but now he began to wonder where Gerry was. He thought Gerry and Colette might already have left Dublin for Paris.

And there was another thing; he thought this might all be tied up with what they'd been planning, in which case they'd been betrayed. But, he asked himself, by whom? Only the three of them knew the operation was underway, and the idea that Colette would have betrayed them was quite unthinkable.

He was confused. He couldn't think clearly, but it was getting dark and his instincts told him to get out. He looked at the man from east Tyrone, who was still smoking. 'Give us a smoke,' he said.

The man thought for a minute before picking up the gold packet of Benson & Hedges, lighting a cigarette and putting it gingerly in his mouth. He was a big man, fat even, with sorrowful eyes and pink cheeks. Paddy spoke quietly. 'You'll be dead when I get out of here.'

The man's voice was soft and slightly camp. 'Who says you'll be getting out?'

Paddy shivered involuntarily. He felt the first pangs of fear. 'Don't be an arsehole.'

'It's not my business, I'm not the boss, but from what I hear this is going to be a one-way ticket for you.'

Paddy had wanted to be angry. He had wanted to frighten the man, to intimidate him and use him to get out, but he felt the certainty draining out of his body. He was beginning to feel genuinely afraid. 'Untie my hands. I need a piss.'

The man shook his head slowly. 'You think I was born yesterday?' He gestured with the pistol. 'Piss in your pants.'

Paddy fell silent. He knew this was serious. There was no respect and no caution. He thought the man was right; this was going to be a one-way ticket. But he was confused and uncertain. If they knew about the attack in London, had they taken Gerry and Colette too? He didn't think they could kill them all. He didn't think they could get away with killing Gerry.

The night came on quickly and nobody inside the house turned on any lights. As the darkness descended, Paddy's fear gathered force and, by the time they came for him, all the early defiance had disappeared. They put a hood over his head and retied his hands carefully before helping him down the stairs and pushing him roughly onto the floor of a van. Paddy felt one of the men climb in beside him and he felt his sphincter muscles weaken as his fear grew again. He felt like he was swimming in darkness and his mind already seemed to be spinning out of control.

As the van started off he wanted to scream, but he knew it would be useless.

He knew the game and tried desperately to keep himself under control.

He told himself he was a big wheel. He told himself they'd no proof of anything. He told himself he was a hard man and this was just like the peelers: say nothing and they'll prove nothing. But whatever he tried to think, he couldn't convince himself he wasn't frightened.

O'Hanlon drove fast and Paddy began to feel the first waves of sickness. He didn't know where they were going, but he thought they would take him to south Armagh.

That is what he would have done. South Armagh was the safest. Wherever it was, he was sick long before they arrived, the liquid dribbling down his chin and the smell festering and foul.

Eventually, they seemed to pull off the tarmac road and onto a potholed track. After a few uncomfortable minutes, they stopped. Paddy heard the doors open and felt the hands taking hold of him.

They dragged him inside and strapped him to a chair. There was no heating in the house and it was extremely cold. They pulled down his trousers and his underpants, but left the hood on. He was still feeling groggy and he didn't fight. They left him for a while and he heard them unloading the van. He heard a few bottles clinking together and he thought they must have brought supplies with them. He thought they might be preparing for a long stay.

They came to him later, though Paddy had no notion of the time. When he heard O'Hanlon's soft voice, he felt a brief surge of anger. He tensed his muscles, as if consciously trying to break loose. 'Go fuck yourself, O'Hanlon,' he said quietly.

Inside the hood the smell was overwhelming and he had to stop himself from retching again.

The voice was steady, soft and pedantic. 'That's not the right way to talk, Paddy. That's not going to help, is it?'

'Go fuck yourself.' He felt dizzy again.

'Look, we want to make this easy on you. Just tell us everything and we will. Don't be hard on yourself.'

'Fuck off.' Every time he spoke, Paddy breathed in deeper and almost retched.

'Easy, Paddy, easy. We're going to be here a long time, you and I. We'll start with the simple. You talk nicely and we'll take off the hood. You go on like this and we'll keep it on. See?'

Paddy was silent for a moment. 'Fuck off.'

'OK, so the hood stays on. We've got plenty of time, Paddy. Plenty of time.'

Paddy felt the anger beginning to fade and the horror return, but he forced himself to sound defiant. 'You're fucking dead, O'Hanlon. You're fucking dead.'

The voice was icy in the darkness. 'We'll see about that.'

Paddy heard them go and, as the minutes ticked by, he tried to keep a check on the time. It was so hard to keep a sense of perspective on anything in the darkness, but he'd received his anti-interrogation training from the IRA and he knew he had to keep track of the time and of what they were trying to do to him. He knew he had to concentrate on their tactics and fight them minute by minute. He began to believe he might yet win. He was sure they had no proof and, even if they did, he didn't think it was likely to be that serious an offence. He didn't think they'd get away with killing him.

The thoughts came tumbling through his mind; perhaps O'Hanlon was a police or MI5 agent and had been tipped off by them. Perhaps one of his conversations with Gerry had been recorded and O'Hanlon had been instructed by his handlers to remove the plotters by any means available. His confusion and uncertainty grew.

He thought they had been gone about two hours – that was his guess – and when they came back, the voice in his ear was just the same. 'I hope we feel a bit more co-operative now. I hope we've had time to think things through.'

The stench was worse than ever. 'Gerry'll skin you alive.'

The voice was sarcastic, mocking and self-satisfied and it sent a shiver down his spine. 'Gerry? Gerry? I don't think so. Gerry's been helping us. Gerry helped us with the last little test.'

Paddy's fear was real now.

'Gerry was very concerned about it all. Indeed he was. Didn't believe it was you, of course. No, don't worry, he was very loyal. Going to be very hard for him to accept his brother's a tout.'

'What are you talking about?'

The voice was even more pedantic now, as if he were a child. 'Tut, tut. Let's give up the pretence, shall we? Gerry was very helpful. He told you about an arms movement into Hugo Street, but the mistake you made was that he *only* told you. Nobody else knew it because it wasn't really happening. It was a test, Paddy, a *test*. Your handlers weren't very clever, I must say, staging a roadblock like that *right* next to Hugo Street and telling the media it was a chance discovery. Our little dickers, they saw it all. Dear me no, not very bright. I don't think they can care much about you, Paddy, because they weren't very subtle . . .'

Paddy tried to shut out the voice. He wanted time to think. Nothing made any sense.

They still waited. Colette stood up again and lit another cigarette. They'd been here two hours now and her nervousness had increased with every passing minute.

She could see the truth written on Gerry's face. There was trouble. Something had happened. Paddy wasn't coming.

It was almost warm in Paris, the late evening sun filtering through a straggling cloud and falling

353

upon the left side of her face.

She watched the children playing in the small sand-pit in front of her and without realizing it she found herself smiling. She'd never been to Paris before and she was overwhelmed by what she'd seen: the beautiful boulevards, the cafés spilling out onto the streets, the noise and the bustle. She sat back down on the bench and listened to the heartbeat of the city.

There were few people in the small garden at the bottom of rue Mouffetard and she got up again to wander past the fruit stalls that seemed to run all the way up the centre of the avenue. Gerry watched her go, but said nothing.

As she walked, she found herself fantasizing about being here without fear and panic. Maybe just shopping, or . . . even just walking around. Maybe with the Brit . . .

Stupid notion.

She turned round and, when she got back to the garden, Gerry looked irritated and nervous. They walked to the hotel in silence and returned to their room.

They sat on the bed and played cards until it was dark outside. Gerry said little, but he was being kind to her. Eventually, as she was picking up a card, she asked him, 'Are we going to die?'

He shook his head. 'No.'

'It's not a suicide mission?'

'I don't believe in them.' He looked at her (she noticed how dirty his glasses were again and thought they hid so much) and raised the corner of his mouth, as though not quite able to smile. 'You've got respons-ibilities, so have I. I wouldn't do it to you.'

'I don't think I could stand going to prison again,' she said.

'You won't have to.'

'I think I want this to be the last, you know . . .'

He nodded. 'You've done your shift.' He chucked down his card and touched her shoulder. 'We need', he said, 'to get some sleep.'

She went to brush her teeth – Gerry didn't bother – and then stripped down to her T-shirt and knickers and came to lie next to him on the bed, pulling the sheets and blanket over her and trying not to touch his body. It was cold and she found herself shivering. Gerry was already asleep, or seemed to be, and she could hear him snoring gently.

She found herself thinking about being here without him. She thought about being in this room with the Brit. She wondered what he was doing.

She wondered if he knew she'd gone yet. She considered his anger and didn't know how it affected her.

She got up and looked back at the bed. Gerry was still sleeping, naked but for his underpants and lying face down, with the sheet and blanket wrapped loosely around him. She put on her sweater and went to the window and looked down on the rue des Gobelins. It was deserted and quiet. She stared out across the dilapidated rooftops for several minutes and then she turned back to look at Gerry.

Justify yourself, you bastard, she thought.

She wondered if he was the price of freedom, but knew in her heart that it was so much more than that. So much history. She thought of the dreams that had plagued her and tried to get some kind of picture of what she was. She felt a deep sense of fatalism again and wondered if it was best that way.

She was frightened about tomorrow and yet a part of her said, You *can* save yourself.

Another part told her that it was over. 'You're a dead woman,' she whispered.

CHAPTER EIGHTEEN

Paddy tried not to think about it, but he couldn't tear his mind away from the fact that he needed a piss.

He felt like an idiot, sitting there with his trousers and underpants round his ankles. He couldn't see his naked legs, but he felt the humiliation. It was a small thing, but it lowered his resistance and made him feel vulnerable.

He needed a piss and he was hungry – and cold. It was unbelievably cold. He could only guess at the time. It was morning, perhaps. He thought it had to be morning because he was very tired. He desperately wanted to sleep, but every time he tried to find something to rest his head on, somebody shook him and pushed him back into the chair.

More than anything, he hated the darkness of the hood.

He decided he could hold it in no longer and he let the water come gushing out of his penis in a thick warm stream which he could feel splashing against his legs. Just as he finished, he heard the voice again. 'Dear oh dear. No self-control, have we?'

He didn't respond. He felt weak and confused and the night-time hours had brought little enlightenment.

'Are you going to help us now? Can we conduct this in a civilized fashion? I think we probably can. Take off the man's hood, Chico, and let him see daylight.'

Paddy felt a huge surge of relief as the sack came off and he was able to breathe in clean, cold, fresh air. For a moment, he kept his eyes shut and savoured the sense of freedom. He opened them slowly. All three of them were there, O'Hanlon standing in the centre of the room in front of him, his legs apart and his hands on his hips. He waved one hand in front of his nose. 'What a smell.'

Paddy saw he was in a bedroom. O'Hanlon sat down on the small double bed, crossed his legs, lit a cigarette and looked at him. 'Now I hope we are feeling co-operative – or that sack goes right back on again.'

Paddy looked at him blankly. He was still relishing the fresh air and didn't trust himself to speak without causing offence. O'Hanlon took a drag on his cigarette and then waved it in Paddy's direction. 'Let us start at the beginning. When were you recruited?'

Paddy stared at him without speaking. O'Hanlon's expression betrayed a flash of irritation. 'Let's get on with it, or the sack goes on again – for good.'

He was speaking to him as if he were a child, but for the moment Paddy felt too tired to be frightened. Against his better judgement, he found himself saying, as he shook his head, 'I don't know what you're talking about.'

O'Hanlon leaned forward, his face suddenly animated and alive. 'I want to make this easy for you, Paddy, believe me I do. But you're making it very hard. You're going to make me hurt you and I don't want that. I'll ask the question again. Who recruited you and when?'

Paddy shook his head. 'Look, you can go on like this,

you can finish me off, but you'll not get nothing out of me, because there's nothing to tell.'

Now O'Hanlon was shaking his head. 'Well, we're going to have to part company on that one. I think you've got a lot to tell. The only question is how long I'm going to have to sit here until you tell it.' He suddenly seemed to lose patience and got up to go, waving his hand airily at Paddy. 'Do him.'

As he closed the door behind him, Paddy looked at Chico and felt real fear coursing through his system for the first time. He realized with a sickening shudder that he faced a slow, painful death; his ordeal likely to be lengthened by his innocence. Chico advanced towards him, grinning inanely. He saw the fat man from east Tyrone stand up and disappear through a side door which he hadn't noticed until now. He heard the sound of a bath running and shivered again.

They dragged him into the bath and bent him over the edge, the enamel rim cold against his skin.

The water was even colder and, for a few moments, he enjoyed the sensation of being clean. Then his body told him he wanted to breathe. He tried to hold on and wait, but the pressure grew until he was desperate and fighting for breath. His lungs and his mind felt like they were bursting and he pushed backwards with all his strength. But they held him. His lungs felt like they were going to explode when, suddenly, they pulled him up by his sodden hair.

They let him take three or perhaps four gulps of air and then he was plunged forward again, his lungs weaker this time and the pain more intense. He fought, his horror and desperation increasing, and they pulled him out only seconds before his lungs gave in and took in the water. He didn't feel he could last much longer.

But he did. He didn't know how long it went on, but

it seemed like for ever. They must have put him under twenty or thirty times – at least it felt like that – and by the time he got back to the chair he wanted to cry.

Chico sat down on the double bed and Paddy closed his eyes to try and blot out the reality that surrounded him. When he opened them again, Chico was on his knees in front of him, smiling inanely. Paddy struggled, but they'd tied his hands to the back of the chair and he found he couldn't move. He pushed himself sideways and hit the floor, the impact noiseless because of the thick, magenta carpet. They picked him up again and Chico took hold of his testicles. He fondled them gently and looked up. 'A perfect pair.'

Paddy looked down at him. He was horrified. Chico was grinning. 'Be a shame to ruin them.'

He squeezed and Paddy felt a searing pain shoot up through his body. He screamed, more out of shock than anything else, and the man from east Tyrone took a step forward and punched him across the side of his face.

Chico eased his grip and began fondling them again, the gesture oddly soothing after the pain. He was still grinning. 'You mustn't scream here, Paddy. No point in it, because there's no-one to hear you and nobody to help you.'

He squeezed and Paddy screamed again. He didn't think he'd ever felt such pain and, as Chico loosened his grip, he felt the words dribbling out of his mouth involuntarily. He wanted it to stop. He thought he'd do anything to make it stop. 'Christ, stop it,' he said. 'Please stop it.'

He felt pathetic, humiliated, and Chico was still grinning at him. 'Just think about it, Paddy. This could go on for weeks and weeks. A little gentle pain every day.'

He was saved by O'Hanlon, who put his head briefly

round the door. 'Car coming. Keep him quiet.'

The silence seemed blessed. Chico was still grinning and cracking his knuckles slowly, but for a few moments at least he didn't feel threatened. The windows were behind him and he'd noticed when he was being pulled from the bathroom that the curtains were drawn, but he could hear the wind. He thought it was a horrible day outside. If it was still day.

He heard the front door open and the faint sound of voices in urgent conversation. It lasted ten or fifteen minutes and then a door slammed and the car started up again. O'Hanlon came back to the room. He waved Chico away and sat down on the bed opposite Paddy. He looked puzzled. 'Curious. Most curious.'

Paddy stared at him blankly.

'Your brother has disappeared.'

Paddy didn't answer. He tried to keep his face expressionless.

'Hard to believe that both of you were touts.'

He felt his anger return. 'Don't be a prick.'

O'Hanlon got up and swung the back of his hand across his face. 'Mind your manners.'

Paddy's face stung, but his anger remained. 'For Christ's sake. Neither of us is a bloody tout. I don't know what the hell you're on about.'

'Then where's your brother, eh? What was he doing at Dublin airport on his way out of the country with nobody knowing where he's going?'

'None of your bloody business.'

O'Hanlon struck him again, harder. 'It is my business, I'm afraid. It is very much my business. He's leaving the country because he's a tout. You're both a filthy pair of touting rats.'

'He's on business.'

'Well, nobody knows about it.'

360

'He's no more a tout than I am.'

'That's not to say much. If he's not running away, then what *is* he doing?'

Paddy was becoming exasperated. He knew he was locked into this madness and he couldn't see a way out. He knew he was going to die here because of the paranoid rantings of a lunatic he detested more than anyone else he'd ever met. 'I told you, he's on business.'

'What business, Paddy? Touting business? Well, you'd know all about that.'

Paddy tried to summon his strength. 'He'll make you pay for this, O'Hanlon. Believe me, he will . . .'

Colette stood up too quickly and she felt Gerry tugging at her side. As she sat down again, he whispered, 'Steady,' in her ear.

Everyone else was on their feet now, though the plane had not yet come to a halt. The overhead lockers were being opened. A coat fell on her head and a man bent down to apologize. She smiled at him, mechanically.

The plane stopped and, a few minutes later, people began to shuffle down towards the exit. Gerry nudged her and she got to her feet. She waited for a gap in the line and then stepped out and reached up for their bags.

They walked towards the exit. The stewardesses smiled and said goodbye and she nodded at them without speaking.

They were in the terminal now and there was a curious excitement mixed in with her fear. But as they approached the control zone, fear dominated.

There was a queue and they waited.

She felt a tightness in her chest again.

She was there. She fumbled in her bag and produced

the small red passport. It was a false name and false identity, but she knew she looked pretty in the photograph. She smiled at the man, but didn't speak.

He didn't smile back. He looked down at the passport and then up again. He looked down once more and then put it back on the counter for her. His eyes turned to Gerry. She walked slowly, waiting for Gerry and trying to resist the temptation to run.

She sensed Gerry on her shoulder and heard him whisper, 'Bingo.'

They walked down to the tube. They had to wait only a few minutes and then a train arrived and they got in. They waited for a few more minutes and then Gerry nodded and they got out and walked down the platform to the other end of the train, Gerry looking over his shoulder as they did so. Colette got in and Gerry waited on the platform. Just as the doors began to shut, he jumped in and came to sit next to her.

They sat in silence and Colette looked at all the adverts for theatres and books and films. There was so much happening here.

Gerry nudged her as the tube was pulling in to Piccadilly Circus and she picked up her bag and followed him into the throng. It was already dark outside, the bright lights of Piccadilly beaming their message out over the crowds below. She followed Gerry past the statue of Eros and a group of Japanese tourists posing for the inevitable holiday snapshots. They waited to cross the road and then walked up to the Regency Crest hotel. They checked in as Mr and Mrs Peter Jennings, occupying a twin bedroom at £59 a night. Colette did the talking. Her English accent was more convincing.

The Regency Crest was not particularly luxurious, its long, anonymous corridors giving way to small, newly painted, but still shabby rooms. Colette put her bag on the floor, lay on the bed and closed her eyes. She fell asleep and, when she woke, Gerry was standing over her and suggesting they go and get something to eat. She nodded weakly and they walked down to the Pizzaland at the top of Lower Regent Street. They ordered and Gerry looked around him carefully before leaning forward to speak to her. The room was empty, but she had to strain to make out what he was saying.

He told her he had been preparing, for many months, a plan to assassinate the British prime minister as he spoke at Prime Minister's Questions in the House of Commons. He said they would enter the press section of the House using forged passes, emerge at the key moment, shoot and then escape via the terrace that ran alongside the Thames. A small rubber inflatable would be waiting.

He told her he had sent one of his best people over six months before to prepare and plan.

Colette felt sick.

She excused herself politely and disappeared into the ladies' loo. She shut one of the cubicles and sat on the seat with her head between her legs.

She thought he must be mad.

She went back to the table and asked him to go over the plan again in detail. He was still vague – deliberately so, she thought – and told her simply to trust him. After a while, conversation petered out and she stirred her cappuccino in silence. As she sucked the froth off her teaspoon she considered the man who sat opposite her and found it hard to believe she'd spent so much of her life trying to impress him and win his respect. At this moment, she thought she hated him.

She tried one more time to get through to him, as if subconsciously willing him to give her a reason to change her mind. 'What'll the leadership think if tomorrow works?' she asked.

'It will work.'

She stirred the remains of her coffee and shrugged her shoulders. 'I know, I know, but I mean, what will they think?'

Gerry readjusted his spectacles and looked at her intently. 'I have some support. I'm not alone.'

'But what will they do?'

'They'll do nothing. Their so-called peace process will be over and they'll have to get on and fight.'

Colette tried to sound encouraging. 'But they'll do nothing to you – I mean to us?'

'They won't touch us. They wouldn't dare.'

Colette fell silent. When her second cappuccino arrived, she tried again. 'When will it end, Gerry? I mean, how much longer do you think it will take?'

She noticed the muscle along his jaw twitching. 'Like I said before, it will end when it ends. It will end when we've won. It will end when we've got the Brits out – when we've broken their will to stay – however long it takes, whether it be five, fifty or five hundred years.'

Gerry stopped abruptly. He had raised his voice slightly and said more than he should, and he looked round to check they had not been overheard. He got up and indicated to Colette that she should follow. They paid at the front counter and returned to their room.

After Gerry had turned off the lights, she lay awake long into the night, thinking. She didn't think she was going to be able to sleep. She was just considering getting up when she heard Gerry sniff and realized he'd also been lying awake. He said only, 'I hope Paddy's all right.'

She realized she had hardly thought about Paddy.

* * *

364

When they picked up the hood again, Paddy knew he was finished. Perhaps, if he'd had time, he would have been brave at the end, but the whole thing had been such a shock and such a surprise – such an outrage, because he knew he was innocent – that he hadn't had time to gather himself.

When he could think of anything but the pain, he thought they must have been ordered to beat a confession out of him – any confession – because they seemed to have consciously abandoned all restraint. He hadn't seen O'Hanlon again.

The confession made no sense. He just agreed with whatever they put to him.

They taped it, as evidence.

He wanted to fight as they dragged him to the van, but he found himself pleading. They threw him into the back and he hit his head against the metal seat strut. It began to bleed, the blood running into his eyes. In the dark, in his blindness and fear, he began to cry like a baby. 'Please, God, please. Please. Please . . .' He didn't know which one of them sat next to him and he didn't care. 'Please. I'm no tout. I hate touts more than anyone.'

There was no answer. His existence was pain, darkness and despair. He called out, but nobody answered him. In his last hour of life, he was to be denied even the comfort of another human voice. He shivered violently and curled his body into a ball, as if consciously trying to return to the safety of the womb. He begged, 'Christ, please. God, please. Ask Gerry – ask anyone – I'm no tout. Please, please, please . . .'

He heard nothing, saw nothing. He felt dizzy, his head dazed by the beatings and by the journey. It seemed to go on for ever, but he didn't stop pleading. There was no reason to it, no logic. He knew what was going to happen, but he'd lost his dignity and courage. He'd never imagined it would be like this, never imagined it would come so slowly and so inevitably. He'd never imagined that he would understand and recognize the march of death, never believed he would stare death in the face and not have any power to prevent it. He cried all the way. Cried like a baby. Cried for anyone or anything to help him. He cried as if what he was doing would make a difference, as if it would unlock some long-hidden sense of humanity and compassion in the hearts of his tormentors.

The van stopped and they pulled him by his feet onto the tarmac, the impact blowing the wind out of his lungs. They pulled off his trainers and his socks and he knew the moment was closer than ever. He struggled briefly and then cried again. 'Oh God. Oh Christ. Please. No. Please no, please . . .'

They yanked him to his feet and he felt the mud squelching between his toes. He felt helpless, but he couldn't and wouldn't give up, and he kept pleading, his cries ever more pathetic and desperate.

They took him – walked him – for a mile or more, and by the end his feet were bleeding, though he certainly didn't notice the pain. He felt curiously light-headed, the pain deadened by his desperation.

They forced him to kneel and he cried harder than ever. He pleaded, still babbling incoherently and calling for his mother. He felt the barrel of the pistol at the back of his head, but he didn't hear the shot.

The men walked away, laughing.

There was a small huddle outside Grant's office and they all fell silent as Ryan approached.

He didn't care. He told himself he just did not care. He was embarrassed, angry even, but he didn't care enough to let it worry him. The others were career men and he looked at them with contempt. He set himself apart.

Grant was businesslike, in that detached way of his, his manner vague but his mind sharp. There was not enough room for all of them, so some stood, including Ryan.

Grant twisted his half-moon glasses round in his hand and gestured at him. 'Let's just go through this again, shall we? What is the explanation? What do we know?'

Jenkins answered before Ryan could open his mouth. 'We know we have a rogue agent. We know there has been a breakdown in supervision.'

Grant cut in, his voice icy. 'I'm not interested in blame at this juncture, Jenkins. I want to go over what we know.'

Ryan made as if to speak and then thought better of it. Jenkins picked up. 'We know from the RUC' – he mouthed the letters as if they were contagious – 'that an IRA hit team, including our woman, is on its way to London – or is already in London. We know there are two of them, but there could be many more. We know that they are due to attack within the next two or three days – or, at least, we *think* we know that. And that is about all we do *know*. We believe the target may be a royal, possibly Prince Charles.'

Jenkins paused for effect. Ryan thought he was enjoying this and his dislike of him escalated another notch. 'One thing we do know: they're travelling via Paris. We alerted Jefferson at the embassy there as soon as we heard, and he in turn has organized our French colleagues. They have saturated both airports and all the channel ports. They're being very thorough.'

Grant cut in again. 'They have pictures?'

'Yes, as do our people. We've launched a massive operation and have all points of entry fully covered. If they're not in already, they've very little chance of getting in.'

Grant twiddled his glasses again, asking Jenkins a question to which he already knew the answer. 'Do we know how many are involved in total – who is providing the back-up?'

'We do not.' Jenkins pushed the top sheet of paper to one side and opened up a computer printout. 'Targets. Well, we can't be absolutely sure, but it seems this is actually going to take place in London – that is the intelligence we have from the RUC, for what it's worth. As you know, the Queen is away, in New Zealand, and there is only one significant royal engagement to-morrow.' Jenkins paused again and looked up before delivering his ace. 'Prince Charles is due to lunch with Thabo Mbeki at South Africa House.'

Grant grunted volubly. He looked round the table. 'Any suggestions, gentlemen?'

Silence. One of the analysts at the other end of the table looked round to see if anyone else was going to answer before saying what was on all their minds. 'He'll cancel, surely?'

Jenkins was curt. 'We've asked. He won't.'

The analyst tried to expand, but Jenkins waved his hand airily. 'He won't entertain it. We've been through that already. We'll just have to tell the police to beef up their security.'

Grant sucked one arm of his glasses. 'That's not easy either. Hard to have the whole place awash with security without people asking awkward questions. Not to mention the difficulties of protecting the source for our friends in the RUC . . .'

Jenkins smirked. 'Under the circumstances, I don't

think we need worry about that unduly.'

'Well, perhaps not. If we don't know for certain that it is him – and I must say the idea of this lunch going ahead makes me bloody nervous – then who else?'

Jenkins looked down at the sheet in front of him. 'Take your pick. Cabinet ministers, former prime ministers – current prime minister, come to that. Dignitaries, former military figures who've served in Northern Ireland. The list is very long, naturally.'

Grant looked directly at Jenkins. 'The PM?'

'Nothing today. Tomorrow only Prime Minister's Questions in the House.' Jenkins half smiled. 'We've asked already. He won't cancel. Especially since the subject he's likely to want to address will be the current propaganda jamboree being enjoyed in America by one Gerry Adams.' Jenkins leaned forward again, his expression deadly serious. 'The position really is this: we have to assume Prince Charles is the target and take maximum security measures tomorrow – if he still insists on going ahead with this ridiculous lunch. We're working on the Palace to try and knock some sense into him. We'll take appropriate measures with the PM also. But in my view, the principle hope lies in picking up these people between now and whenever they are planning to go ahead. We've had intensive discussions with the police and with the Army. We've circulated the photographs. We have surveillance teams in place already. We have taps on all relevant phones, including the McVeigh family home in Belfast. The only thing we have going for us is that they don't know that *we* know. We had better just hope we get lucky.'

At the end of the table, Grant scanned the faces of those around him, but nobody spoke; one or two simply nodded their heads silently. He had to go and see the director-general, the cabinet secretary – and others – and he dismissed them briskly. Except Ryan. He was left standing in the middle of the room whilst the others filed out.

Ryan was reminded of school again. The feeling was different. He was penitent. Grant spoke quietly, almost gently, and Ryan thought he sounded very tired. 'What went wrong, David?'

'I don't know, sir.'

'Don't call me, sir.'

Ryan smiled briefly. 'I'm sorry.'

'The RUC say you may have got too close to it. Jenkins says you're incompetent.'

'I was committed to our agent.'

Grant put on his glasses and looked down at the papers on his table, an act of dismissal that Ryan had already learned to recognize. He threw a last comment as Ryan reached the door. 'I hope it pays off, or we'll all be finished. Sleep by that phone – and pray it rings.'

Ryan went back to the incident room and sat on the desk. He looked down onto the Thames, the river itself just visible in the darkness, and wondered where the hell she was and what she was doing. He felt a curious sense of loneliness.

The room was quiet, the others long since gone to the flats designed specially for this kind of emergency.

The building was new and Ryan had never been here before. His desk had been moved over from Gower Street two weeks earlier. Their new premises and offices were a vast improvement, though he had barely taken in the change.

He wondered now if this was his fault and if it could have been averted. Shadow Dancer was his agent – *his* – and he wondered if he'd fucked it up.

He wondered if she was lost to him.

At the back of his mind he could not eradicate the faces of Hopkins, Long, Brian Allen and even Grant. He knew they were all blaming him and knew there might only be a few hours left.

He looked at the phone and prayed it would ring.

CHAPTER NINETEEN

Colette slept fitfully and, when she woke, Gerry was standing by the window, already fully dressed. She felt full of sleep and thought it must be late. She got up, went to the bathroom and shut the door behind her.

She brushed her teeth first, then showered. For the first time in weeks, even months, she put on a little make-up. As she looked in the mirror, she could see she was pretty, but did not consider it a blessing. She'd spent her life fighting the superficial judgements of those who were impressed by her beauty and she thought it a burden to be overcome rather than a gift to be treasured.

But as she looked at her reflection, she felt, at least, the certainty of where she was going. She had made up her mind now and there was no turning back.

When she emerged, Gerry was sitting on the corner of the bed with the phone to his ear. His knuckles were white and she could tell something was wrong. A terrible premonition crept over her. She sat down quietly on the other side of the bed, twisting her body to face him. He put down the receiver. 'I phoned Ma,' he said.

She looked at him inquisitively.

'Paddy's dead.'

Time stopped.

She looked down and scrunched her eyes painfully shut.

It was as if she'd waited her whole life for this – the pessimist in her always imagining the worst.

Her mind was swimming. A brief glimmer of hope, a notion it couldn't be true, that it was too enormous to be true, was drowned out in the panic of total certainty.

She pressed her hands into the centre of her eyes and pushed until the pain was intense.

She wanted to remain in the darkness.

She became conscious of the silence in the room.

She heard herself ask why and looked up to see the harshness in Gerry's face. 'Because he was a tout.'

For a brief moment, she had the strength to view him with utter contempt. Whether responding to the look on her face or not, he went on, his voice still sour, 'They suspected him and we devised a simple test – a stupid test – just some arms coming into the city. Only he knew about it. Only he and I and Internal. The police were out searching in force. He must have tipped them off . . .'

Colette couldn't control herself. She ran to the toilet bowl and retched violently, her body shaking and her legs weak. She sank to her knees.

Eventually, she became aware of Gerry standing behind her. He spoke quietly. 'I'm sorry, Colette,' he said. 'It's hard for all of us.'

No it's not, she wanted to say. Not for you, you bastard, and not for me because . . . She felt another sudden wave of nausea.

It should have been me, she thought.

She turned back to him, still kneeling. 'Don't you care *at all*?'

'*Of course* I care. Of course I do. But we can't survive if we allow touts to live. He knew the penalties better than anyone.'

'He's our *brother*.'

Gerry was silent for a few seconds. 'He *was* our brother,' he said casually. 'He's nothing if he's a tout.'

She looked at him, caught between desolation and hatred.

'He was a tout, Colette. Do you understand what I'm saying? Do you understand what that means? That means every hardship we've endured, every man or woman we've lost, every sacrifice we've made and every year we've spent in prison was for nothing. He knew all of that, he watched all of that, and every step of the way, every day, he was betraying us. He was betraying us when Davey died. He was betraying us when you went to prison.'

Colette pushed the hair out of her eyes. 'He's still our brother,' she said quietly.

'No, not after all that. Not after he's betrayed everything we've ever done. Everything we've ever stood for. What about the Loyalist attack on Ma? Maybe that was him too?'

'He's not a tout.'

'It's too late for that now.'

She sobbed uncontrollably. 'It wasn't him,' she said. 'It wasn't him.'

'It *was* him, Colette. The truth is I've suspected him for some time – since the attack on Henderson, or maybe even before that. I didn't want to acknowledge it, didn't want to admit it to myself. When the truth is like that, you don't want to believe it. You'd do anything not to believe it.'

He moved towards the door. 'We've got to go,' he said, but she had her eyes closed again and was sinking

374

into the depths of despair. She felt his hand on her shoulder, gently at first. His grip tightened for a few seconds and then he thrust his hand underneath her arm and tried to pull her to her feet. 'Come on, Colette,' he said.

She tried to pull away, but suddenly he gripped her violently, pulled her back towards him, and slapped her hard across the face.

'We've got a job to do,' he said, 'and we'll do it whether our brother was a traitor or not.'

Her face stung and she put her hand to her cheek to relieve the pain. She felt the tears in her eyes again and this time, as he grabbed her, she did not protest.

He almost dragged her along the corridor and into the lift. There was nobody else in it and she caught sight of her reflection briefly in the brass corner fittings. She looked a wreck.

In the lobby below she tucked herself in behind Gerry as he approached the front desk and asked for the bill. She waited, looking at the floor, unable to think clearly.

'Are you all right, madam?' she heard someone ask.

'She's fine,' Gerry said.

'Are you all right, madam?' the woman asked again, her voice tougher this time.

Colette looked up to see a plump, blonde woman leaning on the counter and looking at her with an anxious expression on her face.

Colette tried to smile and felt a brief flicker of pleasure as she imagined Gerry's discomfort. 'I'm . . . I'm all right,' she said slowly. The woman reluctantly turned her eyes away from her and went to the computer printer to rip off the bill. Nobody spoke again and Colette kept her eyes on the floor.

As they emerged from the hotel a few moments later,

Colette felt Gerry's hand on her arm again and she moved forward with him.

They passed the pink Dunkin' Donuts shop and the smell wafted past her.

They stopped by Boots and waited to cross the first part of the road. She was on the right of Gerry and she noticed, to *her* right, a man dressed in a grey suit leaning against a pillar. He had his head half turned away from them and was talking into a mobile phone. She wondered if he was part of a surveillance team.

The pedestrian light went green and they crossed and waited on the island for the next section. There was a family to the right of her now, with American accents and skullcaps – the boys, anyway. She looked up slightly and saw a man in a pinstriped suit looking at her. He was middle-aged and a little overweight, and she wondered for a brief second if *he* was watching them, but he looked at her for too long and she felt a moment of hurt as she realized it was for the usual reasons.

As they were waiting, one of the old red buses passed them with a giant picture of a baby on the side. A beautiful baby.

The light went green and they crossed. She recalled the day Pa had brought back a model of one of those old buses on a trip from London. She remembered the excitement – they didn't often get presents – and her disappointment when she realized it was for Paddy and Gerry, not her. She remembered Paddy and Gerry arguing over ownership and Gerry winning, as always.

As they passed the Eros statue, Gerry still had his hand under her arm and he led her towards a big building with 'Lillywhites' written in big green letters on the outside.

Inside, she saw quickly that it was a sports store, and

Gerry told her to start looking as though she wanted to buy something. Mechanically, she pulled out and carefully examined the shirts around her and, even here, even now, she couldn't help feeling the quality of the material and thinking how happy little Mark would be to be brought back a present.

She lost track of time completely in the store. They seemed to look round for ages, going up and then down several floors, but eventually Gerry led them back out into the street. It was bright now and, as they stepped out onto the pavement, she caught sight of the top of the Houses of Parliament in the distance and felt her stomach tightening. There was a tall pillar before it, on top of which was the figure of a man who looked to be standing with the careless arrogance you'd expect from a British imperialist. It looked like a shorter version of Nelson's column.

They walked a few paces and she felt a momentary sense of pleasure as she caught sight of a blue Bank of Ireland sign. Her bank. She realized, with a start, that she hadn't thought about the new account – *their* money – for, well, weeks. So much money. Enough to change everything.

They crossed the road at the bottom and gently walked down the steps by the statue, passing a group of tourists talking in Japanese and looking at their map.

They crossed the Mall and entered St James's Park. The trees were bare at this time of year and she felt the desolation of winter. An elderly man wearing a strange cap with feathers in it approached them, puffing a cigarette. She wondered again as he passed if they were being watched.

They crossed another road, this time walking towards a security barrier and, despite herself, Colette felt another sharp twinge of nerves. She looked at

Gerry's impassive face and even now she couldn't help a sneaking admiration for his courage. They passed the checkpoint and entered a huge gravel courtyard with a long, almost impossibly elegant white building ahead of them.

She remembered passing here all those years ago, wandering – sightseeing – after one of the surveillance missions.

A soldier appeared from under the archway, looking absurd in his high black boots, white jodhpurs and dark-blue tunic. A ridiculous tourist attraction, except . . .

She shivered inwardly and felt suddenly more oppressed than ever, as if a fatalistic cloud was hovering over her. As they turned onto Whitehall, they passed another soldier, this time on horseback, and for a second she found herself looking into the beast's eyes as it bent to nuzzle the hand of a tourist. They were trusting eyes.

She shut her own eyes again and wanted to be enveloped by the darkness.

Ryan stood up to make, once again, the short journey to the coffee machine.

The room was buzzing around him, but there had been no real developments overnight. The atmosphere was tense and tempers were running short. There had been nothing new to discuss at the early meeting. Everyone was waiting.

A few minutes after he'd returned with his coffee, news came from GCHQ that a phone call had been made to the McVeigh home in Belfast, and traced to the Regency Crest hotel, off Piccadilly Circus.

Ryan didn't pause to wonder whether he should stay by the phone. He picked up his jacket and ran.

It was a bright day in London and, as always at this time, the streets were crowded with people still making their way to work. Ryan sprinted the first few hundred yards, but his legs and lungs began to tire and he slowed to a fast jog, his knees absorbing the full impact of his footfall through the thin soles of his penny loafers. It was not warm, but by the time he reached Piccadilly Circus he was sweating.

He ran into the lobby of the hotel and saw the look on the face of the detective standing with his back to the counter. He was wearing a fawn-coloured raincoat and Ryan recognized him from one of the many anti-terrorism conferences he'd attended, though he couldn't remember his name. The man didn't wait for introductions. He simply smiled and shrugged his shoulders. 'Gone. Gone, I'm afraid. Checked out ten minutes ago. Could be anywhere by now.'

By the time Ryan left, they'd gone over the room with a fine-tooth comb and found nothing. They were fanning out to search the streets around, but Ryan thought it would be like looking for a needle in a haystack.

He crossed the road and stopped by the Eros statue in the centre of Piccadilly. It was quite sunny now and a couple of latin-looking girls were lying by the fountain, as if exhausted. He looked at them for a few moments and then glanced up at the signs towering above him: McDonald's, Foster's, Coke, Samsung, Carlsberg. He turned and strolled slowly – there seemed no need to rush – down towards Pall Mall and St James's Park. He looked carefully about him, scrutinizing faces, knowing there was no chance of seeing them.

He passed the Bank of Ireland and was reminded, with a jolt, of the account they'd promised to set up there. It hadn't been done yet, of course. Probably never would be now.

He wondered if she deserved the money – if she'd *ever* deserved it – and felt the same sense of nagging doubt and failure that had been plaguing him ever since the news had broken, or even longer. Where, he asked himself, did the truth stop and the lies begin? Did the truth begin? He wondered if she'd ever really told the truth about anything.

He crossed Pall Mall and walked past the statue of Frederick, Duke of York, younger brother of George III; he knew, since he'd once bothered to stop and look at the inscription. He skirted St James's Park and made for the great square off Horseguards, leaving the Northern Ireland Office to the left of him. As he walked under the arch and onto Whitehall, he noticed the soldiers in all their finery and felt the bile in his stomach.

If she was going to die, then maybe that was justice. Could anyone say she didn't deserve it?

By the time he reached Parliament Square that thought had sunk in. He suddenly felt sick.

They were upstairs drinking coffee in Grandma Lee's. The café was beside Westminster tube station and right opposite the Palace of Westminster. Gerry was nervous, more nervous than Colette had ever known him. He'd seen the heavy security presence from the window – he could hardly have failed to since the whole place was now crawling with policemen – and he'd cursed Paddy under his breath. He thought the whole operation might be compromised.

She'd never seen the man who'd been waiting for them before, though Gerry said he was from Belfast. He looked like he'd assimilated into English society, because he wore a smart suit and spoke with an English accent. He was clean-shaven and well groomed and he and Gerry spoke to each other in whispers, though there was no-one there to hear them. Gerry was still agitated. 'What's with all the security?' he asked.

The man was even more jumpy than Gerry and his eyebrows kept twitching. 'I don't know. I don't know. I think we should abort.'

Gerry's voice was firm. 'No way.'

'For Christ's sake, this place is crawling with peelers. They must know something—'

'It could be for a hundred reasons.'

The man was getting more agitated by the minute. 'It could not! I've never seen it like this. Never.'

'I said no, and that's it. We've come a long way with this and we'll see it through.'

'For God's sake—'

Gerry leaned forward and sunk his fingers into the man's forearm, his voice laced with menace. 'I said *no*, you hear me? I said no. Now get a hold of yourself. Give me the guns.'

The man could see from Gerry's expression that further argument was futile. He looked carefully about him and then passed the small black shoulder case under the table.

'Now something has obviously happened to get these people excited,' Gerry said quietly, 'but it's only *just* happened, so I think they'll still be off-guard, We're going to bring everything forward and go in now. Understood?'

The man looked as if he would strangle himself on his nerves. 'For God's and Jesus' sake, we've got to abort this. It's madness. The whole area is crawling.'

Gerry's voice was firm. Colette noticed that the muscle in his cheek had stopped twitching. 'It will be all right. They can't possibly have any specific knowledge, so we'll be all right. The security in the underpass won't be so tight.'

381

'You haven't a hope. You've no chance.'

'It will work. We've just got to hold our nerve – *you*'ve just got to hold *your* nerve.'

The man clearly couldn't believe what he was hearing and he paused for a second before continuing. 'But even if you get in, you'll never get out.'

Gerry looked at him with contempt in his eyes. 'You leave that to us. Just get the boat there.'

'The river will be crawling with police; there's a helicopter up there, for God's sake.'

Gerry raised his voice for the first time. 'Just get it there.' He looked around. The room was still empty. 'Get it there, or I'll kill you myself.'

The man got up, the threat still hanging in the air, and Colette wondered if her legs would move, but Gerry put his hand underneath her arm again and almost pulled her from her seat. He stared at the man, grim-faced, and then took her towards the stairs.

At the bottom he eased his grip on her, and as they turned out onto the street she considered running for it, but why and to where? She felt weighed down by inertia and fatalism.

She was beside Gerry as they descended the steps to the underpass and she hesitated for a second as she saw the peelers at the gate to the Commons. There were two of them and she felt the fear return. She watched Gerry as he strode confidently towards them, half a step ahead of her, and, as he fingered his pass and lifted it slightly, she did the same. Gerry was smiling – Christ, she thought, he could charm the devil if it came to it – and she looked at him and not the men ahead of her.

'Morning,' Gerry said, still smiling. His accent was all right, but she knew if he had to say more . . .

They were level now and she looked up into the men's faces. They were both elderly, or ageing at least, both with white hair and both looking relaxed. The one with the glasses stepped forward a pace to take a closer look at their passes, but Gerry continued to edge slowly ahead, as though indicating the examination of the passes was routine and he was in a hurry.

The man glanced at them only briefly and then looked into their faces – an uncomplicated look that seemed to lack suspicion.

And then they were through and Colette was conscious of the inertia receding. Perhaps it was fear and adrenalin, or perhaps – hard to admit – excitement.

They were walking under the arches and to their right was the cobbled circuit where the cars came sweeping into the Commons. A man crossed ahead of them and Colette felt another stab of fear and excitement as she realized she recognized him. A minister, certainly, though she couldn't remember the name. A taxi pulled in to the right of them and a large man in a suit and a handsomely dressed woman stepped out. She felt a little stab of hatred.

They passed through a door and entered what seemed to be some kind of turret. They started climbing a narrow stairway, the walls a dirty yellow and the carpet a faded green, and Colette quickly grew out of breath. The staircase turned and turned and seemed to go on and on – and then they were on a landing and she saw a sign saying 'Lower Reporters' Gallery'. There was now a door ahead of her and Colette could see the room was lighter and she could hear voices. Gerry suddenly turned, taking her arm, and began descending the stairs. When they had walked down two of the flights, she whispered, 'What is it?'

He stopped. 'Fine – just checking. Don't say anything.' As he went ahead, Colette couldn't help admiring his professionalism once again. He seemed to know where he was going and what he was doing, or at least that was the impression he gave. A man in a suit and a well-dressed woman in a mauve jacket and cream blouse passed them, but didn't seem to take any notice. At the bottom of the stairs, they came out and turned left, going deeper into the House. They passed a small car park, where Colette noticed that a van was being turned round on an ingenious rotating metal drum in the floor. There clearly wasn't enough room to turn any other way.

To her horror, Gerry turned left again and walked past a series of cashpoints. They crossed what seemed to be some kind of road and then walked out onto the terrace that ran alongside the Thames. It was more or less deserted and they turned round and walked straight back into a steward. Gerry mumbled an apology and the man looked at him snootily. He stepped aside to let them pass. 'This *is* for members only, sir.'

They retraced their steps and began to climb the stairs again. Another man in a suit flashed past them and said, 'Morning,' but he was gone before she could consider whether or not to reply. Colette could feel the sense of excitement slipping away.

As they reached the sign saying 'Lower Reporters' Gallery', two men came out of the room ahead of them, both clutching bits of paper. They didn't seem to be in a hurry and their eyes fell casually on Colette. Her insides felt like they were disintegrating and she tried to manage a smile. Gerry paused to allow them to climb the next flight of stairs and one of them looked over his shoulder at her again. It was inoffensive – curious, perhaps admiring.

They reached another sign with the words 'Upper Reporters' Gallery' written on it, and this time Gerry went straight ahead. The two men went on up the stairs and she saw the same one look over his shoulder again as they turned the next corner.

Then they were in a darkly lit corridor. She saw a tiny poky office to her left, with newspapers piled in its window. The door was half open, but she couldn't see anyone inside and the corridor was quiet. Gerry was standing still, as if unsure of what to do. He took her arm again and led her to the end of the corridor, towards a door with the word 'Gentlemen' written on it in gold. He paused for a brief second and then took her in. It was a small room with two urinals and a single cubicle. 'Perfect,' he said. He took her into the cubicle, pulled down the top of the loo seat and motioned for her to sit. He shut the door and leaned against the wall.

They were silent and she bent her body and put her head in her hands. She wanted to cry, but the tears wouldn't come.

'If anything happens to me,' Gerry said, 'that is where the boat will be to get away – that terrace we just saw. That is the way to it. Just remember that route and run like hell. The boat will be waiting and, if needs be, just jump into the water and he'll pick you up.'

For a brief second, she was almost tempted to admire the audacity of what he'd planned, but other instincts prevailed and she felt anger. It was suicide, without question. It was risky under normal circumstances – her head had cleared enough to gauge that – but today it was suicide. She wondered what had caused the increased peeler presence and struggled for a moment to think of a rational explanation, but it defeated her. She wondered if they had been watched, if there had been surveillance, but in that case what were they doing here? How had they come this far? It didn't make sense. How did they know anything anyway? She'd told them nothing. No-one else knew anything at all. Except Gerry. And Paddy.

Paddy. The name exploded in her head now and she felt the tears welling up in her eyes.

She imagined the moment they had come for him. Would he have been surprised? Would he have fought? Would he have been frightened, or angry, or both? Would he have cried and begged?

She wondered what she'd have done. What if it *had* been me, she asked herself. The thought came to her that, even if it had been an open choice, even if Paddy had been aware of *all* the facts, he'd still have gone in her stead. His courage was decent, just as Gerry's was evil. Or so it seemed now.

She wondered what they'd have done to him. For all the intimacy of her knowledge and association with the organization, she couldn't actually have said what they *did* to you. Not many people did know. Perhaps it was deliberate. That was part of the fear.

She imagined the final moments. She knew about that and could imagine it vividly. Would he have cried then? Can there ever be courage at the moment of . . . ?

She imagined him being dragged. She imagined the fear in his body and the hood and the damp and cold of the mud. She imagined the loneliness and the cruelty and the hatred and the darkness . . .

She wanted to scream.

She screwed her eyes shut.

She imagined Gerry standing above her, his groin at the level of her head. She wanted to punch him.

She realized she'd crossed a barrier. She'd betrayed them, sure, but her instincts were human – to protect Mark and Catherine. Even before – even before the betrayal began – she wouldn't have executed someone

386

for touting. Dislike them, maybe, hate them even. But she would not have condemned her own brother to death for it. She didn't believe Paddy would have done so either.

She thought Gerry was a monster. Her eyes were dry now. She looked up and saw he was staring impassively at the wall behind her. 'What's the time?' she asked.

He looked at his watch. 'Nearly there,' he said, and she hated him some more. 'Stay here,' he added. 'I've got to make a final check. I'll knock three times.' He opened the cubicle door and was gone, the bag still resting at her feet.

She pushed the lock back.

The room was silent. She looked at the bag and pulled it towards her. She picked it up and felt the heaviness of the metal.

She thought of little Mark and his toy gun and then felt paralysed by the sudden clash of hope and fear.

The room was silent, but for the dripping of the cistern behind her.

She stood up and eased back the lock on the cubicle door, opened it a fraction and listened. She could hear nothing. She wished now that she had a watch. She stepped gingerly forwards and caught sight of herself in the mirror. She wondered idly if it would be the last time she'd ever see her own image. She walked across to the lavatory door, opened it a touch and peered out. The corridor was empty and quiet.

She stepped out. The door closest to her was half open and she stopped outside. She couldn't hear anyone inside.

She pushed open the door gently and went in. She saw two desks, two chairs, two telephones and several piles of newspapers. She closed the door a fraction and sat down at one of the desks. Fear almost prevented her from picking up the phone, but, after a moment's hesitation, she found the courage.

She called the Freephone number and a man answered, her world suddenly slowed, as if she were living in a dream. She told him it was Shadow Dancer and she needed to speak to the young man – the spook – now, urgently, this second. It was life or death, she said. The man said he was sorry, but the young man was away, would the other do? She said no, it must be the young man, it had to be Ryan. Life or death she said.

He asked her to wait. She was terrified, waiting for the tap on the shoulder and the turn to see Gerry's face, puzzled and inquisitive. She couldn't bring herself to look round. More waiting. Waiting for what seemed like for ever, then the man again, saying he had a number if she had a pen. Fumbling in her handbag, still like a dream, and trying to find something to write with, to write on.

She got there eventually and then cut the connection and dialled again. There was no tone. She tried again and then a gentle tap on her shoulder sent a giant shock through her system.

It was the man she'd seen earlier – the one in the suit who'd been looking at her.

She recovered. 'I'm so sorry,' she said, somehow managing to smile. 'I just desperately needed to use the phone, a personal call.'

He frowned for a second and then shrugged his shoulders and half smiled. 'I'll be back in a second,' he said.

She didn't stop to think. She dialled again and this time heard the tone. She almost wept when she heard his voice. 'Shadow Dancer?'

'I've no time. I'm in London.'

'I know.'

His voice was calm and her nerves settled further. 'Will you get us out?'

'I will.'

'All of us. Me, the kids, Ma if she wants to come?'

'Yes.'

'You swear?'

'I swear. I said we'd look after you.'

'Saying's not enough.'

'I promise you – on everything that matters to me.'

'Bring the kids out now. You'll do it now?'

'We'll do it now. Today.'

She paused for a brief second before plunging on. 'It's now, any minute. We got in through the underground press entrance at Parliament. We're in the press gallery. The prime minister, as he stands up—'

'Thank you. I won't forget.'

She put down the phone and stood up, suddenly feeling triumphant. The door opened and the man stepped back in. He looked as if he expected an explanation, but she smiled broadly and walked past him. 'Thanks,' she said.

She stood in the corridor again and looked both ways. How long to go? She wondered if the man in the office behind her would hear or sense her going into the loo at the end, but she thought she had no choice. There was no ladies' to be seen and anyway Gerry had told her to wait. She opened the door gingerly and was relieved to see the room was empty. She walked across to the cubicle and tried to go in.

It was locked.

She turned away from it. She walked over to the basin and turned on the tap, wetting her hands briefly. She went over and pulled down a stretch of white towel and dried her hands.

She thought she heard someone outside, but whoever it was quickly passed.

She stood in the centre of the room. It was quiet. She

crouched down to peer underneath the door, but she could see nothing. She didn't understand.

She walked up to the door and rested her knuckles on the outside. She paused for a second and then knocked, three times.

The door opened. Gerry climbed down off the loo and she saw the anger in his face.

'Where the fuck have you been?' he asked, pulling her in savagely.

She kept her head down.

'Well?'

'I was worried about you,' she said, looking up into his eyes and seeing the hostility, anger and uncertainty. Doubt me, she told herself. Doubt me and ruin your shitty fucking plan.

She wondered what he'd heard. She wondered if he'd listened. How could he not have heard? Perhaps he went and came back the other way. She wondered if he would kill her. Could you, could even he, stoop that low?

He looked at his watch. 'It's three thirteen,' he said. 'Two minutes to go and then the bastard will be on his feet.'

It was so close. She'd had no idea. She wondered if they could ever make it in time? How would they get here, or who would they tell and how . . . ?

Gerry unzipped the bag and took out the guns. He checked the ammunition cartridge in hers and then handed it to her. She put it in the pocket of her jacket without looking – without even looking at him.

He opened the door and led her across the room. It was unreal now and, as they stepped into the corridor, she no longer considered running. The sense of fatalism that had been with her all day enveloped her again and it was not uncomfortable. As they came towards the stairs a man and a woman ran past them, armed only with notebooks.

They hovered in the recess, waiting, and Colette was suddenly conscious of the truth of this. This was not, as she'd once thought, part of Gerry's leadership ambitions. It went beyond that. This *was* suicide, or close to it. It was martyrdom, a place in history.

Death or capture.

I hope they shoot you, she thought.

Back at Millbank, Ryan ran down the corridor into the incident room and threw open the door.

'Shadow Dancer called. It's today. It's now.'

He was out of breath, but they were all staring at him dumbly. 'They have forged press passes and are somewhere in the press gallery. They are going to shoot the prime minister as he stands up in the Commons.'

For a moment there was a stunned silence, and then Ryan saw Jenkins recover and pick up his phone.

Then he turned and ran, taking the stairs down to the lobby in giant leaps. Jenkins would have passed the information to the control centre up at Scotland Yard, but Ryan was running on instinct.

The hall was full of people coming back from lunch and he barged through the middle of one group, waited impatiently as he cleared himself through the space capsules that acted as security barriers and careered into the swing doors and out onto the street.

Then he was running again, his knees quickly sore from the impact of the road. But he barely noticed. He imagined her slowly walking down the steps, a gun in her hand. Would she still have murder in her heart?

Suddenly, he had fixed in his mind that moment on top of the Mourne Mountains, when they'd both been aware that their emotions were leading them somewhere quite different. He asked himself why he hadn't acknowledged it, why he hadn't given her some indication.

He asked himself why he hadn't kissed her when she'd wanted him to.

He imagined her lying on the ground, her body caked i n blood.

He ran harder, his tie blowing over his shoulder and his hair swept back by the fresh winter wind. As he approached Parliament Square, he tried to cut across the road and nearly got knocked down by a car pulling out from a street on the left.

He kept on running towards the main gate. He didn't know where to go, or what to do. Where was the press gallery?

He ran through the gate, out of breath, and heard the shouts of a policeman behind him. He stopped and saw the anger and shock on the man's face.

'Where is the press gallery?' Ryan asked, trying to get his breath back.

'What in the hell—'

'I'm from the Security Service. *Where* is the press—' Behind him, he saw a group of armed police officers charging towards the corner of the square. He ran, ignoring the protestations of the policeman behind him.

Colette put her foot on the first step.

She heard a heavy footfall behind her and she turned, startled, but it was only a journalist hurrying to catch the prime minister's words.

She could hear the chamber now. She could hear the prime minister's voice and the roar from the opposition benches as his opponents scented blood.

She thought of the man. A neutral figure to her,

despite what he represented. She'd seen him so often, but knew nothing about him. Did he have a family? Did he have friends? What did he . . . ?

The world was slowing down.

She thought of Ryan's voice, sounding so near and so reassuring and so confident.

How could he stop it? How could anyone stop it now?

She put her hand in her pocket and felt the handle of the gun, searching for the trigger. She wanted to cry suddenly, to beg forgiveness.

She imagined Ryan running, his face set, determined to . . .

No, it wasn't going to be.

Gerry had stopped, as if trying to gather himself.

She stood beside him, no longer caring that they were going to die together. There was a moment's clarity. What do I have to say and think before I go, she wondered. What will I find when I have gone? Death, which had always terrified her, suddenly seemed routine. There was no time for fear or panic. It was inevitable. Perhaps, she thought, it is no more than I deserve.

She felt the tears welling up in her eyes again. Her sense of calmness began to disintegrate. 'All right,' Gerry said and he began to descend again.

They reached the foot of the stairs.

They turned into the lobby outside the chamber.

She saw the Brit walking across towards them. There were policemen everywhere. She wanted to shout a warning or a plea for help, but her mouth was frozen.

Gerry turned to her and she watched his face as the reality dawned. The Brit shouted, 'Not the girl.'

And then darkness.

393

CHAPTER TWENTY

Colette listened to the clock. She watched the hands, but they didn't seem to move perceptibly.

She picked up her book and tried to read. Once again, she was at the end of the page before she realized she hadn't taken anything in.

She put down the book. Its tattered cover depicted a man and woman standing on top of a mountain and a gloved fist clutching three bullets. It was a love story of a sort, about a Brit and a Republican woman from west Belfast. *He* had suggested it and she'd found it in the local library – the woman behind the counter had heard of *Harry's Game*. What she liked most about it was the smell and feel of home. It was tangible in the description of the streets. It made her ache inside.

She thought of getting up, but lethargy glued her to the sofa. She looked at the clock again. Time was crawling by.

There was always so much time.

She heard the sound of a car and instinctively leaped to her feet. She raced to the front window and waited for it to turn into the gravel drive, but it passed on, the sound dwindling as it descended the hill away from the village. She stayed at the window until the silence returned.

She walked across the room to the back window and looked out at the garden. She could still feel the warmth of the summer.

Loneliness enveloped her like a cloak.

She went into the kitchen and then out of the back door onto the patio. She stopped and smelled the rose that climbed up the rear wall of the house. The petals were smooth and cool against her skin. She stepped onto the grass and walked out to the centre of the lawn. She felt the peace of the garden acutely. Even after six months, the peace was blessed.

Eventually, she returned to the sitting room and the sofa and sat down on the left-hand end. The cushions felt like they'd been made to fit her.

She looked round the room with a detached sense of indifference. There were bright, floral curtains and a picture of a large old biplane dominated the wall opposite her. The furniture was dark. The clock was dark. The sofas were old-fashioned. Only the television was her choice. She'd insisted on it.

She closed her eyes. She heard another car and hated the overwhelming burst of excitement it generated. She forced herself to stay seated, but this time she listened to it slow and pull into the gravel drive. She darted to the window and saw the distinctive green Rover coming to a halt. She stepped back and bent down to look at herself in the hall mirror. She pulled a strand of hair from her eyes. She counted to ten before opening the door.

He was wearing jeans and a white cotton shirt. He smiled broadly, and seeing the genuine pleasure in his face brought butterflies to the pit of her stomach.

He kissed her on the cheek. She thought he must have shaved recently because his skin was soft and smelled of soap.

He went into the sitting room and looked out at the garden. He walked further and then turned to glance round the room itself, as if assessing his surroundings for the first time, as if weighing something unseen in his mind. 'Are the kids in bed?' he asked quietly.

She nodded. 'Do you want a drink?'

He said yes and followed her through to the kitchen.

She poured him a beer and then they stood opposite each other, in silence.

She opened the fridge again and took out a Coke for herself, pouring it slowly and laboriously into the glass.

'How's the office?' she asked eventually.

'Fine. Busy. Look, I'm sorry I haven't been down for a while, but—'

'It's all right,' she said sharply. 'It's not compulsory.'

He looked out of the window. She was conscious of the sound of the birds in the garden.

'How are you getting on?' he asked eventually.

'All right,' she said. 'In fact, you'd have been proud of me. I took Mrs de Montfort up on her offer the other morning.'

'And how was it?'

'I think she was a little shocked. She told me to call her Vera! Don't think she knows quite what to make of me.'

'What have you told her?'

'Said my husband had died and I wanted to come somewhere new. I think she views me with suspicion. We don't really have a lot in common, do we?'

He was looking down and she thought now that she could see the tension in him.

'What's going to happen at the trial?' she asked.

'What do you mean?'

'There'll be pictures.'

'Not outside the court, there won't. You'll be going

in the back of a van, which I know you'll like. Old pictures I don't know about – but you look so different now and, anyway, the people round here probably don't watch the news that closely. With any luck, Gerry will plead guilty.'

'Fat chance.'

'I think you'll find the leadership will be encouraging him to go down quietly.'

'How is he?'

'I'm told his arm has fully recovered. Other than that, rehabilitated, in the main. A real Republican hero.'

'You sound like them.'

'Who?'

'Your owners.'

She watched him turn to look out of the window and knew it had hurt. She thought she'd meant it to. They were silent.

'Can I change your mind?' he asked eventually.

She shook her head.

'I don't understand,' he said and she didn't respond. The silence grew.

'Perhaps I'm missing something,' he said quietly, almost as if speaking to himself, 'but what is the point of committing suicide? Paddy is long dead and buried and some kind of guilt trip to his grave is not going to bring him back.'

'That's not it.'

'Isn't it?' Ryan was looking at her intently. 'I've told you many times that it wasn't you.'

'It *was* me.'

Ryan sighed and looked exasperated. She smiled at him. 'I'll be all right.'

'No, you won't. They know who you are, they'll find out you're there and they'll kill you.'

'I'll be all right.'

'For Christ's sake, Colette.' He cursed under his breath. 'There will be no escort, no security.'

'I don't want any.'

'I asked. They say it's suicide and, if you go, that's your—'

'Funeral?'

'It's insane. You're compromised. They know who you are and have an idea of what you did. We are implacably opposed.'

'We?'

'We – because they may fleece you. I because they will kill you.'

'Still thinking like a professional, then.'

'It'll be the end of my association with Irish terrorism.'

'I thought that was over, anyway.'

'Not necessarily for ever.'

'I thought you'd screwed it up.' She laughed bitterly. 'You're a selfish bastard.'

'You'll be committing suicide.'

'I'll make it.'

'You won't.'

'I'll be in and out before they know.'

'You won't.'

'Is that a threat now?'

'Don't be stupid.'

Silence. She kept her head down.

'It's a free country,' she said eventually. 'I just want to say goodbye, I want to see Paddy's grave, I want to see Ma—'

'She could come here. We've said we'll fix—'

'It's not that. I've said. I want to feel at home one last time.'

Silence again.

'All right, if that's what you want,' he said and, as he

398

did so, she thought she saw something in his eyes. Hurt perhaps, or worry – or maybe just guilt. She couldn't be sure. 'You go if you want,' he said, 'but I'm *telling* you—'

'Oh, come on.'

'Well, why then? Haven't we done enough?'

'*Why*? *Why*? Don't you understand? Don't you have *any* idea?'

He looked surprised by the venom and passion in her voice.

'Do you know what my life *is* here? Do you know what I *do*? Do you know what I *am*? I'm nothing. I *do* nothing. I *am* nothing. I don't belong anywhere.' She pointed at him. 'I know what I am to you: a nuisance, an *ex*-agent, a loose end that needs to be tied up, but what am I to me? *Who* am I? What am I doing here? Where do I belong? I'm a nobody – stateless, pointless, scarcely with any existence worth mentioning. What do I do all day? Nothing. Nothing. Nothing, nothing, nothing. Live, wrapped in a blanket of loneliness, wondering who I am and what I'm for? So you ask me why? I'm going home to be real, to find out who I am and, if I'm killed, then for God's sake what have I lost?'

If she'd expected sympathy, she saw only the hostile set of his jaw. She understood now what it meant. He looked away. 'A little gratitude wouldn't go amiss,' he said quietly, as if talking to a third party at the back of the room.

'Gratitude?' she said, bitterly. 'For *what*?'

He looked at her. 'For saving your life.'

'You've killed me as certainly as if you'd pointed a gun and pulled the trigger.'

'*You* chose.'

'I chose nothing. I had *no* choice.'

'You've *had* choices. Don't cry about where they've led you.'

For a few moments more they stared at each other, then she was past him, slamming the door behind her. She climbed the stairs, went into her room and closed the door there quietly. She sat down on the chair by the bed and pushed it back against the wall. The curtains were half drawn from her afternoon sleep, the duvet pulled back and rolled neatly at the end of her mattress. The sheet had been tucked in tightly again and looked crisp in the fading light. She could just see the sunlight reflected in the mirror on the top of the wardrobe. She leaned back and closed her eyes.

When she opened them again, the room seemed darker, the shadows longer. The pink and blue floral curtains had lost their colour, but not their pattern; a poor bargain, she thought. They billowed ever so slightly in the breeze, as if dancing, lazily. She looked at her bed and thought of lying down, covering her head and sleeping.

She was wearing a black cotton dress with thin white hoops and she pulled it clear of her knees and straightened her long brown legs. She touched them. Her skin was soft. She shut her eyes again.

She heard his footfall on the stairs. He came up slowly, as if thinking as he walked, or reluctant, or just tired. His leather boots were noisy against the wooden floor.

He reached the top and she found herself holding her breath.

He paused. She heard him take a pace and then another.

She waited to hear the door latch being lifted.

He moved on. The footsteps seemed slow, deliberate. She opened her eyes and turned to the window, listening for him. There was no sound at all from next door.

She heard him move, still leather on wood, his steps quieter now. She assumed he must be looking at the dying sun and she stood and walked silently to her own window, imagining herself standing parallel to him.

The sun had disappeared, the horizon streaked with red, broken only by a small group of clouds that seemed to be on a long march home. The impending darkness seemed exciting, as if the night were timeless and tomorrow only a distant possibility.

She waited for him to move, but there was no sound.

She watched the light fade from the sky.

She turned and walked to the door, barefoot and silent. She lifted the latch quietly and slipped out into the corridor, turning only briefly towards his door. There was no sign of any light. She walked three paces to the bathroom and ran a basinful of warm water. She washed her face slowly in the half darkness, enjoying the sound of the water running through her hands. She took the bar of soap and massaged it, applying the lather gently to her face. She lowered her head and washed it off carefully. She kept her eyes shut and fumbled for the towel to her left. It was pleasingly soft. She dried herself, then dropped it onto the box beside her.

She let out the water and it gurgled away. She brushed her teeth, gulping down several mouthfuls of cold water.

She turned off the taps, returning the house to silence.

She dried her face again and looked at herself in the bathroom mirror.

She put down the towel, folding it neatly over the

401

metal bar beside the basin, and walked towards her room. She stopped in the doorway for a second, looking down the corridor.

There was a candle in her window and she found some matches and lit it. The flame flickered in the breeze, but held. She stepped back, took hold of the bottom of her dress and lifted it up over her head. She was naked underneath.

She looked at herself in the full-length mirror on the wall. Her skin seemed dark in this light. She imagined her stomach swelling, thinking of herself with child. She turned sideways.

She walked to the bed, turned over her pillow and brought out a thin, white cotton nightdress, slipping her arms in and then letting it fall down over her.

She half turned towards the mirror on top of the wardrobe and then stopped.

She could see his face, reflected in the half-open window next door.

How long had he been watching her?

She held his gaze.

She blew out the candle and turned away, her heart beating fast. She lay down on the bed.

The house was silent again.

She closed her eyes.

She breathed in slowly, deeply.

She heard a shuffle, then back to silence.

She raised her knees, opened her eyes and then closed them again. She felt apprehensive, nervous even. She thought of how it had been before, how it might be different. She wondered what the darkness might hide and what the morning might bring. She thought of consequences – of afterwards – and that seemed as distant a possibility as tomorrow.

She wondered if he had hate in his heart still. She

asked herself why she didn't care.

She listened. She could just make out the sound of the big old chestnut in the garden opposite, wheezing quietly.

She heard footsteps in the corridor, softly – barefoot.

She stood and hit him in the doorway, their teeth snapping together as she threw her arms around his neck, kissing him angrily and passionately, gripping the back of his head, digging her nails into his scalp, running her fingers through his clean, curly hair.

She jumped, wrapping her legs around him, forcing him momentarily off balance, tipping them both back into the door, which banged loudly against the wall. He widened his legs, holding her with one hand, her face in his neck now. He was wearing a T-shirt and boxer shorts, but her nightdress had ridden up and she could feel his hand against her flesh.

She heard a cry in the night – Mark woken by the noise. They both stopped and listened.

They waited. She could feel and hear him breathing, his passion driving his chest in and out.

The house was silent again.

She pushed her head against his chest and closed her eyes, clinging to him.

Eventually, he lowered his face to hers and felt the tears on her cheeks.

He let her down gently, pulling her to him.

He kissed her, slowly.

She stroked the smooth skin of his upper arm, running her fingers up underneath his T-shirt. She slipped her hands into the sides of his boxer shorts, pushing them down gently. She picked up the end of his T-shirt and then allowed him to lift it over his head, watching the shape of his chest and arms as he did so.

He felt the curve of her back, scrunching the nightdress into his hands and then lifting it up.

For a second, they stood apart.

They touched. She closed her eyes, her breathing ragged.

She took his hand and led him backwards, lying down on the cool cotton sheets. Her knees were raised and he kissed her tenderly, half lying over her, stroking her face with his hand – gently, as if touching something priceless. He searched for her lips again and then they were pressed together, she rising above him, stretching across him and letting her hair fall in his face.

She pressed down, arched her back and closed her eyes again. She breathed in deeply, slowly, unevenly – not caring if ecstasy had a tomorrow.

Later she sat close to him, in the silence, in the dark.

She couldn't be sure of the time now, but the temperature had dropped and the night seemed somehow darker. She was not quite touching him, her legs curled up under her. He lay on his back, breathing quietly and, she assumed, sleeping deeply.

His chest was bare, the sheet just covering his waist.

His face was turned to one side and she had to resist the temptation to run her hand through his hair.

She felt as if she was guarding him.

She wondered if he'd had time to think before sleep. What would the morning bring in him? What could it bring in either of them? She'd never experienced ecstasy. She didn't know whether it *did* have a tomorrow.

She woke to watch the first rays of sunshine quietly intrude. The breeze had not strengthened and the curtains still danced lazily. She lay still, enjoying the warmth of him against her back.

She slipped gently off the bed and stood next to him. He lay, face-down, away from her. The sheet was loosely wrapped around him now, as if he'd been looking to hide the intimacy of darkness from the morning light. His feet protruded. His body seemed long.

She felt guilty, as if her careless sleep had allowed the night to run its course.

She moved round and stood in front of him. His hair was tousled, his cheek slightly distorted by the pressure of head against pillow. She smiled at his sudden ugliness.

She picked up her nightdress from the floor and placed it on the chair.

She walked to the mirror and stood sideways on, no longer sticking out her tummy.

She looked to the window. The light seemed to be brightening before her eyes. She watched him for a few seconds more, listening to the sound of his breathing, then picked up her black and white hooped dress, slipped it over her shoulders and turned towards the door.

She wavered, her resolve slipping. She looked down at the bag by her feet, packed, it seemed now, in a different time.

She waited.

She picked it up and passed on, closing the door quietly behind her.

He must have heard them at breakfast. He smiled at her once as he came in and she tried to smile back, unsure of herself. He ruffled Catherine's hair, but did not touch Mark.

She busied herself, not looking at him. She cleared away the children's bowls and put them into the dishwasher, closing its door quietly and setting it off. She

405

took the packet of Frosties off the table and put it in the corner, next to the toaster. She told the children quietly to get their coats and go and wait in the car. They left silently.

She washed and then dried her hands.

She turned round and looked at him. He leaned back against the sideboard and raised his eyebrows. For a chilling moment, she thought he might be laughing at her.

'We'd better go,' she said and turned away, folding the tea towel in her hand and placing it next to the sink. She put her head down and walked to the door.

They had only two bags and he picked up both in the hall before she could get to them. She followed him out and pulled the oak door shut after her, wondering if she should even bother to lock it.

She stood in the middle of the gravel drive and looked back. The window of her bedroom was still open, but she did not want to return to close it. It was a pretty house – red brick, yellow roses, low doorways. It was a perfect house. She turned round.

In the car, he drove. She sat in the back with Mark and Catherine on either side of her. The journey took more than an hour, but nobody spoke. To begin with, she thought one of them must talk, but after the first fifteen or twenty minutes, certainly by the time they reached the motorway, it didn't seem so unnatural any more.

Perhaps it had been because she was going, she thought.

How could it have been anything else?

As they pulled into the airport, she found herself touching his shoulder. He went first to find a trolley and then took both bags out of the back and placed them on it. For a second they stood awkwardly opposite each other, Mark and Catherine on the pavement beside him. She thought he might say something and stepped forward to stop him. As he tightened his arms around her, she thought she might cry.

She walked away, Mark's hand in hers, Catherine's in his. At the revolving door she stopped and watched him drive away. He looked back once and waved, just as the Rover twisted out of sight.

She stood and watched until Mark tugged at her sleeve. 'Come on, Ma, come on.'

She walked through the terminal. The check-in process and the security checks were now cathartic. She began to feel detached.

On the plane the man next to her, on the other side of the aisle, had very brown arms and she felt an almost irresistible urge to reach over and touch them. She wondered how Mark and Catherine could be so quiet when she'd expected them to be excited. It was as if they sensed something in her which she wasn't able to recognize herself.

She ate the food that was put out in front of her and found herself thinking again of the holidays in Donegal. She found she spent so much time living in her childhood memories now. It was as if that was the only reality she could accept.

As the plane began its descent, she looked out over the green fields and felt the first flutter of excitement in her stomach. Mark and Catherine seemed to sense the change in her mood. Catherine clutched her hand as the plane landed.

They were almost the last to leave.

As they walked down the aisle, Colette thought of how her mother would be with her. They'd spoken on the phone and they'd written, but the subject of what she'd *done* had never been mentioned. They'd talked about Paddy's funeral all those months ago and Gerry's impending trial as if the two events had nothing whatsoever to do with her. They'd talked often and Colette sometimes thought they'd never been closer, as if the unspoken horror of what she was and what she'd done had somehow brought them together in a way she couldn't quantify.

She saw their bags on the carousel and yanked them from the conveyor belt onto her trolley. She was running now – running down the new exit tunnel with its ludicrous patterned carpet and trying to stop the excitement from making her cry. The kids were with her, Catherine on top of the bags, Mark dropping behind as she ran.

She reached the double doors and almost exploded with joy as she went out into the afternoon sunshine.

She stopped. Ma wasn't there. She'd expected to fall into her arms and she wasn't there.

'Hello, Colette.'

She turned. He was wearing sunglasses, but with his ginger hair he was unmistakable.

'Hello, Martin,' she heard herself say.

She felt Mark and Catherine by her legs. She looked at Mulgrew and Chico and felt the fear surge through her.

'Where's Ma?' she asked.

Mulgrew smiled. 'We're just looking after her for an hour or two. But there's no need to worry. Chico will take the kids down to her and you and I are just going to take a little ride and have a chat.'

Chico reached out, but Mark clung to Colette's leg. A car pulled up behind them and Chico stepped forward to open the door.

They all stood in silence. Nobody moved.

Colette felt a sudden and overwhelming sense of

resignation and self-loathing. She bent down slowly. 'It's all right, love,' she said. 'It's all right. It's only for a few hours.'

As they were put in the back of the car she looked at their faces and felt the tears run down her cheeks. Mark seemed to sense, at the last minute, that something was desperately wrong and he opened his mouth to scream, but Chico put his hand over it, dragged him down from the window and shouted at the driver.

Colette felt Mulgrew's hand on her shoulder and she wanted to scream or shout or run. She looked up to see Chico's car speeding down towards the main road and she felt the pain bursting inside her.

She doubled up, her face contorted by a silent scream.

Mulgrew was kneeling beside her. 'It's all right, Colette,' he said. 'It's all right.'

EPILOGUE

The constable was looking up at him, waiting.

Brian Allen nodded and the young man set to work, cutting the bag gently from the end that looked ... from the end that looked like the head.

The rain was hardening, landing in large drops on his face. His hair was soaking wet. The young man looked up at him again and Brian Allen breathed in deeply and crouched down. For a moment he looked at the bag, and then he slowly peeled back the plastic. It felt wet and greasy in his hands.

It was her; he saw that immediately. It was certainly her. Her face was white and her hair blackened by the damp of the earth.

He wanted to recoil, but was conscious of the faces of the young men and women around him. He pulled back the black sheeting and turned to the young constable who had been doing the cutting, indicating with an outstretched hand that he wanted the knife. The young man stepped forward and gave it to him.

Slowly, he cut the bag further.

She was naked and he saw the cigarette burns on her breasts immediately – ten, or perhaps more, little black marks on her skin.

410

He wondered what she'd told them of himself and David Ryan.

He was glad Ryan wasn't here to see this.

He stopped cutting when he reached the base of her stomach. He saw now that she was completely naked.

He looked at her face. The bullet exit wound was on the other side and from here she looked almost peaceful. There was a kind of frozen beauty to her.

He looked down again and, for a moment, tried to look scientifically at the black marks that surrounded her nipples. He counted twelve. He admired her bravery. She hadn't made it easy for them.

He wondered what it had been like at the moment of darkness. So often, he thought, death came quickly, but she would have had time to contemplate it and turn it over in her mind. She would have had time to stare into the blackness, wanting to prevent it, but knowing she could not.

The men would have enjoyed that, he thought.

For him, wondering how she had been at the end was almost an academic discipline. It was his life's work: the study of human nature in extremity.

In this case, it was hard to tell. The cigarette marks told their own story. Only the very brave, or the very reckless, were capable of a last act of defiance.

He imagined the two little kids standing by their mother's grave, windswept and forlorn, and he felt a brief surge of emotion.

He stood up. 'Right,' he said. 'Get on with it.'

He walked slowly up the hill, wondering if the woman was still there somewhere. He still didn't understand why she would have wanted to come here or how she'd found out. Somebody must have seen them and told the IRA, he supposed, and *they* must have told her.

If only they knew the *real* truth, he thought.

He got into the car and looked down at the tableau ahead of him. He thought about the mother and the irony of it all. The truth was that the first time Ryan had asked him who Foxglove – the other tout – was, he hadn't known, but had enjoyed pretending to be omnipotent. It was one of the few pleasures in dealing with a green young man from across the water.

But he'd read the files and he knew now that the mother was Foxglove. She'd been recruited after the death of her son Sean, at a time when another son, Paddy, looked certain of going to gaol for life for murder. She had hated the war and had done it all these years in order to try and protect her children.

For a while, it had worked: Paddy's case was dropped on a technicality and he'd escaped prison. But, Allen thought bitterly, you can't protect your children from themselves. Not for ever.

He thought of the body in the bag and the woman who had stood watching. Mother and daughter. He wondered what each would have done if they'd known about the other.

He watched as they lifted up Colette's body unsteadily and carried it to the waiting ambulance. He was glad once again that Ryan was not here to witness this. He'd spoken to him once since her disappearance. Ryan was compromised, of course, and his career here finished, but Allen had heard he'd been moved to the Middle East Department, so maybe he was more ambitious than he'd been prepared to admit.

Allen wondered what had occurred between him and Colette. He wondered if the rumours were true.

He wasn't offended.

Ryan would carry a burden of guilt, he thought, but he'd survived. Allen believed that was all that counted.

412

He started up the Granada, turned it round and edged out of the quarry and back onto the road.

A hundred yards further on he stopped the car in a lay-by and put his head on the steering wheel.

'Christ,' he whispered.

He thought of Colette's children again and told himself at least things would be better for them.

He told himself it couldn't last for ever.

He thought of the naked white corpse and the vulnerable – for that was the image that now came to mind – young woman she had once been. For *her* now, he felt a deep and melancholic sense of pity.

He gathered himself. He sat up straight and briefly looked over his shoulder.

He saw her coming.

He was on a bend here and could watch without craning his neck. The window was misting up, so he rubbed it gently. She was walking slowly, with her head down, looking misshapen and beaten and old.

He opened the window, so he could hear the rain and feel the cold air.

As she came closer, he heard the sound of her footsteps on the gravel. He wondered if she would look at him. He wondered if he should speak to her and, if so, what he should say.

She was closer still. He felt nervous, suddenly, and uncertain.

He wondered if he should get out. He put his hand on the door handle but didn't open it.

She was almost upon him. He wanted to look away, but could not.

She passed and, as she did so, she looked up. For a moment, he saw quite clearly the agony and beauty in her face.

And then she was gone and he was looking at her

back, watching her methodical progress away from him, the image of her agony imprinted vividly on his mind.

He thought she looked like Colette, or Colette like her. There was a beauty and elegance to their features that was unmistakable.

He raised his hands to the steering wheel and noticed they were shaking. He watched the figure ahead of him and swore quietly under his breath. He got out of the car and stood for a few seconds by the side of the road. He took a few paces back towards the quarry and breathed in deeply. When he turned round, the woman had gone.

He looked at the empty road ahead of him and felt the rain running down his face.

He forced himself into the certainty of his past.

He got back into the car and turned round, heading off towards the airport road. The warmth of the car, the beat of the windscreen wipers and the darkness of the night were somehow comforting. He found himself able to think abstractly of the victims – all the many thousands of them – and, as he did so, he felt his heart harden and the sense of melancholy slip away. There was so much to remember: so many colleagues murdered, so many children disturbed, so many wives bereaved, so many innocents blown to pieces, so much suffering in countless ways over so many days.

What was it he had said to her? 'Those who live by the sword . . .'

By the time he reached the motorway and turned back towards Belfast, all sense of pity had gone.

THE END